MEET THE CREW OF
JERICHO 52

SHAG JORDAN—Once he served time for killing the man who murdered his wife. All he wants now is a little time, a little love—and lots of money.

VANCE BRADY—Branded a traitor for turning tail on a fail-safe mission, he buries his shame in his work, waiting for the risk that will redeem him.

LEW HEATH—A great British bear of a man, Heath is lusty, violent, and uncontrollable—and the best mechanic on either side of the Atlantic.

PAM KREINER—Love is her trade. But she'll swap top dollar for Shag—if she can snag him for a lifetime.

Together they made a top-notch team determined to take what they wanted any way they could, bent on storming the skyways to seize a bold, outrageous dream.

Novels by MARTIN CAIDIN

Selected other books by MARTIN CAIDIN

Messerschmitt Me-109
The Zero Fighter
The Mission
The Silken Angels
When War Comes
It's Fun to Fly
The Power of Decision
Flight Manual for the Ju-52/3m
Flight Manual for the Bf-108b
Rendezvous in Space
Man-in-Space Dictionary
Spaceport USA
The Astronauts
War for the Moon
I Am Eagle!
Rockets Beyond the Earth
Red Star in Space
Jets, Rockets & Guided Missiles
Rockets & Missiles
Vanguard!
Planetfall
Destination Mars
Countdown for Tomorrow
The Greatest Challenge
Aviation & Space Medicine
By Apollo to the Moon
Man into Space
New World for Men
Why Space?
First Flight into Space
Worlds in Space
Overture to Space
etc.

JERICHO 52

Martin Caidin

A DELL BOOK

Published by
Dell Publishing Co., Inc.
1 Dag Hammarskjold Plaza
New York, New York 10017

ISBN: 0-440-13183-9

Printed in the United States of America
First printing—December 1979

FOR
DEE DEE,
COPILOT

It is based largely on reality.
Much of it is factual.
It could be true.

JERICHO 52

1

The water burst through the sudden crack at the edge of the cockpit windshield, a knifelike jet impelled by a wind howling at more than two hundred miles an hour. The blow caught him full force on the left side of his face, stabbing just above eye level into the curve of his temple. Shag Jordan jerked with pain and sudden astonishment, unable to believe that this was really happening to him. The dim world in which he fought the controls of the creaking old transport plane was a madhouse of uncontrolled violence. The great thunderstorms that breed off the west coast of South America at night are like that, mad and mean and speared periodically by searing bolts of blue lightning. This one was as bad as any he had ever known.

The turbulence hit them without pattern. There were no steady chopping blows or separated blasts of vertical wind. For half an hour they'd fought for survival itself, plunging through invisible rivers of air rushing upward and tumbling earthward. The updrafts smashed him and the two men with him downward into their seats, which were soaked with their own perspiration; they gritted their teeth and an instant later a gust banged against the side of the airplane and hurled it over on a wing, and he fought madly with rudder and hard-over aileron to right the machine.

You had to struggle for breath, try to suck in air between each fistlike crack against your neck, between the wildly swinging side-to-side motions, the cartwheeling yaw of the nose. Then, just when you felt you'd beaten this stinking storm and could breathe deeply and normally, *just this once, goddammit!* the downdraft came and the DC-6 plunged sickeningly earthward and only your painfully cinched seatbelt and shoulder harness kept you from flying upward to slam into the overhead. But it sucked the air from your body so that when the next blow came you really weren't ready for it and your lungs were full of stale air and carbon dioxide instead of the oxygen you needed, and you knew you shouldn't do it, but oh Jesus, you gasped for air and suddenly you were hyperventilating. Shag Jordan was doing that; he didn't want to and he'd almost had it whipped and then the windshield cracked and the water jet speared him. He saw the bright lights and spinning colors before his eyes and he knew he was in trouble. "Take the fucking thing!" he yelled as loud as he could, and relinquished the controls.

To his right, Vance Brady was ready. He had been waiting for just this moment because he knew it had to come sooner or later. He tightened his grip on the yoke he'd been caressing lightly, pressed harder with his feet on the rudder pedals, and began flying the big Douglas. Shag Jordan gasped several times for air, squeezed his eyes shut, and saw red lights dancing eerily on his retina. He ignored them and forced himself to breathe slowly, deeply. Screw the storm, screw the pounding and slamming. Self-control and long experience won out and the lights faded. He opened his eyes, in control again, and saw that Vance was struggling to fly the airplane through this charnel house of a storm. Shag was a big man with thick, powerful muscles, but right now, even with all his enormous strength, he felt like he'd stood up alone against the best defensive backs of Notre Dame and they'd all taken huge delight in kicking the hell out of him. He was surprised to discover he hadn't released his death clamp on his sodden cigar; well, automatic responses counted for something. Lew Heath, the third man in the cockpit, seated between and behind the two men at the controls, reached forward and handed him a towel.

Shag took it and wiped his face. Fat lot of good it was going to do. They had water all over the frigging cockpit from a dozen leaks, but he wiped the water and the sweat and the blood from his face and—

Blood? Where the hell had that— Oh, Jesus, the water jet had done it. When the windshield cracked the water had come at him like a bullet. Now it came through in a fine spray and he tried to jam the towel against the crack. Lew leaned forward with a screwdriver but was unable to reach the windshield, strapped in as he was by the flight engineer's control panel. He stuck the screwdriver into Shag's hand. "Shove it in the hole!" he bellowed. "Maybe it'll stop it up for a while!" It seemed a futile and ridiculous thing to do, but somehow it helped, diverting the water against the left side of the cockpit and then to the floorboards beneath them.

Shag turned back to Lew Heath. "How's number four holding?" he shouted. Lightning crashed in a jagged bolt just in front of them and, for an instant, the stubble-faced Lew, his old flight suit as greasy and stained as his baseball cap, appeared not in the red light of their instruments, but in the stroboscopic effect of the lightning.

"Not very bloody well! The oil pressure is still going down and the temp is coming up and we're sitting right on the hot seat, we are! It's going to burn and I'm going to have to shut it down, and if you two loonies don't get us the hell out of this storm right quick, this is likely to be your last bleedin' flight! Got it?"

Shag grinned and nodded. Lew was a superb flight engineer and mechanic. He was also a pilot's pilot and he wasn't telling Shag and Vance anything they didn't know, but it felt better to yell when and if you could. Complaining about a rotten deal somehow always seemed to help. Why whimper like a cur when you can curse like a trooper? Shag turned back to study the panels before him. They were still descending, trying to get through the worst of the storm, maybe even break through its dark heart. He glanced to his right at Vance and couldn't help shaking his head in wonder as he studied the man at work.

Vance Brady was a lanky, high-strung poet of the skies. He was soaked through with his sweat and the water in the cockpit, but was still in full-dress airline-captain uniform, four gold stripes on his sleeves and the fifty-mission-crush cap on his head. He was flying the battered and groaning old DC-6 as if he were on a scheduled flight from Los Angeles to Chicago and impatient for the stewardess to bring him his coffee. But this wasn't Los Angeles to Chicago and this wasn't any scheduled airline and there were no stews, only the three of them and their contraband cargo, and the airplane coming unglued all around them. They were in real danger of structural damage because control was being wrested from them by the turbulence, and life had become a matter of flying attitude only; forget the goddamned airspeed and the altitude and do everything to hold her wings level and the nose in some semblance of a horizontal position. The only way to keep from breaking metal and tearing away the wings was to let her ride like she was on some demented roller coaster. Basically, if you could keep the wings level and those four big props turning you had a chance and, oh Jesus, the lightning bolt and the sudden glare of orange light from his right all happened at the same moment. He heard Lew shouting and cursing and knew he was already feathering number four. Shag yelled to Vance, "I've got it! Find out where the hell we are! We can't hang on in this stuff with only three . . . I'm going down!"

He took the controls, saw Lew's hands moving knobs and handles and buttons, and felt the ship shudder as the big engine groaned down while Lew fought to get those enormous propeller blades knife-edged into the wind. Their best bet, their only real chance now with all that power stripped from them, was to keep control by taking her right down to the ocean surface. Brady was trying to make sense out of their navigation instruments. They needed VHF to get through this storm. The ADF with its low-frequency signals wasn't worth a damn.

"I've got us," Brady called back, the only man Shag had ever known who could shout loud enough to be heard in a shotgun-booming washtub and not seem like he was raising his voice.

"Well, let's not keep it a bloody secret, shall we!"

Lew's gritty tones cut through the cockpit as he tried to see the chart in Vance's hands.

Vance tapped the chart. "We're right *here*, fifty miles out of Piura. We're just below the Ecuador border, coming into Peruvian airspace. We—"

Two things happened at once. A final jagged bolt of lightning crackled madly around them and they were spit from the storm, just as neatly as if they'd been flying in a tunnel through a mountain and had emerged on the other side. In that instant the violence vanished, and they were left dazed in the stream of calm air. They gazed down on the twinkling lights of cities on the coast of Peru to their left. Lew turned back to his engineer panel, readjusting the power, picking up some additional manifold pressure from the remaining three engines, playing the keyboard, trading off power and airspeed in an effort to get the best result from a bad bargain.

"We head for Piura," Vance said as unperturbed as if they hadn't been in a storm for a year. Even the water had stopped its crazy rush into the cockpit. "It's our checkpoint. We make Piura and then we turn east and fly up the mountain road between Las Lomas and Suyo. Right? There's a crew waiting to pick up the cargo. We unload, we get our cash, and we take off and bug out of Peru. Everything's right on schedule."

Shag chewed the cigar to the other side of his mouth and grunted. "You're crazy, Vance. We're going to get into a mountain field and then get out again on three engines? In this dung heap?"

"Nothing to it," Vance replied, dismissing the problem. "I know the field. Downhill takeoff, and we'll be light."

"Sure, sure," Shag mumbled. "Just like the old days, huh?"

Vance let a smile tug the corner of his mouth. "I always thought you could do anything, remember? You—"

"Oh, shit!" Sparks showered from the control panel behind them, prompting Lew's cry of alarm. "There goes the bloody electrical system! *And* our radios and navs. Jesus, what a bloody pile of crap this thing is!"

Vance was studying the coastline lights as Shag eased the crippled DC-6 into a steady left turn toward the Peruvian towns. "Better take her all the way to the deck and then climb up," Vance advised. "I'll be ready with the landing lights. We'll have to climb as soon as we reach the coast. Mountains out there, you know, and—"

"What the hell do you want to give away altitude for *now*?" Shag barked at him. "We've got the coast made and—" He let his voice trail away. The coastline lights were dimming rapidly. "Oh, wonderful," Shag groaned.

Then they were in the next storm and the world was madness again.

2

This one was easy. There were a lot of bumps and the nose swayed from side to side and the rain smashed steadily against the windshield and drummed on the skin overhead, but it was a pleasant enough sort of violence. They weren't worried about the wings tearing off or lightning crashing into the fuel tanks. They could deal with the tropical storm rain, and the occasional lurch kept them honest so there was no real danger of flying into the ocean. That would have been a hell of a cute way to end it. What with the power lost from the dead number-four engine, Shag rolled in slight nose-down trim and kept her headed for the big drink, still invisible below them. The altimeter read two thousand feet but it was as trustworthy as a hungry whore. With all the barometric pressure changes they'd encountered on their long flight down from the States it could be off anywhere from a few hundred to a thousand feet. He gave himself a mental "No lower, baby" when the needle rolled around to a thousand feet above sea level. His eyes were starting to get tired from studying the gauge, and Vance anticipated the problem. "I'll call out the numbers," he said just loud enough to be heard. "What's the lowest?"

"One grand," Shag replied. "We can't trust those gauges beyond that."

"Very good. One thousand feet it is. Okay, we're coming down through seventeen hundred right now." Vance glanced to his left and behind him. "How's that electrical system, Lew?"

"Just ducky, Admiral. But it ain't the electrical system that bothers me. It's the—"

"Hey! Open sky ahead of us, you guys. I can see the coastal lights again. Piura is coming up fast." Shag rubbed the sweat from his brow. "We got it made now. Vance, give me a check on those landing lights."

Vance hit the switches. Three rows of brilliant light stabbed through darkness ahead of them, shining through mist and illuminating the choppy surface of the water about fifteen hundred feet below. "I'm going down another three or four hundred," Shag told them, "and we'll hold about twelve hundred indicated until we have to start climbing. Hey, Lew! How does the world feel now, you pessimistic old bastard?"

Lew didn't answer for a moment. He felt the solidity of the big transport once again as the wings flexed to take the vestigial turbulence reaching out from the storm. The Douglas, strangely enough, felt good. She was as stable and reliable a machine as had ever been built, but her best days were behind her and she'd been unattended and forgotten for years in a surplus storage area. That was suicide when your lives hung on her being reliable over a long and arduous flight, such as the one in which they were now embroiled. Lew sighed, as much from frustration as exhaustion. He hated being the wet blanket. He'd much rather be flying this beautiful but crotchety old airplane that had once been a flagship for United Airlines, but—well, that was yesterday and today was now and he leaned forward so Shag could hear him better.

"Pessimistic, am I, you hairy ape?"

"Damn right. Worried about one lousy old engine. Look ahead of us, you worrisome fart. Ever see prettier lights in your life?" Shag pointed and Lew admitted the lights looked very good. Far better than the others knew. "It's a bed of roses from here on, and—"

"Never mind the music, *Mister* Jordan," Lew broke in. "Wherever it is we have decided to descend to the blessed earth, you two bastards had better do it a lot sooner than you planned."

Two heads turned to him at once. "Number three is starting to go," Lew announced somberly. "I think she's all screwed up on fuel flow. The storm and the turbulence must have separated a fuel line and it's slowly been getting worse. We're losing pressure and I don't think she'll hold much longer."

Shag turned his full attention to the controls. "You ready to get on the trim with me?" he said to Vance.

The answer came crisply: "Ready. I'll go on rudder with you. Lew will handle feathering and I'll retrim."

"Okay. Look, over there to the left. That's Talara. I *know* this view," Shag said. They saw the lights twinkling through mist, hazy glowing pearls along the night coastline. "We can make our field now. It's almost a straight shot and I know the way."

Lew tapped him on the shoulder. "If Talara's got a field, laddie—"

"It's got one," Shag snapped. "So what?"

"Then you'd better be thinking of putting down in Talara. It's at sea level and pretty soon, when number three goes, I don't think even you can keep this thing flying with only two engines on one side. Not with that load we have back there."

Shag shook his head. "No way. That place is crawling with local police and the worst military you ever saw in your life. It's a corporation down there. They control everything that moves in or out of the area, and unless you've got it all set up and paid for in advance, people like us get stood against the wall and filled with holes. We can't go into Talara. We'd be better off ditching if we had to."

"Then find somewhere else, dammit!" Lew's voice was rising and they discerned all the danger signals. His voice would go up in proportion to fuel pressure for number-three engine going down. "We're just about to lose the engine and I don't want raw fuel spraying inside that wing!" He turned back to his panel. He'd said his piece and that was that.

"He's right," Brady said in the silence that followed. "I don't think we can make it to Suyo on two. The terrain rises too quickly, faster than we could climb with three and four dead weight on us. How about Sullana?"

Shag didn't answer for a moment. The coastal lights were much closer now and should have been getting brighter, but they were dimming, flickering intermittantly. "They've got rain showers over the land," Shag observed. "It could help, you know. You don't see much of an airplane at night in the dark. Christ, I forgot. Kill our position lights and beacons—quick." Vance hit the right switches. The wingtip lights and taillights and the flashing red beacons atop and beneath the fuselage went out.

"Sullana, huh?" Shag had picked up the conversation begun a few moments earlier by Vance. He mulled over the choice, chewing on his cigar. "You can't come up with anything better than that?"

Vance shook his head. "It's not exactly dealer's choice, you know."

Shag nodded. "I know, I know," he said grumpily. "Goddammit, it's an outhouse of an operation in there. A loser. Even if we get down okay, *we* lose." Vance arched an eyebrow at him. "Hell, it's on their main highway, so even with the rain and the dark we're liable to attract attention. No way we can hide this thing after we're on the ground, and—"

A deep spasm racked the transport. Conversation died instantly. At a moment like this you listen and you feel with your ass as much as your hands the shuddering gasp that's a message from the airplane. And they had it now, a belly groan from deep within the right wing. Lew Heath spun around on his seat, stabbing buttons and switches. The propeller to their immediate right began slowing, and something in the bearings or the governor was coming apart. That was the groan, the spinning of metal against protesting metal, a cry of despair that shivered through the metal and communicated itself to their bones. Lew was banging his hand on the feathering button but nothing was happening. "She won't shut down!" he bellowed to the others. "You're going to have a time of it, lads!" He was right. The big prop was windmilling out there and creating an enormous drag effect. They could have overcome the drag with their three other engines, but now three and four were out. They had unbalanced thrust and they were short of power.

"Take her through the gate!" Shag called out, and instantly Lew's hands were on the throttles and number one and two engines, the power from the left wing, screamed with increased manifold pressure and maximum thrust from the props.

"You can kiss your baby-pink ass good-bye in fifteen minutes if we're not on the ground," Lew told Shag through gritted teeth. "Because that's when we run out of time and temperature, bucko."

Shag nodded. "Tell me something I don't know, you fat bastard."

Lew glared at him and turned his attention to Brady. "And what in the hell are you looking over here for? Someone's got to navigate, you nit!"

Vance chuckled. They were right on the coastline now and he'd picked out the marks he needed. He pointed more to their left. "See the main street of Talara? The airport beacon is well beyond it. Stay to the right of that beacon at this altitude and they probably will never know we're going by. There's a big hill right off the airport, so keep a good distance. As soon as we clear it we'll pick up a highway and the lights of a town, and—" His voice hesitated. "All right, hold this course. Just what you've got. Easy, easy; I'll go on the pedals with you."

Shag nodded, not needing to reply, feeling the foot pressure ease off as Vance went heavy on the left rudder pedal. The DC-6 wanted to swing more and more to the right with all that power from their left wing and the drag set up by the one dead engine and the second engine worse than dead with its windmill propeller. But, forget the problems *and fly the airplane,* Shag told himself. That was the cardinal rule you followed. *Maintain thy airspeed lest the ground reach up and smite thee,* and he had been smitten enough for two lifetimes already. So he flew the sick machine as best he could and, seeing the rotating beacon of the airport, he eased to the right as Vance had advised. He couldn't see the damned hill in the dark and the rain, and he didn't want to take a chance yet with those landing lights. Once those mothers at Talara knew someone was putting down in an airplane *without* clearance they'd swarm over them like jackals for the kill.

Then the beacon vanished in blackness. "Landing lights!" Shag called. They couldn't be seen from Talara's airfield if they couldn't see the field themselves.

He stamped right rudder and the DC-6 heeled with a sickening motion. The lights had picked out dark vegetation too damned close for comfort by their left and they thundered past the hill, below the crest, using the long stabbing beams of light to find their way. Then he saw a broken thread of light on the ground, and before he said a word Vance flicked off their brilliant beams and they were guiding themselves by the highway winding into the interior from Talara. "Better start your climb now," Vance warned. Shag had made the decision before Vance spoke, and he came back gently on the yoke, but they didn't have the muscle anymore. Everything was swiftly going to hell on them. The terrain was rising faster than they could climb and that meant it was the same as flying into a box canyon. There'd be no way to turn and get out.

"Give me everything she's got!" he said to Lew. "Takeoff power!"

Heath's face was grim. He didn't have to tell Shag that in just a few minutes, the temperatures within those already overworked engines would be crawling through their redlines and into the fire-danger zones. But for now the slight increase in power gave them an extra three hundred feet a minute. The engines were howling at them but the props were worse, screaming as they gave everything they had with maximum rpm.

This was the way you burned up these big engines. Yet she was holding her own, climbing slowly, and giving them barely enough height to stay ahead of the terrain.

"We'll have to make it straight in," Shag announced. The other two men already knew that.

"Just follow the highway and we'll make it," Vance said quietly. "If I remember, the main strip is just to the left of the road so you'll be dead-on for the approach."

Shag nodded. "Lew, climbing flaps." Heath brought the flaps down for better lift and the DC-6 seemed a hair easier to hold in the straining ascent. "When I line her up and call it out," Shag went on, "be ready to give me everything we've got. Gear down and then dump the flaps and don't waste any time."

"Righto," Lew answered quietly. He studied the engine gauges with a frown. "How much longer, Vance?"

"Three or four minutes."

"That's all you've got," Lew told them both. "In five minutes your left wing is going to get very bright. We shall then be on fire, gentlemen. Everything is starting to let go."

"You're a charming bastard, Lew. I ever tell you that?"

"The Queen's own favorite," Heath retorted to Shag's remark.

"Up the Queen," came the reply.

"Both of you shut up," Vance said as mildly as if asking for another drink. "Lew, pass the handguns up here. We might need to get the devil away from the field right after we stop."

Lew nodded, reached back in his compartment, and handed two Colt automatics to Brady, who tucked them both in his belt. "I've got the shotgun back here," Lew reminded him. "I really can't believe all this, you know. I've been shot at by two dozen kinds of uniforms all over the world, and here I am getting ready to fight my way out of an airplane filled with television sets. My God, what a rotten script!"

"It looked good to you when we lifted it from that warehouse in Fort Lauderdale," Vance reminded him.

"Yeah. The TV king," Shag added. "You figured it out, remember? Television sets and computers, worth a quarter of a mil down here. Just fly into Suyo with that neat little manifest you worked up and—"

"Shut up," Lew told him. "Gear coming down, *now*." The field was on them almost before they'd seen it. Grimy yellow lights bordered a spattering of green to mark the runway.

Shag saw it clearly through his windshield and used the highway for depth reference. "Full flaps," he snapped, and the DC-6 shuddered as the gear came out in the airstream and the flaps unwound behind the wing. A fraction of a second before it got dangerous, Shag shoved forward on the yoke with his left hand and rolled in trim with his right to set her up. There would be one chance only, a straight-in approach, and it had better be right because there was no going around from this one, and there were mountains on the other side of that runway. At least it was slightly uphill; that could help a bit, and the ground might even slow them down. Rain splashed against the windshield and the landing lights were on, cutting through it all, and they rocked gently as Shag took her down the slope, aiming as much as flying, desperate to get the gear planted on the ground as close to those green lights as he could. They wouldn't be able to use propeller reverse because the sideloads would spin them around, so it was braking action only, and that at night on a rotten and wet runway.

There was no time for fancy maneuvers above the ground or putting her down smoothly. Just before the green lights disappeared beneath the nose Shag chopped all the power and let her drop down like a sinking barge. She slammed hard, spraying water in all directions. He kicked left rudder wildly and got her straightened out. Vance was with him on the controls, and they were applying brakes desperately, using everything she had, slewing from side to side, almost but not quite beyond control. They began a sideways motion and fought to bring the nose around, but it was no use because of the water beneath them. One gear leg was hydroplaning, skimming over the water, not even touching the ground, and the other was dragging so that the world inside the cockpit turned into a maddened vibration that blurred everything, even their own hands on the controls. They were still slowing and they had a chance to make it when a set of wheels skidded sideways into a deep pothole in the runway and metal snapped with a screaming howl. Sparks shot along the belly of the DC-6 and Lew Heath punched every fire-bottle switch he had on his control panel, spraying carbon dioxide into the engines and the fuel tanks and the wings so that a fire wouldn't even have a chance to get started. He killed the engines on the left wing and then came the sound they had hoped they wouldn't hear. It sounded like a bedsheet a mile long and a mile high tearing right down the middle. They skidded, one wing low, into a parked airplane and the tearing ripping sound was from metal doing precisely that. More sparks and those ear-splitting sounds of metal, a terrible final lurch that jerked them wildly in their harnesses, and all movement ended.

There was still a chance of fire and the only prudent thing to do was to abandon ship. Lew led the way until Shag called out, "Hold it!" They stopped to look at him. He pointed through the crazily tilted window. A swarm of jeeps and trucks, red lights flashing, sirens screaming, were racing toward the broken DC-6. Several uniformed men were already standing in a small knot outside the cockpit.

"It's the local fuzz," Shag explained unnecessarily, "and we are going to have to play this tune *very* carefully. That means words instead of weapons, good people. Get rid of anything that can shoot or cut and get rid of it here and now." The weapons emerged from belts, boots, secret pockets, and neck holsters, and were shoved into a carton marked FUSES. Shag nodded his approval. "Vance, you're the hero with the gold stripes. You're first outside, sweetheart, and don't forget to smile when they point those machine guns in your direction."

Vance hesitated a moment. He cocked his head as he studied the grinning Shag. "Did anyone ever tell your folks," Vance asked slowly, "that their abortion *didn't* take?"

3

Captain Jesús Rosario of the Peruvian Air Force studied the three men in his office. He went through every physical motion with a practiced and deliberate air, something that Shag Jordan noted with extreme interest. This was undoubtedly a man who strutted before a full-length mirror behind closed doors, Shag decided. He had an ego that demanded flattery and deference, and Shag adjusted his survival thinking to this newly discovered condition. If status was the meat on which the good Jesús Rosario feasted, then he was quite prepared to give him a flaming barbecue of bows and scrapes.

Shag reached into an inside pocket and the Peruvian officer froze, the riding crop in his right hand suspended in midair. Very slowly Shag removed the cigar from his jacket. He didn't turn to watch the guns leveled in his direction from behind him. He held out the cigar. "Commander, could I please trouble you for a light?"

The riding crop was mobile again, swishing about

with the motions so long practiced before the mirror Shag was convinced Rosario kept in a closet. Then he tucked the crop beneath one arm and stepped around his desk. The practiced flourish again, Shag noted, as he snapped open his tunic pocket, and a solid gold Dunhill lighter offered its flame to him. Shag leaned forward, puffed the cigar until its tip glowed, and gave his host a slight bow. "Commander, you have excellent taste."

"It is captain, amigo. Not commander. But you are kind. My name is Captain Jesús Rosario of the Royal Peruvian Air Force. I am also the commandante of the police at this airport, and the director of the customs office. I see that we shall have much to talk about tonight. But first, may I compliment you on your landing? Ah," he smiled, "I do not make the joke. That is a big machine and this is a short runway, and the wind, it was poor, no? And the rain and the wet runway, and you only destroyed one other airplane on the ground. But that is of little consequence. It belongs to a Canadian, and he is in our jail, anyway, for trying to smuggle illegal goods into my country." The eyes squinted in the finest Bogart tradition.

Vance moved in. "Sir, I am glad to note that a person of your obvious caliber is in charge here. I am First Officer Vance Brady, and—"

"Yes, yes, I know. We have your papers." Shag was still taking Rosario's measure. The simonized boots beading the water and mud from the field, the too-starched uniform that had to be giving this ass a beaut of a crotch rash, to say nothing of the red lines already forming on his neck. But the gold Dunhill, the expensive watch, and the gleaming diamond on his ring told Shag what he needed to know. Rosario was a cheapie, a local thug who held all the marbles, and to get out

of this one alive he was going to need all the shrewd-
ness he could muster. So for the moment Shag waited.
He knew his own men. They'd taken the measure of
the two cows with guns in the office behind them. Assholes, both of them, but they'd fire only if they got
too rattled or Rosario screamed at them to cut loose.
Left alone, they'd be no problem. Everything centered
on Rosario. The captain picked up a sheaf of papers
from his desk, tapped them with the riding crop, then
held them straight out.

"It is *these* papers that interest me. Your manifest. It
shows that this cargo was intended for Suyo. That is
only forty miles from here."

Shag nodded. "That's true, Captain."

"But you landed here."

"Of course. We lost two engines in a storm. We had
to make an emergency landing."

"It is too bad you did." Rosario slammed the papers
back to his desk. "These are worthless. What is your
cargo again?"

"Electronics equipment," Shag replied quickly.
"Television monitors and receivers, calculators, that
sort of thing. That manifest *is* accurate."

"Of course, of course." Rosario walked slowly to his
seat, sat down in a very military manner, motioned to
an aide with the riding crop. Immediately a glass of
rotgut was in Rosario's hand. "Now, I am sure the
manifest is correct as to its contents. But there was no
clearance for it to be flown into Peru."

"I don't understand," Vance said, his face screwed
up in what he hoped looked like honest confusion.
"We had an order to deliver this cargo to Manuel Armandaz at Suyo airfield. He would sign for it and a
letter of credit would be drafted to our bank in Miami, and—"

"No cash?" Rosario broke in.

"Why bother with cash?" Vance shrugged. "An honest man doesn't need cash money, Captain. We always deal openly, pay the required customs fees, and—"

"Then it is too bad for Armandaz," Rosario broke in. He smiled across the top of his glass as he sipped, then thought better of it and tossed off the contents in a long swallow. Shag won a private bet with himself; the starched bastard couldn't resist wiping his mouth on his sleeve. "Because," continued Rosario, "we have talked with Armandaz. He was found to be carrying approximately two hundred thousand dollars— American money, I might add—in a suitcase. It seemed he was waiting for a special delivery by air tonight. The money was stolen, of course. It has been confiscated."

Brady's eyes narrowed. He'd known Manuel Armandaz for many years. Shag sensed his friend tighten and he prepared himself to cut off any unexpected reactions from Vance. He knew what was coming next. With his cheap black tie and Sam Brown garrison belt with its stitching unraveling, Rosario was a predictable type. His only joy in life came from dealing harshly with anyone who came within his sphere of authority. "Tomorrow morning, at dawn, we shall shoot him, of course."

Shag's heavy boot applied pressure to Vance's foot. Shag didn't like the way this whole affair was shaping up. Rosario was giving it away. The entire scene was a sham, from beginning to end. Someone on top, much higher than Rosario, had known about this delivery tonight. They hadn't questioned Armandaz *tonight*. They'd most likely tapped into his communications setup, found out the basics of what was going on, and then stuck hot needles into his testicles or raped his ten-year-old daughter repeatedly until he spilled the details. They weren't very sophisticated in these parts. When they needed information, they got it fast, and if they had a little fun on the way, that was okay, too.

Jesús Rosario was proving Shag's worst fears correct. He came around his desk to stand before them and brought the riding crop up to rest its tip against Shag's chest. It was an old move used to intimidate and it worked quite well. The instinct was to flinch, to withdraw, to lean back away from the riding crop and the man holding it. Instead, Shag imperceptibly leaned forward and the weight of his body pushed the riding crop back toward Rosario, catching him off balance. His eyes widened as the crop slid through his hand, and he tightened his grip just as Shag eased his body from the stick, so that Rosario was left squeezing a riding crop not touching anything but his own hand.

It also pissed him off. Shag had taken the upper hand away from the Peruvian and had done it so slickly that no one else had even noticed the put-down. At least, Vance and Lew made certain to keep playing dumb, but they'd used the same move on a thousand different cops and military officers and secret police and interrogators in the couple of dozen wars they had between them. Well, if nothing else, it was speeding up the cat-and-mouse game.

Rosario placed the riding crop beneath his armpit again and wiped the sweat from his palm as unobtrusively as possible. "Do you know why I am not going to have you shot tonight?" He looked from one to the other.

"You're afraid of things that go bump in the dark."

"I do not understand," Rosario said to Shag.

"There are night people and there are day people. You're one of those who can't make up their mind?"

Shag crossed his arms and blew a cloud of smoke over Rosario's head. He kind of had it figured now. The cat-and-mouse scene was real. They weren't going to be shot, not in cold blood, anyway, and this Peruvian son of a bitch had something up his sleeve. So it was time to play with the little bastard with his slick mustache and greasy face. "You're not going to shoot us, Captain."

Rosario snickered. "You seem very sure of yourself."

Shag hated himself but he had to play it out. If he got this little bastard too riled up he could get trigger-happy. "The way I figure it, Captain, you're running this show. You didn't get to be commandante by being stupid or wasteful. So you've got something in mind. I don't know what it is, but I'm damned sure you've thought it out pretty carefully."

The swagger stick came forward to tap Shag on the shoulder, but this time it was not a hostile gesture. "I admire you, Jordan. You are a perceptive man. Yes," he added, returning to his side of the desk, "there is a method to all this." Shag began to hope. If he could keep this wart talking he might be more interested in being clever, even greedy, than in being lethal. You don't see the sun come up the next day if you rake the dumb bastard with the firepower too roughly over the coals. *Play him cool, baby,* Shag warned himself.

"I have a minor problem," Rosario went on, back in his seat and toying with another neat four fingers of local swampwater in his shot glass. "This cargo must be delivered, of course, and Colonel Dorsch would be very unhappy if he did not receive this sort of materials. We have a shortage of such equipment, and—"

Shag was caught by surprise as Lew Heath rumbled forward. "Hold it right there, mate." Rosario shared the surprise of the others and reached frantically for his riding crop. He had trouble speaking without it. "Did you say Dorsch?"

Rosario tensed. "Why, yes, I did. Why?"

"*Basil* Dorsch?"

Rosario's eyes widened. "You know him?"

"Old Basil? Of course I know him." Lew drew himself up tall and the rumpled cargo jockey suddenly achieved an unexpected stature. Lew turned to his friends. "Bloody Nazi bastard, that's who we're talking about. He's one of those people who had his private little concentration camp during the war. Medical experiments on people while they didn't have any anesthetic, that sort of thing. Dorsch was famous for putting people in pressure chambers without oxygen, dunking poor blokes in ice water until they was froze near to death, and then seeing how long it would take the poor bastard to thaw out with a couple of women on each side. Filthy fucking rotter. The Israelis would pay a pretty penny to get their hands on old Basil, they would." Lew turned back to Rosario. "You could make yourself a bloody fortune if you passed on his whereabouts to certain people, you know. No questions asked and no answers wanted except the number of his little hideaway. He's a stinking—"

"*Enough!*" Rosario had become as nervous as a cat walking a hot griddle. "I don't want to hear another word of this . . . this . . . these *lies*. Be careful with your tongue or we will stake it to the ground, my friend. Colonel Dorsch is a very important man. Why," Rosario's chest swelled with pride, "I have met him personally. His power reaches everywhere in the continent. He is a close personal friend of our Presidente. And *I* will deliver to him the cargo you flew in here so illegally tonight." He held up the manifest. "These papers. You will all three of you sign this manifest, acknowledging payment for the cargo you brought in here."

Heath was still hot. "Payment, eh? In what currency, mate?"

"You *may* be alive tomorrow morning," Rosario said with chilling swiftness. "And then again, your tongue interests me. Staked to the ground it would be interesting to see how you will react when the fire ants reach you."

Lew stayed impassive but Shag stepped forward. "The papers are only a formality, Lew," he said to his friend. "Captain, I'd be pleased to cooperate with you any way I can. Where do I sign?"

Again the knowing nod followed Shag's words. Rosario pushed the documents before Shag and he accepted a pen and signed. Then he shoved Lew Heath forward to do the same. Right now he wished he'd brought their hardware with them. These two guards and Jesús Rosario couldn't have stopped a nun with piddling biceps if she wanted out of here, but the hardware was in the airplane and that was that.

But the gamble had paid off. That extra touch of cooperation, that stroking of Rosario's ego; it was survival time, baby.

Rosario was immensely pleased with himself and still as anxious as ever to be the big man. "I am a sporting man," he told the trio. "This situation appeals to me. Officially, you are already dead. Your airplane crashed on landing, exploded, and burned with no survivors. It *will* burn tonight, of course, and we will notify the American embassy. In reality, we shall take you north to the border of Ecuador. And there, my friends," Rosario said with a broad smile, "we will set you free. You have done me a great favor tonight by your presence, and I do not like to see such a happy event go unrewarded. This pleases you, no? I am certain your backgrounds are not, ah, spotless, and before tomorrow is done you will be officially dead." Rosario laughed. "Think of it! All your past sins wiped out in a single stroke! You will return to your friends at home and you can make new identities. You will be—"

"Captain, one moment, please." Vance gestured and Rosario nodded. "How can we be dead without our bodies in the airplane?"

"To be sure, that is a problem," Rosario smiled. "Come with me." He barked orders to the guards and motioned for the three pilots to follow him outside. More orders were spat out and more guards appeared, one of whom opened a locked door. Three wretched prisoners were kicked out into the rain. Rosario's expression was devoid of any emotion. "Kill them," he said calmly.

Rifle butts thudded into skulls and in moments it was over. The guards dragged the corpses in the direction of the wrecked DC-6. The whole thing was no surprise to Shag; he'd spotted the killer in Rosario long before this moment. Rosario still wanted or planned to get something from them, but for the moment what it was eluded Shag. He put the thought aside as they stood near the Douglas lying on its broken wing. The last of the cargo had been unloaded and they watched in silence as soldiers poured gasoline over the wreck. The three men killed by having their skulls smashed in were dropped near their feet.

"Carry them into the cockpit," Rosario ordered. Shag threw one corpse over his shoulder as if it were a sack of meal and crawled up into the airplane. He needed some help in getting the man into the left seat, and then they shoved another body into the right seat, soaking themselves in blood and small bits of bone and brain in the process. Lew dragged in the last one and dumped the body over the flight engineer's equipment. He wanted to get to that box where they had stashed their weapons, but they were being watched too closely. They climbed down and backed away from the plane with Rosario and his guards. Rosario nodded to one of his men; an automatic rifle came up and a full clip was emptied into the gasoline-soaked transport.

It went up like a great fuel tank, an enormous *whooshing* sound that slammed a wave of heat over them. "It is a small miracle, is it not?" Rosario shouted above the sudden roar of the flames. "You are watching yourselves die and it is painless. Now we shall arrange to set you free."

"It would be nice to know you meant that," Vance told him.

"Then you are a fool, not like your friend, Jordan," Rosario said. "You could just as easily be amid that wreckage with your skin peeling away from your body, no?"

"You're right, Captain. Sorry."

Rosario sniffed with mild indignation. "I should hope so. Now, you are alive, I have kept my bargain with you. Officially you are dead. But since I have your signatures on the manifest, if your embassy becomes a bother, we will simply say you were paid by local criminals and you flew off in a small plane that you stole from this field. But we have signed proof, if we ever need it, that you landed here safely. Again, I remind you I am a sporting man. Killing you in cold blood would be no fun."

There's the key, dammit, Shag thought furiously. *Just the way he said that. Killing you in cold blood*

*would be no fun. The little shit has something
planned for us down the line, and—*

His thoughts were interrupted by a rifle muzzle that
had been pressed into his stomach. Another guard behind him snapped handcuffs tightly around his wrists.
The same was done to Vance and Lew. The three
were then shackled together by a chain to their handcuffs, and shoved into the back of a truck with two
armed guards watching them closely.

They saw Rosario enter the back seat of a jeep. He
signaled the drivers to start. The cuffs cut painfully
into their wrists as they began a jolting drive in the
dark, wet night.

4

They were thrown violently from one side of the truck to the other. Being dumped on the bare floor of the truck hadn't helped matters any, but they finally worked out a system where they sat with their backs forming a rough triangle, with Shag's feet pressed hard against one side of the truck, Lew to his back and braced against the opposite side, and poor Vance lurching to and fro against the handcuffs and the chain. The road was a nightmare of deep holes and countless ruts. Several times it smoothed out and they dozed—they were men who were long accustomed to catching forty winks wherever and whenever they could. Several times they were brought alert by voices shouting outside. "We're going northeast," Shag told the others. "I recognized a couple of words. We just went through Las Lomas. Would you believe the son of a bitch is taking us through Suyo?"

They didn't bring up the name of Manuel Armandaz. That kind of stuff was better off left in the past. "Where to from here?" Vance asked.

"If I remember these roads, we're headed for Macará. It's a border town with Ecuador."

"You have any idea why he's going to all this trouble?"

Shag shook his head. "Nope. But whatever it is, it's trouble, and we're going to have to be fast on our feet if we hope to get out of it." He tried to adjust his big frame for more comfort. "Now shut up and try to sleep. It may be your last chance for a while."

They came awake with a squealing of brakes, a jerking stop, and the sight of dawn streaming through the back of the truck. The guards dragged them to the ground and they stood together clumsily, trying to work circulation back into their limbs. No one spoke to them as Rosario huddled with several officers, obviously Ecuadorian, and from the glances in their direction it was clear that the subject of their talk was Shag and his shackled companions. "Look all around you," he told the other pilots. "Look at anything and at everything. That barbed wire there is obviously the border itself. The north side is Ecuador and I think that's where we're going."

The view offered little in the way of personal comfort, despite the stunning scenery of rugged, jungle-strewn mountains in every direction. The rain had stopped and the dawn had brought with it murderous swarms of insects. There seemed to be no wind. From the height of the ridges above them in the distance and the deep slopes far below, Shag estimated their altitude at five or six thousand feet above sea level. He tried to form a map of this border area in his mind. They were standing along the top of a ridge that ran roughly east to west. Well to the east the ground worked its way downward until it reached the ocean, but any movement in that direction was obviously impossible. In the distance he saw a north-south mountain chain and knew it crested at roughly ten thousand feet. That meant that if they could get out of this and work their way generally northward they'd be in thick jungle, but with the greatest chance of working their way along a couple of streams or rivers.

His hurried assessment of the area was cut short by the approach of Rosario and some of the meanest-looking men he'd ever seen in his life. They didn't pick the border teams here for looks or temperament. These were tough professional soldiers who'd spent a lifetime killing. He wondered about that for a moment and then it began to sink in. There'd been a series of local insurrections in Ecuador and the government had begun cracking its whip. The rebels had been getting help from across various borders and the screws were being turned on hard. So these would be among their most seasoned men. Rosario gestured and the guards removed the chain and the handcuffs, then stood back a safe distance. Now they had men from both Peru and Ecuador with guns leveled at them. It got worse all the time, Shag mused, but it's all coming to a head.

Rosario led him to the edge of the barbed wire and together they looked across the fence to where the ridge on which they were standing fell away suddenly and became a long steep floor of jungle growth. "We are about to begin our little game," Rosario explained. "You go that way, down the slope," he added with a sweeping gesture. "These men will give you exactly five minutes to get a good start on them. Of course, they are convinced they will soon catch up with you and then they will kill you. They are expert jungle trackers and there is a handsome reward for American CIA agents."

"We're no bloody CIA!" Lew spat.

"Does it matter?" Rosario asked blandly.

"This is what you had in mind with your sporting proposition?" Shag offered.

"But of course. Consider the alternative, my friend. Being in that burning airplane." He shook his head. "No, that is not to be preferred. This way you at least have a chance. But remember the reward on your heads. And these are poor men. Each one of you brought back here is equal to a year's pay for them." His face hardened and the riding crop swished through the air. "You are clever men. We shall see how much more clever you are than these peasant minds, no? Oh, there is one more thing. The game, the spirit of the affair, is as important to us as the timing. Only three men will be sent after you. That keeps the odds even."

Vance did not try to hide his contempt. "They're expert jungle trackers and they're armed with automatic weapons. That makes it a fair trade, right?"

"Certainly. Are you not the superior Americans? But enough of this," Rosario spat. "Climb across that barbed wire and hold your position until I signal you to start."

They kept their silence, climbed through the barbed wire entanglement, looked back to see the huge grins in their direction. Jesús Rosario lifted his arm, held it high as he studied his watch. "Remember, five minutes. Now—*go*."

"*Move it!*" Shag roared at his friends, and they ran to the brink of the ridge, hesitated a second, and started down. There was a faint path through the thick tropical growth, but the way was slippery underfoot and the vines and leaves scraped and slashed their faces. Several times, gasping for breath, Lew Heath lost his footing and flailed wildly to regain his balance. Within the first three minutes his clothing was in tatters. Shag watched the time carefully. After five minutes he ordered Lew and Vance to stop and move sideways into the deep growth. He ran forward another hundred yards and then doubled back, scrabbling upslope, joining the other two men still gasping for breath.

"Listen to me," he whispered. "We don't stand a chance running. We all know that. They're like animals in this stuff. They're bred to it. They can move through this growth like jaguars and we're a herd of clumsy elephants. They'd hear us a mile away and nail us in no time. And remember, they've got autorifles. It only takes one burst."

"Name the game, dammit," Vance urged.

"They'll expect us just to run for it. That's why I left a clear trail a hundred yards beyond where we are. They'll spot every broken branch and leaf and they'll be convinced we went past where we are right now."

Lew's chest heaved with pain. "But not for long," he gasped. "They'll double back the moment they find we didn't keep going."

"Right," Shag confirmed, swatting an insect off his neck. "So we've got to outfox them and be damned quick about it. I can hear them coming already." They were silent for a moment listening to the sounds of three trained killers speeding through the brush on their trail. "Now, remember that scene we had in Angola? Just like this one? Those blacks were as mean as leopards and a hell of a lot smarter. We've got to take these people the same way. Let's get with it. Remember, we let the first two of them go past us. It's number three we want. Vance, Lew and I will take him. You get his goddamned weapon and be ready to use it, because we'll have company coming back at us, and the moment they catch sight of us the curtain rings down. Okay, let's do it."

Lew broke off sections of branch about six inches long. Shag had twisted off a boot heel and unwound a reel of thin but durable steel wire. They each fastened an end of the wire to the wood, using a section of branch for a handle. Shag slipped across the trail in dense foliage and laid the wire on the ground, then froze in position, waiting. The first man came into view, racing through the undergrowth in leaps and bounds like a gazelle in open country. They held their breath as he crashed past them, grinning, his autorifle at the ready. Then came the second man, a repeat of the first, and they waited for him to break past their position.

Shag tugged the wire and nodded to Lew. They rose to a crouching position, the steel wire stretched taut across the trail, waiting. When the third man came into view, they rose in perfect coordination and pulled as hard as they could on the wire, which was too thin to spot in that jumbled tangle of thick underbrush. The tremendous weight of the running man almost jerked the wire from their hands but they held on tight. There was a sickening gasp followed by a spray of blood as the wire instantly severed the pursuer's head from his neck. The head fell back slowly, blood spurting from the neck. *"Get the gun. Get the fucking gun, you idiot!"* Shag whispered hoarsely.

Vance rushed from his hiding place, almost slipping on the blood smeared along the trail. He dove for the gun, rolled up on one knee, checked the chamber and the safety to off, and looked down the trail. Their two pursuers were shouting to one another, and it was clear that at least one of them was doubling back.

Vance waited, still crouched in thick underbrush, and when the Ecuadorian guard was no more than twenty feet away he squeezed back on the trigger. The autorifle kicked out a small slug, a .223 caliber that tumbled as it spat from the weapon, and the full burst of thirty rounds sawed across the Ecuadorian's chest. Vance stared in morbid fascination as the man's arms started outward but never completed the instinctive gesture. The storm of tumbling lead sawed the torso in half across the chest, just beneath the armpits, and both blood-soaked parts of the body tumbled back into the brush.

The three fugitives now heard shouts from down the trail. Shag was already up and running toward the dead man. He found his autorifle in a small stream of blood pulsing from the severed body. He ignored the rich red froth, snatched up the weapon, and faced downtrail. Lew had already run to the first man they'd killed and jerked the revolver from his holster. He pulled three clips from his belt and ran back to the shocked Vance. "Here, dammit," Lew spat at him. "You're out of ammo! Reload, you nit." Vance still showed the effects of shock. Cursing, Lew grabbed the rifle from his hands, threw away the empty clip, slammed a new clip into the weapon, and banged a round into the chamber. He looked uptrail, then turned and cracked Vance across the face with a stinging slap.

"You out of it, mate?" Lew snarled. He saw Vance's eyes clear but he still didn't trust him to move or to think fast. "Look, Admiral, they'll probably be working a sandwich on us, see? So I'm going to cover uptrail, and you get your ass over to those two bodies and start collecting everything they got on them, hear? Take it all—knives, belts, canteens, guns, ammo, compass, *anything*. It's all we're going to have in the world. Now move it!" He shoved Vance hard and the pilot stumbled away toward the first grisly corpse.

"Shag!" Lew called out in a desperate whisper.

"I'm here," came the reply, but Lew couldn't see a thing. So much the better. "The third one's doubling back. I'll set them up."

"Right. I'm going back a bit. I think they'll have some others coming down."

"Go, fatso."

Lew grinned and started up the trail. He reached a slight bend, leaned back with his body against a tree trunk, and waited. The friends of the guards were calling to them, then cursing, and he knew a few of them were on their way. He set himself up carefully.

Moments later the roar of an autorifle burst through the jungle. There was an immediate scream of birds and animals and a thrashing among the higher trees, and then a strangled, gurgling cry as the man who had taken Shag's burst in the gut collapsed in the undergrowth. That took care of the original three hunters, but Shag was certain that Rosario had sent a number of reinforcements after them with a single order—kill the gringos. And sure enough, he could hear more men moving through the jungle toward him. He sighted carefully, waited until he could see four men in a ragged file, and then squeezed off a series of steady bursts. He saw the first two die where they stood. A burst tore away half the skull of the lead man and took the second high in the chest. The third was fast enough to dive for cover, and Lew didn't know if he'd nailed the fourth. He wasn't waiting to find out. He squeezed off one more burst and then took off back down the trail. He had their attention, all right. Several long bursts of autorifle fire sprayed the jungle around him, and there was a gasp from somewhere down below.

Lew lurched to a halt, pivoted, and fired another long burst until the clip was empty. He jerked out the dead clip and slammed in another and threw a round in the chamber. That last burst should have been enough to slow down those bastards. He came upon Shag bending over Vance, his face white and upper left arm bloody. "Oh, shit," Lew growled. "Admiral, can't you ever stay out of trouble? What happened?" he asked Shag.

"He took a wild slug. Bloody but no real serious damage. I've got the blood stopped. We've got to get going."

"You bet your sweet ass," Lew confirmed. "There's a small army up there after us." He looked around. "Any of these nasties have any grenades?"

Shag's arm came up in triumph. "One."

"It'll do. Let's go."

They left Vance watching them, a revolver in his good hand. They stayed low as they went back uptrail ten yards, stretching the thin wire with which they'd decapitated their first pursuer across the trail and securing it to stout tree limbs. They then hooked the grenade pin with the wire. Shag looked on the booby trap with satisfaction. "It should do the job. The first one or two will come through and this thing'll go off after they've gone by. That way we'll get some of them in front and back."

"And slow the blighters down a bit, I daresay," Lew added. "Let's get pretty boy on his feet and move on, Shag." He looked up. "Starting to rain again. It'll help."

Shag pointed through an opening in the thick brush. "See that ridge over there?" They looked at a high jungle slope, its summit disappearing into heavy clouds. "That's where we've got to go. Once we reach the base of that slope and start up we'll be home free. In the meantime, we've got a job on our hands. Let's move."

They took everything of any potential value from the three torn bodies, dragged a wincing Vance to his feet, and started running for their lives.

Ten minutes later a dull thump echoed far behind them. They stopped for a moment, uncertain as to whether they had heard a shrill scream mixing in with the distant blast of the hand grenade exploding on the trail. "Okay," Shag said. "Now all we got going for us is distance and smarts. We get off the trail right now and work our way north-northeast toward that ridge. You help Vance," he told Lew. "I'll try to break a pathway. Let's move out."

They stopped to rest for five minutes of each hour. By the end of their first hour they were scratched and scraped almost everywhere from vines and creepers and branches that seemed to lash out at them as they ran. They were also providing a feast for a thick cloud of insects that kept pace with them. They did their best to listen for any sounds of pursuit, but their own heavy breathing, the normal background turmoil of the jungle, and the buzzing swarm of winged man-eaters plaguing them made it difficult. Vance sat quietly, black flies buzzing around the blood on his shoulder and arm. "I don't think I can keep going like this much longer," he said. "I'm all right now, but another few hours of this and—" He shrugged and let the silence speak for itself.

"We've got to take you along, you know," Lew told him. "That way your body will still be warm when you croak, and we'll be able to cook fresh meat. Human flesh spoils pretty fast in this climate. One of the bad things about the tropics, you know."

Vance laughed only briefly, his face screwed into a grimace of pain. "They're right, you know," he gasped finally.

"Who's right?" Shag responded.

"It . . . it only really hurts when you laugh." He tried to shift to a more comfortable position. "Jesus fucking Christ, but it *hurts*," he said, using his good arm to wipe the sweat from his eyes.

"It builds character. Let's get him on his feet," Shag told Lew. They stood Vance up and prepared to move out.

"It feels like the slug is still in there," Vance said through clenched teeth.

"It is," Shag confirmed.

Vance seemed astonished. "Then why the hell don't you take the goddamned thing *out*?"

"No time. We'll have to build a fire. That means smoke, and we don't dare try that yet. Grit your teeth, buddy boy, and hang in. Come on, move."

"I'm moving, I'm moving. And just for the record, I've been doing so much bloody gritting my molars are already down to nubs."

"Shut up and save your breath," Lew admonished.

The next hour felt like a week. A brief rest, then they were on their way again. They had to keep moving while daylight was still on their side. They wouldn't be able to move at night. Shag wasn't sure if this was jaguar country, but there were big snakes and poisonous creatures of all kinds, plenty of wild boar, and hundreds of screeching monkeys in the trees. Anything they faced in daylight wouldn't stand a chance against their automatic rifles. But there was every chance that their pursuers were still after them, and nothing else in a tropical jungle sounds like a .223 slamming out its firepower. The sound also carried a long way.

Their luck took a turn for the better at sundown—they found a stream. Shag judged the speed at which the water was flowing. "It's coming down fast," he told the others. "That means we're at the base of that ridge we've been heading toward all day. It also means the water's probably safe to drink."

"But we won't drink it, will we, laddie," Lew said. It was more a statement than a question.

Shag shook his head. "Nope. No water-purification tablets. Not even any iodine. Lew, see if you can scrape together some rocks or dig a hole or something. We stay here for the rest of the night."

"Thank God," Vance murmured, sinking to the ground.

They ignored him for the moment. "We got one canteen from those bodies. Pour out the water and put some in from the stream," Shag directed, but Lew was waving off further instructions.

"I've been in places like this before," he said. "I think we'll have to risk a shot or two, you agree? Ah, good. Then get us some dinner, if you don't mind."

Lew propped Vance up against a tree trunk, and the exhausted wounded pilot fell asleep almost immediately. Lew took out his handkerchief and draped it gently over Lew's face; at least it would help keep the insects out of his nostrils and his mouth and give some protection to his eyes. He went to work quickly on the fire they would need, because they didn't have a flashlight between them and it would be darker than a loan shark's heart all too quickly. He scraped out a wide and shallow depression in the ground, banked some rocks and tree limbs to deepen the crater effect, and broke up as many twigs and leaves as he could find. Everything felt wet, but he was still confident he could get the fire started. The key was keeping it going later. When he had collected enough material he broke open several rounds of ammunition, sprinkling the gunpowder onto his kindling. He scraped a cartridge against a rock for sparks, and the gunpowder lit with a low flat hissing sound. Suddenly they had their fire. He worked it carefully and built it high, for it was getting dark swiftly and Shag would need the flames to guide him back to camp.

Lew was startled by three shots in rapid succession. The shots were somewhat muffled, and there were no echoes. "Good, very good," Lew grunted to himself. That sound wouldn't carry far enough for anyone else to hear. Several minutes later Shag came into the clearing with his kill over one shoulder. He sat heavily on the ground. "Found you by the smell of the smoke more than anything else," he said finally. "Couldn't see a thing out there until I got in real close. No one else will smell it, either."

They kept themselves busy while Vance slept. They boiled water in the canteen so they could drink it safely. They made an overhead shelter out of thick fronds and leafy branches, and kept the fire smoking thickly to help ward off insects. They removed Vance's tattered shoes to let the air at his feet, wrapping them lightly in a shirt to keep away the biting insects. Shag skinned, cleaned, and prepared their kill, cooking it over the fire on a spit which Lew turned slowly from time to time. Then he removed a knife he'd taken from a dead guard and held the blade over the fire.

"You'd better hold him. It's going to be nasty," Shag said.

"I'd better cold-cock him, you mean."

"All right."

Lew waited until Shag nodded that he was ready. Then he removed the handkerchief from Vance's face. "Wake up, lad," he said. He pressed his palm gently against Vance's forehead. It was an old fighter's trick. A man coming out of sleep, feeling that soft and warm pressure, involuntarily reverts for a moment to childhood. Vance's eyes opened trustingly, just long enough for Lew to smash a big fist against his jaw. Vance went out like a light. "Do it, dammit," Lew urged.

Shag ripped open the shirt, cursed softly at the sight of the raw wound, hesitated a second, and then went in deep with the knife blade. Lew held Vance, but he was out of it and it took only a single deep twist to remove the slug. "He's still out. Quick!" Lew urged.

Shag held the blade in the fire again, brought it out and pressed the red metal flat against the open wound to cauterize the flesh. Vance burst out of unconsciousness with an open mouth and bulging eyes, started to scream, and passed out again. "Thank God for small favors," Lew muttered. "That could have been a lot worse." He looked up at Jordan. "You're a pro with that blade."

Shag wiped off the blood on a leaf. He just nodded in reply and Lew let it go. An hour later Shag turned back to him. "Wake him up. He needs food and water, as much as we can get into him."

"Righto." Vance came to and moved his good arm to his opposite shoulder. "What the hell happened? I feel like I've been stuck with a spear." He winced. "Good Jesus, that *hurts*."

"It'll heal." Shag held out his hand and gave Vance the bullet. "Here's your little souvenir."

Now Brady understood. "You mean, you . . ."

"And don't expect an apology if your jaw hurts," Shag told him. "Lew got the job done, but he was sort of sloppy at his work."

"It *does* ache, now that you mention it," Vance said, rubbing his chin. "What hit me?"

Lew held up a massive fist. "Anesthetic."

Vance was quiet for several moments, looking from one man to the other. "Thank you both," he said finally, and he meant it, and it was enough.

"Chow's on," Shag told him, and offered a chunk of well-cooked meat stuck onto a branch.

"What is it?"

"Eat it, for God's sake," Lew growled. "Or would you prefer music and napkins with your meal?"

They ate in silence, and Lew and Shag made sure Vance drank the entire canteen. Lew refilled it and hung it over the fire again to boil. When he turned back, Vance was sound asleep. He remained that way for almost another hour. He looked better when he woke up.

"I think I'm going to live, actually," he told them. "By the way, that meat was very good. What was it?"

"Monkey."

Vance stared at them hollow-eyed and with a sudden convulsion threw up. He gagged and choked, but neither man went to help him.

"Strange," Shag mused aloud. "Man's starving, needs food, you feed him cooked meat and it tastes delicious and it *is* delicious, and it goes down and it saves his life. Then you tell him it's monkey and he pukes all over the place. If people like Vance could just shut their goddamned mental movies off they'd be a hell of a sight better off."

Lew nodded. "I've seen men eat fried grasshoppers and rattlesnake—"

"Tastes like chicken. Better than chicken, in fact."

"Right you are. Also, they'll eat crayfish, which is about the ugliest thing going, and some men like okra, which will crawl right up your fork and try to bite your hand. They'll eat pig and horse, but tell them they're eating monkey and—shit." He shook his head, grinning at Shag.

"I don't think old Vance would do very good with possum pie, either," Shag commented.

"Gimme some goddamned water," Vance choked, wiping the vomit from his mouth. "And don't *ever* feed me that stuff again!"

"Right," Lew chuckled. "Next time, Admiral, we'll just let you die. There'll be more monkey for me and Shag that way." He gave him the water. "Besides, you kept it down long enough for it to give you some energy. By the way, you ever eat pussy?"

Vance blinked. "What?"

"Didn't you ever eat pussy? You know, go down on some chippy."

"Why, I—"

"Then what the hell's wrong with monkey? Shit, never mind. We'll find some fruit tomorrow to keep us going. Go to sleep. Shag and I will take turns on watch."

Vance lowered the canteen slowly, returned it. "That's my share, too."

"Shut up before I have to knock you out again. You'll need all your strength tomorrow."

"We're moving out at first light," Shag added. "It's uphill all the way to the top of that ridge, and then we have to work our way to Celica. Two days, maybe. They hate the soldiers there and we just might get some help."

"Why don't we just take the road?" Vance protested. "It would make things easier."

"Because that's just what that son of a bitch Rosario hopes we'll do," came the scornful reply. "The road is staked out. It's a sport and we're the game. But this is one animal that's got teeth, and Rosario knows it. So we stay out of *his* hunting grounds. They won't bother us on that ridge. They don't even believe a white man can get through. But you know what?"

Vance waited.

"We're getting through. The three of us. Even if we have to drag your dead body into that town."

5

They made it to the village of Celica in the two days Shag had promised, and Vance's iron will, briefly subdued by the lead that had slammed into his system, brought him walking into the jungle settlement under his own steam. They were footsore, bearded, gaunt-eyed, tatter-clad, miserable human beings, but the autorifles in the hands of Shag and Lew were as deadly as anything carried by a storm trooper in full battle dress and commanded immediate attention. The natives who stared at them fell silently to each side as they walked slowly along the one main dirt road of Celica. Shag knew what to expect. In the center of the town they stood in a group, their rifle muzzles pointed down, posing no threat. He didn't need to look beyond the woven mats hanging by the huts and mud buildings to know that old rifles and arrows were pointed directly at them. He'd been in the back country of Ecuador before and he knew what villages were considered dangerous to the government. Celica had a bright red pin on all official maps of the back country.

They stood quietly, waiting. Five minutes went by, and the ogling crowd of adults and children grew steadily, silently. Finally one man approached, his wide-brimmed straw hat held before him deferentially. But Shag knew better. The older man, his mustache snow-white, stopped before them. There was the slightest hint of a bow. Much of what would pass between them in Celica would not be expressed in words. Understanding the subtleties of these folk meant everything.

Shag's autorifle came up. He could *feel* the watching crowd grow tense. In a slow and smooth motion he let the weapon swing in his hand and then lifted his arm so that it was extended to the old man butt first. A smile flickered briefly. "Lew, Vance. The guns." The other rifle and the handguns were held out. The old man gestured and others came forward to take the weapons.

The old man said, "Come," and turned to walk to a large hut. Inside it was cooler and there were chairs by a crude round table. The old man motioned them to sit and, moments later, gourds of sweet fruit juices were brought to them. "Drink," they were told. "But slowly, slowly. Then you will eat."

The meal passed without a word. They all knew the need to take in the food slowly, to eat only so much and no more, or they would be puking their guts out. When they finished, a young boy came to the table holding out cigars. Shag's eyes lit up. "Thank you," he said quietly, and he lit up and inhaled deeply as the boy held a burning match for him. He closed his eyes and sighed, then opened them again. "Thank you," he repeated.

"I am—Rodriguez," the old man told him. "The leader of this little place. You know much of our ways."

Shag made no comment; it was unnecessary. "My name is Shag Jordan. This is Vance Brady, and this is Lew Heath. Brady and myself are Americans. Heath is a British citizen."

"To answer a question you will not ask," Rodriguez smiled, "I am the man responsible for reporting once a week to the soldiers of our government. But there is no cause for you to be alarmed."

"I'm not," Shag said, and they smiled together. "You speak English extremely well," he added.

"A long time ago I taught it to our young people. But that is not important. Tell me." A trace of a smile accompanied the words. Rodriguez's hand moved to scratch the ears of a dog that had ambled to his side. "Who are you? What brought you here?"

Shag had long before taken the measure of this man. This was a former professor, a very learned man. Somewhere in the constant toppling of governments and the regular sweeping out of university intellectuals he had escaped with his life. Until the regime now in power was gone he could never return to a city. But he was a survivor, and Shag liked him. "We crashed in the mountains," he said finally. "A bad storm. The airplane burned and we lost everything we had. All our papers. We've been working our way north until we could find a river."

"And from this river?" Rodriguez toyed with a cigar that remained unlit.

"From the river, if we go east, we reach the coastline. Malacha. There is an airfield there."

Rodriguez nodded. "And at this airfield?"

Shag exhaled a long plume of smoke and leaned forward. "There are airplanes. If there are airplanes we could steal one."

The old man's eyes flew open and a gnarled hand came down to slap his knee as he let out a burst of laughter. "My God, it has been long since I spoke with a gringo whose tongue was not forked!" He moved forward and clapped both hands on Shag's shoulders. "I am pleased. I am grateful you spoke to me this way." Again the smile tugged at the corner of the mouth. "It would have made me very unhappy to have you killed. There is something about you. The three of you. We are—*simpatico,* eh?"

"I dearly hope so, guv'nor," Lew murmured.

"The truth is a wonderful thing," Rodriguez said. He paused to order a powerful whiskey, then stared at Brady and spoke swiftly in his native tongue. "We do not have much time. While we talk a doctor will attend to that wound."

"Thank you," Shag said.

"Ah, a pleasure. Now, listen to me. There is a reward for you three. A *large* reward. Every village along these roads has been alerted. Already a traitor among us is running down the road so that he can alert the military. But we know this. We let him go. By the time they can return you will be far from here, we hope. But we must make it look as if there was a fight and that you escaped. By the way, where did you crash?"

"Sullana."

"Ah, in Peru. Then you must have met up with Jesús Rosario. He makes a game of this. It is sport to him."

Shag's face was dark. "We know."

"And he wants *you* very badly. So do our soldiers.

You killed many. They lose much face because of your escape. I think you are very dangerous men."

"We gave you our weapons."

"That is why you are still breathing. The one *policia* here is my nephew. You are safe that way. But not for long, because the reward is very great, my people are poor, and you are, after all, gringos, no?"

Shag nodded.

"We will give you food, water, some whiskey, and machetes. But no guns. The guns are our proof that we captured you, and then you escaped." Rodriguez gestured to several nearby young men and as Shag, Lew, and Vance watched, four men stood stoically as they were battered by fists and knocked to the ground. They did not resist.

"You see? Those are the men you beat to make good your escape." Rodriguez leaned forward, more serious now. "We will tell the *policia* and the others that you fought and overpowered them and ran away. No one else will say different. We will tell the *policia* that we overheard you talking about going to Piedras and that from there you would make your way to Malacha. They will believe us for the same reason you told me. We will also give them one of the automatic weapons as proof we tell the truth. The others?" The smile again but this time without humor. "They will be put away until the day comes for which we have waited so long."

Lew moved closer. "With all due respect, sir?" Rodriguez nodded. "It seems to me that if we don't get to Malacha our goose is cooked. Know what I mean, sir? We can't *walk* out of this territory. It's just too big. We'd never make it. So what do we do?"

"You go to Pinas. There you can cross the highway. You must be very careful, and I would suggest you cross at night. Once you are past that highway no one will be looking for you. I am sorry, but that is wild country, and it is dangerous. You go toward Saraguro, but be careful. Do not approach the town. It is only a few huts. You go around Saraguro. You go to the west around the village, and there you will come across a trail that goes up along the mountain."

Behind them Vance groaned as a doctor probed his wound. But there was no pain from his arm. The words had brought on the misery. "Oh, God, not another bloody uphill journey."

"Shut up," Shag told him.

"Twenty miles beyond Saraguro," Rodriguez continued, "you will be between that village and the next one of Pasaja. That is where you must go, between those two places. Pasaja is—well, no one lives there for a long time. They were all taken from the town and none have ever gone back."

Shag drummed thick fingers on the table. "Pasaja, Pasaja . . . something about that name rings a bell, señor. But for the life of me I can't remember—"

"It is the place of an old military airfield. It is not on any charts. It is from the war many years ago, and all records of the place were destroyed. Nothing exists about it officially."

Shag and Lew exchanged glances. "It's a mystery to me," Lew said, "and I know every field in this part of the world."

"But not this one," Rodriguez told him. "No one has been there for many years. And the men who were there before spoke a strange tongue to my people. They wore uniforms that were different from any others."

Shag and Lew were instantly alert. Rodriguez

picked up a stick and cleared a space in the dirt floor, then drew lines in the ground. They looked down at a swastika.

"Yes," Rodriguez answered the unspoken question. "They were men who came from the place you call Germany. The—I do not know the words, but there was a number with the name. The—"

"The Fourth Reich," Shag broke in.

"Yes, yes, that was it," Rodriguez confirmed.

"You mean," Lew said incredulously, "that there's an old Nazi airfield way up there in those bleedin' mountains?"

"Obviously," Shag said dryly.

"Then how come no one's ever seen it?" Lew protested. "You know how many bloody airplanes have flown over this country? The whole place was mapped under contract by your own government, for Christ's sake. They used Hercs for the job. And what about the satellite photos? You can't hide a whole stinkin' airfield!"

Rodriguez smiled. "You can if it is atop a plateau that is almost always covered with clouds," he told Heath. "It lies off a mountain range. The rain there is heavy. Clouds sweep across this plateau almost all the time, day and night. Sometimes it is open, but not often, and if you are not looking—" He shrugged to dismiss the matter.

"I *do* remember now," Shag said, crashing a fist into his palm, and whatever memory had come back intrigued the old man. "It's where Basil Dorsch fits in! Don't you see, Lew? A bunch of the old Nazis make it out of Germany, they fly down to the desert area outside Dakar, and they load up a couple of old bombers or transports with long-range tanks and head for Brazil. It's only fifteen hundred miles across the drink and if the winds don't screw them up, they could make it easy enough. Plus God knows how many came ashore by sub. The way I've heard it they had a big thing going, but the real zealots began to die out and those who were left decided to scatter all through South America. Dorsch must have been part of that crowd. You know, they escaped with jewels. No weight and worth a fortune to set up their operation, and they had plenty of friends over here, too. Americans aren't that popular in a lot of places down here, you know, and—" He turned back suddenly to Rodriguez. "How long has that field been abandoned?"

The old man shrugged. "Six, maybe eight or even ten years. No one has gone near the place in all that time. The weather is bad and it is, I am sorry to say, located in very bad country. Still, it is better to go there than to Malacha, no?" Rodriguez climbed slowly to his feet. "If you are caught by the *policía* you will wish you had a gun so you could put a bullet into your own head. I have told you. They have lost face and they are very angry, and you will die very slowly in their hands. Now, you must leave right away, for if you are found here then many of us will die the same way. Including children. They make what you would call an object lesson of children. It is very effective, I assure you."

"How soon is right away?" Brady asked.

"*Now*. It becomes more dangerous every minute. If you are not gone soon we will have to kill you ourselves, for the sake of our people." He went outside and they followed. They stood in a small group as several men brought them woven bags of food and gourds of water and the whiskey Rodriguez had promised. Then a machete was handed to each of them.

Shag extended his hand. Rodriguez clasped it with both his wrinkled hands, then leaned forward to kiss Shag Jordan on the cheek. *"Vaya con Dios,* my friend. Good-bye."

6

For a long time they walked in silence, drenched with sweat from the blazing heat, drawing a cloud of stinging and biting insects as they hacked their way through a dim memory of what had been a trail. Again they followed their routine of stopping every hour for a break, drinking water slowly, eating some food for the energy they needed in this land that sucked strength from a man's muscles without his even being aware of the drain. But these were three men who knew and understood survival. They did not fear the land. There were poisonous snakes here but that was an oddball chance, and the big cats that glided through the underbrush were more disposed to go after smaller game. The trick was not to get into situations you couldn't control. That meant staying out of large streams, if they found any, because there were all kinds of carnivorous creatures in those waterways; the piranhas had fifty cousins if they had one. The highlands were free of the caymans and crocodiles, or alligators, or whatever the hell it was that made the lower and wider rivers so deadly. So it was a matter of keeping away from obvious dangers, of doing whatever they could to stay clear of snakes, and if they encountered something big and mean, the thing to do was to stand fast and let the wild animal consider the situation without making an overt threat. The odds were it would go away.

That happened no more than four hours out from the village. They came around a bend in the trail and stared at a formidable pair of tusks and fierce little eyes. That boar must have been three hundred pounds, and against a creature like that the machetes were next to useless. Getting into a tree would have been their only way out, and they didn't even want to try that. So they stood still as the powerful animal studied them, pawing at the ground with one hoof. "Easy, easy," Shag said in a hoarse whisper. "He's letting the herd get away. If the others clear out then he won't have any fight with us. Steady, steady . . ."

Some invisible signal reached the powerful animal and, finally, with an indifferent snort, he turned and trotted away, his powerful flanks cutting through the thick undergrowth. Lew wiped his brow. "Vicious bastard, that one," he gasped. He'd been holding his breath for a full minute and was slowly turning purple. "They move like greased lightning once they get their dander up, you know."

The men went on. "I wish we could have him in front of us," Shag said.

"What for?" Brady asked. "He an old friend of yours or something? He did look like an old girl friend of Lew's, at that."

"Save your breath for the TV funnies, Admiral."

Vance ignored the comeback. "Why were you so fond of old tusker, anyway?" he pressed Shag.

"Because they love snakes. They swallow them down without even biting. Their skin and the layers of fat make them immune to the venom. You got those porcine buddies around, you don't find any snakes. But they didn't seem to care much for our company. Let's keep moving it, troops."

By nightfall they'd put two lower ridges between them and Rodriguez's village. They camped for the night, after slashing the growth around them to form a safe clearing and building an overhang of thick leaves and branches, which was one way to keep spiders and centipedes and even snakes from dropping unexpectedly from above. After they got their main fire going, they started several smaller fires around the outer rim of the rough circle they'd hacked out of the jungle. The combination of flames and dense smoke from the green vegetation would serve to alert most animals to stay away and allow them precious hours of sleep.

They followed a routine they never broke. Two men slept while the third remained awake and alert, feeding the fires, listening for the approach of anything large enough or dangerous enough to present a threat. On their first night something very big and powerful moved close to them, and Vance, then on guard, picked up his machete, his heart pounding, as two huge eyes gleamed brightly in the reflected light from the fires. He nudged the others awake and neither asked any questions, just watched the man who had brought them out of their sleep. They stared at the glowing coals in the jungle. Then whatever it was gave a deep-toned snarl from his powerful chest and moved off in the blackness.

"Good God," Vance said finally. "What the hell was that?"

"Jaguar, most likely," Shag said, and was instantly asleep again until woken for his watch.

In the morning they hacked walking sticks from small trees, sharpening the ends and holding them in the glowing embers of their main fire so they could serve as spears if need be. They ate wild fruit that they knew was safe for them, drank some water, and took a shot of the fiery liquor. It brought them fully awake. Shag studied the sun and marked a mental path for them. "Vance, you're navigator. You had training in that, didn't you?"

Vance nodded. "Can you keep us on a straight path by the sun?" Shag went on.

"Uh huh. It may be a bit erratic, but not much."

"Good."

"How far is this Saraguro or Pasaja place?" Vance looked displeased with himself. "By damn, I'd never even thought to ask before."

"Straight line from Celica, about seventy miles."

"That's a straight line," Lew grinned. "But we're not birds. We go up and down hills, remember? Double the distance if you're counting actual ground travel."

Vance stared. "You mean we're going to have to walk a hundred and fifty miles through this flaming *jungle*?"

Shag didn't even smile. "You got any better ideas, Lew and I are on your side. Okay, I'll start off on point for the first hour."

Each of the next ten days was a repetition of the first—except that each day got worse. Insects burrowed into their clothes and took up residence in their hair and skin. At times strange creatures followed behind or alongside them, and they kept their spears and machetes ready for whatever it might be. Their ration of whiskey was gone by the fourth day, and whenever they found water they boiled it and poured it carefully into their canteens.

They ran out of food on the sixth day. Finding more food was a matter of survival. There were small deer in the jungle growth, but without a gun—or even a bow and arrow—at their disposal the odds on their sneaking up on a deer were far from good. They went two days without any real food. As even the fruit they could eat became scarcer their bellies growled for attention. Their tempers grew shorter and they were wise enough to keep conversation to a minimum; they couldn't afford any emotional clashes. That could kill them off as effectively as any poison or wild animal.

On the seventh day they were stopped by a sudden commotion, the sounds of undergrowth snapping and breaking off to their right. They froze, ready for anything, but whatever it was had no interest in them. A shrill scream, a strangled bleat of a sound, tore through the air, followed by a deep inhuman snarl. There came a final animal shriek, silence, and then the rumbling cough of a big cat.

"It's a blasted jaguar," Lew whispered. "Got to be. Don't think they have leopards in this part of the continent."

"Who cares?" Vance told him. "As long as it stays away from us. Let's get the hell out of here!"

Shag held them still with a sharp motion of his hand. "No! Stay right where you are. If that was a jaguar and he's got a kill, then we wait for him to finish his meal. Lew, see if you can get a fire going. Vance, you help. Make some torches if you can. Bundle up some grass."

Vance was stunned. "Do you mean to fight that animal for whatever it was he killed?"

"Not quite." Shag was trying to see through the thick growth. "From those sounds we heard I'd say it was a deer of some kind he got. If it was big enough he'll eat his fill and after that he won't be dangerous. The chances are he'll leave and come back later."

"And if he sticks around?"

"That's where our torches'll come in. We've got to get in there and get a hunk of that meat or we're going to be goners. If it's a big cat he'll watch us. We'll have time to use a machete and cut us some dinner."

"But what if he doesn't agree with your plan?" Vance persisted.

"Then we use the spears and the torches and even the machetes if we have to! Shut up and get to work, dammit!"

They waited an hour, then started forward, Shag slicing the undergrowth with his machete, the others close behind, one torch lit and smoking heavily, another held ready to be ignited. They broke through the edge of a large clearing by a stream and looked on a magnificent jaguar, his face bloodied from tearing apart a horned deer. The big cat was on his feet, watching them closely, tail slowly inscribing an arc. He didn't move when he saw them, which to Shag was the best sign in the world. He was sated, and fighting was the last thing that interested the animal.

Shag remembered his own lessons of survival in the wild. When faced with a completely new and possibly very dangerous threat, an animal that isn't endangered, that isn't hungry, will almost always back off. The path of least resistance is the law of the jungle or the forest or anywhere else. It was worth the gamble. "Light that second torch," he told the others, never taking his eyes from the animal, which stared back at him with fearless intensity. Lew handed him the blazing torch, which he held in his left hand. His right hand held his machete, which he had no intention of using against that killing machine. "Okay, get ready," he told the others.

"What the hell are you doing!" Vance hissed at him as Shag started forward. Shag ignored him, stepped into the open and stood erect. He held the torch high and slightly in front of him, and without any warning he let out a tremendous shout and ran forward like a madman, yelling crazily. Startled, the great cat backed away and went into a crouch. Shag stood by the bloody carcass, staring at the jaguar and its great bared teeth. But the cat wasn't moving.

Shag didn't take his eyes away for a second. "Cut off a hindquarter, goddammit," he ordered the others. "Just cut it off fast so we can back off."

He stood that way for the sixty seconds or less that it took Lew, his great bulk slamming the sharp machete into the mangled carcass, to cut away a large chunk of hind leg. "Got it," he told Shag. "We're starting back. Vance has the meat. You start back now."

Shag backed up slowly, and knew all was well as the jaguar slowly sank to the ground, his belly full, willing to let these strange scavengers make off with a portion of his kill.

They moved steadily for another two hours until they came alongside a stream where they dropped exhausted to the ground. "Lew. The fire," Shag said. Shag forced himself up, told Vance to work with him, and thirty minutes later they were in their safe clearing again, several fires going. They cut branches to hold chunks of meat and started to cook their first meal in days.

The meat was indescribably delicious to them. They forced themselves to eat slowly, knowing the well-cooked meat would have to hold them for the next several days. Lew hacked open the leg bone, scraped out marrow, and ordered the others to share it with him. "Your vitamins and minerals, gentlemen," he said. "God knows we all need it."

When they were done and darkness embraced them again, Vance sat with his chin propped on his knees, staring into the fire. "You know, I'll never be able to look a vulture in the eye again."

"I should think not," Lew agreed. "You're liable to find your own brother looking back, right!"

By late afternoon of the sixteenth day they had it before them. "There it is," Shag said. "We'll be there tomorrow." They looked up at the great sharp-edged plateau under a heavy mantle of clouds that streamed down from the high mountain range beyond. Every so often they had a break in the running mist and the plateaus showed with remarkable clarity. "You ever see Grand Mesa in Colorado?" Shag asked. "Except for the trees and those clouds they could be the same place. It must be nine thousand feet above sea level, also."

"Or even higher," Lew grunted. "But whatever it is it looks marvelous. I'm flamin' grateful to be here."

Vance sighed. "Optimism is a disease with you two. I'm glad to be here, too. But just where the hell *here* is I don't know."

"We'll find out tomorrow when we're up there," Shag offered.

Lew grinned. "Be funny as hell if all we found was more trees, wouldn't it?"

Vance's latent irritation broke through his carefully

guarded reserve. "Fuck off," he snapped at his friend.

Lew remained unpertrubed. "That's how they settle a tie in a bathing-beauty contest, isn't it?"

"We'll make camp here for the night," Shag said, and separated the two men before things got out of hand.

They made the climb slowly, aching in every muscle and joint, fighting a precipitous, slippery mountain that guarded its approaches with gnarled undergrowth and thorns almost every foot of the way. They had no breath left for talking, the air getting thinner but at least offering touches of blessed coolness as they ascended tortuously but relentlessly. Their clothes were in tatters, they had blisters on their hands, and fiery rashes under their arms and around their groins, and yet this mysterious plateau and whatever it held had been the goal that had kept them going throughout this final, savage, all-day struggle. They stopped only to drink their remaining water, and the last pieces of meat were chewed slowly and swallowed slowly in order to give their twisted stomachs a decent chance of keeping it down. The hours disappeared in an unvarying dialogue of grunting and gasping, of dragging themselves up the slope, of helping one another, of accepting this last challenge as the worst of all they had known in this brutal country.

Finally, though, they stood upright, triumphant, knowing they had beaten the jungle and the miles and the lack of food and the unknown. They still didn't know what they would find here and they didn't care. They'd made it. For the moment that was all that mattered. The sun was low over the distant horizon when they sank slowly to the ground. They were exhausted, their chests heaved, spots danced before their eyes, but they began to appreciate the coolness and their strength came back faster than they would have believed possible.

Shag was the first to break the long silence. "We're here. We did it. We beat that stinking Rosario and we beat the headhunters and we beat the goddamned jungle." Involuntarily clenching his massive fists, he stood like a great statue in this quiet moment that represented something more than survival. He did not understand it all, because just staying alive had been his prime concern for so many weeks now—through the violent storm that began to tear apart the innards of their DC-6 to the wild landing and crash; the toying with their lives that Rosario had so enjoyed, the setup to nail them for sport by the guards across the border; and then the worst of all, the weeks in the jungle and their miraculous avoidance of a dozen diseases, a dozen violent deaths. It was all still something of a mystery to him.

Then again, it was really no mystery at all. The three of them traveled from one strange country to another as a matter of course. Jungle, desert, tundra, mountains—they might be found anywhere from a high peak to a dismal swamp, and they all adhered religiously to the first rule of surviving that sort of movement. Every six months they were poked and prodded and stabbed with needles that warded off typhoid and typhus, malaria and yellow fever, cholera or dengue fever, encephalitis. Now it had paid off in spades in a way they'd never anticipated. No fever, no disease. They were hardened by their arduous trek. Even Lew had shed twenty or thirty pounds, or maybe he hadn't lost that much and had simply converted his porcine bulk back into muscle. They all looked like hell but those looks were deceiving. They had turned their ordeal into an endurance test they had not experienced for many years.

Reborn. The word echoed through Shag's thoughts until Vance's words interrupted his reverie.

"Okay, people. We did it. We beat the jungle and all the bad guys. So what? We're in a bowl of fog on top of a plateau in the middle of nowhere. What do we do now? Start a lost colony?" He swept his arm through the air in an angry gesture. "The mystery airfield isn't even here. It's just high jungle grass and a lot of cold air and all this stinking fog. Jesus!"

They looked around. Clouds scudded overhead, bathed in the orange light of the setting sun. Their ears no longer pounded madly from their exertions and for the first time, really, they heard the wind as it blew their tattered clothes and bent the grass around them. It *did* seem as if they'd been separated completely from the rest of the human race.

Shag clapped Vance on the shoulder. "You're wrong, baby. We made it, all right. We're here and so is that mystery field."

"Where, goddammit!"

"You're standing on it."

Vance looked at his friend as if he'd lost his mind. "It's all grass, Shag."

"Well, maybe it's a grass field," Lew volunteered.

"Uh uh," Shag said confidently. "Stamp your foot against the ground."

"What?" The word chorused from both Vance and Lew.

"Stamp your damn foot," Shag repeated, the first touch of impatience showing. The men did.

"Okay, now my foot hurts," Lew complained. "What's it all about?"

Shag held his machete high and brought it whistling

down to slam into the ground. They were convinced he was crazy, even more so when he looked up at them, grinning. "There! Hear it?"

"Hear what?" Vance asked.

"Open your damned ears and *listen* when I do it again." The blade went up and came down and this time they heard the metal clank against something hard.

"You must have hit a rock," Lew remarked. "Wonderful."

The blade whipped down again once, twice, three times, each time in a different place, and each time there was that same dull, ringing sound. "It's not a rock, you idiots. That's concrete under this stuff. You're standing on a runway that's covered over with grass."

They bent down, poking the ground. Lew tore away a section of grass and turf and chopped away with his machete until a tiny shower of sparks glittered beneath the blade. "Glory be . . . it's here. It's really here."

"Which means it's got to go somewhere," Shag said, bringing them back to reality. "We just came up the end of the damn thing, so we go that way," he added, pointing with the blade in his hand. "Spread out. It's going to be dark soon and we're going to need to find a place out of this wind. It's going to be a bitch tonight."

They walked steadily, each man a dozen feet from the next, the sinking sun throwing long shadows, touching the rim of the mountains behind them, toward the Pacific. Suddenly Shag signaled with his hand. The others froze, straining to hear.

A discordant, banging sound came to them. There was no pattern to it, but it was certainly not natural, nothing that grew or lived in this country. Fingers tightened on machete handles and their spears instinctively came up.

"What the hell is it?" Vance whispered.

"I'd know that bleedin' sound *anywhere*," Lew said, relieved. "I've heard it all my life." He saw the others waiting. "That's a hangar door. The bottom rails are loose and the noise we're hearing is the door blowing up in the wind, and then banging down against the rails. There's some kind of building up ahead of us." He started out without hesitation and Vance and Shag ran to keep up with him.

"They were here, all right. Dorsch, maybe even Bormann, all of them at one time. Look." An old truck had been pushed off into the high grass, stripped of its valuable parts, the faded paint on the side unmistakable in its presentation of a once-blood-red swastika. "Let's keep moving," Lew urged. "We're almost there and we ain't got much light left."

The ghostly sounds grew around them: doors that lifted and banged in the wind, fingers of wind curling around corners and whistling through unseen spaces, drumming off wires. Large shapes loomed in the deep orange fog: walls, power poles, more old trucks, each of them adding to the thumping, creaking, whistling, groaning chorus.

"There's an old barracks," Vance said, pointing.

"Uh huh. And here, to the left. Looks like what used to be a hangar," Lew added.

Shag had walked off to the side. "Old power station here. Some of the wires are still up."

"This place gives me the creeps," Vance mused. "It's like something out of an old Vincent Price movie."

"All we need is Errol Flynn in a leather flying helmet, right?" Lew shot back.

"Shut up. Find anyplace for us to sleep tonight?"

"Let's look beyond that building over there."

"You and Vance go ahead," Lew said suddenly. "I'm going to see if any of these trucks still got some oil in them. I can rig us a lamp that way. Anything to give us some light tonight."

"Okay. We'll be right back."

"Righto. Sing out so we can find one another."

Shag and Vance walked together in the dimming light. The sun was just about down and with these clouds around them it would get dark swiftly. All around them was high grass, old equipment, more buildings than they ever thought could have been put up here secretly. "They must have had an army here," Vance observed.

"That was the general idea," Shag said. "Or at least the beginnings of a new army. They must have brought millions in rare jewels and stuff like that."

"They looted all of Europe. It would have been easy."

They talked as they moved around the perimeter of the strip, dense undergrowth all around them. "This thing sits right at the edge of jungle," Shag remarked. "Hey! Where—"

Vance was running to their left. The last spears of the sun falling beyond the horizon had blossomed in the scudding clouds and sprayed a final pink glow down onto the jungle growth. Shag caught up to the now-standing Vance, whose voice slowly tapped out words, as if on a typewriter: "I don't believe it. I just—do—not—believe—it!"

Shag couldn't see a thing in the fading light. "Believe *what*, dammit?"

Vance lifted his arm and pointed to what they had hoped to find—something that could fly. What Shag saw had wings and the shape of an airplane, but any resemblance to a *real* airplane, one that might be capable of flight, ended there. They walked closer and in the gloomy shadows they faced a hideous wreck of what had once been an airplane. A huge three-engined, slab-sided, corrugated monster, sagging on its haunches. Even in this first glance they saw it was scarred and covered with scabs and gripped by what had to be at least ten years of vegetable growth that chained it to the heart of the high jungle.

"I think," Vance said slowly, "that I am going to pass out. Is that thing really an airplane?"

Mercifully, night was now upon them and only a faint outline remained visible. "It was, I guess," Shag replied. "Right now it's more like a leper colony with wings."

They worked their way back to the flicker of a fire started by Lew. "You know something?" Shag said to Vance. "I was thinking of all the people we killed, how far we've come, everything we've done, hoping we might find something to fly out of here, and then we found . . . *that*."

"Got any ideas?" Vance asked.

"Yeah. Move over. I think I'll pass out with you."

7

They slept in a long and ghostly barracks, able to see by the light of two oil lamps Lew rigged from congealed engine oil, some frayed rope, rocks, and old buckets. Smoke rose in thick clouds, but a steady breeze moved it away from them and offered some resistance to the swarms of insects that had received invitations to the feast by whatever secret odors the men's bodies sent forth on the winds. They were wise enough to overturn the metal cots they found and kick aside the mouldy mattresses, perferring to rest their bodies on the open leaf springs. God only knew what might be living in those mattresses, some form of venomous spider or centipede, no doubt. They followed their established rule of two sleeping and one awake. During the night Shag awoke and joined Lew on watch while Vance slept.

"What about that flying machine you saw with Vance?" Lew asked.

"No way to tell," Shag said. "I know it's got leprosy,

just for starters." He saw Lew grin. "But until we look inside," Shag went on, "who knows?"

"You're right," Lew agreed. "But all those buildings. You never know what we might find inside them. Anything."

"Or nothing," Shag cautioned. "Turn it off, Lew. Get some sleep."

"I'll try. It's just all the noise in here keeping me awake."

"You mean the wind?"

"Screw the wind. It's my stomach. It thinks my throat's been cut. Nighty-night, mate."

They stood side by side at the edge of the jungle. They'd made a quick walk through every building in the long-abandoned secret German base, and the only complete thing with wings still on it rested like a great heap of scrap iron within the edges of the jungle bordering the field. Now they were back to the sorry mess, studying it more carefully.

"There must be five hundred pounds of birdshit on that thing, not to mention what's in it. The goddamn stuff is everywhere," Shag said. He squinted into the brief shaft of bright sunlight that lanced down through a break in the clouds and brightened the underfoliage. He heard a flapping sound and the three men looked up to see a large black shape fluttering down through the leafy blanket before them. A great condor lurched to a clumsy halt on the tail of the airplane. The bird studied them through red eyes, and with the nonchalance only a successful scavenger can assume, defecated on the corrugated metal.

"Make that five hundred and one pounds," Shag sighed.

"At least Lew can clean up that kind of mess,"

Vance said quickly. "We're lucky we've got a mechanical genius with us. Who knows? Maybe the earth will tremble again when he brings that phoenix back to life. I wonder, though. What in God's name are those engines like, and—"

"Screw off," Lew broke in. "Who appointed you chief mucky-muck for jobs around here?"

"You're the mechanic, aren't you?"

"Dead on you are with that remark, Admiral, and you better get something straight right now. I fly airplanes and I fix airplanes, and for a long time there's going to be a hell of a lot more fixing than there is flying. If there's anything to fix, that is. But let us not forget our priorities. I will work and you will work with me and maybe you two will be heroes again in the big bright blue, eh? But I do not scrape birdshit off airplanes because some fancy-pants Yank gets a bug up his bum. That is a community project. I scrape, you scrape, we all scrape, and I hopes you've got long fingernails. But even that comes later. There's a bleedin' army living inside that thing."

"Army?" The word echoed from Vance.

"You better believe it. It's been in the jungle all this time, and you know what's inside there? Snakes and scorpions and rats and centipedes and spiders and birds and mice and wasps and roaches and beetles and moths and more things than God ever dreamed up in His worst nightmares. They'll be inside the wings and the engines and the fuselage and in every hatch and space you can imagine. That's a living horror, that is, and this is one chap that does not intend to go running off at the mouth or making a stupid move and getting bitten, chewed, stung, or whatever. There's a better way."

Vance looked at Shag. "He's just spoken more words

without stopping than he has in all the years I've known him. I think he's in love with the idea of rebuilding that monster." Vance turned back to Heath. "What, pray tell, *is* that iron creature?"

"It's a bloody Junkers."

"Junkers?"

"You pronounce it Yonker, if that means anything to you. It's a Ju-52. First one flew back in 1932."

"That's nearly fifty years ago!"

"Don't matter none," Lew said with a touch of pique. "Look, friend, if there's one thing I know in this world, it's airplanes, right?"

"No argument there."

"All right, then. What I'm trying to get through your thick head is not to judge this thing by what we're looking at. Underneath all that birdshit and everything else is probably the greatest airplane ever built." They studied the iron crosses and the swastikas barely visible through the curling and flaking paint and all the debris heaped on the machine. "They was Hitler's main airplane for the war. You name it, this thing has done it. Started out as a commercial airliner five years before the DC-3 ever made its first flight. Bomber, paratrooper aircraft, assault plane—if there was a job to do, this one did it. Look aft of the cabin door. It's still got one of its turrets. It's got the kind of engines you could shoot full of holes and it would still keep flying."

Lew had an almost mystical look on his face. For a while he kept his silence and shook his head slowly as memories flooded his mind. She was ancient and battered and yet, knowing what he knew, she still tugged at his pilot's heartstrings, slab-sided, corrugated, creaking son of a bitch that she was. It didn't look as if it could fly even when it was new and then, if they managed to get it off the ground, it would be only by lurching clumsily into the air. But no airplane was as misleading in its looks as the old Junkers. Lew Heath felt a strange hope rising within him. No airplane could ever look so bad and still have as many possibilities as the battered old Ju-52.

"You know what the krauts called her?" he asked his friends. Shag and Vance were reluctant to break in on Lew's reverie, because they both understood he was seeing beyond that scarred exterior. "Iron Annie. The ship made of iron. The airplane that could do anything." He turned suddenly to the other men. "You guys are hero pilots. You've both pushed airliners. You ever know an airplane, especially an airliner, that didn't have a redline on it?"

"They never built one," Shag said at last.

"You're wrong, matey," Lew said. "You're looking at the only one. No redline. They ain't got a speed for this thing that's dangerous. That's right. There's no airspeed limitations on this machine. You fly her as hard as you want and as fast as she can go and you'll never break those wings. They got eight spars in each wing. She's built like a bloody tank, with a trussed, cantilevered bridge for the wings. Would you believe that—"

"Hold it, hold it," Shag broke in. "Would you believe I'm thirsty and I'm starving and we'd better do something about that little problem before we do anything else?"

"Well, there's got to be water up here," Vance said. "They had a whole army living here. That's obvious. And they wouldn't be flying in water, so they had wells. Probably drilled down into the mountain until they found a water table or an underground river or—"

"Good thinking," Shag interrupted again. "Go find

that well of yours, and we'll set up a system for boiling the water in quantity this time. Lew, what do you think about food?"

Lew Heath showed a crooked smile. "You think you're such a smart bastard, don't you? You know as well as I do that where you find a condor or a vulture you'll find animals, because if there wasn't any around those flipping things wouldn't be here either. And from all that bird poop on Annie over there, the pickings can't be too bad."

"What about weapons?" Shag pressed.

"Got the makings of a bloody arsenal all around us. With all this metal and wiring and springs and stuff like that, I can make us some nifty crossbows. A hell of a sight better than a bleedin' bow and arrow, unless one of you two just happens to be Robin Hood?"

Shag nodded. "They must have had generators here. Think any of that will be working?"

"If it ain't I can get one of them truck engines to run. If there's any fuel, that is."

"What about batteries?" Vance queried.

"Don't need 'em," Lew sniffed. "Work up hand cranks if we have to. Also make a windlass sort of pulley to turn over an engine. First open one up and clean it out and get it turning over. If they still got the makings I knows how to do the fixings. But Shag's right. First things first. Get off your bum, Admiral, and start looking for the water. Shag, I think we'd better make an inventory of everything we find."

"And a safe place to stay at night," Shag added. "This is jaguar country and the next one we run into could be a lot hungrier and meaner than the one we met before. That means a steady fire and a building we can make into a stronghold."

He hitched up his pants and ignored the bellow of

complaint from his empty stomach. "Gentlemen, it's time to play Robinson Crusoe."

Within five days they were new men with a new lease on life. Not only was there fuel remaining in the tanks of several different vehicles, but they found the underground storage tanks with several hundred gallons remaining of gasoline and oil. When the Germans left this eagle's nest of a secret airfield they scattered through the buildings and the grounds all manner of equipment they'd used to support the base. By the second morning, Lew had a gasoline-driven generator working, and it was only a matter of hours from that point before they had lights, a grinding wheel for tools and weapons, a working air compressor, and more power than they could handle. The equipment was old, sometimes ancient, and belts kept breaking and hoses kept leaking, but they got it to work and they could repair what broke and that meant an entirely different world. With the generator working and the grinding wheel available, a rusty old razor was honed to a gleaming edge, mirrors were cleaned, old soap bars frothed in tin cans, and each man enjoyed a blessed shave, with Shag electing to trim rather than scrape away his luxuriant beard. They boiled water in huge pots, built a working shower and lathered and scrubbed themselves furiously. There were three wells, not one, and to the best of these Lew jury-rigged a pumping system that kept the water flowing into a holding tank. They collected all the best parts of every vehicle scattered through the place, and in one workshed they found a truck in remarkably good condition—even its tires were usable.

"Someone had an eye for machines," Lew observed.

"Whoever jacked this thing up did us a bloody great favor, they did." He cleaned the engine, turned it over by hand, ran power to the ancient battery he had cleaned up and although the battery remained so much slag for starting power, the generator was enough to get the truck engine started. They recleaned the plugs and the distributor and the mags, and oiled and cleaned and greased, and within three days of starting a triumphant Lew Heath drove across their field.

As each step was completed and they had more tools and power at their disposal, the next series of events became more clearly defined in terms of need and capability. Food remained their single greatest problem and even copious amounts of water wouldn't help anymore. True to his word, Lew knew how to fashion weapons. The others worked as his assistants as he ground the materials for the crossbows he had promised.

"I thought we might not need these things," he explained. "Found me a machine gun in one of them sheds, but it's no good to us. Pretty well rusted out and there's no ammo anywhere. Bits and pieces of rifles, even parts of some Lugers around, but none of them could or should be trusted. So we'll play in Sherwood Forest, we will."

The crossbows were deadly. The metal arrows had great killing power, propelled as they were by springs from old trucks and machinery. Their aim, however, was rotten, and Lew came to screaming several times that he wasn't a Krupp munitions works with a limitless supply of arrows. They killed several parrots—at an average of thirty-four arrows per bird, but the meat kept them going. Lew muttered he wanted better food than "a couple of flamin' carrier pigeons," and Shag turned to a combination of his own skills in the wild and the instruments Lew fashioned.

They built hair-trigger traps that netted them several small furry animals that looked something like a cross between a raccoon and a possum, and judging from the taste, a liberal amount of wharf rat thrown in. Using the crossbows, Shag rigged a series of triggers at the edge of cleared spaces and along trails. If an animal hit the tripwire, the movement released the crossbow and a long steel arrow impaled the creature. The first time they tried their new device it worked beautifully, but whatever it was they hit was a long ways from dead and took off in a crashing escape through the undergrowth with the arrow imbedded in its body.

They solved that problem by attaching a heavy steel wire to their arrows, and the uproar they heard in the middle of the night brought them running from their bunkhouse, crossbows in their hands. Lew kept the generator running all night for lights to cover the area around them and they dashed to their animal traps to find a great boar tearing apart their equipment. The arrow had slammed into his belly, but it takes a great deal more than that to kill a wild tusker. He would have gotten clean away except that the wire tangled in his short legs and he was lurching about in circles. He took one look at his tormentors and with a shrill squeal of rage hurled himself in their direction. The wire tripped him again and Shag stepped to the side and fired a crossbow bolt directly into the animal's head. It still took him twenty minutes to die, but the three pilots were ecstatic at the prospect of their meal.

There's only one thing that tastes better than wild boar cooked over an open fire, and that's the wild boar you caught yourself. They gorged themselves, and afterward, resting around the fire, they talked quietly among themselves. They were past their survival syndrome. They knew they had food and water and weapons and power. Now it was time to think beyond that point.

"It's strange," Shag told his friends. "Look at us. We're wearing rags. We haven't had a drink or a smoke for God knows how many weeks. We've eaten the most basic of foods and—you know what? I haven't felt this good or been this content in—well, I don't know how long. The rest of the world could have died off, for all we know up here."

"Piss on 'em," Lew said, following his remark with a great belch. They grinned at one another.

"I know what you mean." Vance nodded. "Somewhere out there, beyond those mountains and that sea, there's a world and a life that doesn't belong to this time or this place. It's almost as if we went down a different tunnel than the rest of the world. All our problems can only be solved with our hands and our imaginations. You know something, you two? I haven't gone to sleep like this for years. I'm tired, I'm absolutely worn out, but it's like a cool breeze has been blowing through my mind and cleaning it out, and I haven't thought about a hydrogen bomb in weeks."

He fell silent, and Shag and Lew looked at each other in astonishment. They'd never heard this Vance Brady before. And what the hell was this crap about a hydrogen bomb? They made a silent decision to let it be.

Shag climbed to his feet and stretched. "There's just one problem I think we need to solve." The others looked up at him. "I really can't stand the sight of you two ragamuffins anymore, you know. You look like beggars in those rags, the both of you."

"Sorry, darlin'," Lew sneered. "Tomorrow night for dinner I'll wear me pink bra and remember the lipstick."

"Don't forget me for the first dance," Vance offered.

"Ah, if you only knew," Shag told them.

"Knew what?"

"It's time to dump these rags, troops." Shag clicked his heels together. "We are due to rid ourselves of these homes for fleas, ticks, lice, ants, and assorted and sundry other bugs that have been feasting on our bods, lo these many weeks."

Lew jerked a thumb in Shag's direction. "He's flipped his wig, he has."

"Think it's the altitude?" Vance asked.

"I think it's the pig. Maybe he thought he was eating a member of his own family. Royal pig, of course," he added hastily.

"See that building?" Shag asked, and watched them nod as they looked at a barracks. "In there, earlier today, I found a treasure, a stack of sealed lockers with wondrous goodies within."

"Shag, clasp your ass to the earth and hang on," Vance urged. "It's a long fall from the top of your looney head to the ground."

"Never you mind. Remember, now, you two cats wait here until I call you. And no peeking."

"Peeking?" Lew was openly worried by this point. "Shag, you all right? Seriously now, you are sounding a bit queer, you know."

Shag chuckled. "If I catch you peeking, I'll kick the living shit out of you."

Vance relaxed. "Nothing wrong with him, Lew."

They watched Shag walk off to the building and disappear inside. Ten minutes went by and they heard Shag calling. *"Achtung! Schnell! Komenzee vront und zenter!"*

"What the hell did he say?" Lew asked.

"He bloody well sounds like Sid Caesar to me," Vance said.

"I think he wants us in that building."

Vance heaved himself to his feet. "Humor him. Let's go, laddie."

They entered the barracks and stopped dead in their tracks. Shag stood before them resplendent in the uniform of an SS colonel, boots, garrison belt, peaked hat, insignia, and all. He clicked his heels and threw out his arm in a perfect Nazi salute. *"Sieg Heil!"*

"Jesus Christ! Where the hell did you—"

Shag turned around slowly. "Nifty threads, won't you say? There's a whole bunch of foot lockers filled with these things. Army, air force, SS. Of course, the brass is tarnished and the boots need polishing and there may be a lot of dust in the pockets and some lint here and there, but—" He shrugged. "Take your choice, gentlemen. Whatever fits you best. And then we shall burn this shit we've been wearing."

Twenty minutes later three ghosts out of the Nazi past emerged from the barracks. "I could use me a monocle, I could," Lew said to himself before a broken mirror. "That and a swagger stick. Who do you think I look like, Vance?"

"Fatso Goering. The Reichsmarshall himself."

"He was a flippin' fag, you bastard."

"You know what they say, Lew. If the uniform fits—"

"And if I had that swagger stick I'd ram it right up your bleedin' arse."

Burning their old rags was a deeply symbolic gesture for them. By tomorrow morning they would have met all their survival criteria. It was time to check out the phoenix.

8

They sprawled on the ground, exhausted. All were filthy, oblivious to the insects marching over their clothes and through their hair. It had taken them four hours of steady, brutal slashing and swinging with their sharp jungle knives simply to cut away the vines and heavy growth that snared the great German tri-motor to the ground. Now she was, if not free, at least unfettered, and only her ponderous weight of eighteen thousand pounds resting on three tires squashed flat along their bottoms, the two main and the one tail-gear, kept the Ju-52 chained to the spot from which she had not moved for ten years or more.

Lew Heath dragged himself up onto one elbow. "I'll get the truck with the compressor, lads. See to those tire valves."

Still prone, Shag lifted an arm in compliance. "Let's go, Vance."

"Get the number of that truck that ran over me, will you?" Brady asked.

Lew was on his feet. "If you're still there when I get

back, bucko, there'll be tread marks across your balls."
He climbed into the cab of the old German truck,
reached out to the cable clamp rigged to his generator,
locked it onto the starting wire, and turned the key
switch. It still amazed him that the old truck kicked
over with its faithful clattering roar. But then again,
he thought smiling, why be surprised at anything an
old Ford could do. That airplane might be German
and the clothes he wore were German, but almost all
the other equipment had been brought down from the
United States. Smart. He released the clamp, shifted
into gear, and rolled slowly toward the two men and
the airplane. Vance waved him to the left side of the
old machine, and Lew backed the truck beneath the
great nose engine and propeller. The hose would reach
from there. He climbed down to join Vance.

"It looks better than I expected," Vance said with
obvious surprise. "I mean, these tires are weather-
checked, with some splits along the surface, but they're
in amazing condition. In this climate I thought that
rubber would never have lasted this—"

"Not rubber. It's buna. Don't look so surprised.
They also called it plastic. These tires are pure synthetic," Lew told him.

"From the Second World War?" Vance didn't believe him.

"They started making these in 1943. They last forever. Now, how about that valve?"

"Some crap in it, but I think it's clear."

Lew looked doubtful. "How much air?"

"Until it looks good. Best gauge in the world. Let's
go."

They hooked up the air compressor, Lew revved the
truck engine, and they watched as the old tire began
to swell slowly along the bottom, and then to fill.

There was a terrible, deep groan as the tire kept taking air.

"By God, that's the strut!" Shag exclaimed. "It's still free. It's moving . . . *look at it!*" He was right. As the tire inflated, the big oleo strut of the gear leg began to push itself upward, and the noisy complaint they heard was metal coming unstuck.

Lew untwisted the hose, showing relief and astonishment. "I can't—I mean, even the tube has held up!"

"Don't waste any time. Let's get that other one," Shag ordered. "We don't know if we've got a good tube and tire seal and we'll never move her all the way up without tires."

The second main tire went in much the same fashion. Now there was the tail tire, and Lew busied himself backing the truck under the wing through the path their machetes had hacked free. He was less sure about the tailwheel tire. Then he remembered it bore the lightest load for this machine, so he began filling the tube and, again, the synthetic material from the war decades past was still secure. Rubber would have gone to pieces by now, but that German buna, developed and rushed into production when the oil fields were set aflame, was almost as good as the day the Germans had abandoned this airplane ten years before.

The ground before the tailwheel was rough, and they planned to ease their load by laying down planks over which the tailwheel would roll. Everything they did was only a prelude to studying the machine, to find out if there was even a ghost of a chance of rejuvenating what had become a corrugated corpse. They couldn't do much with the Ju-52 squatting on broken haunches in thick jungle growth. They had to bring her out, closer to electrical power, in order to begin all the work that was required.

Lew lined up the truck directly in front of the nose engine. He ran three cables from each of the two main gear legs to the truck chassis. Then he climbed into the truck, warned the others clear of the cables in case they should break—they would tear a man's body in half as they whipped free—and tested the load. The truck engine kept running and the transmission wasn't tearing itself to pieces, but all he could accomplish before the truck wheels started spinning was to rock the great airplane where it rested. He climbed down.

"I've got an idea," Shag said. They drove wedges behind the rear truck wheels. "That'll keep the damn thing from moving back at all. It'll throw all its pull into the cables."

"It still won't be enough," Lew decided. "We need some more power."

"Can you get another truck running?"

"I doubt it and I don't think we need to. Vance, you get up here in the truck. Shag, you get on one tire and I'll get on the other. On a flat ground I used to roll a DC-3 with just one man and myself. The trick with these tires, which are a hell of a sight bigger, is to put your back to the tire and use all the strength of your legs and your back. Together with that truck I think we can swing it."

"One way to find out. Let's go."

It was just enough to make the critical difference, with muscle power applied directly to the tires. Vance kept gunning the truck engine and they got a rocking motion started and picked up the rock and the chant together. *"Heave!"* Shag cried out, and he and Lew threw their strength into their backs and legs against the tires. She rolled just a bit more. *"Heave!"* And a little more this time. "When she starts don't let up!" he shouted to Vance. "This is the one. *Let's get it.*" They gave it everything. The tires lifted to the slight depression from the rocking motion, and then they were at the edge and Vance was playing that damn truck like a violin, and there came that slight lurch and Shag and Lew dug in desperately and she was free and rolling.

"Don't stop, you son of a bitch! Don't stop! Keep her going!"

She creaked and groaned through every inch of her weary body, but she was out of the jungle and moments later the tailwheel was also on the grass-covered concrete. Lew scrambled out from beneath the great wing. He ran forward on one side of the airplane, Shag on the other, and they jumped and sang and waved their arms wildly and directed Vance carefully to the spot they'd picked. Vance moved her like eggs on a bulldozer and when they wanted him to stop he eased out the clutch. He looked back with widening eyes as the great machine kept rolling, until Shag and Lew each shoved a wooden block in front of the main wheels. A final groan came from the Ju-52 as it ended its first movement in a decade.

Because of the sudden storms that swept down from the mountains and provided the almost constant cloud cover, it would have been foolish to leave the airplane unattended in the open. They chocked all the tires, pounded stakes deeply into the concrete, and tied the Ju-52 earthbound through the gear legs, the tiedowns beneath the wings, and to three different points from the tail. Then they stood back, sweat-soaked, breathing hard, and stared.

"It's like she's just come alive," Shag murmured. And she had. Free of the jungle growth, with the wind blowing across her surfaces, the Ju-52 trembled through her wings and her body. The ailerons began to move, a ghostly motion, the left aileron moving up as the right went down, the rudder twitching, then slamming hard over with a creaking-banging-grinding sound; the ailerons reversed suddenly.

"It's the wind," Vance called out. "I'll get into the cockpit and tie down the controls."

Lew snatched him by the arm. "No, you nit! I told you, that thing is dangerous. Find some other way to secure the controls. Get some planks of wood. We'll drill holes in them and use them as external locks."

When they were done Lew took the truck to retrieve the load of bombs he'd prepared for this moment. They used pliers and vise grips to open the hatches beneath the wings, to unscrew the access and accessory and inspection panels. Even these moves proved dangerous, because creatures of all kinds fell through the open spaces or poised on the edges within the structure to fall upon anything moving within their reach. The bombs were cans soaked in oily rags and dirt to prevent open flame. They burned through long wicks and gave off thick smoke and an incredibly noxious odor. They went into the tail section, into the fuselage, up into the belly hatches, through the cabin door on long poles, in the cockpit the same way, into the wings, until there were at least thirty of the choking canisters within the Ju-52, each pouring forth its foul-smelling cloud. Within minutes the entire airplane was filled with the killing fumes, and the men sat well back on the truck bed, watching.

"We know one thing, anyway," Lew told the others as they waited. "The wind moved those controls. That means they're all still hooked up and working well. The way those ailerons moved I'll bet a quid they're push-pull rods and not cables. If that's true, they'll be corrosion-resistant and we could have a spot of luck going for us."

As the minutes passed they were witness to an incredible scene. Smoke poured from every opening, crack, and seam in the big airplane, and they heard rustling sounds and then frantic movement within the Junkers. Through every opening they came, the insects and the reptiles and God knew what else, crawling, slithering, creeping, sliding, walking, running, fluttering, staggering—whatever movement there could be was visible before them. Lew brought out another dozen smoke canisters, lit them, and placed them beneath the airplane so the winds would carry them along the outer surfaces. "They'll burn for two or three hours," he said. "I, for one, am quite willing to wait, and if I see one thing moving in there tomorrow, we do it all over again."

The next morning Lew opened the cabin door and stepped back quickly. But not fast enough. Something flew out like a bullet and stung him in the neck. He fell to the ground, writhing in sudden violent pain. Shag smeared the sting with grease from the open pit they used for cooking, and an hour later a fist-sized swelling began to go down. Lew was still white and shaking. "Good God-amighty. What in the hell *was* that thing?"

"Yellow, black, red, and nasty," Shag told him. "You okay?"

"I will be when I get through with Annie this time."

They weren't aware of it but from that moment on that was how they referred to their ancient patient: *Annie.*

The second smoke bombing did the job. "Now," Lew said grimly, "we go to work. First we look at everything that's visible, and then we go find what we can't see. Vance, you're the beanpole in this operation. You're going to crawl through the wings all the way out to the tips. You check each tank, you check the fuel lines and hose connections between them. This thing has tanks like barrels and they're held in place by leather and metal straps. You check each one for security. Grasp it with your hand and shake it. If it doesn't come loose, congratulate yourself. While you're on the way out we'll move the ailerons. You check the rods and bearings all the way out, especially where the connectors come out for the double-wing section behind the main wing. Look for corrosion. Not paint peeling away or anything like that, but under the paint. Check the spars especially and the crossbraces. If there's spar corrosion you'll see it right away. Take this knife, and every now and then scrape along a spar. Sometimes this old duralumin gets brittle, but the odds are with us. This stuff was intended to fly for a hundred years."

"Anything else, teacher?" Vance asked sarcastically.

"Never mind the lip, mate. This is no joke. We'll both be right under you all the time and you're to keep talking to us. We shook up the old girl a bit and we may have loosened a fuel line or two. I don't want you passing out from any fumes. They should drop away through all the open panels but we don't want to take any chances. Understand?"

"I think he loves me," Vance said to Shag.

"Move it, Admiral."

"Oh, God, not you, too."

"I still can't believe it," Vance told them. He rested with his back against the big tire, drinking slowly from their water canteen. "Three leaks. That's all in both wings. Just three lousy leaks! And there aren't any leaks in the tanks. Just connecting points in the lines."

"What about the control rods? The push-pull system?"

"A little binding, but some grease or oil and they'll be fine."

"The spars?"

"You won't believe this but I rubbed them down with a cloth—and you know what? They shine like they were made only yesterday. If there's any corrosion it's not inside the wings."

Lew nodded with a quiet but immense satisfaction. "There's corrosion along the belly. I can patch all that. It isn't load bearing. Most of it is aft of the W.C. where the krauts would piss and dump it overboard."

"W.C.?" Shag had a blank look on his face.

"Water closet," Vance translated. "Head, john, toilet, crapper, bathroom—"

"I get the idea. All the comforts of home."

They crawled through the belly hatches, pulled up the floorboards, opened the access and inspection panels to the control systems, followed the push-pull rods back through the long fuselage, aft of the gun turret, into the tail cone where the rods ended in large bell-cranks and strong cables ran all the way back to the rudder and the elevators. "Jesus, I don't believe it," Lew said. "They've got four cables for each control. You could break three of them and still have everything you need for full control."

Shag shined his light on the cables. "How strong are they?"

"Three-thousand-pound test."

"They look dry?"

"You'd be dry too if you hadn't had any lubrication

for ten years. They'll clean up fine. Our biggest problem is scraping all the birdshit and the dead bugs out of this thing."

"That should be our worst problem."

"I know."

They were thinking the same thoughts. No matter how well everything else worked, the engines were the key to flight. And these were ancient engines that hadn't turned for ten years or more. Which meant the seals were bad, the ignition harnesses were a guess, the carburetors and fuel pumps would have to be removed and cleaned and lubricated and tested thoroughly before going back into the airplane. They made a list plugs, magnetos, electrical systems, vacuum pumps, generators, instrument lines, the long and complicated connections of the throttles to the engines. The same for the mixture controls and carburetor heat. And they'd have to blow out every vacuum line through and into the cockpit, and check out the security of both the Plexiglas and the safety glass. Would the hydraulic pump work? How about the hoses? All the clamps and interconnections? The lines carrying oil? The exhaust stacks were corroded and they'd need every kind of Band-Aid their ingenuity could devise.

Yet it was all there. The airplane was amazingly rugged and absolutely brilliant in design. The only power system for the entire machine was in the brakes. "I can tell they used to be an air-bottle operation. Air pressure. The Messerschmitt used to use these, but someone changed them in this airplane and rigged up a hydraulic pump. It looks like they came out of a DC-3."

"We got brakes?" Shag asked.

"You find out when she moves under her own steam. But I doubt it. And the one thing we ain't got here, damn Victoria, is some jacks so we can pull the wheels and find out. Just pray to your favorite saint, buckos, that the wheel bearings are still greased. The jerries were very matter-of-fact about their machines, you know. The thing to remember is that everything always has a purpose in this airplane. If it's in here it has a job to do. If it's not here then forget it. Simplicity, ruggedness. That's the key to it all."

"Like the props."

Lew nodded. "Fixed pitch. Great for us, I'll tell you. No way in the world I could work with a prop governor under these conditions. But these props are fixed pitch. No prop controls in the machine. *Wunderbar!* Hooray for the Krauts, I say. When it's time to go we lean 'em out for our density altitude with the throttles all the way, balls to the wall, and let 'er rip. That's all there is to it."

"Tell me that again after I hear these engines running," Vance said.

"That I will, Admiral, that I will," Lew promised.

They crowded into the cockpit. What they did from the front office of Iron Annie would tell the final tale. They took their time, studying every dial, switch, control, handle, lever, and device before their eyes. They moved controls forward and backward, from side to side, jiggled them, shook them, tapped and banged on them. They identified the throttles and the mixture controls, and then Lew stopped them quickly.

"Look here, now. See the throttles? The mixture's right behind and below them. You move them up to lean them out, but when you come back on power, watch this—" He left the mixture controls in lean position and pulled back on the throttles as if to reduce power. "See? It's autorich. Anytime you're up high and you pull the power you go automatically into mixture-rich. Smart cockers, the boys who put this thing together, I'll tell you."

There were four separate master switches: one in a box panel behind the copilot, on the bulkhead; another to the right of the copilot on his side wall; and two on the quadrant between the two pilots. They found the magneto switches, the levers that moved each mag from center to left to right and back to both. The spark advance and retard baffled them for half a day until Lew figured it out. "I'll bloody well disconnect those buggers," he announced. "They work fine on the Russian front, but this is Ecuador, not Stalingrad, and we don't need them."

He also found a mystifying system of fuel controls in the belly of the airplane. He figured it out slowly. A special fuel was used for starting and shutting down the airplane in extremely cold weather. It was a complication Lew didn't like. He removed the lines and disconnected the tank, then rerouted the lines for direct connection to the fuel filter and flowback systems in the belly between the engines, directly aft of the nose engine. "It eliminates an aspect we don't need," he told the others. "I've wired the fuel-flow connectors into the open position, and wired the vent system to full open so that there's no chance of air blockage anywhere in the lines."

"What about the fuel pumps?" Shag asked. He had been busy from the beginning, working out a checklist they would use in the airplane, mentally reciting that list a hundred times or however long it took to understand the system and, above everything else in the world, to understand the operational procedures of the Ju-52 and get them in their proper sequence.

"One mechanical pump in each engine," Lew replied. "They come into operation, once the engines are running. We use a manual—a hand pump, a wobble pump like the old fighters—to get the fuel to the engines. When they start the automatic pump takes over. You can tell when you've got enough pressure by these gauges, uh, here."

They marked off the gauges to numbers they would understand. Everything was in metric and they converted to basic minimums. One hundred kilometers was just about sixty-three miles an hour and so Shag figured this thing had to have 120 to 130 kilometers per hour to lift safely off the ground.

"What are these two big handles in front of the pilot seat?"

"Rudder trim. Right engine goes out, you yank the opposite handle. It's connected to a cable and the cable to a bungee cord and then to the rudder. Piss on it, mate. The bungees are all crapped out and will split the first time you try them. Don't sweat it, though. See this dial here?"

"Yeah."

"Takeoff trim settings and flap settings. If we're heavy, you set the flaps at the first pointer on the plus side, right here, and you lower the flaps to ten degrees before starting your roll. That's for a standard two-engine takeoff, so I wouldn't be losing any sleep over the trim if an engine conks out. Not to worry, Shag."

"Just gotta know the routine, Lew."

"I'm with you."

They did everything but dismantle the engines. The mounts were as solid as an oak tree's roots in rich soil. They removed the cowlings from the wing engines and the speed ring from the nose engine to gain access to the interior and accessories. Lew was delighted to confirm a suspicion about the engines. "See these things?" he told the others. "They was driving me straight up a wall, and you know why? Too familiar. They're BMW engines, but—and this is a mighty nice but—they just happens to be Yank engines."

"You mean American?" Vance asked.

"Yank don't mean Zulu, you nit."

"You said they were BMW's. That means Bavarian Motor Works—and that's German."

"A cigar for the clever little devil," Lew chortled. "And right you are. But it so happens I've worked for years on Pratt and Whitney engines and I knows them by heart, inside and out and backward and forward, and these BMW engines, matey, are German copies of the old Pratt and Whitney One Six Nine Zero. The only difference between these and the Yank cobs are that the measurements are in metric. I calls that a great piece of good fortune, I does." He patted each man on the back. "And tonight, I have a special treat for both of you. We clean, we regap, and we triple-check all fifty-four spark plugs from these beauties. Be nice to them, gentlemen, because our lives are going to depend on them cheeky little devils."

Shag liked the nights most of all. Their isolation was total. The coughing rumbles from big cats in the jungle beyond their camp had become a kind of doleful nocturnal music to him. They had rigged a double electrified fence around the solid bunkhouse in which they slept, so that they wouldn't have to worry about any hungry or marauding carnivores.

The nights embraced him. The mountain winds changed at night and the low, scudding clouds they found almost all the time during the day often lifted at night, revealing the heavens with an incredible clarity. Shag often spent many hours looking at the stars. Many of them were friendly to him, had guided him through most of his life in the air. He knew them by name and by position, and looking at them also confirmed his isolation and that being alone was a relative term.

A deep roll of thunder fell softly from the night skies more than once, some jet passing high overhead, probably at thirty to forty thousand feet. With the great clearness of clean air he could even see the position lights and flashing strobes, and once in the moonlight he saw the thick contrails streaming aft of the machine that was itself invisible to him. He was startled one night to see an incredible, absolutely silent display of streaming fire high above him, and the pilot's instinctive panic reaction to a burning plane left him only when he realized he was watching some great satellite plunging back into the resisting mass of the earth's atmosphere.

But most of the time he sat quietly, enjoying a peace he hadn't ever known before. You couldn't rush anything here, you couldn't push, there was nothing to own or possess. The three men depended upon one another for their lives and asked nothing back in return. Their camaraderie was based largely on insults, yet they held a deep respect for one another. They were easygoing, garrulous, occasionally even warm and sensitive with one another. Yet each man was a seasoned killer, a combat veteran of wars from one part of the planet to another. They had flown and fought and dealt in contraband and smuggled, and had changed loyalties often but they had never gone back on their promises to the men with whom they fought, for in those kinds of wars and prisons and undergrounds, there are no strangers on the same side.

Each had in his own way busted out of a dozen jails and prisons and execution camps, and the dossiers on them, no matter how incomplete, were all alike in that Jordan, Heath, and Brady were considered extremely skilled, talented, and very dangerous men. Each man had a significant price on his head in at least one part of the world.

If each had been offered his choice of his lot in life, not one would have chosen to fight and to kill, least of all as mercenaries. But few of us really control the dice with which our lot is cast. They were no exception.

Like his friends, Shag had a wife in his past. But unlike the others, there was no split, no divorce, no breakup; there were no nasty scenes. There had of course been healthy lovers' quarrels. Most of all though, there had been a rich love between Shag and Denise.

Shag was a widower. The full facts were simple enough. Denise died in the crash of a DC-3 flown by his partner Matt Ford, in the air charter they owned at the time. Ford lived through the crash. Later, Shag learned that Matt had been drunk before taking off, that he'd stayed on a flask throughout the flight, and that he was stupidly inattentive to his instruments. Letting down from the southeast into the Las Vegas basin, he went too low and clipped the edge of a ridge. He sobered up fast because he had to. His copilot was already dead as the airplane wheeled sickeningly from the night skies and Matt put it down on a street in a small desert community, killing another sixteen people on the ground. Only three lived from the twenty-four aboard the DC-3, and Denise was one of those who burned to death.

The stewardess survived. Her conscience ate holes in her brain and one day she came to Shag and told him the whole story. Shag said nothing and the girl left and Shag waited for the right moment. He got Ford very drunk and put him in a turbocharged Baron. As they climbed up through ten thousand feet Shag put on an oxygen mask and did the same for Matt, but turned off the flow valve for his partner. He cruised at thirty thousand feet for nearly two hours and when he landed Ford was blue. His heart had stopped working a good hour before Shag started down.

There was a coroner's inquest and a grand jury investigation and even a trial for murder. Shag refused to defend himself, but a long string of witnesses testified that Ford was a lush. The jury threw out murder one but they came back with a manslaughter charge and a conviction, and Shag took it stoically and spent eight months in a cold cell before they released him on parole. Shag didn't even bother reporting to his parole officer. He left the country the same day and went to Central America, where there was a banana war. Shag didn't much care which side won. He'd work for whoever got to him first with a contract and cash on the line. He was very good with his hands in an airplane and they gave him a B-26 with eighteen heavy machine guns and rockets beneath the wings and one day he found a convoy on a narrow mountain road and twenty minutes later more than seven hundred men were dead, an equal number wounded. Shag couldn't have cared less. He kept seeing Denise in his dreams and hearing her voice on the wind in the cockpit, and he knew it would take a long time for him to release her to whatever peace she deserved.

Only on this lonely plateau in the jungle had he been able to realize that it had finally happened. Denise was free—and so was he.

He went back inside and saw Lew sitting on his

bunk staring up at him. "Something's happened to you tonight, Yank," Lew said softly, as if he'd been able to feel the moods from deep within Shag's head.

"Yeah." Shag sat heavily on his bunk.

"I think I understand," Lew said finally.

"Oh? Tell me."

"She's let you go finally."

Shag was honestly startled. He didn't try to hide it. "It's a street that goes both ways, Lew. I did the same. It's like a . . . like a peace I didn't know existed. Do you understand? The pain is gone."

"I understand."

He knew Shag far better than Shag realized. They had met in that rotten, vicious banana war in Central America, and Lew flew copilot with Shag that day as he methodically went about the grisly business of killing seven hundred men he didn't even know, crippling the same number for the rest of their miserable lives. They went from bombers to Mustangs in another war and they became the perfect team for air fighting, Lew flying as Shag's wingman, following the system of the old Thach Weave developed in the Pacific during the Big War. Lew always flew a moving scissors on Shag's tail, and they shot down a hell of a lot of airplanes. They made good money and they didn't ask each other questions, but Shag's story was hardly a secret.

Then came their "big one" south of the equator. They were in Argentina—"temporarily between wars," as they put it—when they were approached by two swarthy men with bulges beneath their dark suit jackets. Fortunately for all concerned it was a business deal. A "certain individual" had to be flown out of the country and they were wanted for the job. The still-unknown customer would pay them thirty thousand dollars for a simple flight to the United States.

"Both ways?" Shag asked.

"One way. You land, your passenger is met by a car, and you burn the aircraft."

"How do we leave?"

"That's your problem."

A glance flicked between Shag and Lew. They both knew a cold cut when they ran into one, and this was a deck straight out of a freezer. It had to have a lollipop somewhere.

"Of course, the money will be deposited to your accounts before you even leave here, and you may confirm this in any way you wish."

There was the rub. Who's the customer? It does not matter. Give us a name, dammit. "Carlos Simoza" will do very well. How many passengers? Just one, and one suitcase. What kind of aircraft?

"It is what you call a Learstar. I have the specifications here." They looked at the typed notes and whistled. A converted Lockheed B-34 Ventura. Great big piston engines, paddle-bladed props, triple-duty superchargers, pressurized cabin, wet wings, and auxiliary tanks everywhere. It had a nonstop range of six thousand miles, it could fly at 42,000 feet and it would cruise at nearly 290 miles per hour. On the deck it would do 370 wide open and that would be what they needed. They'd come in very high and then dump it all the way.

They agreed. It smelled to high heaven and they knew it, but the thirty thou was delivered to a banker Shag knew. Later, he and Lew talked it over. "The thirty grand is peanuts. It's the come-on. We take Mr. Big all the way in, deliver him, and they knock us off and just forget the bread in the bank."

Lew nodded. "I know."

"How do you want to play it?"

"You lead, I'll follow. I'm sure we'll dance divinely."

The crooked grin that accompanied that remark sealed their friendship forever. They knew they were being set up, so the thing to do was to think full cooperation and leave nothing for those pros to detect. They picked up Mr. Big and got a glimpse of him. He was a notorious killer in Argentinian circles, an international assassin, and they knew which way they would go long before they got off the ground. Mr. Big was not alone. He had a very professional killer with him. She was beautiful as well as deadly. Of course, they had been told "Carlos Simoza" would be alone, but who could they complain to? They were told to take off immediately. Shag turned back from the cockpit. "I want thirty minutes minimum to study this cockpit and its systems. Anything less is stupid."

He received a nod for reply. Thirty-five minutes later they fired up the big engines, checked her out thoroughly, and she took off and climbed like two howling devils were out there for engines. They knew they were still on the same wavelength when they were cruising at 42,000 feet, Shag took the oxygen mask hanging loose around his neck, slipped it over his face, and tapped it. Lew put his on, opened the flow to full, and very easily, *very* easily, they began to bleed off the cabin pressure. There was a gauge in the cabin so they played it extra careful and kept their passengers at 15,000 feet for an hour until they were well into mild hypoxia. Just enough oxygen deficiency to slow them down, and then they blew the pressurization. The explosive decompression set off a blinding condensation fog in the cabin and jumped the interior to the 42,000-foot level, where useful consciousness because of the body's internal pressure blowout is less than fifteen seconds. Add that to the long exposure to 15,000 feet, the shock of the explosive decompression, the fog, and you're out of it just like that. Yet that female shark managed to fire off a full clip blindly, stitching the cabin and part of the cockpit before she fell back unconscious. Before another minute passed both their passengers were dead.

They changed course and landed at a field where they could rent a car at a nearby gas station, no questions asked. As soon as they were on the ground they dragged the two bodies into the cockpit and held them out of the way of the controls. They shoved two wooden blocks beneath the gear legs, trimmed the bird for takeoff, advanced the throttles of the now-lightened ship to cruise power, dashed outside, slammed the cabin door shut, rolled under the nacelles, and jerked the chocks. Still flat on the ground, they watched the Learstar take off in a slow, steady climb, passing low over a town a dozen miles away, making enough noise to wake the dead. They stashed the suitcase they'd removed from the plane, walked to that gas station for the car, came back for the suitcase, and took off. Three hours later they were in an airlines terminal buying tickets for Boston, their pockets filled with two cases of diamonds the unfriendly Argentinian had lifted from a private vault. Lew knew a fence in Boston and they didn't want to waste any time, so they gave the fence a great deal, pocketed the cash, and were in Las Vegas the next afternoon.

Lew didn't look like a man who gave away secrets, but he felt compelled to lay it on the line with this man. "I know about you," he told Shag bluntly. Shag nodded. "I believe we'll be doing things together."

Shag lifted his drink in silent affirmation.

"I don't want you guessing about me, you understand."

"Your past is your own business, Lew," Shag said quietly.

"Will you listen, though?"

"The way you're offering, yes."

"Back home I was a lot more than a pilot. I—"

"You're a crack mechanic and an aeronautical engineer and you've got a couple of degrees," Shag broke in.

"How the devil did you find that out!"

"I didn't find it out. I've seen it, just watching you. The only thing I don't know is the company."

"Vickers, you bastard." He shared the grin with Shag.

"What broke it up?"

"Found my wife in bed with a guy I thought was my best friend. Few things surprise me. This one did. I got very cold and very angry and I surprised myself. I pitched Timmy through a second-floor window. Busted his collarbone, I found out later. Lying on a lawn with a wet pecker and a busted collarbone draws neighbors like fleas to a hound." Lew took a long pull on his drink, reflecting.

"Iris was another matter. Carried on something awful, crying and screaming. Afraid I was going to kill her. That would have been stupid. A man kills out of passion he's a bloody fool. You get convicted for that sort of thing. The bed was one of them fancy things, lots of silk cords and the like. I dragged Iris down the stairs, naked like she was, with one hand, holding a long cord in the other, and there was Timmy, yelling something fierce. I tied 'em with the silk cord, and shoved them in the back of the station wagon."

He looked at Shag, who was smiling over his drink. "Anyway, took 'em down to Piccadilly Circus in London, tied them back to back with the cord. Timmy wasn't able to do much, and every time Iris squirmed about, she near to killed him with the pain. Then I threw 'em in the fountain, waiting for the bobbies to arrive of course, along with all the picture-takers from the tabloids. By now I'd built up a sort of temper and I didn't take kindly to the bobbies trying to remove them from the fountain. The photogs were getting some right lovely pictures and I thought they shouldn't be bothered."

"How many?"

"Well, I busted my right hand before it was all over, and me and three of London's finest went off to hospital together. I'd done me a bit of professional boxing as a lad, and had been a commando for a while, and they told me they'd busted three nightsticks across me noggin before I went down for the count. It was a fine brawl."

"You do time?"

"What? Oh, yes. In fact, just a year more than you served. Someone arranged for me to get out about two years ahead of schedule. They had a job to do and they needed someone with my fine technical background."

"Difficult job?"

"Not at all. I didn't care a fig anymore about being on the right side of the law, you understand. They needed a private jet to have an accident in flight. A DH-125, in fact. It exploded over the Mediterranean. When my, ah, employers got the word, they gave me a first-class ticket to Hong Kong and ten thousand pounds in an envelope, and I was gone."

They sat in silence in the lounge, the sounds of the

casino in the background. "Ever regret killing those people in that De Havilland?"

"I was surprised I didn't. They weren't real. Like in a war. You sort of suspend your morality. I found that can be very convenient. How many have I killed in these stupid little wars? Two hundred? Two thousand? Who the bloody hell knows or cares? After a year in that dungeon I'd have knocked off the Queen herself if that's what it took to get out. Let me ask you, Shag. I sent seven people in that jet to their Maker. You did the number on just one man who'd killed your wife because he was a drunk. What's the difference?"

Shag set down his drink. "None."

"That's what I mean, then. We both believed it was the thing to do and we did it. Closed book."

They blew all their money in Vegas. Now they were in an airport bar in Mexico watching a tall, thin American fighting off three locals with knives, and doing a creditable job of it. But Lew didn't like the odds. He removed a small bottle he carried in his pants pocket and poured lighter fluid on their tablecloth, wadded it up, set it ablaze and tossed it into the midst of the three Mexicans. Moments later three unconscious forms were on the floor, the bartender was fighting leaping flames, and they were gone. They piled into a cab and hung on grimly during the wild ride to Hermosa Airport. They learned that their new friend's name was Vance Brady and that he was flying a DC-3 on a delivery flight from Arizona to Chile.

"How many in your crew?" Shag asked him.

"Five minutes ago it was a solo job," the tall man said with a rakish smile. "You want to come along for the ride?"

"You got it, guv'nor," Lew replied, and Shag nodded.

They were two hours out when Brady discovered he had two old pros on his hands. Shag was sitting in the right seat of the cockpit, the airliner on autopilot. "I've got to take a leak," Brady said. "Normally I use a plastic bottle, but as long as you're up here, would you mind keeping an eye on things? I mean, you needn't do anything, but let me point out the essential instruments to you, and if anything goes wrong, get your friend back to me."

Shag looked at him in disbelief. "What if an engine explodes?"

"What if an—" The echo died there. "If that happens, pull these two handles, right here," Brady pointed. "That brings the power back to idle and starts the ship down on a steady descent. By that time I'll be back up here, never fear."

Shag sat quietly until Brady returned. "Want to try it?" Brady asked.

Shag nodded. "Sure."

"Ever do any flying?"

"Well, I once saw this movie, you know, and it showed—"

"Never mind. Now, these are the main controls, and here's the knobs for the power, right?" He went on like that for ten minutes and then told Shag to have a stab at it. "I'll be right here so you needn't worry about anything going wrong."

"Thank you," Shag said. "But you'll really let me try, won't you? I mean, unless something bad happens you won't take over?"

"No, no, of course not. All right, I'll disconnect the autopilot." Brady beamed at his new friend. "Go to it, now."

The nose went down and then came up in a steady pull, higher and higher, and Brady's eyes went wide and he started for the controls as he saw the nose start coming around to the left, but his hands stopped a half-inch short of touching the yoke because the DC-3 was coming around in a beautiful, satiny chandelle. Every control was perfectly coordinated and it took only those few seconds for Vance Brady to slump back in his seat and watch.

"I've been had," he said finally.

"I couldn't resist," Shag said.

"Your friend the same way?" Brady went on, eyeing the huge grin on Heath's face.

Shag nodded. "The same. Let's start all over again." He extended a beefy paw, Vance did the same with Lew, and an unverbalized partnership was cemented between the three of them.

Now they were still together on a high plateau in the back country of Ecuador. "And you know something?" Lew said, looking up at Shag. "We still don't know beans about Vance."

"I didn't think it bothered you," Shag countered.

"What bother? I'm interested."

"Why now more than before?"

"Because of what he said a while back. You remember, don't you? It's been weeks since he even thought of a hydrogen bomb. Now, that's a strange thing to hear a man say, Shag. It doesn't fit into the scheme of things. If he doesn't want to talk about it I'll never bring it up again and—"

"What was that about a hydrogen bomb?"

They turned to find Vance sitting on the edge of his bunk, feet on the floor, eyes wide open and staring at them. "I just said the words, Vance," Lew replied. "That and no more. Amazing. We were talking quietly enough not to wake a cat, and there you are out of a sound sleep, as bright-eyed as a squirrel at sunup. All it took was the mention of the two words."

Vance rubbed sleep from his eyes. "They're more than two words," he said finally.

"We thought you might want to tell us about them," Shag offered.

"Why?" They could detect an edge of annoyance in Brady's voice that they'd never encountered before.

"Easy, man," Shag told him quietly. "No one's pushing. I suppose it was the moment. Lew and I were getting a bit sloppy with one another, I guess. Forget it, friend. Go on back to sleep."

Vance smiled sheepishly. "I didn't mean to bite. The words trigger something in me."

"I said forget it."

Vance shook his head. "No, I understand. In a few days, if everything works out, we're going to do something we've done before. There'll be another evening like this one and the morning after we'll be taking some insane chance on something like we've done before. Tomorrow we may die; that sort of thing."

"I've known a lot of tomorrows," Shag said quietly, "where I knew I could die. What else is new?"

"*Something* here that's happened between us is new," Vance countered. "I know it. I can feel it. Since this seems to be the moment for letting down a lot of hair, you tell me something."

"Shoot."

"You broke free of something since we got here." Vance's eyes bored straight into Shag. Before Shag could answer Lew spoke for him.

"More than that, Admiral. Something released him because he released what it was he was hanging onto for dear life. I don't know if that makes any sense, but it's like a steel cord that's tied around your neck and your heart and your mind and—hell, I'm getting it all mucked up."

"No, you're doing fine," Vance said, climbing to his feet and staring through the window at a moon hanging low over distant mountains. "I've never told anyone. And my name isn't Vance Brady. My real name is in the past to protect some innocent people who think I was killed years ago. I let them think that."

"Vance Brady does real fine," Shag said, and received a lopsided grin from his friend.

"It's simple," Vance finally continued. "I'm a traitor."

"*You?* A traitor?" Lew blurted. "That's so much horseshit! I don't believe it. I may not know the details, mister, but I know men and a traitor you're not." He sniffed with indignation. "I don't care a bloody nit what he says."

"I never flew for an airline," Vance told them. "That's a cover. A long time ago I was in the Strategic Air Command. I flew a B-52. I was one of LeMay's crack pilots. Faultless, made of solid steel, unyielding to adversity, unbelievably skilled—shall I go on?" When he received no answer he elected to continue, and as he spoke he drifted away into the past.

"I was part of the red-alert force. We received the signal to go one afternoon and we all drove like mad from the ready shack to our bombers. We'd done it many times before, of course. You know the fail-safe system. You go balls out to an invisible line somewhere around the North Pole, you do a last air-to-air refueling, and you wait for the signal to turn back. Our target was Kiev and we had four big thermonukes aboard. A hundred megatons each. Enough for Kiev and three other targets. Overkill at its best. And I was one of the best. Reliable, trustworthy, totally dedicated.

"We were getting close to the recall line and we were sweating out the signal to turn around and come home. We didn't get it." He looked up and a tiny flame of anguish flickered in those eyes. "Maybe the radios were screwed up. I don't know. But we reached the line and we still didn't have orders to return. That meant, automatically, that we were to go all the way. Hit the target. Bomb Kiev. Obliterate the city. I was going crazy trying to get a signal of some kind. Even if we didn't get the recall I wanted to have the signal to carry out the standing orders to strike. I might have gone on, I probably would have—no, that's not true. Had I received the coded orders to go on I would have bombed Kiev. Or died trying.

"But we couldn't get anything. My crew was gung-ho. They told me I had to continue, those were our standing orders. I refused. I swung the aircraft around and started back. My copilot went crazy. He screamed I was violating orders, that I was a traitor, that the whole nation was counting on me and others like me. He was as brilliant and as trained as any robot could be. He took out his revolver and pointed it at my head and said if I didn't keep flying the course for Kiev he'd kill me and take the plane in himself. So I turned back for Kiev, and my copilot calmed down. He even apologized to me. I asked him for some coffee, and when he turned around to get it I slipped my own revolver from its holster and shot him in the head.

"I was just not going to go in because of some standing order and kill a million people. I knew that something as small as a radio fuckup could isolate us from all communications. I just refused. I killed a man to stand by that refusal. The rest of the crew remained at their stations. They didn't know what the hell to do.

"We were back over Canada when we got our radios working again. SAC headquarters had been trying like mad to reach us. There'd been no signal to strike. The recall had been out all the time, but we weren't receiving it."

"Then . . . I don't understand," Lew said as gently as he could. "Oh, of course. Your copilot. You'd shot him and—"

"That didn't matter. It never even came up. What did matter—and this was everything—was that I had disobeyed the standing orders to go after my assigned target. For disobeying that order I was court-martialed. The board decided that since I had taken matters into my own hands, I was the kind of man who couldn't be counted on if there really was a war. If the strike signal was on, by turning back I had removed an aircraft and four hydrogen bombs from the attack. I was not to be trusted. No one could count on me to kill a million people. I had violated the basic tenets of SAC. Absolute obedience."

"I used to hear that kind of stuff about the SS," Lew said.

Vance shrugged. "I was dishonorably discharged from the air force. Stripped of any benefits I had accumulated after eighteen years of service. I was denied the right to vote, told my government no longer would support me anywhere if I got into trouble. I was, in short, an outcast, a non-person. My friends shunned me. My family was heartbroken, even if they understood. I've been making my living from the air since then, but as you can see, it ain't been easy."

Shag had been looking at the floor as Vance spoke. Now he studied this man who was his friend and realized what a stranger he'd been all along. "You sorry you did it?"

"Sorry I didn't kill a million innocent human beings? No, I'm not, even though I suppose I'm the first man in history to be branded a traitor because he refused to do something as stupid as that."

He stood before them. "Now that you know what I am, what are you going to do about it?"

"I'm going to shake your goddamned hand," Shag said.

Lew turned away. It took him a while to turn back. He didn't want the others to see him crying. Then he threw his arms around Vance and hugged him like a child.

9

"There'll never be a better time. We've made sure there's no liquid lock in the engines. The cylinders move and the valves are all right, and all the lines are connected. We can't do any more than we have with the seals and how long they last depends on what happens when they're running. These BMW's have external rocker arm boxes just like the old Hornets, and they're greased. They'll be fine. We've pulled the props through by hand and I've gotten all the water out of the fuel, so if you two assholes know what you're doing, maybe we can bring this hunk of iron to life."

They listened to Lew, for whatever he said about the Ju-52 was *the* word. "What about the batteries?" Shag pressed. "I know we can use them—"

"They're charged but they're still weak. We want external power if we can get it. But I don't trust the connections with that truck engine. This here flying machine operates on twenty-eight volts. Twenty-four will do, but that truck is ancient and it's all a bit beyond me. We're taking a chance."

"Then let's not do it. What's the next choice?"

"Hand crank."

"Oh, come on now, Lew, you can't crank an engine that big by hand to start it!" Vance seemed to think Lew had popped his cork.

The Englishman was getting impatient. "You're a stupid nit. Don't you know anything about these engines? They're not direct drive for starting. They've got Bendix inertial starters, and you insert the hand crank and turn that dilly by hand, faster and faster until you gets the flywheel or whatever you Yanks call that system, and when it's wound up and you can hear it screaming at you then you activates the starter handles. That's these little darlins right here. When I yells go, you pulls the T-handle up and that engages the starter system and turns the prop and—"

"And then we pray, right?"

"Right. Okay, I'll go outside and get the crank in position. Before I turns it you makes sure everything in here is ready to start. You sing out through the side window so I can hear you. Number three on the right is the first because it's the one with the generator and we just might get those batteries charged up to snuff."

They had all the cowlings off and extra ropes were holding her secure to the ground. They heard metallic clanks and bangs as Lew inserted the hand crank beneath the engine, standing in back of the big propeller. "He's going to have a bitch of a time," Vance said to Shag.

"I know. But we need at least three hands in this crate to work everything right." Vance still looked doubtful.

"Start the bloody checklist!" Lew bellowed from outside.

Vance called it out and Shag went through the movements.

"All switches off."

"Off."

"Fire extinguishers secured."

"They're *empty*."

"Follow the list, dammit."

"Extinguishers secured."

"Fuel selector to both."

"Both."

"Confirm oil coolers open and carb heat to cold."

"Go."

"Primer secured and selector free."

"Go."

"Supercharger back to below nine thousand feet."

Shag hesitated. "That is a question. It's safer in the secure position." He moved the small handle. "Below nine. Go."

"Sparks to advance."

"Lew disconnected them."

"Okay. Bulkhead master behind copilot on."

"You do it."

"It's on. Bulkhead master on switch panel to on. Okay, that baby's on also."

"Good."

"Quadrant ring master up to on."

Shag pulled the big knob up until it clicked. "On."

"Fuel-flow selector for number three—uh, pull back to the open position for start."

Shag moved the throttle-like knob into position. "Go."

"Ignition switch for number three, pull up to on."

"Up to on. Go."

"Check center position."

"Done. Go."

"That the mag selector?"

"Right. Center position for both mags."

"Activate wobble pump." Vance hesitated. "How do we know if we have enough pressure? The damn gauge is frozen on number three."

"Lew said we keep pumping until he sees fuel overflow on the ground."

"Jesus Christ."

"We could use him." Shag pointed to the pump. "Get cracking."

The wobble pump extended from the left side of the copilot seat down through a handle in the floorboards to the fuel system. It was an old-fashioned hand pump that sucked fuel from the wing tanks through the lines and up into the engine and demanded vigorous, nonstop action.

"Keep pumping!"

"I am, dammit."

"Faster, you ninny!" Lew shouted from outside. "That system's old! Put some muscle into it, Admiral!"

Vance's arm flew up and down in a wild motion and the clanking sounds increased as metal banged against metal. He thought his arm was going to break.

"We've got fuel on the ground!" Lew shouted. "Keep pumping, but a bit slower and steadier!"

"Thank God," Vance gasped.

"I'm starting to crank now!" came the cry from Lew.

"Go!" Shag called back.

They heard the inertial system winding up slowly and knew that Lew was throwing all his weight into the back-breaking effort. They could hear the slow groaning whine of the system turning.

"Keep going!" Shag yelled to him. "Keep pumping!" he ordered Vance.

The groaning sound became higher-pitched and then a shrill whine. "Hit it, God damn your soul! Hit the son of a bitch!" Lew screamed from underneath the airplane.

Shag yanked on the T-handle for the number-three engine, felt the starter system engage and jerk wildly. Shit, the throttle; he'd forgotten. His left hand slapped the number-three throttle forward, jerked it back, cracked it a half-inch.

"Keep pumping!"

"I am!" Vance complained.

The big propeller twitched, jerked around, rumbled faster. Smoke curled up through the engine and puffed mightily from the exhausts. The prop kept turning. Shag jockeyed the throttle, jerked the mixture to lean, back to rich, felt the engine shudder as she tried to catch, saw flames erupting in a dozen places—she was catching. Then the starter system was calling it quits.

Lew leaned against the tire, chest heaving, while Vance stared at Shag with glazed eyes. "Hold it, hold it," Shag told him. "That was the first time and we know she's got the stuff in her. Okay, let's start up again." This time he positioned the throttle, called to Lew to start cranking, seared Vance with choice expletives to keep pumping, heard Lew bellow they had fuel on the ground, felt the inertial system grinding over faster and faster, and then repeated the sequence by pulling up with all his might on the T-handle. He watched the prop jerk around suddenly and he knew he would have her if he could just catch her at this moment so he moved the throttle another inch forward and back again and jockeyed it a bit and the whole airplane shook as the engine tried to catch, spat flames and enormous clouds of smoke and there was a sudden roar as she caught, backfired, slowed, caught again, spat out more flames, hurled out gobs of smoke, and the coughing, banging, flame-spewing madness began to change into a rumble and Shag jerked the fuel-flow handle into the running position and it was a miracle, but he got her up to 800 rpm and he kept playing the throttle, and every now and then she'd wheeze and backfire mightily and he advanced the throttle slowly and they went past a thousand revolutions per minute and she was roaring with all that latent power. Twelve hundred, and beside him Vance let out a roar even louder than the engine.

"The voltmeter! She's charging! The goddamned battery is starting to charge!" He no longer needed to pump. The mechanical system had taken over and Lew climbed into the cabin and came rushing forward and looked with wonder all around him. They were taking a charge in the battery and the manifold pressure gauge was working and the rpm needle fluctuated and wobbled and shivered but who gave a damn because that engine was running and still clearing out all sorts of crap from her innards, and they were still getting a full charge on the battery. They were showing amps on the panel gauge and the oil pressure was coming up and the oil temp was holding where it belonged and the cylinder-head temperature gauge was moving slowly, like the damned thing was supposed to move, and the son of a bitch was alive! Shag played her with every touch of sensitivity in his fingertips because the trick was to keep her alive, keep her turning, let her run, get the other engines going.

They were flushed with success, mad with joy, and forty minutes later they were beaten and exhausted because the nose engine refused to start. At least Lew was spared the shoulder-busting job of hand-cranking; they had enough juice now from the constantly charging battery to wind up the inertial starter system, and Lew was convinced it was in the carburetor, so they said screw it, and switched to number-one engine on their left side. She went through a dozen revolutions of the propeller, gave off a tremendous explosion, and settled down to running as if she'd been operating every week for the last ten years. They kept the wing engines running for an hour, then shut down number one, ran three for another twenty minutes and then shut her down by moving the fuel-flow lever back into the shutdown position. This kept the oil feeding to the engine for lubrication but slowly starved the engine for fuel, shutting off the supply at the tank and letting everything in the lines suck into the engine so that when she coughed and sputtered and the big prop jerked to a stop the lines were dry. The silence was almost a blow and they closed off all the switches and levers and handles in the cockpit and looked at one another with a deep and immense satisfaction. There had never been thunder and roaring so sweet to any of them such as they had just known.

"All right," Lew's voice grated, "let's get with it, lads. Outside. We back the truck up to the nose engine for a workstand and we find out what's wrong."

They found it in ten minutes. A busted fuel line. It was fixed in fifteen minutes.

It took them just under twenty minutes of frantic manipulation in- and outside the cockpit to turn over the nose engine. Finally something seemed to free itself in that maze of cylinders and pistons and connecting rods and associated clanking, clattering assembly and she roared and shook, and Lew knew they had two or three days' work to settle down *that* one, but it no longer mattered, because it was only effort and time and there was no longer any doubt of the final outcome.

Lew stood in the cockpit with Shag to his left and Vance to his right and patted the now quiet throttles. "She'll fly," he told the others. "Annie's alive and well."

"I'll drink to that," Vance said warmly.

"Don't torture us, you ninny," Lew complained. "Come on. That nose engine still wants attention. We've got the whole day to work yet."

By late afternoon it was done.

Annie was very much alive and well.

They ate squab that night. Shag had become quite skilled with the crossbow made by Lew. He'd improved on the crude instrument, fashioning balanced bolts so he could pick his targets. He brought down a half-dozen of the strange long-tailed birds, and it was a fitting feast after the day's successes.

They rested around the fire and made plans. "We've got all the fuel that's left in the storage tanks here," Shag said as he reviewed their situation. "A thousand liters in the bird. That works out to maybe two hundred and sixty gallons usable fuel, because the gauges don't work and we're going by those dipsticks in the nacelles. That work out the same to you, Lew?"

Lew gestured with a drumstick. "When we're rich you can be my accountant. Two hundred fifty or sixty gallons will do fine."

"Everything we do when we leave here," Shag continued, "hangs on whatever range we can get with less than half fuel for this thing. What the hell do these BMW's burn an hour? According to Lew, if they're copies of the old Pratt Sixteen-Nineties, we can figure as high as thirty gallons and as low as twenty gallons for each engine per hour. I remember something about the T-6, that if you wanted real economy you went to sixteen hundred rpm. Once we get going we'll try that and see how she acts, but for safety we've got to figure on the high side. Next question."

He fell silent for a moment and then went on. "If we fly three forty-five out of here for a heading we can make it to Portoviejo. We haven't got any charts, but I know the coast and so does Lew and we can cross-check one another that way. Besides, halfway there we cross over Guayaquil. It's a big city and we can use its lights and the airport beacon for a reference. We should also have a good moon and—"

"Hey, hold on!" Vance was sitting bolt upright. "We're going at night?" He watched Shag nod. "You're crazy!" Vance said in an incredulous half-shout. "We've got no lights! Nothing in that cockpit even glows at night. No flashlights, no charts—"

"I know all that. Lew has rigged up a light that will work off a twenty-four-volt system. We can hang it in the cockpit, sort of shield it, and we'll have light for the gauges."

"Runs right off the battery," Lew confirmed. "Bypasses the generator system. As long as we're running that right engine it won't bother the battery none. Don't fret, sonny boy. It'll work."

Shag waited until Vance had settled down. "We make our takeoff at last light from here," Shag explained. "It's a test flight and our way out of here all in one. If she doesn't fly we'll let her go as far as we can and we're no worse off than we are now."

"She'll fly, goddammit," Lew growled.

"I'm not arguing, Lew. Like I said, we take off with some light at dusk. The runway is to the west so we'll have a good horizon reference. Enough to get used to handling this ironmonger before it gets dark. Look, Vance, we've got to take our shot with the night flight. It's a hundred ninety miles direct to our landing point so we figure two hours airborne. If we get a hundred an hour out of Annie I'll kiss her corrugated ass. But we can't land anywhere within that range from here in daylight.

"Jesus, man, we look like shit, we got no papers, we stand out like a green elephant at an airport and we can't get very far on the fuel in the bird. So what we do is overfly Portoviejo. We're not going to land there. Too big and busy a field. But that leads us to Manta, which is on the coastline, and from there I've got a clear shot for a small field I know at Calceta. It's remote and gives us our best chance. The place is just about abandoned at night, but they've got fuel and oil there and—"

"And what?" Vance said angrily.

"And we play it by ear."

"We need more than that going for us," Vance snapped.

"We'll find out. Besides, it's the only game in town. The trick is to get in there, gas up and get oil, and try to hang on until just before first light. We take off and head well out to sea, staying low, and get the hell out of Ecuador. Do you know what happens if they find it's the Gleeful Trio they're dealing with in this boiler with wings? Their pride will be so far up their asses they'll fall all over themselves trying to do us in. So it's get out of this country no matter what it takes."

Vance couldn't fault the basic reasoning. "And after Calceta?"

"With a full fuel load we can get six, maybe even eight hours' flying time," Shag computed.

"That's a high-side figure," Lew warned.

"So we count on six and we see what happens. What I want to do is make it from Calceta to Buenaventura. That's in Colombia, and only a hundred and fifty miles—no, I'm figuring that wrong. This crap of memorizing the coastline sometimes gets twisted up. It's one hundred and fifty miles from Calceta to Esmerelda. That's along the Ecuadorian coastline. Seventy miles on we cross the border into Colombia and that gives us breathing space. There's no love lost between those two countries, and when the Colombians find out we pulled some wool over the people in Ecuador they're liable to play friends with us."

"Maybe, if, liable," Vance muttered gloomily.

"Piss off," Shag said with a touch of impatience. "From Esmerelda to Buenaventura it's less than three hundred miles. I figure to land there."

"It'll still be daylight, right?" Vance said quietly.

"Late in the day, yes."

"How do we hide the Great Iron Hog?"

"We don't, obviously. We do it all by ear and some very fancy footwork. And maybe we have to get nasty."

"With what? Crossbows?"

"It's the only game in town, sweetheart. Remember?"

Vance had no answer for that. Lew heaved himself to his feet. "You two fight or kiss and make up, I don't care. I got some things to do."

They watched him leave and went back to working

on getting back to the States all in one piece. "What you're saying is that it all adds up to this being a hundred-to-one shot, aren't you?" Vance pushed.

"It could be that bad. It could be better. A lot depends upon just how swift we are between the ears."

"Mind if I throw a few realities at you?"

"I'm the only audience you got left," Shag smiled. "Go to it."

"How do we pay for fuel wherever we land?"

"That does pose a problem," Shag admitted.

"You didn't answer me."

"No, I suppose I didn't. There's a hundred ways, Vance. We bull our way through. We threaten or cajole or steal, even if that means finding some American traveling down here, knocking him off and stealing every credit card he has."

"That one is cute."

"Better than getting shot in the back."

"You win that one on points." Vance scratched his chin. "Let's play your game. Suppose we pull off three or four miracles and get to Buenaventura. What then?"

"That's easy. From there it's a straight shot to Puerto Jiminez. About five hundred fifty miles in a straight line." He laughed at the look on Vance's face and then his friend chuckled with him.

"I didn't think you were that crazy," Vance said, "but who knows? Puerto Jiminez. That's in Costa Rica."

"Just beyond Panama," Shag confirmed. "Right."

"Nearly six hundred miles across open water, no deviations, no mistakes," Vance said.

"*You* can fly that leg, baby. You sure got the experience for that kind of haul," Shag reminded him. "We've got to make it to Costa Rica. We land in Panama and we're running for it in the jungle again. They don't like us much in that country."

"All this is a lot of crap, Shag," Vance said suddenly. "Instead of playing parts in some third-rate movie, why don't we get to a field and steal something with range and speed to it and just wing it back to the States!"

"Those are worse odds, that's why. We can't stop to talk to anyone because we don't have papers and we don't have any way of getting the right documents," Shag countered. "Look, one of the things we have going for us is Annie."

"How? I don't—"

"If you saw a three-engined German bomber that hasn't existed since a war that ended more than thirty years ago, would you believe it?"

"No."

"That Ju-52 is like a goddamned UFO. Hardly anybody is going to believe it. More to the point, if someone claims he saw this Flying Dutchman on wings, the big boys on top would probably toss him into the local looney bin and throw away the keys."

Vance chewed on that for a second. "You could be right."

"Well, I don't know, either. But look, friend, as far as I'm concerned the three of us were dead men a long time ago. We haven't a damn thing to lose. So we go into fields without a peso or a dollar. Screw it. We'll figure something out. And we haven't got a nickel's worth of electronics in that airplane. So what? When did we forget how to fly? Sure, we could lose an engine and we might blow an oil line, but those are all ifs and buts and maybes, and sometimes the maybes work out the way you never expected them to. What were the odds of our getting here, and finding the winged washtub in the jungle, and getting her to run again?"

"Nonexistent," Vance said with a rueful look on his face.

"But we did it. Just don't run for the lifeboats yet, Admiral."

Vance snapped his fingers. "You said lifeboats. A boat. We could steal a boat, and—" He shrugged. "Forget it. I get seasick too easy."

"So do I," Shag said. "I guess we—" He broke off as Lew rejoined them. He was covered from head to foot with dirt, grease, oil and rust stains, and he had a look of immense satisfaction on his face.

"You discover oil or something?" Shag asked.

"Just as good. Found a machine gun for the back turret."

They both stared. "You mean a real machine gun?"

"Right you are, lad."

"What about—I mean, what do we use for ammo?"

"Don't need none, I'd guess," Lew said.

"Then—"

"It don't work anyway," Lew interrupted. "But it sure looks good. Mean machine, that's us, lads. The mean machine. Now get to bed, you two. It's up at sunrise and work all day to get ready for the big show tomorrow evening."

10

"The brakes ain't for shit," Shag told Lew. They tax-ied back slowly from their first rumbling tests and Shag swung her around in a wide turn so she would stop as far back along the runway as possible.

Lew nodded. "It's the pump. All gummed up. I haven't got the tools here to clean it. So you use what brakes you got. Try one brake only."

Shag tried to jam his foot through the floorboards. A loud squeal came from below and the Ju-52 began a slow, agonizing swing. All right, now for the other one, Shag said to himself, and as he pressed the opposite brake it squealed as badly as the first. He jammed his toes forward to depress both pedals and discovered a peculiarity of this airplane. The left brake and the right brake worked independent of each other. Hit both brakes and your feet slammed to the end of their stops, the brakes vanished, and the airplane rolled its own merry way. The trick, he learned in those pre-cious seconds, was to whack pressure from one pedal to another. He'd never run into this kind of setup before but it was the result of some field changes some looney German had made at this very place. Suddenly he was very glad they had a chance to test the bird before lift off time.

Getting maximum power from their engines was proving tricky. They tied the Ju-52 securely to her stakes, blocked the wheels, and ran the left engine to full power for a test. They didn't get it. The manifold pressure was far below the thirty-two inches as indicated by a mark on the gauge, and the engine vibrated madly. He and Lew knew the key. They were at some undetermined height above nine thousand feet and they needed more throttle movement, and they absolutely had to lean out the mixture. Back to full throttle, open the throttle stop lever, and keep advancing the power. At just over thirty-one inches the engine was pouring black smoke and the shaking rattled his teeth in his head. Lew leaned forward and began coming back on the mixture until the smoke faded and the vibration lessened, then the engine finally settled down to its normal uproar. They marked the positions of throttle and mixture control on the quadrant and repeated the sequence for the nose and the right engine.

They shut her down to conserve fuel. All that remained was gathering up whatever they wished to take with them and then flinging themselves over the edge of the plateau in what could be their corrugated coffin.

"Uh, laddie, have you taken a real good look at the way the plateau falls off?"

Shag looked at Lew with surprise. "Sure. Why?"

"We might not have all the power we need, you know. Once we're moving and the props load up there could be some back-pressure. The ignition harnesses might not hold up, and—"

"Whoa, there. You sound like Vance."

"I just looked down the bloody cliff and I feel like Vance."

Shag laughed and patted the astonished Heath on his cheek. "There, there, old fellow, I promise to get you home before dark."

For the first time since he'd known Shag, Lew was speechless.

"Trim?"

"Just above the zero mark."

"Flaps?"

"Ten degrees."

"Fuel selector?"

"Both."

"Spark?"

"Retarded. Oh, shit—disconnected."

Vance chuckled. "So are you. Retarded, I mean. You didn't check the mag drop."

"Screw the mag drop. It's balls to the wall. Anything else doesn't matter. Go on, dammit."

"Oil pressure?"

"Oil pressure, oil temp, CHT, CAT, okay. Fuel pressure not reading."

"Tailwheel lock."

"Broken."

"Vacuum system?"

"It's vibrating too badly to read it."

"Voltmeter and generator?"

"In the green."

The tone became a hair more serious. "Mixture settings?"

"Set for altitude takeoff."

"Time?"

"Time?" Shag glanced at Vance. "Who the hell has a watch?"

"*I* know what time it is."

They both looked at Vance.

"It's time to go," he grinned at them.

"That it is," said Shag, and in that instant he changed. "Lew, you've got the throttles and the mixture control. Vance, you monitor the gauges. Lew, once you've got this thing balls out you call off the speed to me. Use miles and not those damn kilometers, got it?"

"Right."

"I'm watching the runway and the airplane and you keep calling off the airspeed."

"You're set."

Shag looked about him. The sun was just dropping below the far horizon and that meant he wouldn't be looking into a ball of fire when he started down the runway on their go-for-broke launching. He laughed to himself about that one. It *was* a launching, starting out like this from a plateau about ten thousand feet high. Shut up and get on with it, he told himself.

He pulled the yoke full back and readied his feet on the pedals, trying to squeeze just a bit of brake out of one pedal. The smallest advantage could be critical. "Okay, give me everything," he barked.

Lew's hand went forward on the three throttles and the thunder around them was deafening. The Ju-52 shook violently as Lew held the huge wooden yoke all the way back against his chest, and the power was still coming up when she began a sideways slide and he knew the last fraction of brake was gone. The wind was only barely in their favor and he kept the yoke full back as she started rolling. It was like rushing along the deck of an aircraft carrier with oblivion just beyond its edge.

Yet she was moving, and faster than he'd believed possible. He could actually feel the acceleration, and a side glance showed him the yellow flame showing in the twilight from the wing-engine exhaust. "You've got thirty-five inches!" Lew bellowed in triumph.

Faster now. He felt the tail beginning to lighten, and he didn't believe it could be happening so fast. He wanted to get the tail up and level the wings with the ground to ease off on the drag of an inclined wing, and he put some forward pressure on the yoke. To his astonishment the tail came up almost immediately, he was already applying the right rudder he knew he'd need to counteract the torque of the propellers, and he walked the rudder pedals from side to side to keep the nose pointed down the runway. They were halfway along that life-or-death strip and he couldn't believe the words Lew shouted in his ear. The tail had started up when Lew yelled "Forty!" and he no sooner had her straightened out than *"Fifty! She's coming up beautifully!"* sang out in his ear.

"Sixty!"

He could feel those wings grasping at the thin air and each second strung out to what felt like a minute or more, because time had slowed for him, he was feeling every motion, sensing every change. At sixty the rudder was effective beyond anything he expected, and he was absolutely astounded with the instant reaction of the elevators in moving the tail up or down. That told him at once he must play that particular control, moving the huge yoke forward or backward, with critical attention and the gentlest of touches.

"Seventy!"

Two thousand feet left to go, but she already wanted to fly. He resisted the temptation to ease back on the yoke. Every mile per hour they had now was money in the bank.

"Eighty!"

She lifted off by herself. He didn't move the yoke an inch. The trim setting and flaps at ten degrees gave them perfect lift and there was still a thousand feet of runway before them, and the takeoff they had found so terrifying in its anticipation was a stunning, marvelous anticlimax as Annie lifted off the ground and climbed away from the plateau.

"Jesus Fucking Christ, I don't believe it!" Shag was still easing back on the yoke because she was accelerating to 100 miles an hour and at this altitude it meant their airspeed was going right through 120 mph true. He held her in a steady and gentle climb, amazed at her solid feel, unwilling to do more now than gain altitude, to get every foot she would give them, for height was the security blanket they needed. He eased her into a gentle turn to the right and the magnetic compass mounted on shock cords above the instrument panel tilted, then followed the ever-so-easy turning motion. At 345 degrees he settled her down, still climbing, and they were through 12,000 feet when he saw Lew's hands return to the throttles.

They had to shout to be heard with three engines roaring all around them, the great props thundering, the wind smashing into the angular, corrugated, wind-resisting shape, pounding through cracks and openings and into windows, and yet it was a sound of power, a song of flight. Lew leaned close to Shag's ear.

"Got to come back on the power! Cylinder-head temp is starting to come up a bit and I want to keep 'em cool!"

Shag nodded, then held up his hand. "Flaps! Milk 'em up and let's watch the speed!"

Lew nodded, pulled the knob in the center of the big wheel on the right side of the pilot's seat, grunted as he pushed the wheel forward, until it locked into flaps-up position. He shoved down on the knob. "Trim her out!" he shouted to the pilot.

Shag dropped his right hand to the wheel, rolled it a bit forward. They were indicating 110 mph, which was incredible—and burning off fuel at a terrible rate. He leveled her off, squinting at the panel. "Light!" he beckoned to Heath, and Lew hooked up the light to an overhead bracket, turning it until the glare softened. Then he went on the throttles and brought them back and back some more until they came down from 1900 rpm to just above 1600. They watched and they waited and Shag was tense for any change in the feel of the controls. But Annie was right in there. The speed bled off to an indicated 85 mph and that meant they were pounding along with these ancient, battered old engines and fixed-pitch props at just about an honest 100 miles an hour.

They had a good moon now, coming up fast above distant mountains, and Shag eased into a turn for direct visual reference, feeling out the ailerons. Watching the compass, he quickly found that to hold heading called for short, sharp jabs and then holding the pedal for the rudder and the nose would swing right where he wanted. In the calm air through which they flew, if he so much as breathed on the yoke forward or back she changed pitch attitude instantly. He couldn't tell much about the ailerons in this kind of air—they had almost nothing to do—but one slight crosswind gust on takeoff had already given him his first hint that in calm air Annie would be as gentle as a great panda. But if the going got rough and they found rocks in the sky, that rudder and those ailerons could help develop a lot of biceps and calves.

By now Lew had the power set and he was playing with the throttles to ease off on a steady and deep harmonic vibration they heard as much as felt. The propellers. There were three of them whirling out there and to get rid of the vibrations those blades had to be synchronized. You did it by feel and by sound and it took Lew fifteen minutes to get them into a kind of sync that didn't grate on his nerves. Shag was holding 345 on the mag compass and looking well ahead of him for the lights he knew would appear along their course. He tapped Vance on the arm and then rocked the yoke gently and felt it answer. Vance had it. He didn't have rudder pedals, only the old-fashioned kind of rudder bar, but for this cross-country flying it was fine. Shag wanted to relax, feel out the airplane, let her talk to him, study the gauges, watch Lew make the scratch marks with a knife that would give them future reference for cruising flight.

The first muffled explosion hardly shook the airplane, but the BANG! was frighteningly clear, like a riot gun going off against the right side of the cockpit. Then a series of staccato *cracks!* raced through the right wing and the floor beneath their feet trembled. Lew was leaning to one side, studying the right engine, and he watched the telltale signs of the exhaust as the flame spattered and changed color and force with each blast. Lew turned back and shouted to the two pilots.

"It's the ignition harness! Ain't worth a wrinkled tit! Too old! Don't worry about it! That's preignition we're getting! I'll watch it and if it gets any worse I'll—"

The next blast shook the entire machine. Immediately Lew had come back on the right throttle, Vance was compensating for the extra pull from the left engine, and then Lew eased off on power for that engine as well. Their speed bled off to an indicated 78 miles per hour, but they were still making a true grind through the air of just about 95, and that would do fine.

They kept flying, the explosions from the right engine easier now with reduced power and load on the harness, and not coming so often. They were settling down, the three of them, getting the feel of Annie, coming to understand her little signals, anticipating the slight swaying motions when a touch of turbulence caressed the wings. Lew kept moving his hands across every control and lever and knob in the cockpit, anticipating what would be needed for the descent and the landing, and Shag watched him and set up his own plans, even as he kept studying the skies and the earth far ahead of them. Lights had begun to appear along the surface, tiny pinpoints of yellow and creamy white that marked small hamlets or a vehicle on a road far below. But there were more and more lights ahead of them, and then the thinly glowing bowl they knew so well from having seen a thousand similar sights in their past flying.

Guayaquil was below them and they saw light reflected off the curving undersides of the wing engine cowls still visible from the cockpit. It was an immensely reassuring feeling, that sight down below, and Lew's hands, together, squeezed the shoulders of the pilots with him. It was all the conversation they needed.

They picked up the airport beacon, the bright flash of white and the duller pump of green as the beacon turned in its housing. Shag knew precisely where they were now, and how to cut the line that would take them closer to Portoviejo. He took the controls from Vance, who nodded with a quiet smile, and they kept plodding northward, guided by the lights and holding as true a course as possible. It wasn't possible to determine wind drift; they were too high and too slow.

The lights before him were partially blotted out and he squinted, trying to make out details. "What the hell is that on the windshield?" he asked Lew.

"Grease. I told you before, this clunker's got external rocker-arm boxes in the engines, and the caps are corroded and they're throwing grease back!"

Shag shook his head in silent wonder because they were still flying, no matter what else was happening.

The left engine shook suddenly, coughed, backfired, then ran smoothly for a while, only to fool them by backfiring with a blast of flame that lit up the whole wing. Shag heard Lew cursing. "Fuel pressure's dropping. I think the left tanks are almost empty! Vance! The wobble pump! Have a go with it!" Lew grasped the handle of the fuel selector and shoved it to the right. If he had this figured, they had more fuel in the right wing than the left. This kind of fuel system always fed the engines more fuel than the carburetors were set for, and the overdump most likely went to one wing or the other, in this case the right wing.

"Bloody good!" he shouted in sudden exultation, for the fuel pressure on number one was back in the normal operating range and the engine was running smoothly. He gripped Vance's elbow and they stuck the wobble pump back into its slot.

Then Shag pointed and they had Portoviejo in sight and he rolled in a touch of nosedown trim. The big Junkers eased her nose down just a hair and they began dropping steadily. Lew studied the meters-per-second gauge. "Three hundred feet a minute," he yelled in Shag's ear.

"Mark it," Shag told him. The scratch mark was what he needed for the future. They felt the increasing pressure and the buildup of wind sound. Far beyond Portoviejo on the still clear night they saw Manta, and Shag moved his gaze beyond the coastal city. He could barely make it out, but there was no question.

"Calceta!" he shouted. "See the beacon! There, off to the right, just about two o'clock from us!"

He started back on the throttles and they were on their way down at five hundred feet a minute.

Just hang in there, baby, Shag said to the big machine under his hands.

"Don't waste any time," he heard Lew's voice. "We're running out of fuel. Get her down as soon as you can."

Shag glanced back at him. "Anything else, sir?"

Lew nodded. "I'll be right back," he said, and disappeared into the cabin.

Vance shrugged. "Maybe he has to piss."

11

He took her down in a steady, descending circle, the engine roar diminished despite the open side windows to improve their vision. Annie settled earthward like an enormous corrugated condor in the moonlit sky. Shag called for flaps down to their full forty degrees. He needed room and time to feel the pitch changes and to determine how much power he'd need to hold ninety in the approach; he'd have to slow her down as much as possible when they landed because this was a short strip and they had no brakes to count on. He tried to remember everything he could about flying a DC-3 on this same kind of approach, and gave himself a mental warning to compensate for depth-perception changes caused by that big nose engine. He knew he would try to land much higher than eyeball judgment and he decided on a wheels touchdown, attitude level with the ground, and then get the tailwheel back and down as soon as he could. Trying to three-point this thing under these conditions was madness.

Lew had the flaps full down and Shag kept the descent at five hundred feet a minute and ninety miles an hour, trimming her hands off for that attitude. He fed in some power and was pleased with the almost negligible trim change. He could live with that for the approach and the flare to touchdown. Landing lights would have helped but they didn't have any, and Calceta was nothing more than two dim rows of yellow lights and a single beacon shining from a building well off the strip. Then there was no more time to think about it. He was following his instincts and he listened to Lew calling off the speed and he held ninety, then he had eighty-five and the lights were closer and he decided the plane was light enough to bleed off some more speed and as he brought up the nose he was all the way back on the power and the speed was dropping away fast. He was a shade behind and she touched down on the left gear, a soft bounce back up with the oleo taking the shock, and then he had both mains planted and he came back on the yoke until he felt the tailwheel touch and Jesus they were running out of room! Right brake, just a hair, then the left, they didn't do a damn bit of good and he was stomping rubber back and forth and without any more warning than that she rolled to a stop with all the room in the world still before them. Sure, with the tail down and full flaps and idling props they had nothing but drag. Lew pounded him on the shoulder and Vance was grinning. "Here, put these on, you clowns," they heard Lew say and a steel helmet was thrust into their hands. "Just put them on," he repeated. "Taxi back to that building with the light. There's someone in there, maybe two people, and when you climb down from this thing I want them to see German officers stepping down from a German bomber, got it? You go on out first after we stop. I'll be along right after you." And again he was gone, leaving them puzzled.

Shag turned her around on the runway, playing it carefully as he started moving back the way they'd come. Now he was able to see what Lew had told them. Two figures silhouetted in the light from an open door. "I can make out a gas truck there," Shag said. "Direct me to it, will you? Anything gets in front of this nose I can't see."

They moved in slowly, Shag pumping a brake pedal madly until she squealed to a halt and they shoved the fuel-flow levers into the shutdown position, waited for the fuel to suck through the lines; when the props finally groaned to a halt they shut everything off. Vance went back first and opened the cabin door and jumped to the ground, Shag right behind him.

They faced a police officer with his hand resting on his holster and a guard behind him with a submachine gun, and neither looked friendly. They stared blankly as the machine out of times past loomed over them, hot metal creaking and groaning as it cooled. A stream of Spanish came from the officer.

Shag walked slowly to him, his body erect, doing everything he could think of to fulfill the role of a Nazi officer. "*Schprecken der Deutsch?*" He forced out the words, hoping to hell this angry little man before him knew both Spanish and English. Most of the police officials knew some English because of all the American planes that came down through here. It was still Spanish and the holster was now open.

Shag shook his head slowly, bunched fists on his hips, showing as much anger as the puzzled man before him. "Dumpkopf! Assholen in zwei geshtunken, nein? Das der Porsche, and gleitz mit der Volkswagen!"

"You speak English maybe?"

Jesus Christ, it worked . . .

"*Ja.* English vill do fine. You are in charge here?"

"*Si!* Commandante Julio Perez."

"Colonel Basil Dorsch, at your service," Shag said, the words springing unbidden from him. It just seemed the right thing to say. He clicked his heels and his right arm shot up in a sudden salute. "Heil Hitler!"

Behind him Vance's voice cracked like a whip. "Gutten job mit der krappenstory. *Heil Hitler!*"

Julio Perez brought up his right hand in a faltering salute, more confused than ever. But he was a tough little bastard.

"Ve vill need petrol for der flying gershtunker," Shag said with a wave at the Ju-52. "*Das schprecken?* Petrol, fuel, fill der tanks mit gasoline, oil—"

Perez's head bobbled up and down like a cork tossed onto a rough ocean. "*Si, si,*" he said rapidly. "I will need your papers, of course, señor. I mean, Colonel."

"Later, later," Shag replied. "You shtart der gasoline in der tanks right now and vile my men are busy, ve go inside your office and ve take care of der paperwork, ja?" He turned around and called to Heath.

"Schnell! Rauss mit der big assenhole and fillenzee der tanks!" Then to Vance: "Get them filled. To the brim. Oil. See if Lew needs hydraulic fluid." Shag spun around and placed a friendly, bearlike arm over the shoulder of the officer who was a good head shorter, steering him toward the office. To his side he heard Vance ordering the guard to bring the fuel truck around, and Shag wanted the head man out of the way before he could tell the man not to move. You always went for the jugular in this sort of situation.

In the office Perez faced him with narrowed eyes.

He was more confused than he was suspicious, Shag judged, but this was his whole world. He was in charge for this shift, and screwing up his world was absolutely forbidden. And if he didn't understand it or couldn't explain it later that meant it was being screwed up. So you demanded papers, you went by the book, you followed the rules, and Shag figured he was running out of time fast and he needed some honest answers just a bit faster. Besides, Shag thought ruefully, he didn't have a passport, visa, entry card, flight permit, license, credit card, or anything. Just the ability to move and talk fast. "Colonel, please, I must see your papers, now." Perez shrugged. "You understand, no? The rules. They call for the papers."

"Of course, of course," Shag said. "Maybe telling me zumthink you can, ja? Can it be possible, Commandante, that your government vould run a whole field like this mitt only two men? One officer und vun enlisted man?"

Julio Perez made a terrible mistake. He drew himself up with pride. "It is not hard, Colonel. At night this is a quiet field. Only two of us are needed. If we expect unusual traffic or if there is a problem," he nodded in the direction of a telephone, "only then would I need to call headquarters. But there is never such a need."

"Zey are close by here, no?"

Perez shook his head. "Two hours, Colonel. The road is not very good. And now, your papers, please?"

"*Ja, ja.*" Shag slid into a chair and through the open door he saw the fuel truck by the Ju-52, the hose passed up to the left wing where Vance was waiting to start pumping into the filler tube. Shag turned back, reached into his tunic, looked up at the only officer on the field, then with a sly smile motioned him to come closer. "El commandante, I can show this to you only." Shag glanced outside. "Your man is coming this way. Before he gets here—"

Puzzled, Perez leaned down toward Shag, and there is no question that he never saw Shag's heavy German boot lift up with terrible impact to smash directly into his face. Shag heard the dull cracking sound as the boot caved in the forehead bone along the sinuses and knew also that Julio Perez was dead long before he slumped to the floor. In an instant, Shag had the pistol out of his holster. He slammed a round into the chamber and stepped outside.

"Do not move, señor."

The pistol hung by Shag's side and it did not move. Not when the guard who had been with Perez stood twenty feet from him with a Russian submachine gun pointed directly at his chest. The guard was too far away to move against him and all he had to do was to twitch his finger to pump lead all through one Shag Jordan.

"Now, the pistola. Very slowly, let it fall."

It dropped to the hard dirt surface.

"Your hands. Get them up."

The barrel of the submachine gun reflected light from the office where Perez lay in a pool of gathering blood.

"If you do not—"

The man stopped in midsentence. Shag stared at him as his mouth opened slowly, his teeth bared in a hideous grimace, his back seemed to cave in as if struck by a murderous, silent blow. His arm jerked upward and the submachine gun was pointing straight up when a convulsive twitch, the last gasping breath of life, shuddered through the man. The submachine gun roared as the trigger finger spasmed in the moment of death and the man fell face forward onto the ground and lay still.

"What the hell—"

Then he saw it. A long deadly steel shaft, fired from a crossbow held by Lew. Shag didn't take any chances. He went forward quickly and picked up the submachine gun, motioned Lew forward and tossed him the weapon, returned to where he'd been standing and scooped up the automatic pistol. "Let's dump him in the shadows over there," he said.

Lew took his arms and Shag his feet, and they tossed him like a crumpled sack of meal into some high bushes by a dilapidated shack. "Where's Fancy Pants?" Lew demanded.

"In the office. Let's go."

Lew chuckled at the sight of Perez lying in the dark liquid pool. "What in blazes did you hit him with?"

"He hit my boot with his face," Shag answered.

"Nasty habit, that. Let's dump him with his buddy."

"Wait." Shag went through Perez's pockets, took out his ID cards, some money, and two clips of ammunition for the automatic. "Okay, let's do it." Perez was dumped unceremoniously by the dead guard, and they started for the office. "What tipped you off?" Shag asked.

Lew shrugged. "He was nervous. Missed his nursemaid. When the pretty boy was out of sight he got more nervous. He left us fueling the bird by ourselves. Nobody in this part of the world does that unless there's a compelling reason." Lew chuckled. "There was one more thing. He shoved a round into the chamber of this little toy. I had the crossbows right by the cabin door. I grabbed one and came in behind him and I said, well, well, now, look at old nasty there and—you know the rest." Lew glanced around him. "How many more here? I figure they ought to be starting this way, and—"

"Just these two."

"That's all?" Lew shook his head. "Something stinks. I think we'd better look around."

"Okay," Shag agreed. "But not until the Ju is loaded to the ass. Fill her all the way. Get all the oil you need. Get her ready to fly and then we look around. Also, you'd better move the plane when you finish. You and Vance taxi her to the dark end of the runway, over there."

"Okay."

"That way when we fire up we don't have to taxi anywhere. We just point and go."

"Neat. What else?"

"Get with it. The commandante said the nearest police or army headquarters was two hours away by car. That figures from the distances involved. He also said there was one phone line, and—"

"Cut it. Now. If anyone calls—well, the phone lines here are shitty to begin with. A dead phone's common enough, Shag. A phone that rings and doesn't get answered is trouble."

"I'll do it. You get with Vance. I'll cover from here. I'll be outside the shack. That way I can see the road from both directions."

Forty-five minutes later they were done, the Ju-52 chocked at the far end of the runway, invisible in the shadows. The fuel truck was parked to the side, and Lew showed up in a battered jeep with Vance at his side.

"Never a dull moment with you two around," Vance greeted Shag, swinging to the ground.

"We got a lot to do," Shag said, and there was no

nonsense in his voice. "We're not thinking. Lew, get back to those bodies and take the wristwatches off them."

"Okay. Be right back."

"Vance, when he's back you take that machine gun. Stand over there in the shadows. Keep the jeep ready for anything. If someone comes down the road, from either direction, stay in the shadows and let them go on by. If they stop we can—get something to lock or bar that gateway into the field to slow up anybody who shows up. If they do turn in, get to us right away."

"And if I can't come around without being seen?"

Shag ignored the problem. "It's easy, baby. You put a full clip in that toy, and if anybody doesn't like the rules, you empty that thing into whatever they're driving, and after they're all dead you come running. Got it?"

Vance gave him a long look, saw Heath returning, took the submachine gun, and walked around the shack out of sight.

Lew jerked a thumb at his departing back. "What's with his nibs?"

"Guard duty. Everything set with the bird?"

"Set. Now, like we was saying before, something smells around here. Only two men? Uh uh. Want to bet one of these old hangars has something inside our newly departed friends didn't want anyone to see?"

"There's a flashlight on the desk. Get it."

He heard Lew rummaging around. When he came out of the shack he had a belt and a holster strapped around his waist. "Got five clips with this thing, too," he offered. "Let's start across the runway. It's too dark over there."

They trotted across the field. The first two hangars

were filled with junk. The third hangar was locked and they kicked the lock free of the rotting wood. Their flashlight played slowly on a white-and-red shape. A big twin. "Turbo Commander." Shag whistled. "The long-range jobbie and—" He held the light on the bullet holes stitched along the side of the fuselage and the smashed side windows. Inside there were two bodies chewed by the gunfire. Blood was everywhere.

"Now we know," Lew said. "You know, the odds are they were carrying something."

"Something worth a lot. This damn airplane is worth nearly a cool million."

"Not now," Lew said. "Engine on this side is holed everywhere. But whatever they were carrying—"

"Right. Must be in the office. Let's go."

It took them twenty minutes to find the false wall and smash their way through. Inside was a heavy steel cabinet with a massive lock. "Whatever it is, it's in there," Lew observed.

"We need a can opener," Shag told him. "Give your gun to Vance and bring back the big one."

It took half a clip to blow away the lock. Inside were several attaché cases. They studied them in silence. The first case bulged with money, currency of several different countries, including American and Swiss notes. The second case was even more interesting. It was filled with passports, visas, identity cards, and other papers in at least a half-dozen languages they could identify quickly.

"Shee-yit," Shag swore. "This is heavy, baby."

"Into the big bird with it. No matter what happens, let's not lose this."

"Make it fast."

When Lew returned he found Shag with a bucket

of paint and a brush. "What the hell are you doing?" Lew said, bewildered.

Shag turned to him. "Look. We got an hour, maybe two before we take off from here. Nobody knows we're here. Got that? Nobody even knows we exist. And when the big honchos get here, because sure as hell they know about that Turbo Commander and those bodies in that hangar, they're going to look for leads. They may talk funny, but stupid they're not. So whatever leads they find is the direction in which they'll travel."

Lew gestured at the can and brush. "You're going to write a love note, I suppose."

"You got it." He stood before a wall, tore down a calendar and painted a huge swastika on the wall. He turned back and Lew was nodding in understanding. "How's your stomach?" Shag asked.

"Let's have it," Lew said.

"Those two bodies. Get a screwdriver, a knife, anything. Carve a swastika on their foreheads, their cheeks, anywhere. And remember, it won't hurt them."

Lew left without a word. Shag painted a swastika on another wall, thought for a moment, then in broad strokes brushed HEIL DORSCH! beneath the second swastika. He heard Lew coming in.

"What now?" he asked.

"Get to that Commander. Open the fuel drains and leave them open."

"You want fuel on the ground?"

"I want fuel everywhere but this building."

"I'll get the Commander and then start with the fuel truck."

"Good."

"Service with a smile, old man."

They met as Lew came around the second row of

buildings, the stink of gasoline everywhere. "Leave the hose running," Shag ordered. "Then get Vance. This place is like a bomb."

They gathered in the jeep. Vance smelled the gasoline, saw the swastikas in the office. "What in the devil are you doing?" He hung on as Shag raced down the runway toward the Ju-52.

"Leaving a message. By the time we leave here most of this place is going up like the Fourth of July. All except the office."

"You think a swastika painted on walls is enough?"

Shag shook his head. "Nope. But I left another message for them to think about. A memo from a Major Hans Bruno to Colonel Basil Dorsch."

"What kind of memo?"

"It names our next refueling point. They should be looking for us there."

"Are you crazy?"

Lew held Vance's arm. "Let him go on. I've got an idea he's about to pay off a debt."

Vance looked at him, waiting. Shag pulled up to the side of the Ju-52 and gestured for them to climb aboard. "According to that note, whatever plane landed here, whatever crew killed these two men and set this place off—well, they're headed for Sullana."

Vance stopped in his tracks. "You mean . . ."

"Yeah, that's what I mean. The note says they're to see Captain Jesús Rosario of the Royal Peruvian Air Force for further instructions."

Vance's smile turned into a roar of laughter. "Beautiful!"

"Let's get cracking. See down that road? They're still a couple of miles from here but we've got company on the way. Probably been trying to call and nobody's answering."

Twelve minutes later all three engines were running. Lew wadded up an oily rag, ran outside to a pool of gasoline, and fired off several shots into the ground. The flame blasting from the shots was enough. Fire leaped up, Lew ignited the rag, threw it toward the nearest building, dashed back to the airplane, climbed into the cabin, and slammed the door behind him. "Go, go!" he shouted.

"We're still chocked!" Vance told Shag.

"So we are," Shag smiled, and went full forward on the throttles, yoke hard back to his chest. The engines howled and the Ju-52 rocked for a moment and then jumped the blocks they'd shoved beneath the wheels. They accelerated down the runway, flames leaping upward on both sides of them. As they passed the office they saw three trucks and squads of soldiers staring at them. Shag lifted the Ju-52 into the air, got just enough altitude and banked steeply to give the stunned soldiers a perfect flame-lit view of a three-engined German bomber making its getaway, and headed off to the south toward Peru and the waiting Captain Jesús Rosario.

12

They flew south for twenty miles, climbing steadily in a clear sky. Thirty or forty miles beyond the coastline they turned right and took up a north heading that paralleled the land. First light painted a gray-pink line to the east, beyond the high mountains invisible to them at this moment. But they'd made it and were on their way. "You take it," Shag told Vance. "As soon as you have good light take her down to five hundred feet and just keep following the coast." Vance nodded and Shag went back into the cabin where Lew was examining the contents of the two attaché cases.

"Forty thousand American," he said. "Another ten or fifteen in Swiss banknotes. There's also a bunch of money here from Colombia, Peru, Brazil, Panama, Ecuador—maybe more. It's a lot, that's all I know. A bloody fortune."

"What about the other bag?"

Lew placed the case on his lap. "Worth a king's ransom. You name it, bucko. Want a passport? Visa? Identity cards? It's all here. See this?" He held up a small metal device. "It's got an official imprint seal in it. Squeeze it together and it raises lettering on any document. They must have them in a dozen languages. Pens in different colors. A slew of rubber stamps and pads. If a man knew how to handle this he could go anywhere in the world."

"Can you make out some for us in Spanish?"

"Me?" Lew snorted. "Might as bloody well ask for Arabic. Not me, laddie."

"How about England?"

"Clod. You mean the United Kingdom."

"I don't care if it's Patagonia," Shag said.

"Look, let's go for Canada," Lew recommended. "At least we know the language and I can do them right off." He saw Shag nod and then added a question: "What names?"

"Our own."

"You're mad!"

"We'll make up a set of German papers later. Go to it. I'll think up some other names for us to fit these uniforms."

"It's too bad they didn't have a haberdashery back where we just took off."

"These are better," Shag said. "As long as you're going to be conspicuous, go all the way. Incidentally, you were a draftsman, weren't you?"

"An engineer. There's a difference."

"But you should still be pretty good with a pen."

"As good as any."

"Well, in a few minutes you'll be guilty of forgery. Get busy, friend. I'm going up forward. Vance doesn't get some shuteye soon he's going to pass out on us. It's been nearly thirty-six hours now since we've slept."

He slid into the left seat, checked all the gauges, fiddled with the throttles, and grunted with dissatisfaction. He just couldn't get these three engines synched out to kill that harmonic. "Vance, get some sleep. I'll take it."

Vance nodded. He adjusted his body, tightened his belt and was out in seconds. Shag worked the throttles again and looked at the left engine. For the first time he wondered about the polished metal mirror on the side of the cowling facing him. He studied the reflecting surface and found himself staring at a curving shadow that kept moving toward him. He cursed himself silently—it had been right there all the time! The curving line was a shadow of the nose propeller, and the reason he could see it was because it was turning at a slightly different speed than the prop on that left engine. He pulled the left throttle back just a hair. The line moved faster and he adjusted the power in the opposite direction, slowly, very slowly, and the line vanished. The airplane felt smoother. He half stood in his seat, looked at the mirror on the right cowling, and repeated the procedure of slowing the curving line until it disappeared.

Annie sang like her engines ran on honey. He marveled at the ancient system that synchronized three propellers perfectly by use of two mirrors. An automatic sync mechanism on something like a twin-engined Convair cost over twelve thousand bucks.

He looked back into the cabin to see Lew hard at work, then eased the Ju-52 closer to the coastline. An increasing number of fishing boats and small bright reflections in the sky, airplanes working to and from the airport, identified Esmerelda for him. He checked his newly acquired wristwatch and figured the time to the border. Forty-five minutes later the words formed in his mind. "Good-bye, Ecuador, and hello, Colombia." Three hundred miles to go and it was getting sweeter with every passing minute. A layer of broken clouds had formed at twelve hundred feet above the sea and he climbed slowly until he was within a hundred feet of the broken cloud deck. Now they had an excellent blanket over them and he could still keep the coastline in sight.

He turned again to look back into the cabin. Lew had stacked his paperwork alongside an attaché case and was fast asleep. Good. Later he'd grab some for himself. His stomach growled and reminded him they hadn't had a thing to eat or drink for nearly twenty-four hours now. Or was it longer than that? Well, they'd be on the ground at Buenaventura in just about two hours.

They'd have to play a different ball game there. This was broad daylight and there'd be people all over the place and they couldn't go barging into that field and start playing war. It just wouldn't cut the mustard. But even so, they were flying into the airfield in as brazen a manner as one could imagine—nothing like marching naked down a street to get everyone's attention, and in a figurative sense they were naked.

He recalled something about Colombia. There'd been a big stink down there in the not too distant past. He racked his brain to bring it all back. Had it been Eichmann? It could have been, but the gist of it was that someone had bribed high officials in the Colombian government for sanctuary. A long-sought-after war criminal, one of the concentration-camp types. Israeli agents found him, tried to sneak him out of the country, and were caught. They did their job, though. Shag remembered that part. When the Colombian police caught up with the Israeli team and took them prisoner, they only smiled. One of the men tapped his watch. But it wasn't a watch. It was a short-

range radio transmitter, and one of the Colombian police remembered later that the prisoner taken by the
Israelis had a heavy necklace. The necklace was filled
with plastic explosives and was set to receive a radio
signal that triggered a miniaturized detonator. They
never found even a piece of his head.

The point was there were probably still the same
kind of people well hidden in that country, and anybody, but anybody, could be bought for the right
price. And if you came in with the sun shining on you
like gold—why, gold's a language all its own.

They entered the pattern at Buenaventura, circled
the field, and slid in to land behind a Vickers Vis-
count turboprop. Shag let her roll to the far end of the
runway, saw a military jeep with a large checkered
flag fluttering from its bumper, and followed the vehicle. A ground crewman directed him with hand signals to a parking spot, and they started their shutdown. "Everybody remember the routine," Shag
warned. "You've got your ID cards. If they ask to see
them, hand 'em right over. It's all smiles and friends
here."

"We hope," Vance amended.

"Faith, brother," Lew offered as the props ground
to a halt.

Shag patted his pockets. Three of them were stuffed
with Colombian currency and he wasn't going to play
games with these people. It just didn't fit the cards.

Shag climbed to the ground, the helmet hot and
heavy on his head in the devastating midday heat. An
official in uniform met him. Shag couldn't tell his rank
and it didn't matter. He clicked his heels and saluted
in the standard military fashion. He received an immediate salute in return and the officer gestured to a

sedan. Lew and Vance followed him inside and they drove off. No one had yet spoken a word. They were driven to a thick-walled building of two stories and a man would have to be blind to miss the positions for heavy firepower from the upper level. Inside, everyone was in uniform, crisp, sharp, armed. Their escort led them into an inner office where a Colombian official in gleaming boots, a garrison belt, a holstered pistol and, above all, row after row of ribbons on his chest, stood to greet them.

"Colonel Arturo Rivera at your service, gentlemen."

They stood ramrod straight and Shag cracked a perfect salute to the colonel which, to his relief, was answered. "Colonel Rivera, with your kind permission, may we be alone?"

Rivera held him in a long gaze, then motioned his aide to leave. Shag stepped into the breach immediately. "One moment," he snapped to Lew and Vance. "Your papers. *Schnell!*" They handed over their identity documents to him. "Wait outside," he snapped.

They left with the Colombian officer.

Colonel Rivera offered a cigarette. Shag nearly swooned at the taste. "I regret not being able to speak German," Rivera said after a brief pause.

"I prefer English," Shag replied. He'd meet this one head to head.

"Good. May I see your papers, please?"

"Of course." Shag handed him the documents for the three of them. Finally Rivera looked up. "Jordan, Brady, Heath. Canadians. They *sound* Canadian."

"They are forgeries, of course," Shag said easily and was rewarded with a startled look. "My name is Ludwig Schwenke. Brady is Bruno Hauser. We are German. Heath's real name is Baron Herman von Faulkenhausen. He is Swiss by birth, international by choice, a swindler at heart."

"You are strangely honest, ah—"

"Jordan will do."

"As you say. Why did you land here?"

"We are out of Cuba, bound for Peru. The time for the *putsch* has come. Our people are gathering from everywhere to meet in Quito and at a secret site near Natal in Brazil. It has taken a long time to gather the, ah, special weapons we require for our purposes."

"Most of the old-timers are no longer with us," Rivera said.

Careful, baby. You're treading on a minefield, Shag told himself. Then, to Rivera: "You talk of men. Ideals remain alive forever."

"Of course, of course."

Shag reached inside his tunic. Rivera stiffened, but only barely, then relaxed as he saw the thick wad of currency on the desk before him. "What is the equivalent of that in American dollars, Colonel Rivera?"

Rivera riffled the notes. "Approximately thirteen thousand dollars American." He sat back and waited.

"I have never seen that money before this moment," Shag said.

Again Rivera bided his time. When he moved it was a silken glide; a drawer opened, the money vanished, the drawer closed. "Tell me what you need, Jordan."

"You are a gentleman, sir. I would like to have the flugzeug—forgive me—the aircraft serviced. If this could be done as soon as possible with my men, I would be grateful. We would be out of your way in a very short time."

Rivera pressed a desk button, his aide appeared like magic, orders were given crisply, and the aide vanished. "It will be done at once."

"Thank you. We should be ready to leave in a half-hour, then. If you have the time, Colonel, there are a few other things, you understand? A shopping list?"

Rivera nodded. "That could be expensive."

"You are a man of taste, Colonel. There is more money. It will be delivered as soon as our engines are turning and we are ready to leave."

Rivera stood up. "We shall go together. You are interested in—?"

"You have a supply office?"

"Yes."

A steady stream began from the supply building to the Ju-52. One hundred and twenty spark plugs, cans of grease, vacuum-driven directional gyros and artificial horizons. Two powerful but portable VHF radio transceivers. Three cases of military rations—marked U.S.A., Shag noted. A Polaroid camera and six containers of film with enough flashbulbs for the film. One case of Scotch. Several cartons of cigarettes. Six boxes of cigars. Lighters and fluid. Two sweep-second watches. Packages of personal supplies. A case of fruit juice. It was hard to tell who was the more surprised—Rivera at the diversity of this man's requests, or Jordan at the ability of Rivera to supply anything.

It was done and they were driving back to the Ju-52. "Are there any other needs, my friend?" Rivera asked. "Perhaps you need some weapons?"

This was the moment for which Shag had waited their entire stop. He laughed heartily. "That is the last thing we need, my good colonel! There is enough poison gas—the deadliest nerve gas ever known—inside that aircraft to kill more than fifty million people. No, thank you, sir, weapons we do not need."

Rivera sat stiffly alongside him, although doing his best to maintain an air of comfortable nonchalance.

At the Ju-52 Shag went into the airplane; he did no more than step out of sight of Rivera when he reached into his other pocket and withdrew the wad of Colombian currency. It disappeared as quickly as before, but he saw an added respect in Rivera's eyes. Whoever these strange people were, thought the colonel, they have no shortage of money. The ancient machine, he judged, must be a ruse. But it would not be wise to ask questions. And he had the feeling he might not like the answers.

Shag stood with Colonel Rivera as Lew and Vance fired up the three engines. They smoked and back-fired until they finally ran smoothly, which only mystified Rivera all the more. "Colonel, one more favor!" Shag called to him over the idling thunder.

"Of course! Name it!"

"I would appreciate your notifying Peruvian Air Control that we will soon be in their area. Our code name is Panzer, and I would like the information passed on to Basil Dorsch. Can you do that?"

Rivera's eyes flared. "I know that name."

"Good! Then I may count on you!"

"You have my word."

They saluted, Shag closed the door, and the mystified audience on the ground watched the anachronistic machine slowly vanish into the distance.

"Vance flies. He's the fucking navigational genius. Anybody who can fly back and forth over the North Pole with Russian fighters hunting his ass can fly a straight line from here to Puerto Jiminez." Shag took a long swallow of Scotch from the bottle, belched searing fumes, and fell back to attacking a fourth can of C-rations. He tossed the can over his shoulder to clatter in the aft part of the cabin. He was so goddamned *tired.* He tore open a cigarette pack and lit up. He wanted a cigar but he wasn't going to be awake long enough to enjoy it. A quick cigarette was all he could handle at this point.

"Listen to me, you British prick. I'm going to sleep. You understand? I'm punchy now. Vance flies, you help. Break open those VHF radios—"

"What?"

"Yeah, yeah. Shut up and lissen . . ." He was starting to slur his words from fatigue. "Get out those radios. Portables, but powerful. Batteries and everything, got it? You feed the general up there in the cockpit. Food, juice, whatever he needs. And you know what? There's over a hundred brand-new plugs in these boxes, too. If you get bored you can change them."

"While we're flying, right?" Lew said sarcastically.

"I don't care if you stick 'em up your ass. Now, go away."

Lew watched Shag prop up his feet on the seat before him, lean back and fall asleep instantly. Lew took the cigarette from his hand, ground it out on the floor. He opened some more C-rations and took turns flying, eating, and taking short swigs from the bottle of Scotch.

Then the right engine began to act up.

Three hours of sleep. Dead to the world. Deep, sound, untroubled, soothed by the rumbling growl of the engines and the slight swaying of the airplane. Like a babe in a cradle.

He felt, perhaps he sensed, the vibrations from the right engine. Shag didn't move but his eyes came open instantly. He was so deep into slumber that he had to force his memory into obedience. He focused slowly on the cabin, then recognized what had awakened him. The right engine was missing. Not the sledgehammer explosions they'd encountered before. Shag rose to his feet, tore open a box, and stuck a cigar in his teeth. He lit up, closed his eyes, and savored a taste dimly remembered. Only then did he go forward, stooping through the cockpit entryway, then standing between the two men. They acknowledged his presence with a nod. Shag studied the gauges. Every time they got a bang or a rumble out of number three the manifold pressure and rpm twitched. That wasn't the harness; he was convinced of that. Plugs or a magneto, most likely.

He didn't touch anything. Lew's hand moved the number-three mag lever from both to the left position and the reaction was immediate. Engine speed fell by nearly four hundred revs. Back to both and it came up almost to where it had been before. He went to the right mag only and the engine smoothed out.

"I think it's both the mag and some of the plugs!" Lew yelled above the cockpit thunder.

"How much longer to go?" Shag yelled back.

"Maybe two hours. The wind's from our left."

Shag looked down on the ocean through the broken clouds, saw the streaks marking the wind. It wasn't with them but it also wasn't hurting any. They'd make it. He remembered something, turned to move the fuel selector to the right wing. They didn't know yet how to crossfeed this monster, and if that right engine quit they might have to draw all their fuel from the left wing. Burn from the right now while they knew they could do it.

Shag went back to the cabin, took a long swallow of Scotch, fiddled with the second transceiver. He heard several aircraft talking from high altitude with a ground station. He was trying to find the frequency for Puerto Jiminez. What the hell. It also handled a lot of military traffic and they should be working 126.2. He dialed it in. They were still too far out and too low for him to understand the crackling of voices, but he confirmed the Puerto Jiminez tower. He went forward and gave that frequency to Lew so he could use it on his own radio.

Back in the cabin he left the radio on high volume and looked ahead of them. The clouds were getting heavier. Vance already had the same idea and he was starting down. Better to get under that cloud deck out here before they reached land and got stuck with a job of penetrating a cloud deck close to the ground, without even a fraction of the instruments they needed.

The right engine tried to swallow itself. The back-firing became worse. Plugs this time for sure, Shag knew. Then it became so bad and flame kept belching out of the stacks that he knew they'd have to shut it down. Damn. They were so close now and—

Lew was on it. He felt the slight swing as Lew cut the right engine with the mixture control and then punched off the electrical system for the engine. The nose was coming up and the Ju-52 was shuddering as Vance flew her at minimum speed trying to rid them of the drag from a windmilling propeller. It worked. They were shaking wildly, barely above stall speed, when the right prop jerked a few times and then stood still. The nose came down, Shag felt and heard increased power from numbers one and two. They must be down to barely 85 miles an hour, he figured, but they'd burned off most of their fuel and Annie would hack flying even on two ancient engines.

He saw Lew waving him frantically to the cockpit. He went forward and followed Lew's pointing hand. A

Boeing 727, making a wide circle, obviously coming around to get a better look at the completely unbelievable. Pan American Airways, from the looks of her. They didn't want that airliner to get too good a look.

"Vance! Take her down with the wheels right along the clouds, got it? Then hold it there for sixty seconds exactly and drop her down!"

He ran back through the cabin, climbed into the cargo hold aft of the main bulkhead, went through the storage compartment into the turret. He paused long enough to put on his helmet and cinch the chin strap, then he climbed up into the howling wind and grasped the handle of their machine gun, their great hunk of rust, with his left hand. Clouds flickered by him, giving an impression of great speed. Vance was holding her halfway into the cloud deck. Shag watched the 727 coming around at a tremendous closing rate, straight toward them. He saw the pilots clearly. That also meant that only the crew, close up and getting closer, could see them. Vance forced himself erect in the airblast and threw up his arm in a rigid Nazi salute. The 727 was still boring in when the world disappeared in scudding gray as Vance took her down through the clouds. He leveled off no more than eight hundred feet above the water and continued on course as Shag returned to the cockpit.

His grin was infectious. "You should have seen those mothers," he chortled. "Those two great big sets of eyes, staring at us." He made mock binoculars with his fingers curled into circles. "And there was this heinie gunner standing up in the turret, machine gun and helmet and all, giving them the old Heil Hitler routine. Vance, you timed it perfectly. I think they had time to blink once or twice and then we just disappeared. It was beautiful."

Vance looked doubtful. "They're probably reporting us right now," he growled.

"No way, baby," Shag told him. "Look, nobody in his right mind reports UFO's or airplanes that absolutely cannot be there. You know what we looked like? Here we are over the fucking ocean, creasing the cloud tops, this bucket of bolts looking like it's just been shot to hell, one engine dead and the prop standing still, and a kraut gunner in the turret giving them the Heil Hitler jazz. You know what? It's like a time warp. The kind of thing they talk about in the Devil's Triangle or something. Who'd believe them? If some guy came to you with this nutty story of an airplane that hasn't been around for more than thirty years, that shows up all shot to pieces, and the gunner salutes him, would you believe the crazy bastard?"

Vance had a rueful look on his face. "No. I wouldn't."

"Might as well report a thousand-foot UFO."

"I can see the headlines now," Lew added. "Close encounters of the worst kind."

"Okay, okay," Vance broke in. "Enough with the yuks. I'm taking her down to about a hundred feet. All we need is to be picked up by radar. We're still in Panama airspace."

Shag shrugged. "Wouldn't make any difference anymore. Sure as hell they were painting that 727 on their scope." He thought about that. "But on second thought, if he was squawking his transponder, it could have blanked us out. We'll know soon enough. With one engine dead we don't have much choice and— there!" He pointed. "See those lights? That's Azeuro Peninsula. Okay, take her down and head for all those neon signs."

Ten minutes later they were passing through rainshowers and all three men were cursing. Visibility was going to hell in a handbasket and it was getting dark swiftly. The minutes dragged and they were more than concerned now about their fuel. They were running off the left wing tanks and it was time to drag out all the good-luck charms they could think of when they saw the lights along the coastline of Costa Rica, and identified Puerto Jiminez.

"Take her straight in, Vance. Don't turn left and don't turn right and don't pass go and don't collect two hundred clams, just straight in to that runway ahead of us. I'm going back into the cabin where I can hear better. I'll let the tower know we're coming in. Oh, by the way, our call sign is Panzer."

Lew turned to him. "Since when?"

"Since right now."

Vance never wavered a foot left or right. Lew had the wobble-pump handle out of its slot and was ready to suck the last gallons of fuel from the tanks. Vance put her down on the main runway, let her run long in the rain-lashed darkness as the runway lights flashed by, brought the tail down gently. The left engine quit as they turned off the active and onto the taxiway.

"Holy shit," Lew said for them all. They had fumes left in the wings.

They rolled ahead slowly on the nose engine. Vance managed just enough brake to turn alongside a military ship, an old C-45. The Ju-52 shuddered to a halt. The tanks were completely dry. They climbed down in a rain pounding harder with every passing minute.

In the terminal building, high above the offices, a man in the control tower had followed their flight all the way to the ground, and then watched the old bomber sigh to a stop. He rubbed his eyes, shaking his head in disbelief. He picked up a pair of binoculars and saw three German officers in steel helmets emerge from the machine. He banged the side of his head with his hand several times, but they were still there.

He picked up a telephone, dialed a number, waited impatiently. "Give me the general. No, this can *not* wait! Give me General von Krueger—*immediately!* This is an emergency!"

13

They were prisoners in the nicest sort of way, in a private lounge with deep, luxurious couches and cognac on the table in front of them. Major Ricardo Castialano, who sat on the edge of a very wide, handsome, richly polished desk, tapped his leg with a swagger stick.

"You will know more in a little while," Castialano told them. "That is all I am permitted to say on the subject of my superior. Relax, gentlemen. Your aircraft—and it is a most remarkable machine—has been towed inside our own hangar. It is safe from prying eyes."

Silence followed. Lew was nodding, his head dropping lower and lower. Then he shook himself awake, stretched out on his couch, and with a barely audible mumble of "Flog the wogs," he was fast asleep. Vance Brady leaned back in a deep armchair, sipping on a cognac, chain-smoking, but was comfortable, his eyes taking in every detail, trying to get a handle on the situation—and drawing a blank.

Shag looked up as the Costa Rican major walked

slowly to his couch. He drew up a chair to face the big man in the German uniform. Shag's helmet was on the floor. He was on his third cognac and his second cigar.

"Until my superior arrives, would you mind answering a question for me?"

Shag nodded. "Of course. If I can," he added slowly.

Castialano nodded in return. "Thank you. I wanted to ask you about your ECM system."

ECM. Electronic Counter Measures. What the hell was this cat talking about? Shag waited.

"You may prefer not to tell me, of course," the major said. "I am not pressing for details. I am familiar with all manner of electronic warfare systems, but I have never encountered this before."

Get the hell on with it! Shag said to himself.

"Can you tell me how you managed to land here without our radar picking you up?" Castialano wasn't on a fishing expedition; his manner and question confirmed that. They also confirmed a wild idea that Shag had picked up after they landed, but this was a for-keeps poker game and he wasn't giving anything away.

"I mean," the major went on, "you were *invisible.* Absolutely invisible. We have some of the most advanced sweep radar in the world. We can pick up the moving propeller on a small airplane more than a hundred miles out to sea. When you landed we had only one definite target and that was a scheduled airliner. Nothing else." Major Ricardo Castialano frowned. "Except for another of those stupid UFO reports. It was in the same area where the airliner was descending, but Jiminez Control spoke to the crew and they claim they saw nothing."

Vance had joined them. "UFO, Major? Fascinating. Can you tell me what kind?"

Castialano's eyes darted back and forth between the two men. "Like I said, a stupid report. Our radar reported they had on their scopes an enormous object, more than a thousand feet across and six hundred feet long, almost hovering. It was drifting in toward this very airport. In fact, according to those fools in the radar center, it hovered *over* this airport."

"What then?" Shag asked as casually as he could.

Castialano shrugged. "It disappeared." He tapped his leg again with the swagger stick. "Now, that other matter. Why did we not pick up *your* airplane on our radar?"

"Simple," Vance said. "We had our transponder off."

"We do not need a transponder. Three engines, all that metal, your size? No, no, my good sir, we should have picked you up and tracked you with absolute precision. We did not. Can you tell me about your system?"

Shag took a long, slow swallow, thinking furiously, and then he tossed the dice in his head and hoped they'd come up seven on the first pass. "I apologize, Major. I can't tell you anything at all. I hope you'll understand?"

Castialano didn't understand and he didn't like it and Shag tossed him another. He wasn't going to play the game by stretching it any more, but this kid-gloves treatment and waiting for Mr. Big, whoever or whatever he was, was simply too much to ignore. "Major, one thing, if I may. Some advice."

If Castialano was really holding all the cards, then being offered advice by a man completely within his control should have brought on a reaction of anger or contempt—anything but a clear indication that he was paying full attention. Which he was. The major nodded for Shag to continue.

"You said the aircraft was in your hangar?"

"It is."

"By that I suppose you mean your air force hangar?"

"Yes."

"Major, would you be good enough to order your men not to search that aircraft or mess around with its systems?"

Castialano couldn't resist the superior smile. "I will consider that. If you tell me why, of course."

Shag leaned back in his seat and took another sip of cognac. When he looked up his eyes bored straight into those of the other man and he was gesturing with his cigar. "Because," he said softly, "I really don't care to die because of someone's stupidity." He fell silent, then shrugged.

"Yes? Please continue."

"I'm sorry. That's all, Major. All I can tell you is that if someone screws with that machinery in your hangar you've signed the death warrant for all of us."

Castialano studied him carefully. "You seem very relaxed to have just made such a statement. Not a concern in the world, and—"

"Major, I don't care what the hell you do. Your ass goes with ours."

A flush of anger crossed Castialano's face. Before he could reply the door opened. Two of the biggest, toughest men Shag had ever seen in his life came in slowly, the first man pushing a wheelchair as if it were a toy. Almost at once Shag ignored the two men. They were trained, professional, very nasty killers. Bodyguards. Shag was big and tough but he wouldn't have wanted to meet either one of those dudes in a dark alley. Their lives had been given over completely to guarding the old man who now had Shag's full attention.

When he spoke Shag's heart sank, for the rasping voice came to him in flawless, native German. All Shag could determine was that this man was introducing himself and demanding to know who they were. From the corner of his eye Shag could see Ricardo Castialano standing at rigid attention.

Shag had heard barely enough. "Herr von Krueger," he said, putting as much awe and reverence into his voice as he could, climbing slowly to his feet. He went into sudden attention.

"Your pardon, sir," Shag told him in crisp, clear words. "My orders. Until we are face to face with Herr Dorsch in Quito, we are forbidden to speak the mother tongue. Our orders are to talk in English only."

The old man looked at him as if he were below an eagle's perch. "Why is that?" he demanded, his English as flawless as his German.

"Orders, sir." And then it hit Shag. He had mentioned the name of Dorsch and this von Krueger had shown not the slightest surprise. So the connection was still open, the Nazi thread still wound its way throughout Central and South America. It told Shag exactly how to keep those dice coming up with the right numbers. Screw the major. This is the man who holds all the cards. This is the man who's got all the power.

The old man—and there was no doubt that he was formerly a general—nodded. Orders. The word explained everything. "Where did you come from?" he demanded again.

"We started from Cuba and flew direct to Belize for refueling and then landed here. Our orders were to overfly Puerto Jiminez out to sea and then approach from the west so as not to reveal our original course."

"Wise." Then the thoughts that Shag had anticipated rolled through von Krueger's mind. "That is foolish. You would have been tracked on radar."

Shag permitted himself the trace of a smile. "No, sir."

"Stand at ease, Herr—"

"My identity card reads Shag Jordan."

"Your name!"

"Shag Jordan," came the stubborn reply. "That is all I am permitted to say until—"

"I know, I know," von Krueger said petulantly. "Until you see that thieving bastard Dorsch. All right. We talked about radar. How could you not be tracked on radar?"

"I cannot say, sir."

"Stand at ease. You cannot say." Von Krueger looked up at Castialano. "Have you talked to your radar people?"

"Herr General, their machine was not tracked. We do not understand it. I checked it out personally. The first we knew of them was when they called into the tower with their code name."

"Which is?"

"They used the name Panzer, sir."

Von Krueger looked up at Shag, who gave an imperceptible nod. The old man stayed deep in thought, disturbed only by a raucous snore from Heath. "Wake him up," he said angrily.

Vance went to the couch and kicked Lew's feet. The Englishman came awake with a start, staring in confusion at the strangers in the room. "On your feet, quickly," Vance snapped at him. "Speak only when the general speaks to you, understand? *Schnell!*"

The old man ignored the two of them as he returned his attention to Shag. "What were you doing in Cuba all this time?"

"Waiting, sir. We arrived there two years ago from Turkey. We had expected to leave sooner, but with all the Russians there—" He shrugged.

"And you waited for what?"

"Our orders, to fly this aircraft and its cargo to Basil Dorsch in Quito."

"Give me your tunic and your boots."

Shag was taken by surprise.

"Quickly!"

Shag removed his tunic, handed it to one of the bodyguards, then slipped off and surrendered the boots. They were brought to von Krueger. He held the tunic close to his eyes, examined it with meticulous care. He spoke briefly in German to a guard, and the lining of a pocket was slit open. Von Krueger felt the material inside, tossed the tunic back to Shag, then studied the boots, inside and out, before motioning for Shag to take them.

"They are original. They were made during the war."

That could only mean the Big Two, Shag realized. What the hell other war had there been for the Nazis since then? But what counted was that the feel and texture and smell of original German equipment had a warming effect on him.

"Your cargo for Dorsch. What is it?"

Shag glanced in the direction of Castialano. "It is all right," von Krueger said. "Speak freely before him. Go on, go on."

"Sir, two of the fuel tanks in the wings are false."

"How many tanks do you have?"

"Six in the left wing and seven in the right. They

are all slightly larger than the originals so that the aircraft holds six hundred and twenty gallons exactly."

"What is in the two false tanks?"

Shag drew himself up straighter. The critical moment was coming. "Answer me!"

Shag appeared uncertain. "I am ordering you to answer!" thundered the old man.

Make him important. Recognize his authority. You've got to bend to his will or he'll feel he's losing control . . .

"Sarin."

The eyes of General Hans von Krueger widened until they seemed like saucers. When he spoke again it was in a hoarse, incredulous whisper. *"Sarin?"*

"Yes, sir."

"Can it really be?" Strange emotions playéd across the strong, ancient face, and hope seemed to emerge from some dark corner and come to life. "Sarin," he repeated. A look of confusion showed. "But I thought Speer—" He looked up.

"Not all of it, Herr General. One submarine with canisters escaped both Albert Speer and the enemy. Now, one false tank in each wing of our machine is filled with sarin. It is in heavy liquid form, of course." He nodded toward Castialano. "That is why I asked the major to keep everybody away from the aircraft. I do not know if he believed me."

Von Krueger looked up at Castialano. "Did you issue that order, Major?"

"Not yet, sir."

"Do it now, you fool! *Now.*"

God, the old man could still shatter plate glass with that Prussian bellow. Shaken, Castialano made a hurried phone call, barked some orders in Spanish, lowered the phone.

"Do you have the slightest idea, Major, what we are talking about?" The old general froze Castialano with a icy glance.

"No, sir."

"Sarin is the deadliest poison gas ever developed. It is nerve gas. It is so devastating that Dr. Albert Speer even defied the orders of Hitler himself against using it. With the British and American bombers outnumbering us the way they were—" He cut himself short. "Major, three pounds, only three pounds, of sarin, mixed with the proper diluting agents and sprayed by one airplane over this city, would kill every man, woman, child, and animal, including the dogs in the streets and the rats in the sewers, in ten minutes. It is the kind of nerve gas against which a mask is useless. A single drop on the skin kills horribly in a few minutes. The gas gave us what once only the Greek gods possessed—the means to render our enemies mad before they died. Sarin attacks the frontal lobes of the brain and the central nervous system, and—" He turned back to Shag. "How much are you carrying?"

"Three hundred pounds, sir. The tanks, of course, are booby-trapped."

"I would expect them to be. I would also expect you to deliver them as quickly as possible to Herr Dorsch. They must continue to be transported in the Junkers?"

Shag could hardly believe the way the dice kept turning up seven on each successive gamble. "Yes, sir. As I said, sir, the tanks are booby-trapped. If anyone interferes with them—well, sir, you know the consequences far better than I."

"Enough of this," snapped von Krueger. "What do you need. How may I help? There is a stirring in my old heart and brain for the Fatherland! Thirty-five years I have waited for this moment! Be quick, man. What do you need?"

"We must rest, sir. We have not slept in over thirty hours, and flying without rest would be dangerous. But there are things we need. If you could arrange for the work while we rest—"

"Get on with it! Major, pay attention. I will be holding you personally responsible."

"Yes, sir."

"We must have the spark plugs for all engines changed, sir. Those that fit the American thirteen-forty models also fit our BMW engines. It would help if we had new batteries."

"Child's play. Go on, go on."

"A general inspection of the electrical system. We also need modern navigational equipment. There was no chance to—"

"What kind? Write it down, Major, you incompetent idiot!" Castialano began writing furiously.

"If the magnetos could be cleaned?"

"Stop asking. Tell me."

"If you have the crews, 720-channel transceivers, two VOR systems with powerpacks and antennas, a digital DME and an ADF. Our flight instruments are old. Altimeters, airspeed indicators, VSI's, directional gyros, gyro horizons. We have some in the aircraft but there has been no chance to install them." He glanced at Castialano. "Vacuum systems only. The left engine operates the vacuum pump. We will likely need some external venturis."

"Do you have all this here?" von Krueger snapped. "Yes, sir."

"Go to work. Use all the men you need."

Heath stepped forward. "Begging the general's par-

don, sir, I request your permission to be with the aircraft during this work."

"You just told me you needed sleep."

"There is no excuse for not attending to duty. These
people are not familiar with the Ju-52. We cannot afford mistakes. I can sleep later while we are airborne."

"Commendable. Go with the major. He will have
food for you as well." He turned to Shag. "There are
rooms over there where you can shower and sleep. In
twelve hours you must be gone."

"Yes, sir. We would like to plan on a night takeoff."

"Yes, of course. I shall see you in twelve hours exactly."

He motioned curtly and the two guards wheeled
him around and through the door. Everyone stood at
attention until he was gone. Ricardo Castialano
breathed a long sigh of relief and grabbed for the cognac, poured a glass and drained it in a long swallow.
Again Shag was drawing information from every small
move, sound, and word around him. Obviously Krueger had the muscle not only with Castialano but with
his superiors. That meant all the way. It was too pat,
too neat, the way those two gorillas had come in here
with that old Nazi in the wheelchair. They just about
owned the place. Costa Rica had no love one way or
the other for Germans or Italians or Russians or Japanese; their best friends reached the top of the list because they paid well. Or bribed heavily. Or bribed
heavily with the promise of much more to come. Obviously it all fit.

Shag pushed it aside for the moment. He wanted to
spell it out with Vance but when you had the mind of
an old German, who might have been SS or Gestapo or
simply an outstanding combat leader, and you mixed
in the ingredients of laying low for thirty-five years,

and there was high political chicanery, you did not talk where you could be overheard. Shag arranged for a hot meal and some drinks, made certain food was sent to Lew Heath, and kept their conversation on the revival of the Greater Germany, fully convinced that every word they spoke was picked up by electronic bugs and was being recorded.

Not until he shoved Vance into a steaming shower did he lay it out.

Vance didn't give him a chance. "Why the hell aren't we out there helping Lew?" he demanded.

"Shut up, you asshole." Shag turned the water on full to create as much hissing and splashing background as possible. He leaned close to his ear. "When I talk, you sing, got it?"

"You've lost your marbles."

Shag cracked him in the ribs with an elbow. "Sing!"

Vance sang. Badly, but noisily, and Shag stayed by his ear. "The whole place is bugged, dummy." Vance sang and nodded. "We're not with Lew because high-ranking German officers don't mix with lower ranks when there's enough manpower to go around. Dammit, forget that. They're setting those engines straight and fitting us out with everything we need to fly that bird all the way back to the States."

Vance yodeled, but the way he rolled his eyes let Shag know he considered him completely mad.

"The old fool has bought everything about a *putsch*," Shag went on. "Can you imagine that old geezer waiting here for thirty-five fucking years for Hitler's legend to come alive again?" He shook his head in disbelief. "And did you see the way he accepted the name of Basil Dorsch? There's a whole fucking network of these Nazis all through this conti nent! Besides—"

Vance spun him around and placed his mouth by Shag's ear. "Now *you* sing, you bastard!" he snarled. Shag sang. "Okay, one sings, the other talks, and their microphones don't get a thing. What the hell do you want?"

Shag sang off-key, but it killed any listening devices. "Where did you get all that crap about poison gas?"

They exchanged the singing-talking routine back and forth. "It's real. I majored in chemistry and history. There's tabun, soman, and sarin. German nerve gases. If they ask you about any others, tell them Green Ring Three."

"What the hell is that?"

"It's an American nerve gas. Based on the German stuff. The three green rings identify the bombs or shells as to what's inside."

"Is it true? I mean, about how deadly this stuff is?"

"It's as bad as that or worse," Shag confirmed. "Listen, we've got to coordinate it all. And we've got to get some sleep—"

"How the hell do we sleep while there's a Nazi revolution going on that we're supposed to be starting!"

"Don't sweat it, Admiral. With von Krueger working this caper we're like a babe in its mother's arms."

"That's what worries me. Milk makes me sick and—"

"Shut up, goddammit. Do you remember that conversation about how they couldn't pick us up on radar?"

Vance's eyes widened. "I was meaning to ask you about that. How in the hell did we manage that little trick? I know radar, old buddy, and what we heard in there is impossible. The military radar they got here can track a gnat's asshole at twenty miles. And what was all that nonsense about some giant UFO? I—"

Shag shoved a bar of soap into his mouth. Vance

coughed and choked and spluttered. Shag sighed. It wasn't singing but it would do. "Just keep your trap shut and listen, will you? Just trust me. We're that damned UFO. Got it? Us. The Ju-52. I'll explain later, but they can't track us on radar. Okay, that's enough. You stay in here a few moments longer."

He opened the glass door and went into the next room to dry off. Vance followed, in time to see Shag finishing a bottle of cognac, tossing it into a chair, and stretching out on a bed. Vance sighed and reached for another bottle. Ten minutes later he was also dead to the world.

They looked in near disbelief at the cockpit and the cabin. There could be no underestimating the local authority of the old man in the wheelchair. A radio rack had been installed behind the pilot's bulkhead, in the cabin, with four rows of power equipment and a dazzling array of avionics. Shag gave the newly installed racks an admiring glance. The arrangement was simple, fast, and effective, and didn't bother with trying to stuff the readout equipment in the panel or elsewhere in the cockpit. It wouldn't win any awards for aesthetics but it sure took the blue ribbon for no-nonsense effectiveness. In the cockpit he saw two VOR heads in the panel. They were now able to navigate by very high-frequency radio, receive weather reports and forecasts, and with the DME—Shag had a love affair with all Distance Measuring Equipment—they would never lack for an exact fix as to their position in the air.

Lew's eyes were red from weariness but there was also a deep glow of accomplishment. "They've had thirty people working on Annie," he said with pride. "Never saw anything like it. Of course there ain't no wiring diagrams, but who cares? They've popped in the antennas where we need them, they've changed all the plugs, put in spanking-new batteries, cleaned the carburetors, attended to a hundred things. She's still the same old bird, of course, but those engines will run a lot better. I wish I'd had an extra couple days here to get inside those cylinders, I do, because—"

Shag had walked away and was staring at the aft turret. He had also seen von Krueger being wheeled into the hangar, so he kept his comments to himself for the moment. He didn't believe what he saw in the gun ring of the turret. The gleaming .30-caliber up there was new. The rusty old relic was gone. And that meant—

He turned and snapped a salute to the old man, whose pride was clearly as great as that of Lew Heath. The general acknowledged the salute with a nod. "You are ready to leave?"

"Yes, sir." Shag didn't need to ask to know the latest charts had also been placed in the aircraft. "It is two o'clock and we would like to do most of our flying under cover of darkness."

"That is wise. By the way, I spoke with Colonel Dorsch."

Shag gritted his teeth.

"He is most anxious to greet you. He is flying up to Quito."

"Thank you, sir."

"Is there anything else? I do not wish to delay you."

Think fast . . .

"Yes, sir, there is. But not for us. There will be more aircraft following us. They will fly from Cuba into Mexico along the Yucatán and work their way down to Ampala. If you could notify your, ah, contacts to assist these crews it could help greatly. We are all using the same identifying code."

"I know, I know. Panzer. Dismiss it from your thoughts. It will be done. Now, you are ready?"

"Yes, sir." Shag was afraid to say another word. His heels cracked together and his right arm went out in a whip-smart Nazi salute. He turned to climb aboard the Ju-52, Vance and Lew following. They went straight to the cockpit. Before them the hangar doors opened and they felt the airplane lurch slightly, then start to move forward.

"They're towing us outside," Lew said. "Listen, what in the bloody hell—"

"Shut up. Both of you, just keep the hell quiet. The moment that tractor lets us loose, get this thing started and get us off the ground before this whole Alice-in-Wonderland scene blows up in our faces. Let's do it!"

They couldn't believe the way the old engines turned over, fired up, built to minimum temperatures and pressures. Lew handed Shag a headset and a microphone. He shook his head in wonder, clamped on the headset, and brought the mike up to his lips. He pressed the keying button. "Jiminez Tower, this is Panzer. Ready to taxi to the active for immediate takeoff."

"Panzer, taxi straight ahead and then to the right on the first taxiway. You are cleared for takeoff when ready."

Shag rolled her steadily. They'd even hung two red lamps on the back of the cockpit bulkhead for night lighting. It was all jury-rigged stuff that worked, and nothing else mattered. Shag followed the blue taxi lights, swung onto the runway.

"Hey, what about the runup?" Vance asked. "We need to—"

"What we need is a lot of air below us," Shag snapped. He went full forward on the throttles and the Ju-52 answered with a wonderful acceleration. In the cool night air and with those new plugs she had a different, livelier feel to her. She was in the air in two thousand feet. Shag climbed out straight ahead, banked to the right at a thousand feet above the ground, and headed for Honduras.

"Ampala, here we come," he murmured. He turned to Lew. "Jesus Christ, get us a drink. I'm shaking like a leaf!"

14

They kept their fingers crossed and their conversation to a minimum as they climbed steadily out of Puerto Jiminez. They weren't guessing or relying on memory anymore. They had charts with them and Vance traced a line from Puerto Jiminez direct to Ampala in Honduras. It was a distance of 470 miles and they had the wind on their tail and Annie felt rejuvenated. They flew at twelve thousand feet with the cloud tops four thousand below them. Scattered thunderheads revealed themselves by lightning; from the cockpit of the Ju-52 they looked like the insides of enormous frosted light bulbs flickering on and off. They would be no problem on this flight.

Lew tapped Shag on the shoulder. "I still don't believe that whole scene back there," he said. "But it can all wait. I'm getting some sleep before I fall down right where I am."

"One thing first. Does that hardware they put in the turret really work?"

"Shag, that is a Class A, mint-condition, air-cooled

Browning machine gun, .30-caliber, belt-fed. It works.
They also put a large crate in this cabin that's packed
with hand grenades. Also of American manufacture, I
should add. And now, it's beddy-bye for me."

Vance climbed from his seat to stand in the cockpit
center so he could be better understood by the other
men in the thundering uproar of the Ju-52. "All right,
let's have it. This radar crap and why we can't be
tracked. And what's this nonsense about the Ju-52
being a UFO?"

Shag brought the nose five degrees to the right and
let her settle down. "It's simple, but we had no way of
knowing what was happening. Their radar picks us
up, all right, but it can't return an echo. It's the corru-
gation."

"The what?"

"The corrugated skin on this airplane, you ninny! It
breaks up the radar beam. The radar hits us but instead
of getting a clean bounce the microwave beam gets all
busted up and comes back in something like a spray.
Something on the order of ten. That's why they've
been getting those tracks and those reports of a UFO a
thousand feet wide and over six hundred feet long. It's
us!"

Vance stared in wonder and Shag whooped with
laughter. "It's the perfect cover, baby! Who believes a
UFO a thousand feet across that's drifting over the
ocean, or wherever, at only eighty or ninety miles an
hour? And when we turned to land at Jiminez, we
were in the pattern, so it looked like the damned
thing—the UFO, I mean—had come to a stop and
was landing. And the moment we got down to a few
hundred feet and ground clutter got on that radar
scope, the UFO just vanished. That's why no one believes anything about it. The track is fuzzy. It's like a

ghost return on the scope. It can't be there but it *is* there. And then it hovers and after that it vanishes? It's impossible—and it's perfect."

Vance drew on a cigarette and thought for a while. He had to admit things were vastly improved. They were tracking VOR stations along their route and two of them were even set up for DME and they had perfect positioning on the charts. But he felt uneasy. That whole scene at Puerto Jiminez had been a fluke. What the hell, that old Nazi meathead could have died the day before they showed up and their ass would have been grass. They couldn't count on that anymore. He told this to Shag and the other man agreed.

"I know. We're not on a flight plan and these people get sticky about that sort of thing. Besides, we don't have landing permits and—oh Christ, Vance, we just play it hard and fast. If the old general still has his connections, then Ampala will be set up for the Panzer code and we won't have any flak from those people on the ground."

"I hope you're right."

"I hope so, too. That's why anytime we land from now on, Lew stays on that machine gun, and one of us stays in the cockpit. Think we can refuel this thing with the engines running?"

Vance looked doubtful. "It could be done. Why?"

"You never know, baby. We might have to get down, load up, and get the hell out. I don't think we ought to shut down those engines unless everything's cool."

"You're assuming a lot."

"Like I told you before, baby, it's the only game in town."

* * *

Their route took them out of Costa Rica and over the entire country of Nicaragua. Ampala, just across the border in Honduras, could be sticky, but if the code name had been sent ahead it might be accepted as a landing permit, and if von Krueger's connections were still as strong as they seemed to be, and if they didn't run into some hard-nosed son of a bitch on the ground, and if the rabbit hadn't stopped to take a shit the hound would never have caught him, Shag thought wearily, well, what the hell. There was an old saying that if everything seemed impossible, maybe the dog will learn to talk, and back there at Puerto Jiminez there'd been a whole kennel of articulate canines. Who knew what would happen now?

They passed over the Gulf of Fonseca, checked their position over El Salvador, where Shag rolled the Ju-52 into a steady right turn and took them over Honduras in a circle of twenty miles, so that when they called in to the Ampala tower they were due north of the field. "Ampala tower, this is Panzer. Do you read? Over."

They were on their toes down there. "Go ahead, Panzer."

"Roger, Ampala. Panzer is two zero nautical DME out of your field landing from the north. We're descending through nine thousand now."

"Panzer is cleared to land straight in runway one-seven. Wind light and variable. Altimeter two-nine-nine-eight. Report coming down through four thousand." There was a pause. "Panzer, are you transponder-equipped? Over."

"Negative on the transponder, Ampala. We have your beacon in sight now."

"Roger, Panzer. Continue your approach."

They came down through four thousand. Vance sent Lew back to the turret, told him to be ready for anything. Shag called in again. "Ampala, Panzer through four thousand, setting up long straight-in to one-seven."

"Roger. Cleared to land."

"Uh, Ampala, do you people have a message on us for immediate servicing? We'll need hundred octane and oil."

"Panzer, we are confirming your request. Everything is ready for you."

"Roger that, Ampala. Thank you."

"Keep your fingers crossed," Shag told Vance. "Sounds like the von Krueger magic is still working."

"Do we shut down?"

Shag nodded. "Yeah, but you stay right here in this cockpit, and Lew stays in the turret. I'll take care of the servicing."

Vance nodded, tight-lipped. He didn't like the gut feeling he had about Ampala. Besides, it was ten after five in the morning and it would be getting light too damned quick to suit him. He checked the automatic from his holster and made sure he had a round in the chamber. He was sweating bullets as he began his final approach.

Shag brought her in with a grease job, got the tail down, and followed tower instructions. They parked the Ju-52 behind a hangar and the fuel truck was ready and waiting for them. Shag let Vance shut her down. The props were still turning as Shag exited through the front cabin door and worked his way down to the ground in the blast from the number three engine. He stood in the headlights of the service truck, giving the hand signals to chock the airplane right away. Without parking brakes, even a slight incline would start them rolling, and they couldn't afford any more dings and dents than this flying ironmonger already had.

The propeller blades jerked to a stop and Shag motioned the fuel truck to stop just before the right engine. He climbed back onto the wing, snapped open the covers for the fuel filler, and called to a service lineman to join him on the wing. The fuel-hose nozzle went into the inlet, Shag snapped open the cover to the oil tank, unscrewed the seal, and began dumping in oil. He didn't know if it was 50- or 60-weight and he didn't care. He went through twenty-four cans of oil, six gallons in all, which meant their oil consumption was getting less with each flight. He slopped a lot of it on the nacelle and the wing, and ignored it.

Vance was already ahead of him with the nose engine. He was standing with his feet on the cockpit quadrant, leaning out through the top hatch, the nose-engine oil tank open and waiting. Shag climbed down the right wing after closing the oil and fuel fillers, climbed onto the left wing, and motioned furiously for the truck to move up to the next position. He went through the same routine, letting the fuel pour into the wing tanks until they heard the overflow splashing on the ground. Shag was locking the left-wing fuel and oil caps, and Vance was cleaning the windshield when it all began to go to hell.

A jeep rolled up to them. Four men climbed out slowly and just the way that first one moved told Shag it was bad news. Shag went to the cockpit window. "Get ready to crank over this mother. Poppa Bear just showed up and he looks like somebody stole all his porridge."

Vance nodded and started flipping switches. But how the hell was he supposed to start this antique son of a bitch by himself? You had to pump the Bejesus out of that wobble pump and work the inertial starter, first down and then up, and have the mags ready and jerk back on that infernal fuel-flow control and work the throttle and—

He got her on the edge and thanked whoever who looks after dumb pilots that they had new batteries and plenty of power, and then he moved the wobble pump slowly up and down, starting to build the fuel pressure so he could reduce every step to its minimum. He didn't like what he was watching outside.

A Honduran colonel was arguing with Shag. Not talking, but arguing, and he was very angry about something—

"I am Colonel Roberto Salvador Baccero and you have broken several of our laws already," he heard. "You do not have a landing permit for Ampala, and—"

"Colonel," Shag broke in, "we were cleared to land by your tower. I agree we don't have a permit in hand, but it was phoned in. Your tower already had it."

"I have been on duty for only an hour tonight. I know nothing of such a call. I must check it out before you can leave."

"Colonel, we don't have time to wait here. We're on a tight schedule and—"

"You are insufferable," Baccero glared. "Like all German pigs." Shag groaned inwardly. The dude was building to one very hot head of steam. Somewhere he and other members of the glorious Third Reich had clashed head-on, and now was his chance to exercise his authority.

"Your arrogance is beyond belief," Baccero continued. "German uniforms. My God. You are even wearing that filthy swastika. Why someone has not shot you out of the sky is a mystery to me. You are not going anywhere until I have had the chance to check you out thoroughly."

We're fueled. We've got to get the hell out of here before this character brings up reinforcements. "Colonel, I'm sorry. I don't think you understood what I meant." Shag gestured to the Ju-52. "Our aircraft is very old—"

"It is a garbage dump," Baccero said with a sneer.

"Sir, you're right. It is just that and our engines are not in the best of shape. We need every foot of that runway, and we need cool air. Once that sun starts coming up and we get a density-altitude situation, we might not be able to get off the ground until tomorrow. I mean, until it's night again."

"That is regrettable."

Bite, you son of a bitch . . . Take the bait and swallow it . . .

Baccero bit. He turned and barked out orders to his men. The fuel truck and the jeep roared off. They rolled onto the runway at midpoint, headlights pointing straight down the runway. "Now, the problem is solved," Baccero smiled. "You need the full runway and there is only three thousand feet from the end to where those vehicles are stopped. Now that you cannot take off, you are no longer in a rush, are you?"

"Goddammit, Colonel—"

"Watch your mouth, pig!" Baccero's holster was open and an automatic was in his hand. Shag brought his hands up slowly, his eyes wide.

"Hey, I apologize, Colonel. I didn't mean to—"

"You will do more than apologize before I'm through with you. Now, you will follow my orders. You are under arrest until I have checked you out. I know nothing of your stupid clearance from somewhere else, and furthermore, I do not care."

"Yes, sir."

"You are not so insolent now, I see." Two men were standing behind Baccero, their rifles no longer slung on their backs, but cocked and pointing at Shag. Which pleased Shag immensely, because no one seemed to be paying much attention to Lew in the aft turret.

"Colonel, if either you or your two pinheads gets nasty, you'll be spread all over this flight line in little pieces." Baccero watched with incredulity as Shag lowered his hands. "Look behind you, Colonel. That's a .30-caliber pointed right at you. You get off the first shot, he empties the whole belt into you and your men."

There was a long silence, and the pistol returned to its holster. But Baccero didn't back down. "It seems we are at an impasse. I will not order those vehicles off the runway. You cannot take off in what runway you have, and I seem to have lost the upper hand. For the moment only, of course," he tacked on.

"What's your deal?" Shag asked.

Baccero studied him. "You are not so stupid, I see."

"The deal, Colonel. What's the next move?"

"Turn over your weapons immediately. I promise you fair treatment."

"Really?"

"Really."

"All right. Let's get aboard. We'll taxi where you tell us and then we're in your hands."

"A wise move."

"I think maybe you better tell your men first what's happening."

"They understand English very well. They have heard every word. They know you cannot take off, so they will be patient, and they will walk along with us as we taxi." He snapped out a command, one guard ran to the other side of the Ju-52. "See?" Baccero smiled. "You have a machine gun and your machine gunner has a rifle aimed at him from either side. It is a standoff, I would say."

Shag offered a slight bow and gestured to the door. "After you, Colonel."

Shag boosted him into the cabin, climbed up and closed the cabin door. Baccero eyed him with suspicion. "Why did you do that? Close that door?"

"We're going to taxi with all three engines, Colonel. Our brakes are shitty. When that left engine starts it slams the door and breaks the handle. Okay?"

They went forward. Vance had moved to the left seat and looked back with a blank stare. "Turn 'em over," Shag said. "I'll take the pump." He started the wobble pump going, looked outside for fuel, then worked the inertial starter as Vance played his tune with fuel flow, throttle, and the mags. Baccero looked on with open disbelief at the complicated maneuverings until all three engines were running. "All right, Colonel, where do you want this thing?"

"You will park to the left of the tower. We will then decide where to place this grotesque machine."

"Whatever you say."

Shag pulled up the knobbed handle in the middle of the trim wheel and began cranking backward. "Roll her down to two-five," he told Vance, and told him a lot more that was unsaid.

"What is he doing?" Baccero asked.

"Setting the flaps."

"Why? We are only going to taxi."

"Well, that's a matter of opinion. I say we're going to take off."

Baccero's right cheek twitched. "I should have had

you placed in irons immediately," he said through clenched teeth. "You cannot take off! You are mad!"

"Colonel, look out at that right wing and tell me what you see."

Colonel Roberto Salvador Baccero had a splendid view of the corrugated expanse of the right wing and as he looked he exposed a splendid profile of his jaw to Shag, whose hamlike fist thudded with a bone-crunching impact against the unsuspecting Honduran. Baccero spun around, unconscious, falling to the cabin floor. Shag leaned down and removed his holster. He ran to the back of the airplane and leaned into the baggage hold. "Lew! Lew, goddammit!" he shouted. Heath heard him and leaned into the aft fuselage.

"Get the one on the right!" Shag shouted. Lew's face disappeared. Shag went to the cabin door, forced it open and called to the watching guard. "The chocks! Colonel Baccero says to remove the chocks so we can taxi!"

He waited until the soldier returned and gave him the thumbs-up signal. Shag waved him closer. The soldier came to the side of the fuselage, directly in the blast of the idling engines. "Hold the door open!" Shag yelled. "The colonel wants you to come aboard!"

The soldier nodded, reached out one hand for help, and Shag took the man's hand in his own. He waited until the soldier had one foot on the cabin-door step and was completely unbalanced, brought up the automatic he'd taken from Baccero, and shot the man clean through the heart. He released his grip and the body fell back, and almost in the same instant there was a short burst of machine gun fire that vibrated the entire aircraft. He stuck his head back into the baggage hold. "Lew!"

The face peered down at him. "It's balls to the wall!"

he shouted. "As soon as we're wheels up you cut that tower to pieces! Got it?"

A thumb jerked before him in the up position and Shag ran forward to the cockpit. "Get to that runway! Soon as you hit the end give her everything she's got! Lift her off at seventy and then turn in toward the tower, but keep it on your left, okay?"

Vance gestured frantically. "Those trucks—"

"Fuck 'em! With these flaps we'll be in the air long before we even get there. Move it, God damn you!"

Vance rolled her as fast as he dared with those rotten brakes, started a long, wide swing to the runway, and as he straightened her out poured the coal to the engines. Thunder screamed at them and almost immediately the tail was coming off the ground and she was accelerating faster than Shag would have believed possible. He stood just aft of the cockpit and looked through the windshield at the approaching headlights. They were still more than fifteen hundred feet away when the Ju-52 left the concrete beneath them and clawed for the sky, leaning into an immediate left bank. Shag grabbed the still unconscious Baccero by the shirt collar and belt, shoved his body against the front cabin door to force it partially open in the thundering windblast, and heaved Baccero onto the wing. A final kick and the body plummeted in an arc toward the runway. Shag watched the dark shape smash into the windshield of the fuel truck on the runway. The next instant the Ju-52 vibrated from nose to tail as Lew opened up with the machine gun. Shag pushed into the cockpit, standing to Vance's right as he held the left turn perfectly, and they watched the tower vanish in an eruption of shattering glass, the blue-white brilliance of electrical systems shorting out, and then a dazzling blast as the heavy power cables blew.

Then they were gone and the tower was behind them. Before them they saw the first streaks of dawn and huge cumulus clouds reaching upward in all directions.

Vance turned to him. "What brilliant suggestions do you have in mind now?"

"Take her up to eight grand, baby. We play hide-and-seek in that stuff ahead of us. Set up zero-two-zero, lean her out and play guided missile. Lew hasn't come out of the turret. I'm going back to check on him."

"Hold one," Vance said. "Where are we going?"

"There's a nice vacation spot called San Miguel. It's on an island off the Yucatán."

"I know it. Cozumel."

"Right. See that weather up ahead? It must go on a long ways and I think we can hack getting into San Miguel and getting out again with no trouble. A little greasing of a couple of palms and who knows? Straight ahead, Admiral."

He went back to the baggage hold and cursed. Blood dripped down from the turret floor and a white-faced Lew Heath was slumped beneath the machine gun, gripping his leg.

15

Lew gritted his teeth, thought better of it, and assaulted Shag with a stream of profanities. Shag grinned as he held Lew down and poured Scotch into the bloody wound. Lew's gasp was loud enough to hear over the engines and Shag felt him slump. "Christ, it's only a flesh wound. Didn't touch the bone."

"Only a—!"

"Pipe down. Stop squirming like that. We don't have a first-aid kit, so I'll have to tie a tourniquet with one of the seat belts. Here, drink the rest of this stuff." Shag busied himself, nodded, and patted Lew on the shoulder. "It'll hurt a little but I think you'll live. How the hell did it happen? I thought you nailed that guard right off."

"In a minute. Help me into a front seat so I can use the headset." Lew grimaced in pain as Shag dragged him forward and stuck him in a seat. They were taking some turbulence and Shag secured the other man tightly with his seat belt. "Okay."

"The lap of luxury," Lew said between gritted teeth. "Started to tell you it wasn't the guard. I got him with a burst in the head. He went off like an overripe melon. It was that jeep on the runway. They were working us over and I couldn't depress the Browning enough to have a go at them." He blinked his eyes. "Strange bit, that. As we went by something blew up the cab of that fuel truck."

"That was the colonel. I tossed his nibs out as we took off."

Lew thought that one over. "Neatly done. You do have a certain flair about you, you know."

Shag flicked him a salute. "Put on your headset. Hang on. It could be a rough ride."

He went into the cockpit and took the right seat and pulled his belt tight. He couldn't believe the sky in front of them. In just minutes the high clouds had closed in and they were flying through crap. San Miguel had a low-frequency radio beam and Vance was trying to home in with the ADF, but between them and Cozumel there was a lot of lightning that was twitching their needle. Shag glanced at the man next to him. "You get anything on the weather?" he shouted.

"It stinks! I think we'd better—" He held off talking as a tremendous gust slammed into the old Junkers, almost standing them on a wing. Vance fought her back level. "We better get down while we can! It's solid up ahead of us and there's no way to make an instrument approach to that island paradise of yours!"

Shag nodded and Vance went to the gauges, starting downstairs into the soup. "They're reporting fifteen hundred for the ceiling!" he told Shag. "I'll take her right about ten degrees! No mountains that way!"

They could hardly hear one another in the thunder

of engines and the sudden rainshowers through which they were descending. Lightning flashed steadily and Shag wondered what the hell they were running into. They kept going down through dark gray. There were occasional breaks to show them they were between layered clouds, and enough water to turn the cockpit into drips, sprays, and splashes from every side.

At fifteen hundred feet, the ceiling Vance had received on an hourly report, they were still in the soup and the pucker factor for all three men was rising steadily. They had no way of knowing just how bad it was down below, and the altimeter read eleven hundred feet when they caught their first sight of whitecaps below. Shag let out a long sigh of relief, gestured for Vance to swing to the left to keep the coastline in sight, and they pounded and rocked for two hours before Cozumel came into sight.

Shag held up seven fingers and Vance took her down to seven hundred feet. It was wild below, and from the water streaks and whitecaps they judged the wind at twenty or twenty-five miles an hour, but with gusts going as high as forty. It was going to be an interesting landing. They flew over San Miguel Airport at the same seven hundred feet, banked steeply to judge the wind, and Vance started into a turn that would bring them around into the runway. Shag leaned over and rolled in forty degrees of flaps. Coming down the slope, they seemed to be standing still, their speed over the ground about forty or fifty miles an hour, but with the nose swinging sharply from side to side. Vance kept in the power, ready for anything, and he put her down on the main gear just beyond the runway end, kicking rudder like a madman to keep her from veering sharply to one side. He got the tail down and sucked the yoke into his gut. "Jesus!" was all he said.

Shag opened his side window. "We're in luck! The storm must have gone through here yesterday. Look, the place is just about deserted. Take her over to the right. Can you see the fuel pumps?"

"Got it."

"Good. Be ready for anything."

They stopped by the pumps and shut her down. Not a chance of refueling in this crazy weather with those props turning. One slip and a man would tumble into those slashing blades. But Shag had to play it very tight. He wanted whoever was on the field to come to them. It was a matter of waiting it out. He decided against Vance going back to the turret. Too early for that. He needed their head man here, inside the Ju-52.

Mexicans always waited. It took five minutes before an old truck with an Esso sign rolled out to them. A beefy man in a yellow rain slicker climbed out and walked slowly to the cabin door. Shag went to the door and held it open. The beefy man took his hand and Shag helped him into the cabin. He eased the door closed before the wind could catch it. The big man looked at them in confusion. "I do not understand, señor. Where are you from? We have no flight plan for you. And why are you flying in all this crazy weather?"

"You ask a lot of questions."

"What kind of machine is this?" The big Mexican wiped water from his face. "It is a bad day. The radar people, they call me from the mainland. I am to look for a giant thing in the sky. What you call it? A great saucer, I think."

"UFO?" Shag offered.

"That is it. Have you seen such a thing?"

"No. But we didn't land here to stay. Only to refuel, and be on our way. We are flying down to Honduras."

"In this machine? In this weather? You are crazy, I think."

"Fuel and oil, amigo."

"Maybe I do not think it is so easy. No flight plan, *sí?* And your papers. I must see them, and—" The voice died out.

Lew had turned around in his seat and was holding an automatic dead on the Mexican. He froze, but his lips twitched. "Sit down, laddie," Lew told him. "What's your name?"

"It is Salvatore. Angel Salvatore. I am at your service."

Shag stood over him. "I'm glad to hear that. I have a proposition for you."

"*Sí.*" The head bobbed up and down. "I am listening."

Shag extended his left hand. "Five thousand dollars American," he said. "And in my other hand . . ."

He pulled back the hammer of the gun in his right hand. Angel Salvatore's eyes were very big. "I have a choice?"

"You do."

"Then I am your friend, señor."

The hammer came down gently and the package of money went into Salvatore's hand. He held it, not moving. "Money is bad for the memory," Shag said.

"When you are gone I never see you before, señor."

"I'm glad. Now, you go into that cockpit, and we will turn on the radio. Then, in a normal voice, you call your operations shack over there, right?"

"*Sí, sí.* I will do that."

"You tell them to send over two men to refuel this aircraft. We want the tanks filled all the way. And we'll need a lot of oil. You have fifty-weight?"

Salvatore was all cooperation. "Also, tell them to bring over a first-aid kit. A big one."

"I will do that."

"Get a grease gun," Lew added.

"I will do that, too."

"Let's go."

Vance hit the master switch and turned on the radio to the frequency Salvatore requested. The Mexican airport manager noticed that Shag's weapon was out of sight, but the automatic was still very much in evidence in Lew's hand. Rapid-fire Spanish ensued. Salvatore cursed out the ancestry of several of his men, and two men soon came running to the airplane.

"Vance, you're it," Shag told him. "Fuel, fill the oil tanks, check the hydraulics, and you'd better do a number with those rocker arm boxes." Shag turned to Angel Salvatore. "You stay in here. You're our guest."

"It is my pleasure, General."

"Where'd you get the general bit?"

Salvatore smiled with dark teeth. "You give me money, no? You have a strange machine, like nothing I see before. That machine gun I see is real?"

"You bet your ass it is."

"Ah. You have a real machine gun. Many weapons. You are dangerous *hombres*, I think. But you are nice to Angel. So you are general." He widened the smile. "If you want you can even be *El Presidente*."

Shag laughed and turned to find Vance in the doorway. "That first-aid box. It's here." Shag went to get the kit and returned to the front of the cabin. "Angel, you move into that cockpit and you sit on the floor and behave yourself."

"Excuse. You fix his leg?" Shag nodded. "I was medic, as you say, in Mexican Army. I am very good."

Shag looked at Lew, who nodded. The gun was passed to Shag and Salvatore went to work. He whistled slowly. "It look bad but not so bad." Lew hung on after a long slug of Scotch, shared the bottle with the Mexican. Ten minutes later Salvatore was done; the wound had been cleaned and bandaged neatly. "I think he smart if he get tetanus shot soon."

"We'll take care of it. We cleaned it out with whiskey."

"Ah. Very good." Salvatore leaned close to the window. "They are almost finished now."

A severe gust shook the airplane. During their time on the ground the Ju-52 had rocked almost ceaselessly to the rising-falling cry of the wind and rain slashing against the corrugated skin.

"Maybe you tell me where you come from?" Salvatore asked. He had been studying the uniforms and the weapons.

"Berlin."

Salvatore took that one without so much as a blink. "And you go to Honduras?"

"On the way to Quito."

Salvatore sighed. "I am glad you make the gift to me." He took a long pull from the Scotch. "Nobody will believe me about you." He sighed again. "I will pay for the fuel and the oil and I will say a DC-3 land here."

"You're a wise man, Angel."

"Thank you, señor. I leave now?"

Shag shook his head. "You stay with us until we're on that runway. Just before we take off it's time to say good-bye."

"As you wish, señor."

"Angel, this place is just about deserted. How come?"

"Big storm yesterday. Many people go to the mainland. Others, they stay home." A flash of lightning and a deep rumble of thunder accompanied his words.

"Yeah. So I see."

Vance came back into the airplane. Water streamed from his helmet and he was soaked to the skin. "Thanks for the trip," he said sarcastically.

Shag ignored his discomfort. This was the big one ahead of them, the last one. "We all set?"

"All set."

"Let's fire her up. Angel, you stay here with Martin Bormann," Shag instructed Salvatore. The automatic was back in Lew's hand, and he gestured to Salvatore to take a seat and relax. He watched in fascination as they turned over the three engines, warmed up the radios, went through a mag check.

"I told them to pull the chocks on a hand signal after we were started," Vance said. He opened his side window, spat out rainwater, and signaled the ground crew to jerk away the wheel chocks. They taxied slowly, the Ju-52 rocking severely. If anything, the winds were stronger than before. They turned carefully onto the runway facing into the wind and stopped, Shag holding the yoke full back. The winds were so strong that without brakes he needed some power from the nose engine to hold their position.

"Vance, take our friend here to the door. It's time for him to leave. Angel! It's been a pleasure. See you around."

Salvatore was on his feet and he nodded to Shag. The Mexican was convinced he had only a fifty-fifty chance of getting out of this airplane alive, and he was astonished when Vance helped him through the cabin door to the ground, and tossed him a careless salute.

The door slammed closed and Angel leaned into the screaming gale of three engines pushed to full throttle. He couldn't believe what he was watching. In the high winds the big German machine was off the ground and starting its turn only three hundred feet from where he stood. He reaffirmed his decision never to mention that airplane or its occupants. He would be shot for drinking on duty. When he looked up again that strange machine had vanished. Was it the clouds? The rain? Or had it just disappeared?

He didn't know. He patted his inside pocket. The money was there. Angel Salvatore smiled. Not all crazy dreams are bad.

Shag pounded Vance on the shoulder with a massive fist. "We did it! Goddammit, we really did it! We're on our way home now, baby! Zero-three-zero and just hang on to that heading and before the day is over we have got it made." The slashing rain, blasts of lightning, the worsening turbulence, water streaming into the cockpit and the cabin—none of it bothered him. The grin stayed on his face as he rolled out of the turn from takeoff and settled down on his course of thirty degrees.

"Look at that water down there, sweetheart?" he chortled. "See those waves, those streaks? They're with us. Hear that, baby? A fat tail wind and a free dividend of thirty, forty, maybe even fifty miles an hour. We'll cover distance like greased bacon through a goose's ass."

Vance didn't seem impressed. "Sure, sure. Where the hell are we going?"

Shag fought the controls. "Right where no one

would ever expect us to go. Right across the Gulf of Mexico and up into Florida. Home, sweet, home, baby! That's where. It'll be dark by the time we get there, and we've got that beautiful wind with us. You know, I figured we'd just try to get into the swamp area, down by Marcos or somewhere like that. But with this wind I've got another idea. A better one. A place we can land and no one will ever see us and we can hide the bird when we're on the ground."

"You got it all figured out, huh?"

"Sure do."

"You know why we've got this wind, Shag?"

"No, and I don't care."

"You crazy bastard! We're flying straight into a hurricane!"

"Wonderful! Who's going to look for a UFO in a storm like that!"

16

They weren't flying anymore. Not in this charnel house of turbulence. The Ju-52 was flung from one violent blow to another, wallowing across invisible mounds of air, plunging down the other side to slam into updrafts that jarred their teeth and rattled their bones and turned the airplane cabin into a dust-strewn chaos of boxes and equipment, food and cans, weapons and oddments, all tossed and banging about wildly. In a moment of wide-eyed horror, Lew snatched the half-empty case of Scotch in midair, secured it safely with a seat belt, thought of his situation and grabbed a bottle to soothe his nerves and to temper that hellish throb in his leg.

He waited for a rare respite in the shuddering, wallowing motions and shouted for Shag as loudly as his lungs permitted. The pilot turned back to look at him and grinned widely, waited for just that moment of respite and grabbed for the bottle. "You got it!" he bellowed to Vance, passing control to the man in the right seat. Vance, struggling with this berserk mountain of corrugated metal, stared unbelievingly as Shag took a long pull on the bottle, passed it to Vance, and signaled that he had the controls again.

"You know something?" Shag bellowed. "You can taste the fucking electricity in the air!" He was right. The grinding storm was building enormous areas of positive and negative charges of electricity. The Ju-52 was a natural receptor for a static charge and the flat metallic taste was everywhere, in the dust strewn about them, in the spray lashing into the cockpit, in their mouths and nostrils and ears and hair. All that metal and those whirling propellers and their magnetos and spark plugs and discharging batteries and the passage of metal through supercharged air was simply too much for the old Junkers. It couldn't rid itself of the electrical charge as fast as it was taking it on. All three men were familiar with the edginess that crawled through and under their skin.

Shag had elected to go down and stay as low as possible. If they went any higher they'd be entirely in the soup, flying blind. Here they could see, and the white-lashed dark sea beneath them was a welcome reference, no matter how rough its surface and the almost instant death it promised should they have to ditch the Ju-52.

Shag fought to maintain attitude. He didn't care if they wallowed or shook or trembled. The rule was to fly your airplane. Screw everything else. Keep up your airspeed, stay above the water and below the clouds and make the line plunge straight ahead.

Beneath their seemingly cavalier attitude was a deep seriousness which encompassed the machine, the elements, and their own roles. There are varying degrees of turbulence and they were already nibbling through what was regarded as violent, characterized by moments when control was literally taken from them by the fury of the storm.

They were hurled inverted only eight hundred feet above the water. Shag did the only thing possible and it was the wrong thing to do with an airplane of this size, but still it was their only hope. He and Vance jerked the yoke full back. There was no hope of stamping rudder and working aileron and rolling this monster straight while they maintained altitude. They lacked speed and control and they were subject to gust stalls, and they needed above all else *airspeed*, and the only way to get it was to suck back on the yoke to drop the nose earthward, below the horizon. They had to get their speed immediately, within seconds, or nothing else would count and they would drop like a lead weight into the raging waters below. As fast as he came back on the yoke, Vance helping, Shag snapped the overboost lever to full forward, into the position normally used for flight above nine thousand feet, and banged the engines into overboost. Normally they would have managed to get thirty-two inches of manifold pressure from the throttles. Now the needles jerked around to forty inches and the engines, old and battered as they were, literally screamed with the internal hammering. But they got power and the props even jerked into the air a bit harder than before, and the Ju-52 dropped earthward, nose sucking down swiftly, into a wild split-S maneuver, all the time the controls under their hands dancing and vibrating madly. The speed was building swiftly and they were a hundred feet over the water when she was level, and they prayed there would be no downward mushing movement or a sudden downdraft, and they barely held the hundred feet and they were indicating over 160 miles an hour and Shag took advantage of the speed to claw her around so that they could return to their original course as shown by the directional gyro before him.

Shag had come back on the power and they were heaving upward to eight hundred feet, and Lew was cursing quietly because he could see the oil thrown from the engines under that brutal punishment and he knew irreversible damage had been done.

They plowed on, hammering, pounding along, and Shag was swept up with the fury and the wonder of it all. To him, the storm was a gauntlet flung at his feet, a challenge hurled straight into his face, and he accepted it as such. The longer they flew, the wilder the storm, the more the hammering pounded them, the greater the exultation in his soul. Sweat poured down his body in rivulets and then streams, soaking his body, his clothes, mixing with the rain tearing into the cockpit.

A great explosion enveloped them. At first they thought an engine had exploded or part of the cockpit had failed under the ceaseless punishment, then the cannonade was recognizable when they heard the sound from everywhere around them. A windshield on Vance's side cracked and sent a shower of splinters through its entire surface. *"Hail,"* he shouted. "Turn her! Turn her fast!" The hail could have torn them to pieces. It would have ripped through the windshield of another airplane, battered the leading edges of its airfoils to blunt-edged disaster. But not Annie; she took it all with a stoic acceptance, rejecting the shotgun blasts of ice, bouncing them off her tough skin. Shag continued directly ahead, easing off a bit of power, reducing their airspeed to lessen the impact of the blows.

"Carb heat!" he yelled, but Vance had already anticipated what was needed and he turned three handles to route exhaust-system heat into the engine intakes and carburetion systems so they would continue functioning and not choke themselves with swiftly changing temperatures. There was a heat system to guarantee proper operation of their airspeed indicator under such circumstances, but they had never looked for it before and now was no time or place to start.

As swiftly as it came the hail was gone. It occurred to them that no one had thought about time, no one had measured time against fuel burned or remaining, because it really didn't matter. But now, even as they churned through that final gauntlet of hail, it appeared they might have punched through the worst of the last pressure trough, that the storm was abating or they simply had survived its worst temper. The ceiling had dropped and they were down to five hundred feet, but it could have been four or seven hundred; they had no way of knowing what sharp changes of barometric pressure surrounded them and the truth was they didn't care, just as long as they could see before them. The ceiling had also flattened out. Indeed, they were surprised with the gentler skies. Visibility had increased greatly and the turbulence through which they flew was as old-hat to them as flight itself.

They had seen several ships, merchant vessels wallowing like bloated pigs in a bottomless sea of mud, when Vance shouted loud enough for even Lew to hear him from the cabin. "There! Off the nose at ten o'clock!" They strained to see, Lew swiftly out of his seat and bracing himself in the cockpit entrance, and there it was. "Dry Tortugas," Lew exclaimed happily, and it was, sandspits showing through the heaving swells and a small island standing bravely against the watery onslaught.

"We got it made!" Shag yelled. He leaned over and clapped Vance on the shoulder. They grinned at one another, for Dry Tortugas was a brilliant beacon in the darkness of the storm.

Shag eased into a turn to the right. Now he could judge the winds better and he knew if he flew due east, they would run into the Marquesas Keys at the very end of the island chain curving down from the Florida peninsula. They were dangerously low but the turbulence continued to abate, and Shag knew the kind of weather into which they were moving. Low and leaden skies, but a flat belly to the clouds and the visibility getting better, with intermittent showers, none too heavy, to be expected. It was also getting darker and that combination disturbed Shag. Flying low when you could see was one thing, but flying low when the world was slowly being absorbed into a dark cotton blanket was akin to suicide. Yet their survival had risen several points on the probability scale, for the end of the Keys came into sight, and now there was the chance to put the Ju-52 down where they could reach land, where they wouldn't have to worry about drowning.

Shag laughed aloud and his friends wondered at him as they felt the confidence radiating from him. Why worry about the fall of night when that meant all kinds of lights down here? This was the chain of islands that made up the Keys and that meant lighthouses, airport beacons, highways, towns, small villages, all sorts of roads, shopping centers. From the air, even at this altitude, they were all markers, outlines, identifying signs. And no one could tell what or who they were by looking into the sky. There was a steady light rain that would keep most heads indoors, and airplane engines were a familiar enough sound in this area. Besides, no one would get more than a glimpse. The night was both the latest navigating beacon in a continuing series and their cloak as well.

Just so long as they didn't run into any goddamned towers.

They thundered by Pine Island, lights ripping by in blurred streaks. Shag noted Pine Island carefully, waited exactly one minute, then turned to a heading of 045 degrees; this would take them directly to East Cape in the southwest corner of Florida. He noticed they were covering ground faster than before; catching the wind directly on their tail was enough to increase their effective range by well over forty percent of normal.

They waited out the turbulence, now nothing more than a comfortable rocking motion to them. Shag still gloried in that supreme confidence of his, Vance flew as he always did—carefully, seriously, quietly—and Lew was having kittens over the slowly rising temperatures of the engines. That slam into overboost, no matter how life-saving it was at the moment, had damaged the engines seriously and he knew their continued operation, especially with a diminishing oil supply, was now a very ugly question. They could start coming apart deep within themselves and their first real warning would be an unexpected clattering, grinding noise and, perhaps, a glimpse of pieces of engine going in all directions, followed immediately by a fire.

He banged Shag on the shoulder. "Where we putting down?" he shouted.

"Hobe Sound! Up near Fort Pierce!"

"You're fucking crazy! We can't make it that far!"

That inevitable, supremely confident grin showed. "The hell we can't! With this wind we got it knocked!"

Vance leaned closer to them. "If we hope to get anywhere, you idiot, we can't stay at this altitude!" He gestured ahead of them. "I know this area. It's filled with antennas and towers three to five hundred feet high and we'd never see one of them before we hit it! We'll have to go up the coast!"

"The whole bleedin' world will see us!" Lew shouted in protest.

Shag shook his head. "No way, baby! Who the hell will look, and if they do what will they see? A blur? This place is lousy with planes, remember? No one pays any attention. We'll slide off the coastline far enough so they can't get a look at us!"

East Cape and the coastline raced by only three hundred feet beneath them. Darkness. A bitch for flying in this weather, but there were occasional specks of light. In many cases they were more dangerous than helpful, but Shag didn't fall victim to the old trap of misjudging a ground light for a star near the horizon. *No stars tonight, or if there are, they're damned wet ones* . . .

The air settled down to only moderate turbulence with long minutes of dead calm. They were flying beneath the overhang of an enormous pressure wave, almost as if they were within protected space, with the violence now behind them and following. They'd punched through.

Shag figured that, except for an occasional helicopter on a local patrol, the only planes that would be in the air would be on instrument flight plans, all under radar and traffic-center control. This whole area of south Florida was absolutely lousy with radar, civilian and military. The closer they came to the built-up areas the more baffling would be their scattered-buckshot radar return, for they were low enough for any scope to mix the ground clutter of buildings and antennas with that of the skin bounce from the Ju-52. There were going to be some totally freaked-out radar people tonight.

He saw dazzling flashes in the distance, low on the horizon, and he was puzzled for several moments until his memory registered something. "Hang on," he told Lew and Vance. "I just saw a street sign I recognized." They watched in silence with him and then Vance was bolt upright in his seat.

"Are you crazy? You can't—for God's sake, Shag!"

But nothing would stop him now. He couldn't resist. He took the Ju-52 right down to treetop level—there were few enough trees in this grassland and swamp area—and then they were rushing swiftly to the high-intensity approach strobe lights of Homestead Air Force Base. To those on the ground who heard the sound and turned to look, there was a sudden swelling thunder from the west and an apparition that emerged from the darkness. Reflections of the strobes and the runway lights of the air force field bounced back to astonished observers on the ground, and when Shag figured they had enough of a look to see the Ju-52, he horsed back on the yoke to spear into the belly of the cloud deck, held his course at seven hundred feet for exactly two minutes—enough for radar to get a good lock on that thousand-foot UFO—then pushed forward on the yoke again to emerge below the cloud deck, completely invisible to anyone straining to see the dark shape that had appeared and vanished.

Minutes later the coastline was in sight and it was all Mark Three Eyeball flying from here. The good visibility let them see forever. They punched over the isolated areas, saw cars on roads and the lights of houses and then a dark area ahead that they knew was the beaches; going north from there meant open coast-line. To their left the world was an amphitheater of rich light; the reflections of Miami and Miami Beach and Fort Lauderdale and all the communities pouring light into the skies, to be reflected downward from the low cloud base. To Shag this was as good as daylight. No, better. He could see everything and nobody could see them. Neat, baby. Made to order. He went a good mile off the beaches, turned left to fly north, using the dazzling beach for navigation. Fat, dumb, and happy—and it couldn't have been better. He knew Lew was sweating bullets about the engines and their lack of oil and how low their fuel might be, but if an engine coughed he'd fly her on two and if they dumped it all he'd put her down somewhere and they would just take off and disappear on the ground. None of it concerned him. He flew without conscious effort; all his thoughts were on trying to remember details of what lay ahead.

He knew it all here. They winged past Pompano Beach, Deerfield, Delray, Boynton, the big interna-tional field at West Palm Beach, and then he saw what he'd been waiting for—the lighthouse at Jupiter Inlet. "That's it," he told the others, pointing. "Just about five minutes more to go."

He was on the money. The lights of Hobe Sound came into view. Shag picked out the reference points he knew so well, wracked the corrugated condor into a steady left turn, and rolled out on a westerly heading, studying the ground. There; the superhighway, and then St. Lucie Canal, and Shag pulled open his side window for an easy study of the land and began to circle and—"There it is! See it? That grass strip runs north and south and the wind's just right to land to the south."

"I can't see shit," Vance complained. And he couldn't, because it was darker than hell down there and unless you knew exactly what to look for, a grassy flatland without lights or markers is like looking into a barrel of black.

"Gimme everything!" Shag shouted to Lew, and he felt the flaps coming down as Lew's voice bellowed in his ear:

"You got forty!"

Full flaps and that stiff wind, and Shag let her coast down on the slope at eighty miles an hour indicated though they weren't doing more than forty or fifty for ground speed. He could barely make out the strip from the dim reflected light off a small canal that paralleled the abandoned grass runway and then they touched. He yanked the last sigh of power off, brought the tail down, and with that wind and wet ground and high grass they didn't roll six hundred feet and the brakes didn't matter a bit. Even the ones they didn't have, Shag thought with a private smile.

"Lew, get the top hatch open. You should see a hangar to the right at the far end of the strip."

Lew pulled back the hatch, winced as he put a foot on each seat and heaved himself up into the airblast of the nose engine. Shag taxied with the wing engines, moving slowly, and Lew called down, "Got it!"

Shag threw off his seat belt. "Vance, you take this seat. Just look for me." He climbed into the cabin, grabbed a flashlight and a revolver, and disappeared from the plane. They saw the light bobbing as Shag ran through grass toward the hangar, then an orange flash.

"He's shooting off the lock," Lew said.

"He has his ways," Vance muttered.

They could barely see in the darkness, but then it

was obvious that Shag was pushing back huge doors hanging from rails. Then he signaled them with the light, indicated the space between the doors, and motioned for them to taxi directly toward the light. Vance played the power carefully, slowly, watching one side while Lew watched the other, and Shag guiding them in carefully. Shag played the flashlight on a wooden block in his hand and they understood. Then he held the light up against the far wall of an ancient wooden hangar. Vance kept her creeping in, the light disappeared, and he felt the Ju-52 jerk to a stop, telling him that Shag had thrown the block beneath a tire. There were some thumps as other chunks of wood locked Annie in place, and Vance started shutting her down. The engines died slowly and in the crashing silence and the aftersound of ringing ears they could barely hear the hangar doors closing and the wind whistling through cracks in the old wood.

They gathered beneath a wing on the dusty floor, the great shape hovering above them, and they listened to the sounds of engines cooling, and they could hear a slow dripping of oil that spattered into the dust. They looked up at her and wished they could exchange words or feelings.

But they were struck as dumb as the airplane. The enormity of where they were at this moment, alive, of what had preceded this moment, a journey that—they had been squeezed dry. Several times Lew started to say something. But he managed only a frustrated gesture, a meaningless motion of a hand. Finally he turned to Shag, rested a hand on his shoulder, and squeezed gently.

He looked up into Shag's eyes, those mysterious pools of strength that so long ago had seen as far as this moment. Shag looked back and he nodded. "I know," he said, and it was enough.

The sound brought Vance out of his own shock. "I guess we'd better sleep here tonight."

Lew turned to him. "I wouldn't feel at home anywhere else." They climbed back into the cabin, leaving the doors open for a touch of breeze. Lew held up a bottle. "You first," he said to Shag. Then the bottle went to Vance, and finally back to Lew. He held it in one hand, studied it for several moments.

"Here's to Annie," he said, and took a long pull. Then he set the bottle down, and they were asleep without another word.

17

A blast of thunder just outside the hangar brought them awake, sore and stiff. They moved slowly, letting the reality of where they were sink in with a delicious acceptance that they had beaten the whole goddamned world. They struggled to elbows or sitting positions. Lew's leg felt as if it had been lanced by a hot poker.

They were ravenous, and after the eye-opener they sat quietly eating rations, draining cans of fruit juice, listening to the heavy rain and the almost steady thunder. "It caught up with us," Vance said, referring to the storm. "I've had enough of this stinking weather."

Shag wiped his mouth on his sleeve. "I haven't. We still need it."

"What the hell for?" Vance threw back at him.

"This trip ain't over yet, buddy-boy. We're here and we're alive, but staying alive and free takes a bit more than we got." Shag snapped his fingers. "Lew, gimme your knife."

He pulled off his jacket and began cutting every piece of insignia. "You, too," he said, looking up at

Vance. "And cut some rips and tears in your pants. Don't leave a thing that shows where these clothes might have come from." He thought for a moment. "They'll be soaking wet. That's gonna help. Lew, let me have about six hundred bucks. American. What kind of ID we got?"

Lew counted out the money. "Only six hundred?"

"That's all. More than that makes people think too much. What about the ID?"

"Great for where we were. But who needs a passport in Florida?"

Shag nodded. "You're right. We'll have to work it out somehow. Now, both of you, listen to me. This field is off St. Lucie Canal. We're near Lake Okeechobee, but we're also isolated. Friend of mine owns this place but he hasn't used it for years. It's an old duster strip. He operated a chemical-spray outfit from here until his lungs filled up with the crap and he had to go out West to keep from dying. The only road that comes in here is made for goats and it's in lousy shape because nobody uses it. So no one knows we're here and for a while we've got to keep it that way. The nearest big town is Okeechobee but it's a bit too big for us. South of us is a little fishing and airboat village. Sherman. That's where we're going."

"*We*'re? Who's that?"

"Me and Vance. You can't walk for crap with that leg. You stay here and you stay buttoned up until we get back. We've got things to do and I don't want to waste time talking about it. Vance, you still carrying that automatic? Okay, leave it here. I'll do the same."

"But—"

"We can't waste time shooting the shit, Admiral. Let's move it."

Vance exchanged a long glance with Lew, who nodded slowly. Vance had the idea Lew would follow Shag anywhere. Then he smiled to himself. So would he, when it came to that.

They went outside in the hammering rain, started along the old road, now a muddy sea of grass beneath them. "There's a two-lane road about three miles out," Shag explained as they squished along. "We hit that and go south to Sherman. You know what's happened to us?"

"I haven't read your script," Vance reminded him, earning a chuckle from Shag.

"We live in, uh, let's make it Alachua, near Gainesville. We came down here a few days ago for a vacation. Airboat freaks, that's us. Gigging frogs, fishing, that sort of thing."

"I don't know shit about airboats," Vance said.

"You don't need to. I do. And we got caught in that storm last night and lost everything we owned. We had a boat. The name is, uh, *Myrtle—*"

"Who the hell is Myrtle?"

"Who knows? I want our stories to jibe, that's all."

"Okay, we lost everything. Then what?"

"You leave it up to me."

"And what happens, great wizard, if we run into the law?"

"That, baby," Shag said with a knowing smile, "is just what I'm hoping for."

Deputy Sheriff Eddie Carter squinted through the windshield, moved the wipers to high speed, and began slowing his cruiser. He turned on flashing blue lights as he made out the forms of two men on the side of the road, waving their arms frantically at him.

Carter picked up his microphone. "Twenty-six to Central."

"Go ahead, Two-six."

"I'm eight miles north of Sherman. Two white males on the road with hand signals for me to stop. Looks like they're in some kind of trouble. I'll call in after I talk to them."

"Okay. Want any assistance?"

"Nah. They look half-drowned. Probably some dumbheads who lost their boat. They're lucky they're alive."

"Never saw anything like it, Sheriff. One minute we're out there and the water is calm, you know, maybe just a bit on the choppy side, and the next—"

"That chop is a warning, Jordan. Anybody knows these waters runs into chop like that, he can see the storm coming and, why, he just hightails it but fast for the nearest shelter. And I'm not a sheriff, I'm a deputy." Eddie Carter glanced at the big man next to him. "Anyone else with you two?"

"Uh uh."

"You're lucky."

"Don't we know it." Shag's hands lifted and then fell back into his lap. He dragged deeply on the cigarette Carter had offered. "I mean, you know, there we were and *pow*! End of the line. That airboat just stuck its nose up and rolled over. Everything we owned was on it. Wallets, our driver's licenses, all our clothes."

"Well, at least you two aren't at the bottom of the lake. Lots of people seem to be missing from this storm. It's a bad one. We even had a couple of twisters last night. Anyway, once we get you into town we'll dry you off and get you some hot food. Anybody you want to call?"

"Alachua. We just moved there. Used to be down in Harlingen. Ran a spray-plane outfit. Thought we'd try our hand in Florida."

"Where's this Harlingen place?"

Vance leaned forward from the back seat. "It's the armpit of the old U.S.A. Down near Brownsville in Texas. Farm valley. Got too damned many Mexicans for us."

Carter snorted. "Stick around. Way them Cubans is working up from Miami we'll be overrun with them soon enough. You know, we used to have a spray out-fit here. Old man, guy named Douglas, ran it. Got sick in his lungs, had to leave. We need that kind of stuff pretty bad around here. You set up in Alachua yet?"

Shag laughed. "Been there two weeks. Stayed in a motel, came down here for a vacation we'd waited two years on."

"Why not look around here? You might like it."

Shag nodded. "Could be. Say, is that Okeechobee ahead?"

"Yep. Home, sweet home."

"Can we rent a car here?"

"I can get you one, but—" Carter chewed on his cig-arette butt. "Be tough without identification. Shee-yit, you ain't even got a driver's license or nothin', right?"

"Just some hard luck and some cash." Shag pulled the soaked bills from his pocket. "Couple of hundred here. Figured maybe we could buy some clothes, rent a car, then get back to Alachua. Still got some stuff there. We could call Harlingen and, you know, get a telegram with our driver-license numbers and—"

Carter held up a hand. "We can make do. Every-body here knows everybody else. Sheriff's Department will vouch for you about the car. You're paying cash anyway, so leave 'em a deposit. Tell you what. I'll drop you off at the clothing store. You get what you want, I'll pick you up in about thirty minutes. I'll have you squared away by then."

"Goddamn, this is just great luck for us," Shag said with a smile.

"Shucks, ain't that hard being neighborly, is it? Glad to help out."

Shag and Vance tapped the horn by the hangar, climbed out, and ran for the door. They came up short at the sight of the automatic barely extended through a crack, then moved inside as Lew pulled the door wider. Lew stared at them in jeans and field jackets, glanced at the bags they carried. "Shag, if you fell into a pit of jackass shit you'd come out with a rose in each hand and one in your teeth," Lew remarked. "Where did—"

"Never mind. Inside the cabin. We've got a change of clothing for you. As soon as you're dressed we're on our way. Let's go. I want to be out of here while it's still raining."

Twenty minutes later Shag swung away from the hangar, Vance by his side, Lew in the back of the Ford sedan with his leg propped up on the seat. In the trunk were the attaché cases with the currency of several different countries, the case for forging papers, and the gold coins they'd picked up in Peru. "So this guy, Carter, he couldn't be more helpful. Even set us up to drive off without a license. Our buddy. Told me a lot. That field really hasn't been used for years, and he thinks we're interested in it for a sprayer operation."

"You let him think that?"

"Uh uh. I let him think he came up with the idea. And he's right. We are interested."

"In crop-dusting?" Vance and Lew shook their heads together. "You're not smoking them funny cigarettes, are you?"

"Both of you, listen to me. You got a handle, you're legit. Clean, smooth, upright citizens. You've always got to have an answer for any chickenshit questions, understand? Right now Deputy Sheriff Eddie Carter is talking all over that alligator-piss town of his about these big Texas sprayers who he was smart enough to talk into coming down here. He's a hero. So we back him up, he struts his stuff, before you know it everybody there is pulling for us. But it's first things first in this business."

"What business is that?" Vance asked.

"Survival, and busting out big, baby, that's what. Now shut up and listen to me. We're heading for Miami. I know some people there I flew with a long time ago and—"

"So do I," Lew broke in. "Some very heavy Cubano types."

"What line they in?"

Laughter came from the back seat. "If they're the Cubans I know, you can start with murder, robbery, arson, guerrilla warfare, forgery, bum checks—you name it and they're experts at it."

Shag glanced back at them. "They to be trusted?"

Lew sobered. "A few. I can reach them from a certain hotel."

"Name it."

"Flagler. Right in Little Havana. Ducky place, if you don't mind the sound of knives being sharpened and that sort of thing."

* * *

Shag and Vance walked into the lobby, and let their limping friend go to the front desk while they stood back just far enough to let their presence be felt. Lew was right. Shag could feel it. The goddamn place was a thieves' den, a gathering place for the Cuban underworld in Miami. Yet Lew was relaxed, despite the rapid-fire conversation he was carrying on in low tones. The desk clerk rang a buzzer. A swarthy man with a Pancho Villa mustache appeared out of nowhere, but the smile on his face when he saw Lew was genuine enough. There was more talk, looks in their direction, and a bellhop with a scarred lip and a permanent snarl took their few bags. The carpet was worn and frayed, the wallpaper faded and peeling. There was a grotesque parody of an elevator that smelled of rotgut whiskey and urine. The elevator jerked to a stop on the eighth floor, and they followed their scarred bellhop to the end of the hall, a trail of further destruction and desecration. They went into a room of sagging beds and broken furniture, and Shag was just about to explode when the bellhop closed the door and locked it, went to a curtain that he drew aside, and opened a concealed door, leading them into a beautifully furnished, modern, spanking-clean suite. The hunched posture vanished and the simpering-idiot snarl twitched away.

"This is Sanchez," Lew said. "He owns this hotel." They shook hands all around. Shag and Vance held back their questions. It didn't take much to figure out the operation. What better cover, what better role to play than a degenerate bellhop?

"We are very old friends," Sanchez explained, pointing to Lew. "This man saved my life."

Lew sprawled on a bed. "Piece of cake. Some very

unfriendly niggers were doing their best to cut Sanchez into fish bait."

"Bahamians," Sanchez chided Lew gently.

"Okay. Bahamian niggers, then. Black, nasty, and murderous bastards, they was."

Sanchez nodded. "Four shots, four dead Bahamians."

"Enough of this palaver, Sanchez," Lew said with pain. "We got a matter of business to attend to. A good deal. And we can start with a doctor, if you would, old man."

Sanchez went to the phone, then returned. "He is on the way. We have a full bar here. Can I make you something? And while we get to know one another better, we can talk of your needs. Rest assured, amigos, that for this man here," he nodded at Lew, "all is well."

Shag accepted his drink. "I'm glad to hear that. Maybe you can call an old friend of mine while we're at it. I think he'd like to see me."

"Of course. Who would that be, señor?"

"Major Don Carlos Valdez."

Sanchez looked at him with a mixture of awe and hostility that baffled them. "I find that hard to believe," he finally responded to Shag.

"That doesn't matter, does it?" Shag smiled.

"Your organization, then?"

"The Black Watch."

Sanchez offered a slight bow; from this man this was the ultimate honor. "I will attend to everything," he said softly.

They spent three days in Miami. Major Don Carlos Valdez was a walking shrine among the Cubans who had fled their native land and more than anything else wished to rip Cuba free from the Castroites. He and a man named Shag Jordan had flown together several times and had rubbed shoulders on a savage commando raid in which most of their number had been killed and from which Valdez emerged unconscious and bloodied, carried on Shag's powerful shoulders. He was not a man to forget such a debt, and within hours word of Valdez's visit had passed through the expatriate community. From that moment on everything went swiftly.

On the fourth morning they were driving north in two cars, Shag at the wheel and Lew by his side in the first car, registered in Lew's name, with Vance following in the car they had rented in Okeechobee.

"How much did we realize from the foreign currency?" Lew asked.

"Better than I'd hoped. Sixty thou American."

"And in your greenbacks?"

"Thirty-five."

"Thousand? That's a pretty bundle, Shag. Nearly a clean hundred thousand dollars. Fifty thousand quid. Neat, that. It could take us a long way, you know."

"Got the travel bug? Your leg must be a lot better."

"Better? I could do a jig. But maybe you're right. It's time to set our sights somewhere. And with that much money we could—"

"It's chicken feed compared to what I've got in mind. Besides, there's more."

"More?" Lew echoed.

"Remember those gold coins we snagged in Peru? They weren't just gold coins, friend. They were collector's items. Worth twenty big ones."

Lew whistled. "Better than I thought. And we've got driver's licenses all neatly made out from that bloody shithouse of Harlingen, and proper business cards, clothes, this here car, pilot's licenses, and the medical forms—the lot. We're legitimate, I'd say."

"That we are," Shag agreed. He lit up a very expensive, very beautiful Havana cigar.

"What's all this muck about it being chicken feed, as you so crudely put it?"

"Shit, how long would we make out this way? Having the bread doesn't hack it, Lew, because sooner or later it runs out and you're back in the middle of nowhere. You really think a hundred grand, even two hundred grand, is a lot? Your brain must have taken more shock than your leg. If we lived well we'd go through ten grand a month and at the end of a year we'd have piss in a boot to show for it. You've got to keep it coming in, or else do something to make the really big hit." Shag snorted in disdain. "If we wanted to get into the flying business, and we bought just a new Bonanza, like the A36, know how much we'd have left? And that's just for a single-engine job that can carry six people."

Lew thought about it, then shrugged. "You tell me."

"We wouldn't have a dime left. We could buy a used twin, like an Aztec or a 310, something like that, but if it's worth anything at all it's got to go for fifty to eighty grand. And then we'd need facilities, insurance, go through federal inspections, seed money to keep going, and—"

"I get the idea," Lew said with a sour face.

"About time," he was told.

"So what are we going to do?"

"I told you. Go for the big one."

"How much is big, laddie?"

"Couple of million." Shag exhaled a perfect smoke ring and laughed at the choking sounds from his companion.

"Couple of—? You've slipped your cog, you have. Loose wheels. Clockwork tangled. Gears—"

"*Each,* Lew."

"Each what?" Heath shouted.

"Couple of million each."

Sarcasm hung in the air. "Going to tell me how?"

Shag chuckled. "Thought you'd never ask." He held his words as he swung off the highway, took a winding road.

"Where the hell does this go?" Lew demanded.

"Lauderdale Exec. It's an airport. You remember what those are, don't you?"

"Knock off the fun and games!"

"We're going to buy an airplane. Or rather, we're picking up an airplane. Cherokee 300, fixed gear, very cheap. All arranged by Valdez."

"Why—"

"We need to get in and out of that duster strip and we can't spend our whole lives doing it by car. So, we get this six-place jobbie for transportation. We may also buy one or two used spray planes here. They've got some old Stearmans that will do fine."

"They also arranged by Valdez?"

"Uh uh. Duster operation down near Homestead is about broke. The bank will accept the lien on these two birds and we pick 'em up for a song."

"You don't make a man feel like singing with all this strange and mysterious stuff," Lew said darkly.

"Whistle. Sing. Clap your hands. Here we are." He drove onto the entry road to the airport and parked at Bradley Aviation. Two hours later he'd closed the deal for the Cherokee, two used trailers, an airstrip lighting kit, windsock, other goods for the field, and arranged for everything to be delivered in three days to the strip he marked on a chart.

"It's all grass right now," he explained to the sales manager at Bradley. "By the time you get there, just fly eight miles due north of Sherman and we'll be marked out."

Lew and Vance looked on, mystified, until they stopped for coffee on the same field. "Who bought the spray planes?" Vance asked.

"Dillard Sprayers."

"Who the bloody hell are they?" Lew asked.

"Us. Used to know a character by name of Snake Dillard. He got killed down in Harlingen. Drunk, tangled with some power lines. It's a nice name. It's real. Anybody checks, it's been in business for twelve years or so."

"You all through spending our money?"

"Uh uh. Got to get a pickup truck and an old jeep, chemicals, stuff like that. We need an office, but we can set that up in Pahokee. That's on the southeast curve of Lake Okeechobee. We'll get our office there. Won't use it except for mail, really. We'll live out of the trailers at the airstrip. You see, gentlemen, we're legitimate now. Honest businessmen. We've got bank accounts and references down in Harlingen and Brownsville. Solid citizens, that's us. We'll need a few more people, but we'll bring them in as duster pilots and mechanics. It's all a cover, of course."

He slurped coffee, while his friends discussed killing him. Vance motioned Lew to cool it. "All right, Shag. Time to end the fun and games. All this is obviously to keep attention off us. It's a good routine. We're right out in front of the whole world and nobody really sees us because we're so obvious."

"Right."

"But we're really being devious, aren't we?"

"You win a cigar."

"About what?"

"We're going to rebuild Annie. Okay, it's still a long drive back to Okeechobee and I want to turn in that car today. Keep the sheriff happy, too. Let's go."

18

"You know something? You're fucking crazy. You're a bloody lunatic, Shag. It's one thing to fly, and to do what we've done, but this!" Lew threw up his arms in some silent supplication to heaven as they drove north from Fort Lauderdale Executive Airport. Vance followed them, even more frustrated from his inability to even listen to the exchange, which he could see through the rear window of the car he followed. Lew was gesturing angrily.

"You stupid, camel-friggin' pile of shit, do you even know what in the hell you're suggesting?" It wasn't a question but a shouted scream halfway to a physical outburst on Lew's part, and all the more accentuated by Shag's calm demeanor. He drove easily, obviously relishing the rare Havana clenched in his teeth. "You're going to rebuild that Ju-52?" Lew raved on. "In a pig's arse, you are. It's impossible! She's more dead than alive, she's a bloody wreck from one end to the bleedin' other. Don't you understand machinery, you colonial nit?"

Shag rolled the cigar to the side of his mouth, spat out a piece of chewed wet tobacco. "Until you showed up with that mouth of yours working like a windmill with the shits, I thought I did."

Lew's eyes bulged. "Well, you don't! You—you—damn your silk hide, anyway, Shag, do you know what you did to those engines over the Gulf when you went to overboost? You slaughtered them, that's what! Murder. Mechanical mayhem. Irresponsible throttle-jockeying! You—"

"That moment real clear in your mind, Lew?"

"Say again?"

"You remember that real well, huh?"

"Yes."

"Think slow, baby. How would you have handled it?"

"That's a stupid question. There was only one way to handle it and that's exactly what you did. Any idiot would know that."

Shag looked puzzled. "Then what's your beef?"

"Shag, do you think I question how you fly the heavy iron? I'm talking about machinery. You said we're going to rebuild what was once Junkers' finest."

"I did, and we are," Shag said with conviction.

"Look, Shag, I'm as fond of the old girl as you are. She saved us all. But she's a bloody wreck! Her engines are far worse than when we took off from the plateau. Oh, to be sure, in went batteries and plugs and cleaned mags and instruments and the like, but that's nothing compared to what she needs. She's got corrosion eating out her belly and her lungs and—"

"And she brought us home."

"But at the cost of her heart!"

"Her structure is as good as the day she was made. Spars, trusses, braces, gear—"

"No bloody brakes."

"We'll modify some from another airplane."

"The engines are slag!"

"They're BMW's, Lew, and BMW's are copies of Pratt and Whitney's. You said so yourself. We'll get a batch of thirteen-forties and hang them on her. Go to constant-speed props."

"But the hydraulic system—"

"Needs repairing, that's all. Same for the wiring. Tear it all out and stick in new. It's easier than repairs. When we get the engines we get all the systems with them. Generators, vacuum pumps, the works. We buy rebuilt engines as a package. If we need new cowls we do it with a good sheet-metal man."

"Do you know how long that will take?"

"With four or five good men, maybe a month from the day we get rolling on the job."

Lew's voice had lowered. "And the bleedin' cost?"

"The way I figure it, since were not paying for labor, and we got friends in getting the parts cheap, maybe fifty grand on the outside. And that's for everything."

Lew sat back, folded his arms, and stared straight ahead. Shag waited him out but after fifteen minutes of ominous silence, he leaned over and flicked cigar ash in Lew's lap. Lew danced wildly on his backside. "What the hell did you do that for!"

"Thought you were dead. Now that I see you breathing again, oh wise one, tell me something. How come you clammed up?"

"Nothing to say."

"Bullshit."

"Well—"

Shag blew cigar smoke at him.

"All right," Lew blurted out. "I can do it. And in a month. But I don't understand something. Why?"

"We already discussed that. The big one."

Lew scratched his head, then reached down and rubbed gently against his healing leg wound. "I've thought a lot about that."

"And?"

"Talked it over with Vance."

Shag waited.

"We figure we're—well, you know. Blooded."

"Three Musketeers? That sort of thing?"

"Don't make fun of it, Jordan."

The tone told Shag everything. "I'm not. In fact, I don't think I've ever heard anything that—"

"Stow it, mate. You don't need to say it." Lew waited several moments. "But there's the big question. How?"

"Oh, time tunnels, Flying Dutchmen, UFO's. That sort of stuff."

"I was right before. You're not dealing with a full deck. The three of us are going to put together this witch's brew of yours—"

"Good simile."

"Oh, clam up. We put this together and razzle-dazzle them all with footwork, is that it?"

Shag looked at Lew with admiration. "By God, there is hope for you yet!"

"The three of us are going to do all this?"

Shag sobered. "Nope. We need a crew. I've got to contact Pam Kreiner. I've already checked. She's still in Las Vegas. Then I—we—need seven good men. You're going to help with that."

"What kind?"

"Bastards. Like us."

Lew laughed. "Easy enough, I daresay."

"Couple of pilots, trained jumpers, all experienced with weapons. Couple of them must speak German. Couple of them have to be really good mechanics. And not just this modern crap. The fix-anything sort of cat."

"Got anybody in mind? Because I know one who's perfect, and he's an absolute rotter. Name's John Crouse-Hinds—"

"Royalty, huh?"

"Actually, his family is. He's a bloody enormous bloke. Three hundred and twenty pounds and he's all muscle. He's got about every rating in the book and his airframe and powerplant ticket, besides."

"What's he doing?"

"Last I heard he got fired from charter flying. Bluenose crowd, that sort of thing. Got drunk and the insults started. John landed the aircraft on a beach in the Bahamas, personally beat the living tar out of all his passengers, raped the two women, knocked his co-pilot into the middle of next week just to keep it all neat, and stormed off." Lew chuckled. "The judge couldn't understand it all so he fined Johnny a couple thousand quid and sent him packing on the first plane back to the States. Johnny figured it was fair. By the way, he also speaks about six languages, all of them fluently, including kraut. He's also a professional wrestler. Says it's good for his psychological shortcomings. Except he forgets to act his role and he usually ends up bashing heads into corner posts and knocking everyone in sight senseless."

"I don't want any bull in a china shop, Lew."

"Not Johnny," Lew protested. "He's as gentle as a child, really. Strangest thing is, if he's doing what he believes in, and if he trusts the man he works for, he's absolutely loyal, and I means to the death."

"Find him."

Johnny Crouse-Hinds was the first of their crew to
arrive, having driven nonstop from Canada where
Lew's friends had tracked him down. Jolting down
their road in a battered pickup truck, wearing faded
denims and a seedy straw hat, he was everything Lew
had said, and more. He parked the truck, stood outside, and absorbed everything in sight, remaining silent and unmoving until Lew emerged from a trailer
to greet him. He was absolutely enormous and yet a
closer look showed the other pilots that he was also as
light on his feet as a big cat. He shook hands all
around, gave Shag a long deep look. "I think I like
you especially," he said in a resonant bass. "You are
what I would call a very dangerous man, so things
around you will be interesting." He looked at Vance.
"Is this your bookkeeper?"

The rub didn't take. Crouse-Hinds received a thin,
cold smile from Vance. The Englishman smiled back.
"You would make a good Egyptian," he went on. "An
asp, I believe."

"He's a city killer," Lew said, enjoying the moment.
"Better think of your asp as grown up."

Crouse-Hinds showed a broader smile and extended
a hand to Vance. "I will think of you as a very large
python, then." They shook quietly, then the new-
comer turned to Shag. "One man is always at the top.
Is it you?"

"Ask them," Shag said. "It has more meaning that
way."

Vance and Lew nodded. "Good. Your authority is
absolute?"

Shag hadn't even thought of it that way. But thinking of it now, and with what he had in mind, this man was right. So Shag made an instant decision. "It is. There'll be a period of a week to get adjusted and think over things. At the end of that week it's either in or out. From then on, a man screws up I'll kill him."

"That easy?"

"Is killing supposed to be difficult?"

Crouse-Hinds liked this. "No, friend." He stretched and looked around. "Questions. Where do we sleep? Eat? Shower? Laundry?"

Lew was running the logistics. "Until we're set up here it's rations during the day. Everything else we run down to a small town south of here called Sherman. We'll bring in what we need in the way of some extra trailers, get a microwave oven and some other small miracles like that, use paper plates—whatever it takes."

"When do I fly?"

"When I say you fly," Shag said easily.

"Good. Then give me something to do." He studied his own enormous hands and shrugged. "They get in trouble if they're not busy."

Lew motioned for him to follow. "Let's go. Your guided tour will be short. Then you get a map of this place to study. You memorize everything. You drive the roads with one of us and then we'll fly you over it so you know it from down here and from up there, eh? When you can find your way around and you have your cover story absolutely right, then and only then do you get involved."

Crouse-Hinds nodded slowly. "Are you sure this isn't the French Foreign Legion, friend?"

Lew laughed. "Maybe it is. I'm not even sure." He

pointed to Shag. "He's the only one who knows and he's not telling even us."

Crouse-Hinds studied Shag again. "Good enough."

They all showed up in the next four days. Gaston Rademacher was tall with broad shoulders, but his entire frame was flat, like an enormous oaken board. He had a thick crop of curly hair and a mustache that would have turned Pancho Villa green with envy. Rademacher was of Greek-Rumanian extraction. He spoke four languages perfectly, including German. "My English he is not good," he explained on their first meeting. "But it work all right, you think." He had great yellow teeth, and there was no way to tell if he was thirty or fifty years old, but if experience with aircraft counted he could have lived for a century and taught the Wright Brothers. He was an international drifter who'd flown old cargo planes, sprayed crops, smuggled guns; if it had wings and a place to go, Gaston didn't give a damn how it got there or what it carried, just so long as he was behind the controls.

Valdez had found him in Miami and checked him out. He was looking for a war in Africa or South America; he didn't much care which. He would have hired out with the Vietnamese to fight against China. "In between wars," is how Valdez described him. "But we know his background well. If he shakes your hand he is to be trusted. And he knows I am recommending him."

Wolfgang Siedel was another matter entirely. He was as deep in legal shit as the bottom of an abandoned outhouse. Young Wolfgang had flown as flight engineer—because no pilot seats were available—on Condor Airlines cargo flights between Germany and

Canada. "Where's he now?" Shag asked Crouse-Hinds. They were seated in a trailer, chewing on fried chicken with great side helpings of goulash, prepared in desperation by Gaston Rademacher, who was convinced America was hell-bent on gastronomical suicide. It made for an interesting combination with plenty of wine, beer, and good whiskey to wash it down.

"Ah, Wolfgang, I fear, is a romanticist."

"I don't give a shit if he's a Republican. Where is he? And why are we interested in him?" Shag pressed.

"The why of it is first," Crouse-Hinds smiled. "His romantic inclinations bring him grief. It seems he knocked up the stewardess on his airplane."

"I thought he flew cargo."

"Yes, but the captain always took his wife along, and she was on the manifest as a stewardess, and Wolfgang with his wavy golden hair and that Nordic curl to his lips—well, amidst the cargo there were blankets and he lanced the lady good. The captain, dear fellow, had his balls altered some time ago and was quite sure that the swollen abdomen of his long-wedded wife did not spring from his own shaft, and well, they had a terrible fight and Wolfgang—remember I said he was a romanticist—pulled a sabre—not a sword or a rapier, but a sabre, mind you—of fine Prussian steel from his bag and carved flowery lines all about his captain. He beat a rap of attempted murder because it was very obvious to the judge that had he wanted his captain dead, pieces of Condor's finest would have been spread in all directions, so the charges were reduced to assault with a carving knife, or whatever, but there was the mitigating factor that the captain had initiated the assault, cuckolded or not—"

"To hell with your Sabatini romance. What's the payoff?"

"You've got a dark heart, Jordan," Crouse-Hinds smiled. Shag rolled his eyes and the burly man continued. "He's serving two to five, but we might be able to persuade—"

"How much?" Shag pushed.

"Three thousand. Gold in coin or any form. No paper currency. That would buy a parole. Amenities must be observed, but they would forget he ever existed."

"Why do we want him?"

Crouse-Hinds put down his spoon and locked eyes with Shag. "I do not discuss what I think you are going to do because that is neither wise nor polite," he smiled. "But only a blind man could be brought within this circle and not draw certain judgments. You are planning slowly and carefully and you will need fast, tough, reliable men, weapons experts included. I don't need a travel folder, Jordan. I can read the signs on the walls. You're building up to a beaut, you are, and it's my opinion that it's going to make the great London train robbery and the Brink's armored-car ripoff combined resemble a girl-scout picnic."

"Go on, please."

"I wouldn't know this if you hadn't been so open, you understand. You know, leave nothing covered in any way and—"

"Okay. I wear clean underwear and you watch me bathe."

Crouse-Hinds came up short, just a shade perplexed, not sure if he should be insulted. He thought better of it. "Wolfgang Siedel is a German and he looks like the perfect Aryan, which has simply got to dovetail with your painting that ruddy iron beast of yours a solid black. He speaks the language perfectly and he's a Prussian prick, which is a rarity with the youngsters from Germany today, since they're far more anti than they are for war. But Wolfgang Siedel was in the German army for three years. In fact, he was on a terrorist—Christ, I mean, an *anti*terrorist team. Something like your SWAT over here. He's a weapons expert, a trained killer, multilingual, a pilot, and he's sick and tired of having to wait his entire life to make a fortune. I think you're his perfect meal ticket."

"Is he loyal once he commits?"

Crouse-Hinds smiled. "If he's not I swear to you I'll kill him myself. Before it gets to be a problem, and despite the fact that you haven't told me a rat's turd of hard information. But understand one thing, Jordan. I'm not asking."

"I understand very well, Johnny." The two held the look between them. Finally Shag nodded. "Get him."

Phil Bergellini looked down from the front seat of the Cessna 180 and without turning grasped the pilot's arm at his left. "There, my friend. You see it? That grass strip with the wooden hangar? You can see three planes down there and some vehicles."

"I've got it." The pilot eased into a wide turn. "I'll make a run to check the drift," he said.

"Ah, you are a good man," Bergellini beamed. He sat in the right seat of the small plane, exposed directly to the windblast that fluttered his clothing. He watched the ground carefully, saw faces upturned. They were watching. Good. "Hey, the first run I drop the cargo bag, you got it?"

"Right. I'll hold this heading."

At the precise moment Bergellini heaved a heavy bag from the airplane door, saw the static line yank it open, and watched the chute blossom. He also saw two men running to where the bag would land. He turned to the pilot. "You make a very good flight, signor! Good man. I thank you much!" They shook hands briefly, and Bergellini climbed out of the airplane, left foot on the small step and his right foot on the tire. In a moment, while his hands grasped the angled strut, his right foot was rushing through hysterical movement along the spinning tire. His face contorted by the windblast, he had to scream to be heard. "Dogshit! Miserable fascist! Lock the fucking brake, you madman!"

The pilot winced, stepped on the foot brakes, and pulled out the park handle. Bergellini judged his distance again and pushed off with his arms. Immediately his arms flailed out and his legs spread wide in perfect stability and he fell earthward at 120 miles an hour. He judged the distance, yanked the D-ring, and as fast as the sport chute cracked open he was working the toggles to control his descent. He eased earthward under perfect control, swung around in a steep bank to catch the wind, dropped to earth as gently as a kitten stepping out of its sandbox, landing solidly on both feet. He raised his goggles and waved to the group watching him, then shrugged out of his harness. He wore faded jeans, a T-shirt and old sneakers, the antithesis of what one expected on a man dropping from the sky.

Vance Brady was first on the scene and the two waved and grinned hugely as they saw one another. "Aha! Mine colonel!" They hugged tightly, and Vance stepped back.

"You're out of uniform, fella."

Bergellini nodded with enthusiasm. "Just a little more than before, no?" They walked together toward the watching group. "This man of yours, Jordan, he is here?"

Vance nodded. "That's him, in the open shirt. With the beard."

"He is really everything you tell me, eh, compadre?"

"All that and more."

"When do I find out what this is all about, Colonel?"

"You don't until he's ready. But, Phil, before we get there, I trust him with my life. Completely. No questions, no holding back."

Shag watched them approach. Bergellini was a coiled spring, filled with a frenzied energy that showed even as he walked under the load of his parachute. His background was perfect for what Shag had in mind. He had been a base defense specialist in the air force, a select member of a HALO team. HALO stood for High Altitude Low Opening, which meant these men were trained killers, the equal of the old commandos or rangers, who were trained in every dirty tactic and weapon known, were proven to be masters at improvisation, and both protected Strategic Air Command bases and went on offensive missions. HALO troops jumped at thirty thousand feet or higher, at night or in rotten weather, and fell freely down to one or two thousand feet, opening their chutes as low as possible. They were about the most versatile of all combat fighting men.

Shag greeted Phil Bergellini with full acceptance, because this man had been a master sergeant in the air force and had flown several covert missions with Vance. There was no doubting his skills and Vance swore by his loyalty. "He's doing air shows right now," Vance had explained. "The new type of barnstorming circuit. Lot of jumps, the pay is pretty good, and he screws himself silly day and night. He's even tried to do it free-fall."

"Did he ball the chick?"

"Oh, he nailed her, but I think they had to separate before they wound it up. Too low and they had to pull."

"Why do you think he'll join us?"

"First, because we were in the kind of outfit where you never question another man, orders, suggestions, or whatever. Second, because he knows he can't spend the rest of his life jumping and fucking, and the idea of a steady job makes him puke. Third, because he loves nothing more than the kind of bash you have in mind. And fourth and least of all, the payoff looks promising."

"He could get killed in this deal, you know."

Vance laughed. "Go tell that to a man who jumps out of an airplane naked, with a broad who's also naked, and is trying to screw his brains out before they hit the ground."

"Good point," Shag allowed.

Frank Bemis met Lew Heath by appointment in a bar just outside Opa Locka Airport. Frank offered a nondescript appearance, sandy hair, no distinguishing features, and a sleepy look on his face. Somewhere in his background there'd been a stint in the army in Vietnam where he was a seek-and-destroy team leader. He'd hated it. He'd killed more hundreds of people than he wanted to remember, and in his revulsion at wiping out children who ran screaming from burning huts he told the army to go fuck itself and refused to fight again until he could meet his adversary face to face. The army was embarrassed because Bemis had three rows of decorations for courage, valor, heroism, and whatever other labels they pinned on their really good killers, and when they told Frank Bemis he could be court-martialed for desertion he nearly killed the provost marshal who offered the good news. "Add one more charge to your list," he told the astonished military police as he walked by them on his way back to his cell.

A smart major judged it all, quashed the crap surrounding Bemis, tore up the papers, and met with the man who'd disavowed his skills. "I understand you're a genius with your hands," he told Bemis over a bottle.

"I'd rather make things than break 'em," he answered simply.

"You got it," the major said.

"Got what?" Bemis asked.

"You're crew chief on my chopper from now on."

Bemis told the major he was crazy. "That's a Huey Cobra. A killer. No dice."

"You're wrong. You're going to roll the dice every time from now on, Bemis. You go out with me on everything. Firefights, seek-and-destroy, whatever. But you don't touch a gun or a trigger. That's what you want, right? You play mechanic. You keep that goddamned chopper running like a Swiss watch. You take care of me and I take care of you."

For seven months Frank Bemis went out and quietly watched as the major killed and people tried to kill them, and he was astonishingly calm about it all, not even blinking when they shot the chopper to pieces and he knew he'd be rebuilding it. And then one day, while he was lying in his bunk at his home field, a mob of people in their black pajamas came in at night and tore up the defense perimeter and killed the major in bed and blew up a bunch of choppers.

They also put six bullets into Frank Bemis. He survived a coma that lasted three weeks and he woke up in a stateside hospital. When he got out he studied his hands, got every federal license there was as a mechanic and inspector, and buried himself in rebuilding broken airplanes. He'd worked on a couple of iron birds for Lew, and by whatever magic there is in such people they found a bond between them. Lew wanted him on the team. Frank could fix anything, in the field and on the spot, and that could be vital.

"If it all works you can buy your own shop," Lew threw in for a clincher.

"It sounds like it could get nasty," Frank said, toying with his drink.

"Nasty and profitable."

"Some people could get killed?"

"Could be." Lew studied him. "That bother you?"

Bemis surprised him. "No. I don't care about people killing or being killed. They've done it since the first guy picked up a rock a couple of million years ago. Nothing's changed. Only the style. Just so long as I don't kill. I won't."

"Even if someone's coming at you?"

"That's right. Piss on 'em. Something happened to me in Nam. After fourteen months of firefights in which most of my outfit got wasted, three different times, the only time anybody ever hurt me was lying in bed. So let 'em have at it. I know they can't waste me."

"You'll do anything else?"

Bemis grinned. "Sure."

"Okay. You're in."

Shag personally selected the final member of the six-man team, and he was the most unlikely of them all. Sam Bronstein. The man who could do anything, find anything, get away with anything, who didn't need money, because he was lousy with it, who didn't have a spare moment in his life but was bored to tears. And that was the lure with which Shag could get Sam. They'd met in a banana war, when Shag came back from flying a strafing run on which he'd killed a few hundred people on a dirt road and shot some more out of trees where they were hiding for their lives. Shag was hot and sweaty and dog-tired and he went into what was laughably called the clubroom at the edge of the field, with the flies buzzing and the fans turning slowly and the strange bargirls who brought the warm beer and leaned over so their chests would brush against your face.

He was on his third or fourth beer when he spotted Sam Bronstein. The man was so ridiculously out of place that he couldn't help himself. He just flat-out stared at the man in the suit that cost a few hundred bucks, whose shoes were a glistening black sheen, whose white tie was perfect against the light blue shirt. Shag picked it all out: the impeccable tailoring, the diamond cufflinks, the perfect haircut, the long and slim cigars he knew were made to order—but most surprising of all was that the man was as cool and comfortable as the proverbial cucumber, when everyone else was pouring sweat into their boots.

Shag surprised himself by going to the man's table. He scraped a chair to the table and sat down. They stared at each other. "If I'm intruding, tell me and I'll go," Shag said. "I'm on your turf and I recognize it."

"Sam Bronstein," said the stranger. "You're Jordan."

Shag was midly surprised. "There must be a reason for your knowing."

"You cut the bullshit neatly," he was told. Shag leaned back and took in the paradox of the bull neck and manicured nails.

"What in the hell is someone like you doing in a place like this?" he asked.

"Business," Sam smiled at him.

"Do I ask or zip the lip?"

"Depends on why you want to know."

"Intense curiosity."

"Good enough. I sell the airplanes you fly to kill people."

Shag nodded slowly. "So we're both killers."

"Yes."

"You don't seem offended."

"Why should I be offended with the truth? Who among us hasn't killed? Some more than others, some better than others. You're a professional killer, I'm a professional executioner. I buy, trade, deal, sell, arrange. From bullets to full-scale wars. There's a big demand for my business. Look at yourself."

"You sure lay it out without the shit."

Sam Bronstein shrugged. "When your opposite number knows, you don't blow smoke. It's foolish."

"It still seems different. I—"

"You mean it's different to make money selling instead of earning your money by fighting and getting shot at?"

"Uh, yes."

"That's stupid and you know it."

Shag couldn't believe the way this stranger was manipulating the conversation, anticipating his words, thrusting and parrying with such ease. He felt uncomfortable. People didn't play mental tag with him and get away with it like this fellow was doing.

Shag moved his chair. "You're right."

Bronstein leaned forward. "I'm bored. When's your next mission?"

"Late afternoon. For some reason that's when those people like to move their troops by truck. Gets them into position for night attacks, that sort of thing."

"You mind sitting right seat for a trip?"

Shag let that one sink in. "You're asking to take the left seat and fly it?"

"Gamble, Jordan. You know the holy words. What the hell."

"Better change your suit."

"I got what I need. Five o'clock sharp. One favor. I'd like not to bother with the preflight. Will you handle it?"

Shag smiled. "I always do."

"Good. I find it tedious."

They met at five beneath the wing of the B-26 bristling with machine guns and rocket canisters. Shag was almost in shock. Sam Bronstein climbed from a jeep, wearing a brilliant flame-red flight suit and paratrooper boots and carrying a jet helmet beneath one arm. "You got your mission?" he asked.

Shag nodded. Bronstein never said another word, just climbed into the cockpit and when Shag nodded, the stranger fired her up with a honey-smooth touch, did his runup check right where they were, released the brakes, and cobbed the throttles into a swinging turn onto the runway and into the air without losing a second. Sam went across the treetops bordering the field with leaves scraping propeller tips, cranked in a wicked turn through a valley, asked for the target coordinates, found the hapless people on the ground, and proceeded to chew up three or four hundred terrified soldiers and mangle most of a convoy. He brought them home with a few bullets in their wings, landed like a feather, and had cut the switches while they were still rolling to a parking place. When they climbed out he pointed to the waiting jeep and took Shag to a large trailer, which turned out to be a palace in a dung heap. Thickly upholstered chairs, air conditioning, and a wonderful bar, from which Shag offered this man an honest toast.

"Where and when?" Shag asked finally.

Korea had been the beginning. "Flew lead sleds there. Straight-wing eighty-fours on support missions. Shot down three times, screamed for an F-86 and they gave me one. Six MIG's. Felt good. Then a tour of fifty missions in a B-26, but a lot better than that junk heap we just flew. Had to bail out of that one. Flew an Israeli fighter for the short war and added eight more MIG's to the tally over there. Then a couple of scrapes down here, a short but very interesting visit to Africa. Idi Amin lost four of his few transports to me there. Sheep in a barrel. That sort of thing."

"But it's not your occupation." He made it a statement instead of a question.

"Silly to depend upon killing for your living." Bronstein thought that over. "Got to remember that. It has a touch of simple Spartan philosophy to it. But back to what you said. No, I'm an attorney, member of the bar in Florida. Registered munitions dealer. Very legal and proper. Also an airline or two here and there. I dabble a bit, you might say."

"Why'd you fly the mission today? You didn't do it to prove anything to me or to impress me."

"Good God, no. That's theatrics. I was bored and you make good company, Jordan. There's a streak of the philosopher in you. Somewhere in your background, someone shoved a long and dirty knife well up into your ribs and the wounds haven't healed. You hide it well."

Shag thought of his dead wife and the then-dead pilot friend of his. "But you saw it."

"That, also, is my business. I'm a strange sort of a tailor, Mr. Jordan. I take the measure of men."

Shag hadn't called Sam about his new project. He tracked him down through his office—in the Buena Vista enclave of Disneyworld, of all places, and in a sumptuous penthouse suite. Shag laid bare his plans, told Sam he needed international contacts, a crack attorney, financial connections—and then he offered the real oyster. "I'd like you to come in with us."

"I don't need the bread, Shag."

"I know that."

"Then why do you ask?"

"I learned how to be a tailor, Sam. You're bored."

Bronstein nodded and his smile grew slowly. "One condition."

"Name it."

"Only you know the real Sam Bronstein, understand? All the other people are to know is that I once wore the blue suit and I've been flying cargo runs out of Singapore. Common enough and no way to check."

"They won't check."

"Good. I guess I follow your orders, right?"

"I'd feel silly giving you orders, man."

Sam offered a cigar. "Enjoy, enjoy," he said.

Shag had them all together in the trailer they used for meals and meetings. They weren't worried about intruders. His crew had rigged up a dozen surveillance and alarm systems, and they had three of the biggest and meanest attack dogs always on the alert. But their best cover was that the local authorities and populace had become accustomed to their irregular hours, and local coffers had swelled from their business. People around Okeechobee were inclined to enjoy unexpected pleasures without questioning their origin.

"Everybody knows what they have to do," Shag told his group. "You also know how to play our cover, keep things rolling smoothly. Thirty days from now that piece of iron is to be ready to fly. While I'm gone, Brady runs the operation and Heath is right behind him. If there are financial problems, Bronstein here has contacts in the right places. If we need to contact Valdez or anyone else in Miami, only Heath makes the contact. And from now on, nobody ever goes anywhere alone. Two for whatever tango is going on. Any questions? Good. I'm taking that Aztec we rented out West and I'll be back in a week. There'll be one more addition to this group and that locks it."

Crouse-Hinds drummed thick fingers on the table. "Anything else you'd like to tell us?"

"Yeah. Wear your rubbers when it rains."

"This last member of the group," Wolfgang Siedel said. "Do we know him?"

"You don't. And it's a her."

19

He kept his eyes closed. It was delicious, the coolness of sweet juice from a pear trickling slowly along his chest. "That's it," the soft, husky voice whispered to him. "Don't move. Just lie there." The silken fingertips slid along his neck, paused by the tender skin below his shoulders, and traced a slow and wandering journey to the firm muscles of his belly. He twitched.

"No moving. Eyes closed and body still, remember?"

The fingernail moved upward along his thigh, sending the muscles into an involuntary spasm. "You're cheating." Soft hair brushed his face. He gritted his teeth. "I—am—lying—here—absolutely—still." He had to force the words out.

"You have terrible control. You should see this thing. So terribly swollen. Throbbing. Oh dear; it's purple."

The muscles were taut along his neck. "Do you know," he gasped, "how long it's been since I—"

"I can see, love."

A tongue traced the inside of his leg. He moaned like a sick calf.

"Poor, dear man." The tongue moved higher and then he was writhing wildly, her arms holding down one leg. His own hand sought frantically for her body until she slapped him sharply, but she never removed her mouth from him, her fiery tongue flicking like a snake until he thought he would go mad. The heat boiled up deep in his belly, swirled around there until he was helpless, and then he felt his loins throb until he was sure his body was raised from the bed, floating in space, and she edged a tooth with an effect that brought a sharp gasp and almost a scream from him and then there was no more control, his teeth were grinding together and his neck arched back and his climax started with a withering searing through his belly and up along the shaft and, at the instant he started coming, she withdrew for just a second all touch of her teeth and lips and tongue and he wanted to bellow with maddened rage, but then her tongue flicked again and she moved her teeth in an unbeliev-able motion and he knew a climax of such consuming fury and heat that he screamed and started to thrash about and discovered he had no strength in his arms or legs and he fell back totally exhausted, muscles jerked so taut they were cramping, and she was caress-ing him gently. When he tried to talk her lips brushed his. "Shhh. Not yet. Not yet. Just lie there." Her hands moved along his body and he didn't know if it was real or a dream. Good Jesus, was he on an acid trip or what? He floated and he wasn't aware when he fell into the deepest sleep he had known in many, many years.

When he awoke it was to the aroma of fresh coffee. He dragged his naked body to a sitting position against the headboard, not ready to speak, watching Pam Kreiner approaching with a steaming mug on a tray. She placed it by his side. "Careful. It's hot." She was wonderfully sensuous, her age belied by a body still as supple as when he had known it many years before. She sat by his side, her breasts as full and as firm as ever; yet she was older, wiser, her strength concealed as much by instinct as it was by practice. She opened a wooden box on the end table, placed the Havana between his teeth and held the match for him. He took a long drag, savoring the taste with his eyes closed, then sipped at the coffee. He couldn't believe how completely drained he felt. An enormous weight was gone, a chunk of iron the size of a bowling ball ripped from deep within his belly, the chains gone from within his brain.

"You were right," Pam said finally, the words bringing him upward from the lassitude he still enjoyed. "It was a long time."

"Two years. Maybe more."

Her eyes widened. "Are you serious?"

"I sure as hell am, woman."

"You haven't been laid in over two years? You?"

"Haven't cared to."

"How do you feel?"

"Like the part of me that was dead has been revived."

Her eyes moistened. "That's the most beautiful thing anyone has ever said to me."

"Life's a beautiful thing. If you're alive," he amended. "I feel alive for the first time in God knows how long. I think I'm going to fall in love with you, Pam."

"You're crazy," she said with tinkling laughter.

"Always have been. But I mean it."

"How can you think you're going to fall in love with someone, Shag!"

"Because I feel something I haven't felt in too long. No, keep quiet. Hear me out." He put aside the cigar and the coffee and held her hands. "I haven't wanted to be with anyone and I find myself wanting to be with you. I haven't needed anyone and, suddenly—well, suddenly knowing I could be vulnerable again doesn't make me psychotic."

"Goddammit, Jordan, I'm a hooker!"

"Goddammit, Kreiner, I'm a killer!" he said in mocking echo of her words. "What the hell's the matter with you, Pam? I don't know how you live? How all this came about? When Karl was killed and you ran blindly through a forest of nightmares? I've been there, baby. I killed, you hooked. End of the line for the nasty stories."

She looked at him carefully, her head tilted, and he couldn't remember anything so beautiful as those long lashes and that dark, tumbling hair. "You want to get married, Shag?"

He never hesitated. "Hadn't thought of it. Legal stuff and all that. But if you want to, sure."

"Well, I don't want to."

"Okay."

"You want me to live with you? Give up hooking?"

"Answer to the first question, no. Not just live with me. Be a part of me. Answer to the second question, you already have. It's done. Given up. Forgotten. Never happened."

"But it did happen."

"So what?"

"You're a fool."

"Of course I am. It's us mad people who make the world go round."

"I heard you were fighting a war somewhere."

"Somewhere, someplace. They're all the same. Now I've got a very special project going. Aside from wanting you for me, I want you for the deal. But before you answer, it's the sort of thing that could be rough and you could get hurt or killed."

"I've been dead since Karl was killed." She stroked his arm. "Until now."

"Do we team it, girl?"

"Just like that?"

"Just like that. You've got to go all the way. Ask your questions later if you want. All you want. But if you come in with me it's all the way, Pam. It's got to be like that, because that's my heart you're going to be holding in your hands, and if you stumble, I'm gonna get bruised up something fierce."

"That's a two-way street, Shag."

"So it is."

"Make love to me, Shag."

"Can I finish my cigar first?"

They wrestled like two kids, laughing until their lips met again.

In the next three days Pam Kreiner disappeared. They cleaned out her apartment and turned it over to friends. They booked a flight to Hong Kong for her, paid for the ticket one way, bought another for a friend on the way home and told her to go to that exotic port, make herself known as Pam Kreiner, and then pull her own disappearing act and come back under her own name. The girl was a close friend who'd shared laughter and lumps with Pam. She didn't even want to ask any questions, and that was that. Before the three days were up everything Pam had left in the world fitted into two suitcases.

"Meet me tomorrow night at the American Airlines lounge in Los Angeles Airport," she told Shag. "I'm going to complete the job. You want the Pam Kreiner people know to disappear, right? Good. I'll do that, but what I do next is a present and a surprise, and don't ask me any questions. I have a friend in a certain place who will have my identification all set up as Pam Jordan and—" She stopped short for a moment and tried to judge him. "Was I wrong in doing that, Shag?"

He shook his head. "No. It's as right as can be."

"Wonderful. Stay here at the hotel. I want to leave here alone and I'll see you tomorrow. Kiss me good-bye, you impetuous fool, you."

And she was gone. He went down to the lounge and sprawled in a comfortable chair. An old friend saw him and came over for a drink. The casino manager, whose credentials for his present position, at which he had proved a great success, were strange. Al was a former fighter pilot, a jet jockey who'd flown both in tactical and strategic commands, and they had some old times to talk over. They stayed up most of the night and then Shag checked out and went to McCarran Field. Thirty minutes later he was punching through a haze layer in the Aztec on his way to Los Angeles.

He had a busy day seeing an attorney Sam Bronstein had recommended. There was a lot to do with bank accounts, stock certificates, licenses, and other legal garbage only one of these legal beagles could handle. Leo Kalb asked no questions other than those directly touching on what Shag required; Shag had no doubt Bronstein had given him very specific instructions on that score. Then, too, Shag mused, if I were an attorney the last man in the world I'd want to cross would be Sam Bronstein. He probably had a half-dozen motorcycle gangs as clients and they'd do anything, including mass murder, at his beckoning. Shag left Kalb's office with an attaché case packed with papers. Everything was exactly as it should be.

He waited in the lounge for Pam. Eight o'clock came and went but he didn't see her. He also found it difficult to take his eyes off a striking blonde seated at a table near the window. He hadn't seen a woman like her for years. Long hair, a suede leather trench coat and—he gaped.

It was Pam.

He went across the lounge slowly, his disbelief painted across his face and growing with every step. Her smile dazzled him and he sank slowly into a chair. He couldn't help staring. She spoke to him softly in German, and his only answer was a soft, lingering kiss on those beautiful lips.

"Aren't you going to say something?" she finally said in English.

"Can you ride a motorcycle?"

"*What?*"

"You heard me. Can you ride a damn bike?"

"Why yes, I can, but what's that got to do with—"

"I love you. I'll explain later. We're on our way to New Mexico. I've got a meeting in Albuquerque with some lawyers for a mining company. Where are your bags? We'll fly there in the Aztec. Have you eaten dinner yet? My God, you look marvelous."

Her laughter was like tinkling crystal. "You're nuts."

"Yeah, I guess so." He grinned like a foolish ape. "Let's go. I'm hungry."

Three hours later he was in the air. He climbed out to ten thousand feet, settled down the Aztec on autopilot, and sat beneath a canopy of a billion stars, Pam curled up beneath one of his powerful arms, sleeping like a child. He glanced up at the stars. He didn't care what the future held. Right now all was right with the world.

"Ah, we've been expecting you, Mr. Jordan. And this is—"

"You're a diplomat, Mr. Haggerty. This is my wife, Pam."

The attorney led them into his office, offered coffee, accepted their desire to get to work immediately. Tim Haggerty put his elbows on his desk, made a steeple of his fingers and peered over them at Shag. "I spoke with Kalb this morning. He briefed me on your needs. May I review them before my secretary brings in all the paperwork? It will—oh, very good. Thank you, Miss Evans. Now, as I understand it, Mr. Jordan, you represent an organization, Classic Mining Corporation, with the major offices in Ontario and San Francisco?"

Shag nodded.

"Very good. Your credit references are already on file with us here. I understand, also, that it is your intention to work the old mine near Fence Creek—that's the closest community and I'm afraid it's not much to begin with, and it's thirty or forty miles away from the mine. Your interest is uranium, and I understand from Mr. Kalb that the necessary federal documents, as to what procedures are to be followed in the event of a strike, are already filed."

His tone made it clear he didn't expect any great uranium strikes from anything within a hundred miles of Fence Creek. "The company that operated the mine before they closed down operations—"

"Went broke, you mean," Shag corrected.

"Yes, sir, they did. I handled the bankruptcy papers myself. You have more confidence in this project than I do, and frankly, Mr. Jordan, I'd be less than candid if I didn't tell you I believe you're wasting your money."

"We don't think so. Anyway, we're willing to give it a shot. Your lease price is certainly reasonable enough."

Haggerty nodded. "Yes, sir. One thousand dollars a month with a guarantee for a year."

Shag opened the attaché case and handed Haggerty an envelope. "There's a cashier's check there from Classic Mining to your office for twelve thousand dollars. Wasn't that old outfit known as Atlas Mining?" Shag knew the answer but wanted to hear it from this man.

"Yes, sir. They thought the great uranium rush twenty years ago was right under their feet. They were wrong."

"Their extraction methods were lousy," Shag said. "We'll do better. Have you made the proper arrangements with the sheriff of Fence Creek County and the other specifications I requested?"

"Yes, sir. We're thorough if nothing else, Mr. Jordan," Haggerty beamed. "Here's the key to your post-office box in Fence Creek. All your credentials—mining license, occupation permit, lease for one year renewable at the same price for a second year—well, everything is there. As soon as you sign the papers, sir, you're in business. May I ask how you'll operate there?"

If he hadn't asked Shag would have brought the matter up himself. "We'll handle it by air. Oh, a couple of trucks and that sort of thing, but mainly we'll use some old cargo planes to have the ore assessed."

"Please feel free to use our services for that, Mr. Jordan."

"I didn't know you were in that line. You look pretty legal to me."

Haggerty chuckled. "We're not. But we have reliable clients who are, Mr. Jordan."

"Bring on the paperwork."

They were done half an hour later. Shag and Pam got up to leave and Shag timed his last speech for that moment. "One last thing, if you would, Mr. Haggerty."

"Of course, sir. Name it."

"We're tight-lipped about this operation. I don't mean that it's secret or anything like that. Obviously with all this paperwork it's not. But we don't like to be bothered and we don't want people coming around to interfere."

"Mr. Jordan, you're in raw, naked, and terrible desert out there. Even the scorpions seem to avoid the place."

"Charming," Pam murmured.

"Sorry, ma'am."

"It's okay," Shag said. "Do you know the sheriff at Fence Creek?"

"Yes, I do."

Shag reached into a jacket pocket and removed ten one-hundred-dollar bills. "Personal services, Mr. Haggerty. Not on the books. Would you be good enough to pass on the word to the sheriff—"

"Austin, sir. Percy Austin."

"Would you let Sheriff Austin know of my feelings about our privacy? We don't want trespassers and we get riled easy when they show up."

"Consider it done, sir."

"Thanks again. Good-bye."

"A pleasant day to you both, and have a safe journey."

Later, at the airport, Pam's curiosity overcame her discretion. "What was that all about? The trespassers, I mean. The way he described that mining area it sounds like the Gobi Desert. How can you be worried about people barging in?"

"I'm not, really. But Haggerty has a thousand clams for a couple of minutes of conversation, he'll tell the sheriff—ever hear a whacko name like that for a sheriff? Percy Austin. Jesus. Anyway, Haggerty will consider us eccentric, and—"

"The word for you is crazy."

"Okay, then, it's crazy. The point is that he's already got me marked down and typed. The mention of my name will immediately remind him of a bunch of dumbasses who are blowing their money on a property everybody here knows is worthless. The only thing they ever took from that mine is dirt."

"Do you believe there really is uranium there?"

"Hell, no. Let's go see our mining mecca."

"They should have called it 'End of the World,'" Pam said. She rested against an old weathered fence that gave an ominous creaking warning before it collapsed in dust.

Shag laughed and helped her to her feet. "It is grungy, isn't it?"

"It's the pits, Mr. Jordan. How long has it been since anyone's even been here?"

Shag looked down the beaten-up old airstrip where he'd brought the Aztec down for a bumpy, teeth-rattling landing. The sun clamped down on them with

a ferocity he'd never known before. The shacks and
work buildings were literally bleached white, the well
that had been dug would need work. No power; he'd
need generators. Everything was coated with a white,
gritty dust. But what he needed most of all was a large
wooden hangar and it was still standing; it had been
made of sturdy beams and would last a long time to
come. They walked to the mine, peered inside, decided
common sense forbade walking into a mine shaft that
might collapse or harbor snakes or scorpions within its
darkened tunnel, and walked back to the airplane.

Shag stopped with his arm around Pam's shoulder.
"How do you like it, hon? Some place for a honeymoon."

She almost turned white. "You've got to be kidding
me, mister."

"The girl I love? No way. But first we'll give you a
vacation in Florida."

Later, cruising at 9,500 across the desert on their
way to Midland, Texas, for an overnight stop, they
tried it. Autopilot on, passenger seat fully reclined,
and as long as Shag didn't bump his ass against the
control yoke, it was a marvelous place to make love.

20

They sealed off the road at night with a swinging bridge. A car driving to Dillard Sprayers found that the miserable winding road ended abruptly in a deep and wide ditch that could be crossed only when the bridge swung back to complete the roadway. Not quite the castle moat but just as effective, and if an intruder did get past the ditch within three hundred yards he was setting off silent electronic and mechanical alarms. If he was on foot then he'd be busy with three big German shepherds slashing at his hide. All this time, of course, the professional and experienced killers who lived at the isolated airstrip near Lake Okeechobee, would be waiting with amusement to do their own number. To their disappointment, no one had given their system its acid test.

Since their return, Pam had been briefed on the systems, made friends with the dogs, and captivated the crew of mercenaries. But she had yet to see the interior of the hangar, and so, for that matter, did Shag. Since his return the men had barred him from a view of what was going on beyond the great sliding doors. "Two more days," Lew said with fingers upraised. "That's all we ask of your lordship. We want two more days before we let you and your lady rest your optics on the old girl."

"You're acting like a bunch of goddamned kids," Shag growled.

"Aren't we all, really?" Sam Bronstein laughed at him.

Vance Brady cleaned his fingernails with a wicked-looking knife. He had shown a total admiration for Pam and her effect on Shag ever since they returned, and yet, one couldn't very well pass up a rare moment. "Pam, has your hero given you the special news yet? About your assignment?"

She looked at Shag questioningly. "It's not time yet," he said.

But the others sensed the moment to needle Jordan. Wolfgang Siedel stood before Pam, took her hand and kissed it with exaggerated Prussian gallantry. Then he stood erect, clicked his heels, and spoke to her in German. Her eyes widened and she turned in disbelief to Shag. "Did he mean what he said?" she demanded.

"Love, how the hell do I know? I can't speak German."

"I can," smirked Wolfgang.

"Shut up," Sam said.

"All of you zip it," Pam said coldly.

"Yes'm," Crouse-Hinds mumbled. He stood with the brim of his hat in his teeth, a forlorn 320-pound cookie monster being chastised by a lithe and lovely blonde. It was so ludicrous that Pam had all she could do to keep a straight face as she advanced against

Shag. She stopped before him and pointed her hand at Siedel. "Now, what this reject from the Hitler youth movement said was—"

Howls of laughter interrupted her. She waited for the snickering to fade out. "Your young Goering said I was going to do some work as a seamstress?"

"Only a little," he said.

"Sewing?"

"Well, shucks, ma'am," he muttered, shuffling one foot across the other. "Can't be all fun and games, right?"

"*Me?* You want me to *sew?*" She looked down at his shuffling foot. "Your feet hurt?"

"Uh, no, ma'am, just being respectful. Don't hurt none at all."

"Well, it does now," and her booted toes lammed into his ankle and Shag bellowed with the sudden pain, hopping around the room on one foot while massaging the other. Chairs crashed to the floor as he cursed and hopped. Pam lit a cigarette. "Now I'm ready to sew."

"Remind me to buy ready-made clothes," he grinned. "A guy could get killed this way. Besides, hon, it's a special job. We can't trust anyone else to do it."

She looked around. "Anyone else here know how to sew?" Gaston Rademacher moved forward. He looked at Pam as if she was a blond goddess they'd found hidden in a cave.

"Me. I fly, cook, sew, shoot—I do anything. I help you."

She smiled at him. "It's easier already. Thank you."

"The shipment, Shag," Lew said. "It's already here. We had everyone's size and Phil flew up to Baltimore and brought it back."

Shag showed his surprise. "That fast? From that Unique Import place?"

"Import, my ass. That's mostly for the schlock trade," Sam Bronstein said quickly. "They copy stuff. Replicas. That's how we got real uniforms and insignias for everybody. It's, shall we say, ersatz, but it looks absolutely authentic and it's everything we need. We had to guess a bit with Pam, but I think we're close to her size, and a few alterations can take care of any problems."

Pam looked back and forth between the two men. "I'm confused. This is mad. *What* uniform for me?"

Wolfgang offered another Prussian strut, clicked his heels, and bowed. "If you will permit me, Colonel Kreiner, there is not one, but three uniforms for you."

"Get stuffed," she told him. "Shag, what the hell is this all about?"

Crouse-Hinds stepped forward, offered his arm. "In the next trailer, ma'am. If you will give me the honor?"

Shag nodded and Pam shook her head in acceptance. They went to the adjoining trailer and she looked around her. "My God, it's like Gestapo headquarters in here!" It was. Uniforms hung neatly on racks, complete with officer's and noncommissioned officer's insignia. Leather belts, holsters, peaked caps, gloves, steel helmets, boots, canteens—everything. And to one side, three uniforms in her own size, black, with garrison belts, boots, gloves, various hats, and—what startled her the most—with the insignia of the SS. The men crowded in behind her and she found herself ignoring them, looking to Shag for explanation and relief.

"I know this isn't what it seems to be," she said.

"Will you please tell me I'm not crazy. What is this all for?"

"The operation I've been planning for weeks. And before you ask any further, no, it's not an uprising of the Fourth Reich. We're not members of any bund, we're not planning a *putsch,* and there isn't a sympathizer with anything even remotely Nazi in this crowd. I don't have to explain about myself. You knew Heath from before and he needs no words. Sam Bronstein is Jewish and that ends that. Bergellini is an insane Italian who has no interest in the past, but prefers his freedom to anything else. Vance is an old blue-suit type. Johnny over there? He'd kill the first Nazi that ever came within reach. Gaston? His grandparents were butchered by German troops. And then there's Wolfgang Siedel, pure Aryan, the golden knight of the German skies."

Wolfgang nodded, all fun and games gone from his eyes. "I will explain myself. My father was a man of great learning. A professor in Berlin. A Catholic. And very much against a madman whose name was Hitler. I never knew him, but I still have a picture my mother gave me so I might know the past even if I did not experience it. It is a picture of my father hanging upside down by barbed wire in a political prison camp in Germany. About 1938. And—"

"Enough," Pam said quickly. She turned to Frank Bemis. "You look like such a gentle human being. What are you doing in this mob, anyway?"

Frank smiled so softly she wanted to cradle him in her arms. "Thank you. I think I'm here to remind them that there's hope for us all."

"Are you a—well, a—I mean—"

"A priest?" He smiled. "Hardly. But I am a convert. I have made myself content to be a spectator at man's favorite sport of killing other men. I don't mind watching, but I'm no longer climbing down with the Christians or the lions."

"I'm not sure I understand," she said, faltering.

"It's not easy being an ex-killer, miss."

"I'll have to take your word for it, Frank. Thank you for trying to help."

She turned back to Shag. "I can't help it. I'm confused."

He put his arm around her waist and drew her close. "Don't be. One thing clears away all the fog. Trust me."

"Is there any question?"

He shook his head.

Gaston Rademacher stepped forward. "Special tonight. No more goddamned skinny chicken, yes? For you, good woman, Rumanian stew. Very special. Much garlic. Good!"

"Gak," Crouse-Hinds said.

Rademacher stabbed a finger at him. "For that, you wash tonight. All dishes and pots and pans."

"Great," Pam said. "I'll wipe."

She flew out of bed early the next morning. Not willingly, or even knowingly, but she was almost straight up, her eyes wide open, one hand searching frantically for Shag. The crash came again and then the stuttering roar of a heavy machine gun blazing away in short, chopping bursts. Three other weapons opened up and she heard voices shouting. She threw on a robe and dashed for the trailer door, just in time to see several large oil drums still tumbling end over end, spewing oil and smoke as they had been blasted by the wicked firepower.

And every one of those mothers was as calm as a stuffed family after a Thanksgiving dinner.

She waved at them, dressed quickly, and went outside. Shag was holding a Schmeiser cradled in one arm. He kissed her quickly and then pointed to a table. Coffee, doughnuts, and ear protectors. The first blast from the heavy machine gun sent the coffee flying from her hand to grab for the sound-muffler headset. She tried a second time with the coffee and got the cup down without shaking it onto her hands. By her third cigarette she was calm enough to watch carefully as the men tested a bewildering variety of small and large weapons. When it was over they crowded around her.

"That orange barrel over there," Lew said.

"I can't hear you."

Shag removed the ear protectors. "He said, that orange barrel over there."

"Oh. What about it?"

Shag handed her the submachine gun. "Have a whack at it."

She felt the heft of the weapon. To everyone's surprise, there was no gingerly withdrawal on her part. Pam and her late husband had done everything together. He loved to hunt and Pam spent four years learning guns and becoming very efficient with them. She checked the Schmeiser for safety, trigger, balance, and with no warning, spun half around, crouching, leaning well into the weapon to counter its recoil, and emptied the long clip in five short, hammering bursts. The orange barrel was still flopping ass over teakettle when the men crowded around, shouting and laughing their surprise. "No wonder Jordan behaves his bloody arse!" Crouse-Hind shouted. "I could do with a woman who can shoot like that!"

They walked back to the trailer.

"Tonight the Pumphouse and Railroad Gang," Shag gestured to take in the others, "have invited us to see the results of their handiwork in the big hangar."

Pam nodded slowly. "I meant to ask. You know what's in there, don't you?"

"Oh, sure. An airplane. In fact, I flew it in here."

"Then why the mystery?"

"Very special airplane. Lew and the gang have been rebuilding it. Tonight's the prom, I guess."

Sam Bronstein stopped at the hangar doors. "The boys have decided that since you're going to be gawking, Shag, you'll probably trip over your own feet and hurt the lady. We took a vote. Pam will watch the debut with one arm on mine and the other on Johnny's."

"That's like a fawn caught between two grizzlies," Shag said.

"But they're such nice grizzlies," Pam intervened quickly.

Sam was just a bit more serious. "It's Lew and Vance," he explained. "They're so damned proud they've been popping buttons for the last couple of days and—"

"I understand. The lady is in your good keeping."

They stood before the old wooden hangar doors and heard Lew call from within. "All right, lively now! All lights out, you nits! And that goes for outside as well as in here. Quickly, quickly!"

All around them lights winked out; within the hangar, outside its parking ramp, within the trailers and the vehicles, until darkness enveloped them. They waited a few moments for their eyes to acclimate to night vision, and then Bemis and Siedel rolled back the hangar doors. Shag peered inside and could barely distinguish light shadows from darker shadows, but there was no mistaking the great hulking shape before him in that gloomy structure.

Lew Heath's voice cried out, "*Ta-daaaa!*" A light came on by the tail, shining on gleaming corrugated black metal. In the center of the great sheet of metal was a blood-red swastika within a yellow circle.

"*Ta-daaaa.*" rang out again and lights spilled across the right wing. Black paint glistened ominously and two great white crosses could be seen, one above and one below the wing.

The lights came on in a steady succession after that until the entire hangar was gleaming from spotlights raining their glory down on an airplane that looked as if it had rolled from the production line only hours before. Shag had expected a great job from this crew but not a miracle. And he had been given just that.

She shone and gleamed from nose to tail, from wing-tip to tip, from her belly to the top of the rudder. Crosses atop and below the wings and on each side of the fuselage, and the swastika blazing from each side of the big vertical fin and rudder. Shag walked slowly to the main cabin door. My God, could this really be the same airplane?

"Mr. Jordan," Lew said stiffly, "if you'd be good enough to offer me and Vance Brady, here, this mangler of cities, your attention, 'twould be our pleasure to provide a personally conducted tour, with some lack of proper flourishes and a band, of this glorious machine by name of Iron Annie." Shag turned to look at Pam; she nodded in understanding for him to go ahead.

They stood by the cabin door. "We'll do it in the manner of a walkaround, Shag," Lew continued, and there wasn't even a shred of humor remaining. They had crossed that invisible line to where all was business, and damned hardline at that.

"The door. Now, let me show you this dandy little item." Lew pushed in on three snap releases and a curving door hinged down. He reached within the now open space in the side of the Ju-52 and a sturdy aluminum ladder slid out and then down to the ground to form a stairway. "That's only the half of it," Lew said. "You just fold over these two metal bars, and presto! you have a ramp that can handle a motorcycle without any trouble, getting on or off the machine."

"Excellent," Shag said, for he had ordered just such an arrangement and Lew clearly had improved on his original concept.

"Look up at the turret. New windshield, and the scarf gear for the gun is about six times easier to work than before. I built an interruptor into the firing mechanism so that if anybody gets a bit too excited, they won't be shooting holes in our own tail. Now, see this ball socket here by the loo window? It holds either a .30-caliber, or a man can poke a hand-held submachine gun through there and have a steady firing platform. The same arrangement is on the other side of the machine, and there are two more of these sockets inside the cabin."

"Five firing positions, then," Shag voiced his thoughts.

"More than that," Vance joined in. "Look at the cabin door; they've both been modified with sliding windows from vans, and they leave enough space for hand weapons. Also, you can stand up in the cockpit. If you really need to hose out the lead you can have the turret gun for the heavy firepower, plus seven other gun positions."

"Bend down here," Lew instructed. "See the belly along here? There isn't a piece of corroded metal left anywhere on the skin of Annie. Not a blemish left on the old girl."

"Any internal corrosion?" Shag asked.

"There was some," Lew confirmed. "It was easy enough to fix, you see, with this sort of construction. Only two crossbraces and one structural beam of any consequence. It would have flown for years the way it was with no problem, but now you don't even have to think about it."

Shag touched a rounded unit jutting two inches from the fuselage. "External power?"

"Right. Operate off auxiliary, direct electrical or battery."

They walked behind the left wing and there was nothing to question because it was all there right before him. "Now inside these wings," Lew went on after the pause, "I could hardly believe what we found. Or didn't find, rather. No corrosion. Using duralumin and its covering the way the old Junkers people did, they've had the best corrosion resistance in this machine that I've ever known. And would you believe the same for the push-pull rods for the ailerons? But what got me to a real fare-thee-well were the tanks!"

"Problems?"

"Just the opposite, Shag! Those tanks are placed between trusses and crossbraces and then they're held in place by straps." Lew's eyes were wide. "And the straps are both metal and leather. It's the leather that worked me up so much, I suppose. It was perfect! If I had all the time in the world to play with I wouldn't change 'em."

They walked around the wingtip and moved along

the leading edge of the wing. Shag was going straight for the new engine mount, but the strange shape of the tires caught his attention. He bent down and examined them. Real tires. Not smooth or bald. But real, with deep grooves, and twice as wide as the original German equipment. He studied the gear axles and the shock struts and the larger plates against the axle housings. He looked at the other men. "How the hell did you manage all this?"

"Pure genius," Vance said. He jerked a thumb at Lew. "All his. Those are C-46 wheels you're looking at. Just about indestructible. Lew machined axle extensions to hold the wider wheel assembly and cross-braced the extensions with eight bolts on each side. As strong as it was before, it's stronger now."

"She'll take a side load of fifty thousand pounds, maybe twice that much," Lew added, "but before you'd ever reach that force, that indestructible tire the admiral is talking about would be burning its way off this machine." He pursed his lips and scratched his chin. "She'd still handle. In fact, you could take this thing off on its rims if you had to. We used chromeloy steel for those backing plates and they'll hold up the *Queen Mary*, they will."

"But the best part," Vance added with a quiet smile, "are the brakes."

"You mean you fixed them?" Shag smiled himself. "That even I find hard to believe."

"Fixed, my arse!" Lew exclaimed. "We took some C-46 housings and assemblies, sliced those little beauties in half, and put each half on each wheel, and this here baby," he thumped the tire solidly, "will stop so fast you'll be hauling the yoke into your fat gut to keep from nosing over."

Then there were the engines. A job of pure mechanical genius. Shag had been right in his original idea. The Pratt & Whitney R1340 had the same mounting dimensions as the R1690 the Germans built under license as the BMW 132E, and the engines they'd bought for the Ju-52 fit onto the old mounts perfectly. He studied the mounting system and was truly impressed.

"Where'd you get the engines?"

"That outfit in Miami cracked up a Mallard. Two engines came from that wreck and we bought one more with a cowl. These are all Mallard cowls we cut to size for this installation." Lew tapped a knuckle on a propeller blade. "Hear that sound, laddie? Beautiful! That blade is an AG-100D, right from a sprayer. Fat paddle blade, it is, and it makes the engine work like it had half again as much power going for it. If you recall, your worship, this is an organization known as Dillard Sprayers, right? What could be more normal than to buy the same engines and propellers most of the people in this business either use or want to have for their equipment? And you now have constant-speed props, I might add, and not without well-deserved praise for meself and me darlin' crew of lovely cutthroats."

In the center of the underside of the fuselage were two powerful lights, adapted from the landing lights of a Cessna 421. "Taxi lights," Vance said. "Remember the landing light in the flush mount under the left wing? It works now; hand crank in the cockpit. We adapted a Learjet landing light in there. You can see a mile with it. And if you'll ever need them, there are position lights and strobes all around the bird."

They continued around the right wing, along the right fuselage. "The cargo doors work now. Two pins on the outside and one on the inside and they opens like a big bloody clam, they do," Lew said. "Original design and clever. Built-in stanchions to hold the bottom half of the door, wire hooks on top. You can move engines, heavy equipment, anything into the airplane this way."

Around to the tail; Shag stopped for a close look at the tailgear system. "You know what tire you're looking at?" Vance asked. "We were worried about adapting an American tire to that German rim. Turns out the main gear tire from the Aztec is exactly the same size as the original German tailwheel tire and tube. We just put it on."

"The tailwheel lock system works, too," Lew added.

They climbed up the ladder into the cabin. "Just hold it right there, if your magnificence don't mind," Lew stopped Shag. "Admiral, would you do the honors, please?"

Vance went ahead into the cockpit and flipped a toggle switch. "Battery power on," he called to Lew, who worked another switch by the cabin-door entrance. The cabin lit up with flush-mounted lights in the overhead.

"Come back this way first," Lew pressed. He opened the door to the toilet, and Shag almost laughed when he saw the chemical john from a motor home, a neatly framed picture of Adolf Hitler on the upraised seat.

"You can't even take a piss back here without paying your respects to Shicklegruber," Vance said. "Compliments of one Wolfgang Siedel."

They had internal lighting all the way to the back turret and also wires for an intercom system, which meant the man all the way in the back no longer had to play blind guessing games about what might be happening up front. They walked up the cabin. "New flooring beneath us," Vance said. "Three-quarter-inch marine plywood, and we put the carpet on top of that for better grip. Every window's been replaced on each side of the cabin. We used auto safety glass and just cut it to size. It was remarkably easy to handle."

They stopped by the front cabin door leading to the right wing, where Shag looked at something entirely new. The men had rigged a complete electrical panel with monitors, electrical-flow controls, and multiple rows of circuit breakers in the form of toggle switches. "This is Lew's baby," Vance announced.

"It worked out fine. Old DC-3 panel that we cleaned up and modified. All new wiring through the entire aircraft. Each engine has a generator—I mean, each wing engine, of course. Also a vacuum pump in each engine on the wings, and if you lose either wing engine or the generator itself, the other one can handle the full load for the aircraft. Also, if we lose it all, we still have the batteries to rely on. They work. Would you believe those little darlings are Sears Die Hards? Set them up in series, so that no matter where we are we can put in any twelve-volt batteries and be ready to go. Now, put yourself in the left seat."

You always get serious in the front office. They had kept most of the instruments stolen, bought, or given them on the way up from Peru and bought whatever else they needed. They had the works. Three of everything for oil pressure and temp, fuel pressure, carburetor air temp, cylinder-head temp, manifold pressure, rpm—everything. There were also two VOR heads in the cockpit, a digital ADF, a DME, and Shag noticed the VOR heads were set up for localizer and glideslope, and there they were. A jury-rigged box between the two pilot seats with two beautiful, miniaturized transceivers, and a three-marker beacon, and a switching panel.

"Jesus, we can go the whole instrument route in this thing," Shag said with admiration.

"We got Clark headsets," Vance said. "Two for the cockpit, one for the turret, and one for someone working the cabin. The back sets have boom mikes, but we figured they wouldn't work in the noise environment of this cockpit, and the best noise-canceling stuff in the industry are Shure mikes. See these little red buttons here on the yokes? Press them down first, then depress the hand mike and you're on intercom only."

"You mean no screaming up here from now on?"

"Not unless you get nostalgic," Vance said with a satisfying smile.

"And no more beating ourselves to death with that bloody wobble pump," Lew added. "We've still got it but we don't need it except for emergencies. We put a DC-6 pump in a belly hatch, so all you need to do now to start these babies is go to start position for fuel flow, turn on your pump, watch the pressure dial there, crack the throttle, and hit those toggles. Primer, boosters, and starter all under your lovely little fingers, then back with fuel flow into running position and that's it. The days of the Chinese fire drill are behind us."

"Speaking of fire drills, do we have an extinguisher system?"

"No way to do it, Shag," Lew answered. "It would take too much time. What I did was put some thick metal as a firewall aft of each engine. Figured we'd save a lot of time and weight that way. We know she flew well on two of the old engines. She'll do a lot better with these Pratts going for her. You get a fire, you shut down; and that's all there is to it."

Shag sat in the cockpit for an hour, going over everything. The parking brake, the new pedals beneath his feet, the new vacuum gauges and hydraulic pressure gauges. He tried the big trim wheel with the flap knob in the up position and then down. They'd done a great job with the system. It still took a lot of muscle but that was the case when Annie was spanking new. He looked at new windshield glass before him. They'd even eliminated a lot of the old vision-interfering posts and supports.

"What do you think she'll do?" he asked the others.

"These engines cruise best at about nineteen hundred for rpm and anywhere from twenty-five to twenty-eight for manifold pressure," Vance said. "You can cut them back from that but these engines are S1H1 models. I've flown them before and they operate smooth on those settings. Oh, by the way, we eliminated the autorich system and went to straight manual. Full down is rich and you pull 'em up to full lean. The prop controls are here on the quadrant. Standard operation. And you'll notice the old overboost? It still works. These engines turn out thirty-six inches and twenty-two fifty for normal takeoff, but you can overboost them to forty-two inches without hurting them if we need the power on takeoff. Also, of course, we'll pull full manifold all the way up by going through the boost gate if we need to."

Vance leaned back. "We figure she should indicate about a hundred and twenty at basic cruise power. At seven thousand that'll true out to one thirty to one forty and if you want more speed she'll do a hundred and fifty in high cruise. Everything else we'll find out when we fly."

Shag looked around him again. "Gentlemen—and I mean this—I salute you. Annie is one gorgeous son of a bitch."

Three hands clasped in cockpit center.

21

"Okay, let's get down to cases." Shag sat at the head of a table in their meeting room, all business, the fun and games pushed aside. This was the first major active step in his operation and he would keep it low-key but it was critical—as was everything else in this entire scene.

"Vance, you first," Shag said. "You've been keeping tabs on UFO activity, right?"

The others looked up in astonishment at Jordan's words, and felt even greater surprise when Vance nodded. "By God," Crouse-Hinds muttered, "they're bloody well serious about these mucking UFO's!"

Lew cracked an elbow into his ribs. "Clam up," he said sharply.

"I've kept a graph on it," Vance said. "It's the usual crap, but there's been one item that's significant. Not because the report is worth a tinker's damn, but because it's been getting so much attention. You haven't been following the television and newspaper stories. They're apeshit. A lot of people in Louisiana have been seeing strange things in the sky. They see more of them on weekend nights when they're gashed out of their skulls. Must be something about bourbon or swampwater that does it. Anyway, there've been hundreds of reports, and then the story broke about one man in particular who claimed he was picked up by a UFO. You know, forced to go aboard. A strange beam held him in its grip and drew him into this big goddamn saucer hovering over his fields. He's come up with a real lulu." Vance grinned. "He said the aliens forced him to screw a couple of their females, who never took off their helmets and visors so he really couldn't see their faces. Anyway, he had this amazing stiff pecker that had powers he'd never known before and he serviced about six of these alien broads, and after that they dumped his ass out into a swamp, and he's supposed to have radioactive burns all over his dork. The best part of it is that some old millionaire who's staggering around on a cane offered our hero a cool million if he'd tell him the secret of keeping his tool up for so long."

The men laughed. "I'll bet he had nothing to sell," Wolfgang said.

"Okay, okay, just hold it down," Shag said, his expression serious. He turned back to Vance. "Is this kind of story all around this state as well?"

"It is. Big news. A lot of it is kook stuff, but it's been driving the authorities crazy. Everybody is seeing things in the sky."

"Just what we need," Shag commented. He opened a flat attaché case, withdrew a folder and smoothed out a newspaper clipping. "You seen this?" He passed it to Vance, discussed its contents with the others. "It's a story about a shot tonight from Cape Canaveral. Or the space center that NASA runs up there. They sort of trade off with the air force. Anyway, what matters to us is that tonight they're firing a ship to Mars. Big Titan booster with a Centaur on top. It's going sometime after midnight, and we can keep tabs on the countdown by radio, or we can talk with Patrick radar on one-eighteen-four. A lot of planes go up at night to watch these things and that's common practice."

Phil Bergellini was waving for attention until Shag looked at him. "Hey, maybe I'm crazy, but what this all about? So someone spend a lot of money to send a ship to Mars? So what? What the hell do we care?"

"It's time to make our first acid test under a solid radar environment," Shag replied. "I'm taking up the Ju tonight for her first test flight, but that ought to be as exciting, in terms of the unexpected, as last week's breakfast. I need to confirm a few things by flying her up to the Cape. I'll want Vance in the right seat with me, and Pam and Bronstein will go along. Just the four of us; that's all we need. Lew won't be along. He's got a job to do somewhere else."

Frank Bemis shook his head slowly. "You always have a reason, Shag. I know that. But flying up to the Cape during a night shot to Mars? That is pretty wild, it seems to me."

"Just shows you don't really appreciate science, I guess," Shag said, his face straight, leaving the men more confused than ever. "Look, you other people run the operation here. I'm going to take off at about 11:30 tonight. We may want one of the Stearmans up to fly around in flat pitch and jazzing the engine, using all its lights, and generally making a lot of sloppy noise. No one will see the Ju-52, so it's as good as being invisible."

"They'll damned well see you on radar," Crouse-Hinds said unhappily.

"You're wrong," Shag told him. "That's the whole point. I need a major UFO incident tonight, and this is the perfect time for us to make sure one takes place. We're also flying the airplane to check out her performance and find out the numbers we need to work with. You figure out who takes up the Stearman and the rest of you work the lights and maintain security down here." He closed the folder and snapped the attaché case shut. "I've got some work to do. Talk to Brady if you've got any questions. Lew, I want to see you alone for a few minutes. You wait here. Pam, you too."

The men filed out, crowding around Vance with questions and comments on the madness they'd heard in the meeting. Shag had already dismissed from his mind anything they had to say; everything would fall into place at the right time. The room was empty except for the three of them.

"How's the deal in Miami?" Shag didn't waste any time on preliminaries with Lew.

Lew leaned back in his chair and sighed. "It's on. If we really want to go ahead with it, that is. Our contacts are willing to take a cut for supplying the information, but goddamn, Shag, you know how I feel about playing with this stuff." He looked unhappy. "It's worse than nitro."

"Coke doesn't blow up in your face," Shag reminded him.

"It blows up in too many other ways," Lew muttered.

Pam leaned forward, her hand on Shag's arm. "You're not dealing or running that sort of stuff, are you?"

He patted her hand. "No way. That's not my bag, love." He turned back to Lew. "You get your ass down there and handle it personally. Get it all, every scrap of information. Then come right back here. We can't afford to pass this up, Lew. The till's starting to echo it's so empty."

"I still don't—"

"I didn't ask you to approve it, man. Just do it."

The cockpit glowed in the red lights from the panel instruments, on gauges and pointers to their left and right, between them and up behind them on the bulkhead. Shag had sat in this same seat for an hour now, reading down the checklist worked up by Lew and Vance. One complete review set it all up in his mind, two complete reviews made it familiar, and by the third time, which would be bringing the airplane to life, it would be the beginning of habit. He handed the checklist to Vance and told him to call it off. Behind them now were the preflight and cockpit checklists. Master switches were off, seats positioned and belts fastened, full control movement visual confirmation, rudder bungees to neutral, visual check for flap movement and the knob back to trim position, trim set for takeoff, clock set, tailwheel down and unlocked, friction knobs loose, brake pressure rechecked and brakes locked, fuel selector to both, three indices up for carb heat cold, prop controls full back, fuel-flow levers full forward, throttles full back, mixtures full up to lean, fuel pump off, switches for primer-booster-starter off, starter selector off, ring quadrant down and off, three mags down and off, spark advance—he laughed—disconnected, all avionics off, generator switches down and off, circuit-breaker panel confirmation okay. That was it. Ready to go. Pam was in a cabin seat and Sam Bronstein stood behind and between the two pilots, watching every move, not saying a word.

It was unbelievable, Shag mused. It didn't seem possible this was the same battered giant they had flown on their harrowing journey up from South America, through the Central American countries and across the Gulf of Mexico and that wild storm; the airplanes truly were the same but this was something new, the phoenix arisen, and he could feel it, could sense it.

Windows open, props clear, fire guards ready.
Go.
External lights all off.
Off.
Belts?
Okay.
Bulkhead master up to on.
Battery power on and voltmeter showing twenty-five.
Quadrant master up to on, CAT and CHT number-three positions.
Go.
Three mags down to off.
Go.
Okay, now, number-three prop full back, number-three fuel-flow selector to start, number-three mixture down to full rich and number-three throttle cracked.
Confirmed, and fuel pump coming on.
The green light snapped on and the pump in the belly wound up and growled as fuel flowed through the lines.
You got four, okay, now five pounds. Go.
Start selector to number-three position and the light is confirmed. Clear number three.
Three prop clear to start.

Shag's right hand worked four spring-loaded toggle switches on the quadrant; primer, booster, and two starter switches. The moment he closed them the right propeller jerked around, thick white smoke crawled and then boiled through the overwing exhaust stacks. Shag let her turn five times and then pulled up on the number-three mag and just like *that*, she was turning over. He released the toggle switches, felt the throttle, and listened to the sounds, let the prop wind up to 800 rpm.

Fuel flow to running.

Okay. Manifold pressure okay, rpm holding, oil temp okay, watch the CAT and CHT, and the oil pressure is coming up nicely.

And on the eighth day God created the radial engine—

Don't you know it. She sings, don't she? Okay, fuel pressure holding and we've got forty pounds on oil pressure, and give me number-three prop full forward.

You got it.

They watched the oil pressure rising on the gauge and then the oil began to move from the tank up into the prop system and the sound outside the window changed from a steady coughing rumble to a finer, swifter, more razorlike thunder as the propeller blades went into fine pitch.

Setting rpm at eleven hundred.

Very good. Number-three generator, bottom switch, up to on. You got an indication?

Roger that. Generator's on the line.

Let's recheck all gauges.

In the green, sweetheart.

Okay, on to number two.

Three minutes later all engines sang their honeyed

sweet-coughing-rumbling thunder. Every gauge was right on the money. She felt absolutely marvelous.

VOR's on and dial in West Palm.

Got it.

Transponder standby.

Roger.

Comms to—what are we using?

We'll work West Palm.

We leave all lights off. No advertising.

Roger.

Set altimeters, horizons, turn and banks okay, DG's okay, overboost free movement and locked back, electrical panel check okay.

Go. Check your trim again.

It's right on. Let's do the runup here. Brakes locked. You take the yoke.

Okay. Yoke full back. She's all yours. Fuel selector on both, fuel pump off.

Here we go. Throttle to 2000 rpm. Good; nice and steady. Mag check left, now right, max drop is fifty. Beautiful. Okay, three times back to exercise the prop. That response is right on the money.

Everything's in the green for number three. Go for two.

Like a Swiss watch. Now, one. Damn, but she sings! I'll ease her up here. Whooee! but those are brakes, all right. Okay, lined up. Tailwheel lock, okay. Let's tighten the prop friction, please.

You got it.

You ready?

Let 'er rip.

Sam, Pam all set? Okay, let's see what she's got to offer.

* * *

Shag held the yoke full back, eased the throttles forward as he stood on the brakes, got full power, and Annie howled like a mad demon, props spinning at 2250 rpm and the manifold pressure pegged at 36 inches and there was more there if they needed it. He popped the brakes and the Ju-52 rushed forward, a sudden, totally unexpected jolting acceleration. Shag let the torque from those big blades get just a bit ahead of him and he hit right rudder to correct it, walked the rudder pedals, and just as quickly as he lined her down the runway that tail was off the ground and she was rushing forward, riding between the dim lights. By his side, Vance called out the numbers.

"Jesus. I don't believe it. Fifty, sixty, through seventy, we're at eighty and—"

Annie eased into the night air without any movement on the yoke, her trim set perfectly so that at eighty miles an hour she literally flew herself off the ground. Shag climbed her straight ahead on the instruments before him, his whole world a quietly gleaming red light. The world was a black maw and it was strictly instrument flying for now, and he couldn't believe it as Annie slipped up to a hundred miles an hour and he kept coming back on the yoke to keep her no faster. At eight hundred feet he came back on the throttles to 32 inches and eased the props back to 2100 rpm, still holding that hundred miles an hour, and Annie went upstairs at a comfortable 700 feet per minute and he had never felt anything so sweet and solid in all his life. He left the throttles at that setting until they were pushing through four thousand feet and then for the hell of it he firewalled the props and the throttles and boosted those radials to forty inches and

Annie held her hundred miles an hour and climbed upward at better than a thousand feet a minute.

Shag grinned like a kid with a new toy, brought back the power to cruise at 28 inches and 1950 rpm, and Annie leveled off and gave them a true airspeed of over 155 miles an hour, which was better than she could have done before in a dive. Shag had a good horizon now with the east coast of Florida and all its lights and he clawed her around in tight turns and abrupt maneuvers and that damn airplane flew better than it had ever flown since the day it rolled through the factory doors at Dessau. They went to eight thousand feet and passed West Palm, they worked the VOR navigation needles to home in on Vero Beach and Melbourne beyond that, but they didn't need them because the night was splashed with stars and there wasn't a cloud and they could see a hundred miles in front of them, with the Florida coastline laid out like plush velvet with sparkling diamonds and rubies everywhere. Well ahead of them they could see the way the coastline extended out to the northeast and there was the space center. Sam eased from the cockpit, put his headphones on Pam, and sent her forward to stand between Shag and Vance.

"My God, it's so *beautiful*," she exclaimed, and Shag had to remind her that for them to hear her in that thundering boiler room of a cockpit she'd have to use the intercom. She pressed the button and spoke into the mike. "I never dreamed it could be like this up here. It's a fairyland." Orlando glowed into the night sky to their left and they saw the city lights of Melbourne and the coastal communities of Indialantic, Indian Harbour Beach, Satellite Beach, and the beacon from Patrick Air Force Base, and the beacons of Merritt Island Airport and then Ti-Co Airport, but it all paled before the stabbing beams of light sweeping upward from the launch pad just inside the beaches of the Cape.

They heard Sam on the intercom. "Twelve minutes to launch. I've got a local radio station."

"Great," Shag answered. "Give me a five-minute mark. I'll set her up to start our run at that time." He reached down and made certain the transponder was in the off position. Ground radar was used to pick up a transponder on a certain discrete code, which bounced back the radar signal on that frequency and pinpointed a plane's position in the sky. With the transponder off the only way they could be followed was by sweep radar sending out its beam which bounced back from metal and told the ground-radar controllers that an aircraft was where their radar echo indicated.

But not this baby, Shag thought with a smile. We're about to become a UFO . . .

He flew toward the Cape and they watched the great white shape looming from its launch pad, clouds of vapors streaming in the wind, rings of searchlights turning the vista before them into a scene from a science-fiction movie. And it might have been, for that great shape was going to send two ships to land on Mars.

"Five minutes," Sam announced.

"Good. We're going to do two big circles up here and that should start them freaking out in every radar room for fifty miles around." He eased the Ju-52 into a wide turn to the left, completed the turn, and heard Sam announce three minutes to go. Another turn for two minutes and he rolled out, headed straight for the pad. He came back on the power and held her in level flight at eighty miles an hour so that they were just about drifting through the sky as they came to the edge of the Cape, the great rocket brighter than ever. They saw the lights of the emergency helicopters the air force flew for every shot, and the blinking beacons and flashing strobes of other planes, and they were perilously close to the launch pad when everything vanished in an enormous, utterly silent blast of orange-yellow-white flame that raced across the earth in every direction and lit up the entire cockpit and glowed off the cowls and made a strobe effect through their props. The great Titan boosted skyward with incredible acceleration, the light spreading out through what seemed to be the entire world, and then it was at their own level, and all they could see was the silent screaming flame as the Titan tore upward into the waiting vacuum on the road to another world. Shag kept their speed to eighty and flew directly over the launch pad and then eased into a right turn to take them out over the ocean. He held his speed, just floating through the sky until he figured they were fifty miles out, and then he went forward on the power and put the nose down and they flat-assed it toward the ocean until they were barely three hundred feet over the water.

Which meant that on every radar scope that had been following that giant shape virtually hovering in the sky—that same giant shape just inexplicably and impossibly vanished. Shag cobbed the power and they were doing well over 160 miles an hour. He stayed out to sea until they were south of Stuart and there was open, almost deserted beach to their right, and then he swung into a steady turn and went even lower so that they crossed the coastline at no more than two hundred feet in a breathless rush across the coastal highways.

They came to the edge of the great lake and he blinked his landing light four times, the beam spearing straight down from beneath the wing. "There," Vance said. "Come right a bit." The dim yellow lights of their grass runway. Four thousand feet and a narrow strip in the dark wouldn't be the easiest and it was best to use the landing light until the wheels were down, but the crew was ready and waiting and they saw the flashing strobes of the Stearman stooging around and making a racket. Shag brought her in, rolled down forty degrees of flaps, and set her down like a feather on the main wheels, power off. He came back on the yoke as he went to the brakes and the airplane came to a halt in what he estimated was no more than fourteen hundred feet. He couldn't believe it, but it was real. This damn thing flew better than most of the STOL airplanes they were advertising as being the latest advance in aviation. They taxied to the hangar, shut her down after he swung her around, and the men pushed her into the hangar and shut the big doors to hide her from the world.

Lew Heath came back from Miami at 4:30 in the morning and woke him up. "It's on," he said.

"Good," Shag told him, and went back inside to Pam.

22

They crowded into the trailer bearing a cloud of cigarette and cigar smoke, sleepy-eyed, and draining cups of strong coffee. At seven o'clock the morning news came on and they heard a lot of schlock about taxes and wars in different parts of the world, barely paying attention until another set of commercials had passed across the screen and—

"Hold it," Shag ordered. "Here it comes." The newscaster described the launch of the Titan-Centaur with the Mars landers, rolled to a brief shot of the rocket hammering away from the launch pad, and then came back with what had been holding Shag in suspense.

"But the big news of last night's spectacular space shot," they heard, "wasn't the familiar sight of the Titan-Centaur lifting off, or even the news that the Rover vehicles that succeed the old Viking mission are on a perfect trajectory to the red planet. Instead, it's a UFO that has space scientists baffled. Just before liftoff of the Titan rocket, a huge shape materialized in the night sky near the Kennedy Space Center. It was tracked by radar from Orlando, the space center itself, and from Patrick Air Force Base. NASA denies that they know anything about any UFO in the area, but reliable sources indicate that a spacecraft well over a thousand feet in diameter was tracked not only near the launch pad, but directly over the space center itself, and then drifted out to sea and seemed to vanish without a trace. Normally a UFO story, one of many these past two weeks, wouldn't amount to much, but radar technicians are saying that NASA officials are deliberately misleading the public by lying about last night's spectacular radar tracking. Several pilots who were in the air at the same time report seeing a huge shape directly over them, and we are still receiving reports of a strange sound, like a giant electromagnet, that was heard by hundreds of people in the same area. Dr. J. Allen Hynek, famed astronomer and expert on UFO's, has declared that—"

Shag turned off the set and leaned back with a look of satisfaction on his face. "We did it," he said quietly. "By damn, we did it. Frank," he nodded to Bemis, "get to town as soon as you can and bring me whatever newspapers there are. You can take the Stearman to West Palm. You can pick up the Miami papers there. They may have some more details on this thing."

Crouse-Hinds banged a fist on the table. "Will somebody in this looney bin kindly tell me just what the hell we were supposed to have done last night? And what's all this camel dung about a UFO and just what could it possibly have to do with us?"

They looked expectantly at Shag. He sipped at his coffee, lit up a cigar, and began his explanation of radar and the effect upon a microwave beam of a corrugated metal surface. When he finished the trailer was absolutely silent. They were all busy digesting what they had heard, and the implications were slowly sinking in.

Crouse-Hinds leaned massive elbows on the table. When he spoke again it was quietly and with increased respect for Shag Jordan. "Then, this is what you've had in mind, all along, isn't it? All this crockery about a UFO that's got these people in an uproar. You've planned it from the very beginning. If we play our cards carefully, they'll never see us when we're up there, right?"

Wolfgang chuckled. "But they will see a monstrous shape in the sky. Ah, people," he sighed. "You bring to them just a hint of something and they are so quick to believe!"

They were all picking it up. Gaston Rademacher showed great crooked teeth with his smile. "You make Annie invisible, I think."

Shag nodded. "That's right. If you don't see a Ju-52 because you don't even know it exists and you do see something else, even if your senses are lying to you, then that something else is what's real."

Sam Bronstein studied them. "Very neat, Jordan. Very neat indeed. So neat that even with my own devious mind I didn't anticipate it. Now, that strange sound they reported. How'd you manage that?"

Shag shrugged. "Combination of things and all of them based on suggestion and that ever-growing urge to believe in UFO's. So when you reinforce it with radar reports and charges and shouts of lying, people tend to choose sides. They're already halfway there, yes or no, and all you do with an airplane no one can see—because in the dark it's invisible to the human eye and to radar it's a thousand-foot shape that simply can't be—is give them a sound that, combined with everything else, is totally different. You just change the rpm on the engines and you've got three propellers all turning at different speeds and no one has ever heard a Ju-52 before with those angled engines and the really peculiar sound it makes and—well, there it is."

Phil Bergellini slurped noisily at his coffee. "So we are invisible, then?"

"Almost," Shag answered. "Almost, but not quite, and the key is never to remain in one place long enough to give the opposition a chance to find out what you've been doing to them. The trick is to keep them off balance, to dazzle them with some real fancy footwork."

Vance had been listening quietly. "What's next, then?"

"We send two men out to the mining claim in New Mexico," Shag told them. "They also set up the schedule so that when we move the Ju-52 out west all our flying is done by night, fuel is waiting for us in isolated areas, and the plane is concealed by day. If we want to disappear in the night sky—"

Bronstein looked like the Cheshire cat from *Alice in Wonderland*. "I was wondering how you'd accomplish that, being a thousand feet wide, you know."

"It's simple," Shag answered. "When we want to be seen, it's how people see us that counts. So we turn on the transponder and we either squawk the VFR code on 1200 or anything control asks us to squawk. They know what they're talking to in the night? We could be a Cessna 310 or a DC-3 or a Piper Arrow for all they know. They say squawk, we squawk, and their radar gets a nice clean return on the scope. And we, as the Ju-52, simply are never there."

"Goddamn," Sam said quietly.

"Okay, let me wrap it up," Shag addressed the group. "We have two more jobs to do here and then we leave this place semiactive as a cover. But the two jobs are critical. One of them is a blind—"

"What?" Rademacher said hollowly.

"A blind. Decoy, ruse, sham—"

"Ah. A trick," the big man said, nodding his head.

"Exactly. Enough of a trick to set a lot of shit stirring in a lot of pots. We need more rumors, more grist for the mill, we need to mess up everybody's thinking so badly they'll all be squabbling among themselves and by the time they get around to locking that famous old barn door, we'll be long gone."

They thought his words over and then Wolfgang motioned for attention. "You spoke of two operations. Would you explain?"

"For now, only the first one. It's tonight."

"And the name of the game, guv'nor?" Crouse-Hinds asked.

"We attack Fort Lauderdale International Airport."

"Attack?"

"That's right."

"With what, for God's sake!"

"Machine guns, grenades, bombs, stuff like that."

"Oh. Stuff like that."

"That's right. But we really don't."

"We attack but we really don't?"

"You got it, sweetheart. That's the name of the game. Now, hold your questions for later, after we brief everybody. I'll need five people aboard the iron bird." Shag turned to Vance. "You got the weather for tonight?"

"It stinks. You had your good weather for flying your UFO patrol over the space center." Vance studied a notepad. "Tonight you've got low ceilings, showers, visibility standard at five to seven miles, down to one or two in the heavy stuff."

"Those ceilings. How low?"

"They're promising as low as eight hundred feet."

"Great. Made to order."

It wasn't the first time they'd judged Shag as having lost all his marbles, but since he'd always come through before, they kept counsel among themselves and listened intently to the briefing. When they left they were sharing grins and backslaps.

"West Palm? This is Miami Center."

"Go ahead, Miami."

"Hey, we're getting something crazy on the scope. Same thing we've seen a couple of times before, and—"

"You got that UFO again?"

"Yes, but don't pass it off so quickly. Look, we've got everything we have trained on that object, and whatever the hell it is, there's no doubt it's out there. Everything sends back the same pattern. It's a big mother. Over three hundred yards across."

"There's nothing that big in the sky, Miami."

"The hell there isn't."

"Jesus, we—holy shit, we're getting it now!"

"What's your scope readout?"

"Over . . . it's over a thousand feet across and it's barely moving and I don't believe it. You know what happened? We were working an Aztec and it disappeared, and—hold it, we've got a hot line here! That Aztec we were working? It was squawking 4047 and the pilot came into the line, sounded crazy, like he was incoherent or scared—"

"Did you say scared?"

"Scared shitless. Then he said something enormous was coming up on him and it was glowing a faint blue, and we heard a scream and the son-of-a-bitching airplane has disappeared! Like it's been swallowed up!"

"Well, that ought to keep them busy," Shag laughed into the microphone on intercom. Sam Bronstein was flying right seat tonight with him and he shook his head.

"Can't argue with you on that." They drilled steadily through the night sky at 85 miles per hour, holding the Ju-52 in a wallowing drone with ten degrees of flaps, giving the radar people fits with their drifting passage. They flew in thick clouds, bumping gently, the rain a bare whisper over the thunder of the three engines. After taking off from their duster strip, Shag had squawked VFR on his transponder, which alerted everybody within range of his signal, because the weather was strictly instrument flying, and then he called in to Vero Beach, picked up Miami Center on radio, and filed his flight plan. He identified himself as Aztec N6322P, got assigned his slot, and at 140 miles an hour worked the Ju-52 down the Florida peninsula, mixing in easily with the thin night air traffic. When radar had him pinpointed solidly he went into his act, his voice becoming higher and panicky as he reported an enormous blue glowing object overtaking the airplane until, at the exact moment, he screamed into the mike and switched off the transponder.

In the radar rooms the Aztec, represented by a solid glowing blip on the scopes, vanished. And in its place was that enormous unidentified flying object that had plagued the southeastern United States, its presence magnified enormously by rumor, fear, and plain old-fashioned hysteria. And right now, he knew, there was a monumental flap underway to find out just what the hell had happened to Aztec N6322P, and what in the name of God was that strange object they were now tracking on their scopes?

It was going perfectly. Their own navigating systems kept them precisely on course. Shag flew by instruments and those systems, working Palm Beach and then Fort Lauderdale, and he knew every radar along the route was aimed at them, which was precisely what he wanted. The wind was out of the south at twenty miles an hour at their altitude and that meant a ground speed of about sixty-five which made the whole affair even more ridiculous. The showers were broken now and every so often they even caught a glimpse of coastal lights through breaks in the clouds. It couldn't have been better.

He pressed his intercom button. "Everyone set?" They called back, Lew Heath in the aft turret, Wolfgang Siedel manning a socket-mounted machine gun through a side window, and Pam flat on her stomach in the cabin, peering down through number-two hatch with an open door before her. "Okay, team, here we go. Open up on my command and let it rip when I call it out."

He came back on the flaps and cleaned up the wings, advanced the throttles. He listened in on the tower at Fort Lauderdale International, knew the active runway, surface conditions, and what planes would be in the pattern so he could time his approach perfectly without interference from any traffic. The Ju-52 was going down in a long steady powered glide, almost a dive, indicating over 190, banked over steeply and plunging for the ground, flashing in and out of clouds and whipping through the rainshowers. Then he was flying the glideslope so he would come down through the broken cloud deck that covered the earth at eight hundred feet, and the field appeared suddenly before him, approach lights flashing in the wet night, and he had the speed over 200.

"Get ready," he called out. He was almost standing on left rudder from their speed, and the Ju-52 punched and banged its way through mild turbulence and then they were almost onto the runway. The approach lights flashed beneath them and Shag held the Ju-52 barely ten feet over the glistening runway. "*Now!*" he called into the mike, and immediately the Ju-52 bucked and rattled as Heath opened up directly at the control tower with the big machine gun, and Siedel blazed away from the opposite side with his machine gun, while Pam dropped a string of grenades through the belly of the speeding airplane. A series of blinding explosions ripped along the runway and then they were across the entire field, startled faces looking up, an airliner skidding wildly as its shocked pilots had the briefest glimpse of an impossible shape appearing briefly and then disappearing into the clouds.

23

"All right, hold it down! We've got enough trouble on our hands, what with Washington beating us all about the head and shoulders for answers we don't have, without you guys turning this thing into a dogfight." Hugh Harris, chief of the FBI office in Palm Beach, an office almost nobody outside the agency even knew existed, jerked angrily at his necktie. To hell with the book on how to work a meeting of this kind. There weren't any rules here and if the fucking director didn't like it then he could come down here and catch their goddamned ghost. Because that's what they were chasing. A ghost, a phantom that moved through the sky and defied all the laws of reality and science. The astrologers were out in full cry and the demonologists and UFOlogists and every other nut and kook was howling at the moon. It was a field day for the weirdos and God knows that this time they had some gasoline to throw onto the fire that burned all around Harris and threatened to engulf him.

The others hadn't fared much better. This entire affair was so ridiculous that even Jake Torbay had been ordered to attend the special meeting of top government officials in this area, and Torbay, who was one of the best CIA men Harris had ever met, didn't know whether to puke or tell his home office to get stuffed. Torbay was a tall, lean, powerful man who'd fought and killed enemy agents the world over, who was as deadly as a hundred armed men, who knew every waterfront and back alley of every rotten city in the world, and he had his face screwed up in a mixture of disbelief and anger that he was even here. His business had to do with whatever emanated from the Soviet Union, with espionage, murder, secret plots, war plans, with anything except half-baked stories of giant UFO's and mystery airplanes that appeared out of a time tunnel and ripped across a modern jet airport with machine guns and bombs blazing away and exploding, *never leaving so much as a scratch or a mark to prove their existence.*

Harris leaned back in his chair, stubbed out a cigarette, and then tore open his third pack of this meeting. He looked across the conference table in the private meeting room at Fort Lauderdale International Airport and studied the unruffled exterior of a portly, thick-haired, impeccably dressed man he knew for many years and disliked intensely. James Curtin had been with the State Department from time immemorial and the son of a bitch looked twenty years younger than his age. He used shoe polish, Harris mused, to darken what should have been a crop of white hair. He was urbane, smiling, and just about as dull a human being as ever walked the earth.

"Jim, just what the hell are you doing in this meeting?" Harris blurted out. The others turned to look at Curtin, and that meant not only Torbay from the

CIA, but also Bill Woodburn from Customs and Red Thompson from the Federal Aviation Administration. The only man who mattered here was Red, an old friend of Harris. He was a tough, wiry, freckled, nononsense pilot and federal investigator who wouldn't have been fazed by the headless horseman riding the back of the Loch Ness Monster.

"I'm here because I was ordered to attend this circus," Curtin replied after a deliberate pause. He examined his perfectly manicured nails. "All we're missing is someone from Narcotics. Then the three rings would be full and—"

"Why don't we just cut the shit and get to it," Red Thompson broke in. "All you've got to offer here is mouth, Curtin, and Torbay can't find any Communists under the rug, but at least he admits he's as bewildered as the rest of us. So if you can't contribute, stick your hands in your pockets and play with yourself."

Jim Curtin was dangerous, Harris knew, but he refused to interfere. Red was even more dangerous, but the man from State didn't know it. "Thompson," Curtin said softly, "you may be a very big frog but you're in a small pond, and when this is over I will—"

Red's hand shot out to grip Curtin's tie and he jerked the porcine figure hard against the table, twisting the tie so that Curtin found himself with the side of his face hard against wood and strangling for air. "Don't threaten me," Red said in a quiet, pleasant whisper. "Not now, not ever, not even in your dreams. This whole schlock affair goes on and on because you don't know what's happening and you need something for your report. You know how to spell my name?"

A gurgling sound came from Curtin.

"Good," Red told him, "because now you have something to do. Sit over there in the corner and write a complaint about me. At least you'll be quiet." He released his grip and turned his back to the gasping and shocked man from State.

"Hugh, run it past us again, but this is the last time. We either make a decision to recommend some action after this or we simply admit we're out in left field without the proverbial pot to piss in." Red Thompson stuck a slim dark cigar in his teeth and lit up. The smoke somehow managed to drift in Curtin's direction and bring on a strangled cough.

Harris nodded. "All right. First, the UFO. What the press has so delightfully called the Ghost of the Cape, or the Mars Rider, and the rest of it."

"To hell with what it's called," Bill Woodburn said. "What is it?"

"And what are you doing here?" Red demanded. "You going to ask them for their passports?"

Woodburn was unfazed. "Red, you catch those mothers and I'll do just that." Their mutual grins cut away the tension.

"Okay," Harris said impatiently. "We don't know what it is. You've all seen the radar reports, talked to the people on the scopes, listened to the experts. The experts say it's not possible and the working stiffs say the experts are dumb pricks and if they'd been in the radar rooms they'd be believers." He sighed and went on.

"So we narrow it down. The radar people are tracking something. I happen to know they're not full of crap. I know them, I trust them."

"Has anyone ever gotten a visual on this thing?" Torbay asked. "An unquestioned sighting with the old-fashioned eyeball?"

Harris shrugged. "We have a scream from an Aztec pilot who said he was being overtaken by—"

"Scratch that one," Red broke in. "What you really have," he said wearily, "is a voice on a radio and that's all you have. No one is missing any goddamned Aztec with the number of that plane. Okay?"

"Then how do you explain that one?" Harris demanded.

"I don't have to explain it," Red said patiently. "A voice on a radio isn't proof of a damn thing. Maybe the guy thought it was Halloween. How the hell do I know? I won't accept voices in the night—"

"It's on tape," Torbay reminded him.

"So was Richard Nixon," Red said scathingly. "Tape, shmape; it's all worthless. There's no proof of anything."

"What about the radar tracks?" Woodburn asked. "You said they were real. You still agree with Harris on that?"

"They're real, all right," Red told him, "but that doesn't mean we know what radar was tracking. Look, radar is a tool and it has certain limitations. One time the old early-warning radar we had up in Alaska bounced signals off the moon just coming over the horizon and the computers translated it as eighteen hundred missiles lifting over that horizon and we almost had a goddamned nuclear war. You either know definitely what radar shows you or it's all guesswork, so why the hell don't we just forget it until more evidence comes in?"

"We've got some," Torbay said quietly. "At least a series of reports that match exactly what was picked up last night. That same object or force field or whatever it was that can affect the air-traffic radars has its special signature. I've been checking down the line. It was seen in South America and Central America and a couple of months back it was picked up by military radar during a hurricane and—"

"And what?" Red demanded.

Torbay shrugged.

"How about last night?" Woodburn pressed. "What happened right here, dammit!"

This was closer to Harris's own specialty. "You tell me what we had last night," he threw back to Woodburn.

"You know as well as I do," Woodburn retorted.

"Sure I do," Harris said smoothly. "We've got zip, that's what we have. A black machine that showed up in almost the same area as that fruitcake UFO, that appears instantly out of thin air and flies down the main runway of this field—"

"Over a hundred people saw it!" Woodburn shouted.

"Saw it?" Harris sneered, hating himself for the cut but not able to stop it. "What did they see? A time traveler? A fucking bomber that snapped into this temporal time plane from a war a long time ago and machine-gunned both sides of the field and dropped bombs that blinded everybody, that poured machine-gun fire into the glass tower and didn't do any damage of any kind?"

"Maybe they got lousy aim," Torbay offered, smiling.

"Great," Harris told him. "No shell casings anywhere along the runway. No marks on the runway. No fragments of bombs. No damage to nothing. I'll say they got lousy aim. I don't believe the damned thing was ever here, that's what I believe."

"A lot of people saw it, heard it, felt the goddamned concussion wave from the explosions!" Woodburn was almost screaming at him.

Red Thompson waved his hand in the air. "All of you, Jesus Christ, are worse than a bunch of—I don't know what. That plane was here. That much is definite."

He earned a lot of hard stares as the others waited for him to continue. "It was here," repeated Red Thompson. "There's only one proof."

"Not that idiot photograph," Woodburn said.

Red shook his head. "No, we didn't luck out on that one. Somebody was fast enough with a camera to get one picture, but all it shows is a great white light on the film."

"Could that mean something?" Torbay asked.

"Sure it does," Red offered. "A great white light on the film and that's all it means."

"How about a spectrum check? Computer enhancement of the negative?" Torbay brought up the first lead he might be able to push.

"With a Polaroid?" Red asked.

"Forget it," Torbay said.

Harris studied Red Thompson. "You said it was here. How do you know?"

"We monitor this field for noise studies. Got microphones planted up and down the runway." Red was his old professional self again. "All the mikes are on recordings. Any sound over a certain level sets them off automatically. Every mike on the field was activated last night. I've already run a computer readout on the tapes." He paused to relight his cigar stub.

"Jesus, man, don't quit now," Woodburn urged.

"Whatever was here last night had piston engines. Propellers. Multi-engine; that's all the tapes can tell us. We did a Doppler shift on the sound. The speed was about two hundred miles an hour. It lifted abruptly and vanished just as quickly as it appeared."

Woodburn groaned. "Now we got sounds that appear out of nowhere and that disappear into nowhere. Oh, shit, I'm sorry, Red. I didn't mean to be cross. But you sure had me hoping we had a real handle on this thing."

Red sat up straight and glared at Woodburn. "Are you all so dense? I have just made a positive identification that an aircraft, class multi-engine, powered with piston engines, using propellers, flew down the main runway of this airport at approximately two hundred miles an hour, flying from west to east, and climbed out at the east end of the runway. If that isn't a handle, what the hell is it?"

Hugh Harris shook his head. "It's a recording, Red. That's all it is. A recording of some sounds and nothing else."

"Fuck you, G-man. You wanted your positive handle and I just gave it to you. There's not a doubt in the world about it."

"But it just disappeared? I mean, just like that," he snapped his fingers, "it disappeared?"

Red looked around the room. "Are you all complete assholes? Don't you even know how these DB systems work? The sound recording is activated automatically when the decibel level reaches a predetermined factor and it cuts off the same way. That's why you have what you call appearance and disappearance on an instant scale. If we increased the sensitivity we'd pick up a dog farting in the next county. What we do pick up is decibels, Doppler effects, and the like, and that's an acoustical signature that's just as good as any fingerprint."

Harris sighed. "Not for my office, it isn't."

Red stared at him. "What the hell are you talking

about? You use voice patterns for identification in court, for Christ's sake!"

"This is different. My office will reject it."

"Well, screw them, too. What you're asking for is something on a silver platter. Radar is a matter of complex electronics operating in a meteorological and electrical atmosphere that still baffles scientists, and you can't have your silver tray heaped with goodies just because you say so."

"Red, try to understand. Washington is getting all kinds of flak on this thing. Pilots are accusing the government of covering up and we're accusing the pilots of being crazy. The radar crews are so spooked they won't even talk to us anymore—"

"I don't blame them. With your crowd and the Curtin Raisers over there, and Torbay's people nosing around, you'd think that radar bunch—which, incidentally, can never get away from its job of trying to keep airliners from running into each other—you'd think they were the enemy or something. You stupid bastards came down on them hard. Harder than needed. You didn't even have to come down on them. You know what's going to happen pretty soon? They're going to give you all the big middle finger and tell you to run the goddamned air-traffic system, and right then and there about eighty percent of all passenger flying in this country comes to a dead halt. You're leaning on the wrong people and they're not going to take much more."

Jake Torbay leaned forward. "Okay, Red, I agree with you and so does Harris and I guess Woodburn does too, and that peckerhead from State doesn't matter. But Washington won't buy the story we can't tell them what's drifting around in the sky and making all our national defense systems as useless as tits on a boar. And we can't tell them that the myterious Flying Dutchman that popped in and out of time, or whatever the hell this crap is about temporal space, is *real*, because you cut a pretty tape recording. They won't buy it, Red."

Red Thompson got up and walked to the conference door. At the last moment, his hand on the knob, he turned around. "Okay, guys, I'll level with you. You want to know what it is up there?"

They waited in silence.

"It's a UFO. A real one. A big mother over a thousand feet in diameter. And it's Jewish."

They gaped at him, until Bill Woodburn from Customs found his voice. "How the hell are you going to prove a stupid statement like that!"

Red smiled, opened the door slowly, looked back over his shoulder. "I don't have to prove anything. You're demanding an answer? You got your answer. I say it's a giant Jewish UFO. That's your answer. Now we all know what it is. And when you prove me wrong, then we'll all know what the fucking thing is. Tell that to Washington."

He didn't bother to slam the door. What the hell was the use?

The swamp extended for miles southwest of Miami. The surrounding terrain was soggy with water, but certain pilots knew spots where the ground level had been raised and then hardened for a good load-bearing surface.

Exactly thirteen hours and twenty minutes after Red Thompson told his federal cohorts to get stuffed, Mel Baxter, the pilot of a twin-engined Beech 18, slid gracefully down from the night sky toward a barely visible blinking amber light. Several more lights came on and Baxter touched down gently on grass, let her roll and brought down the tail. The airplane stopped easily, and he turned her around and taxied back to where the amber light was now blinking in his direction. He couldn't see much beyond that light, but he knew the layout by heart, where the roads adjoined the special grass field, where they led, who would be waiting to take delivery of that very special cargo he carried . Baxter smiled. When he took off there'd be a half-million dollars in hard cash in this airplane to replace the cocaine he'd flown in, and he didn't care if he ever saw this worn-out piece of twin-engined crap ever again. He watched the lights signal him to cut engines and he leaned out the radials and felt the old Beech shudder as the props ground to a halt. He could see better now. Two vans to split the shipment and leave in two different directions, just as planned.

However, this wasn't your ordinary business deal and there were certain precautions that had to be taken. He lifted the sawed-off shotgun from its rack and let it rest in the slot he'd cut in the back of his seat. You couldn't see the gun but if he pulled those triggers there wasn't a thing in its way that would survive. Business insurance. The cabin door opened and he recognized the contact man. Davis held up three fingers in their own private signal, and Mel Baxter relaxed. "Let's get with it," he said tersely. Other men appeared and began moving containers from the plane to the two vans. It was done within five minutes, Davis brought in the bag with the half-million in cash, they shook hands and without another word separated. This was no time to jaw; they were vulnerable as hell in this isolated area if anyone knew they were here.

Baxter fired up the engines, didn't wait for checking mags or props. Everything was still hot and on the line and he swung the Twin Beech around, gave a fast glance at his trim, and started down the runway with the yoke back in his belly and the throttles full forward. All that took about five seconds, just enough time for a savage light to erupt in the air directly before his eyes. He had stroboscopic view of swamp through a propeller for an instant and then he couldn't see a thing and he thought about taking off anyway, holding the plane steady until he could see, but the decision was no longer his to make when a burst of machine-gun fire snapped a gear leg in two and the airplane fell onto one wing like a dying buffalo. Blinded by the flare, he was jerking up the mixtures to lean and killing switches. His vision just starting to return, he cursed his watering eyes. He grabbed the money bag and the shotgun and started for the door. He had just climbed outside the crazily tilted airplane when another blinding light—a searchlight this time—stabbed his already impaired vision. A voice came to him from an unseen body.

"Lift that piece and we'll cut you in half. Drop the bag and the piece right where you are, man, make a left turn where you stand, and head out into that open field and keep going. You turn around and you're dead. You got three seconds. One, two—"

Baxter was a survivor of many a drug run into the country and he knew above all else when it was time to quit. He also knew he'd been had. Those weren't feds out there and whoever they were they knew what they were doing. He opened his hands and the bag and shotgun dropped to the ground. He groped his way around the wing of the airplane and started across the grassy field.

And he did not turn around when a machine gun roared behind him and he heard a high thin scream.

They weren't shooting at him or he wouldn't be walking. Whoever they were, he was grateful for their own code. They could have snuffed his ass with a single finger squeeze. They didn't, and that meant they were in the same business, only tougher, smarter, and better organized.

"Okay, the fucker won't stop." Sam Bronstein studied the van racing away, ass-end whipping as the tires spun. "Take him out, Lew."

The Cuban driver behind the wheel of the van still accelerating away from the ambush cursed as the sky came brilliantly alive. He heard a great roaring sound from his left and gaped through the window as an enormous dark shape behind brilliant searchlight beams rushed alongside him. He only had time to know that what he was seeing was real, that he was looking at some ancient bombing plane from a part of history he hardly knew. Then a machine gun poured a long burst into the van, tore his body into erupting flesh and bone and spraying blood. The van snapped wildly to one side, rolled over and burst into roaring flames.

"Shit. There goes that load," Lew cursed from the aft turret as Shag pulled the Ju-52 around in a wicked turn. If that van burned like that then the coke shipment inside was gone. But the second van had smarter people. They were standing in front of their vehicle, clear and bright in the lights, hands held as high as they could go.

A voice called to them from the darkness. "You made the right move. If you want to stay alive you start out running across that field in front of you and don't stop to think. Move!"

The two men ran as fast as their legs could carry

them through the tall grass and across the spongy ground. They were well out into the darkness of the fields, already the objective of mosquitoes and other unseen assailants, when a dark shape thundered overhead. They turned, gaping, as a huge airplane settled to earth on the grass strip. In the headlights of their own van they saw a German bomber and steel-helmeted figures moving around.

"I don't believe it. I just don't believe it," one man kept repeating.

"Let's go, you crazy bastard," his friend hissed at him, just as frightened and bewildered, but more determined to stay alive. They ran.

Bronstein and Rademacher moved in from one side, Bergellini from the other. They'd already grabbed the bag with the money from where it lay on the ground alongside the crippled Beech. Now they unloaded half of the cocaine shipment from the second van, ran it over to the Ju-52 and tossed it aboard. They went back to the airplane and the van, tossed in jellied explosives with three-minute timers, and raced back to the waiting bomber. They were aboard in seconds and Shag was firewalling the throttles. He was climbing through a thousand feet when explosions ripped through the airplane and the van on the airstrip. Fire blazed wildly, sending long shadows across the swamp.

Near the shores of Lake Okeechobee, two old Stearmans circled the town and the crop duster airstrip, filling the sky with their thunder, drawing attention to their rotating beacons and flashing strobes. Beneath the canopy of noise and lights a dark shape settled to the ground and, minutes later, had disappeared within the great wooden hangar.

* * *

"Harris? This is Red Thompson. Okay, we've got it again. Southwest of Miami. Same radar return. Also some strange reports of bright flashing lights out in the swamp. A hundred people are already signing affidavits about flying saucers. Be here in five minutes and you've got a seat in my chopper. Oh, yes, bring that idiot Curtin with you. I want him along so he'll see for himself."

Eight minutes later a car bearing Hugh Harris and James Curtin screeched to a stop, and they ran for the waiting helicopter. Red Thompson took it into the air immediately and set off at full throttle for the area where lights, flying saucers, flames, and God knew what else had been reported. They saw it soon enough—the glow from several things burning on the ground.

"Well, this one is for real," Red told the others as he settled in for a landing by two police helicopters. There were already several police cars on the ground, their brilliant searchlights illuminating the area. Red and his passengers looked at the still-burning wreckage of two vehicles and what had been an airplane.

A deputy sheriff came up to them. "Only one body. From that van over there," he said, pointing. "But we've got clear tracks of some other people heading out across the grass, and one chopper's got two suspects."

Red nodded. "Sound like anything?"

The deputy shook his head. "Nothing that will stand up in court. No way to prove they were *here*."

"Did they say anything about what they might have seen tonight?"

The deputy laughed humorlessly. "They were out walking for their health. And that's *all* they would say. But the chopper pilot said he'd never seen anybody more scared to death than those two. He said they were still shaking."

Red Thompson turned to Harris and Curtin. "Okay, you got it all. Our friendly giant UFO on radar, a hell of a lot of activity, three piles of melted slag, one dead body, two people who were here but we can't hold, and a great big mystery about the rest. Tell you what," he added as he led them back to the helicopter. "I'd really enjoy reading copies of your reports. Because you just heard mine. You guys can tell them about that big UFO that runs on chicken soup."

24

He relaxed completely, and that was a tough thing for him to do. He hadn't realized that years had passed since he could enjoy the luxury of letting go completely, of placing complete trust in the two hands kneading his taut neck muscles. Pam had removed his shirt and ordered him face down on the thick mattress, and it took a while to lower his guard, but she had some oil that burned into his skin and to his surprise soothed the muscles beneath. Or maybe it was her fingers. He didn't know and he didn't care; the sound of the three engines in sync was a deep throb that moved through the body of the Ju-52, carrying with it the inevitable vibration of piston engines and flailing propellers, and it was sweet music. He turned his head to look back at her in the red light of the cabin.

"This thing is like a vibrating bed," he said. "I fell asleep for a few minutes."

Her hands never stopped working. He couldn't believe the way he kept falling more and more in love with Pam. He said nothing about it and she didn't ver-

balize her feelings, either, but every look and touch
said it for them. "You were asleep for an hour," she
corrected him.

He took that one in silence. An hour. An hour of
blessed and complete letting go. Jesus. He raised himself up on one elbow and then turned to a sitting position. She handed him his shirt. "It'll keep in the oil.
Put it on."

"Yes'm."

"Lean back against the bulkhead, there," she motioned. He did so and brought a cigar from his shirt
pocket, lit up, and sighed deeply. She was on her
knees, her body weight back, relaxed and as supple as
a cat. He still hadn't accepted that long blond hair
and that tawny shape; it all seemed just a shade beyond his reach. She reached into her bag and brought
out a flask. "Brandy. One long swallow. It completes
the treatment."

He sipped slowly instead. She watched every move
and he knew when he had enough because her hand
reached out for the flask. A short one for herself and
then she moved forward to the cockpit and passed the
flask to Lew and Vance at the controls. She came
back, paused by a side window, and looked out at the
ghostly flames of the wing engine exhausts. "It's un-
real. Up front, I mean. Looking out like that and
seeing a bowl of velvet with those glowing gems in different directions. You know, sometimes I can't tell
which ones are lights on the ground or stars in the
sky."

"Does it matter?"

She smiled and settled herself by him. She took one
of his feet into her lap and slowly worked oil into the
tough skin. "You'd give a water buffalo competition.
You don't need soap. Brillo would do better."

He grinned at her. "I'll give you two years to quit what you're doing."

"Shag, can I get heavy for a minute?"

She was like that, he'd come to understand. As if her mind worked on parallel tracks. She could be occupied completely with something or even engaged in animated conversation, but a part of her mind always seemed free to roam through some other open field of thought. It could have been her background. Though he never cared to meddle into her past, he was surprised to discover that she was extremely well educated (her education included a masters in business and accounting that she'd earned in Munich). It must have been a hell of a road to Vegas, he mused. But that was her business and he would never ask. She had come to some crossroads and, true to her fashion, she had decided the time had arrived to ask questions.

"I haven't got any secrets from you, baby," Shag answered. "Fire away." He inhaled deeply on the cigar. The Ju-52 rocked gently in the night air. Damn, he could stay like this forever.

"What do you think about that man we killed? The driver of that van?" Her eyes met his, held them.

"I would have preferred he stayed alive. Killing is easy, love. It's the not killing that's tough. If he had stopped—" He shrugged.

She nodded. "I know. The other three got away."

"They didn't get away, Pam."

"Sorry. I mean you let them get away." A long pause went by. "Do you think there'll be more of it?"

"Killing?"

"Uh huh."

"The world turns on killing, lady. That's the way the Man Upstairs made the rules. I don't fight if I can help it. I never start one."

"You just finish them," she said, and there was no malice or irony in her tone.

"If that's the way it has to be," he said, completely at ease with the conversation. "A lot of people have tried to plant roses over my ass. A good many of them are growing their own gardens. That's the way it goes."

"That gig we did at the airport; you know, Lauderdale? When we made that crazy run down the field."

He smiled. "Didn't hurt a soul."

"I know that. Remember me? I was dropping those grenades."

"Lew said you planted them right down the centerline." He grinned. "Remind me to get you some bombardier wings."

"Oh, hush. All I did was drop them through that hatch. Shag, I don't understand. I mean, I know about the machine guns and firing the blanks, but those grenades were something else. They were powerful enough to light up everything and even in the plane I could feel the blast waves from them. Why didn't they do any damage?"

He sat up straighter. "When you let those babies go they were a long ways from any structure. Most of the shock effect went into producing light. You do that through heat. What you felt was the detonating charge going off. Actually, the shock wave was scaled down. But if anyone looks into that flare when it goes, they're blinded for a couple of minutes or so, depending upon how far they are from the source. It confuses the hell out of everyone. Look at it this way. A lot of people saw us appear and then disappear. We're firing a couple of machine guns and they hear them and see the flames from the muzzles and the flare bombs going off and the roar of the engines and it's all happening much too fast for most people to figure it out."

"But there are people like you, Shag. They'd know."

"Sure," he agreed. "But first, how many of them are going to pound on government doors and volunteer as eyewitnesses? You know what happens to pilots and others like them who see strange things in vivid detail? They come down on them like the old proverbial ton of bricks. So everybody in the business has stepped back of the line. Shut up, don't volunteer, mind your business and screw 'em all but six, and save those mothers for pallbearers."

She laughed. "You have a quaint way of saying things. Like a rhino walking delicately among tulip beds."

"Never mind the bouquets. Stick with me. Look, good eyewitnesses are what I was after. The people who saw this iron boat coming down that runway saw it from different angles. That means they all saw different things. If they're pushed, they'll answer questions, but the answers from other people with the same qualifications won't come out the same. Now you add that to the people who are confused and believe what they saw was real—well, its the old find-the-pea-under-the-shell game, because finally you don't know who the hell to believe. Take those times when we turned off the transponders and we've been giving them the old razzle-dazzle with the UFO bit. Other planes were in the air, seen from different angles and distances by a lot of people. They call newspapers and congressmen and the police and by the time it's all over no one knows what the hell has gone on. Finally the bigdomes up in Washington, who every day face their own problems of running a country and a world, get sick and tired of it. Machine guns, you say? Bombs? Attacking an international airfield? And nothing was hit and nobody was hurt and the airplane vanished into thin air? You know what happens next, hon? They order everybody involved to mind their own business and to drop the case. Which is just what we need. By the time some of the smart cats begin to fit all the pieces together we're long gone and the smart info on us goes down the drain."

She spent several minutes in silence. "What about that cocaine?"

"What about it? It was worth a quarter mil. We sold it to the Cuban underground for a hundred grand. They'll sell it for a clean profit of a hundred and fifty thou, which means they'll have that much more bread to run their operation. That's why they gave Lew the information for us to get the drop on those guys in the swamp. Hell, we didn't run the stuff. I've never run any of it and I never will. I'm not moralizing, either. It's tough to clamp down on guys running coke and give your blessings to the next crowd that's running napalm."

"I never thought of it that way."

He sighed and relit his cigar. "It hasn't changed since the time of the Romans. Kill a man and it's murder. Put on a uniform and take an oath and kill a thousand and get a medal. It's never the killing. It's the why of the killing."

"You said we might have some more—you know, we might have to do some, uh—"

"Jesus, Pam, don't get squeamish now."

She shook her head, angry with herself. "I'm not. You say to pull the trigger and unless I have a good reason not to, I will. Because I've never believed you to be someone who likes it."

"I don't," he said, and his voice was flat and hard.

Again the silence, the muted engine thunder rolling

over them and the airplane swaying gently. "Do you really want the money that badly, Shag? The big one, as you call it?"

He caught her by surprise. "Nope."

"Nope? Then . . . all this, what's it—"

"Challenge, maybe. Or perhaps I've accepted what I've inevitably come to know as the only real and fast way to get to the top of the heap. The armpits smell bad when they're crowded. Up on top you got room to breathe. But it's not just the money. Hell, baby, nothing in this world is more easy come, easy go than the green. Maybe all this is a reason for living. Maybe it's the odds. It's there, I'm here, and I've been clawing my way up." He seemed to look off into the distance, somewhere back in his memory, then snapped himself back to the present. "You know I played it strictly by their rules before."

"I know," she said, reaching out her hand to touch his.

"So now we play it by my rules. It's still the same old monopoly game, except maybe we're loading the dice in our favor, and—"

She motioned. "It's Lew. He wants you."

Shag climbed to his feet, leaned over and kissed her. "Catch me next time around for the flight under the stars." He smiled warmly. "I liked this session. Amazing how much you learn about yourself."

And myself, she thought.

Lew left the cockpit and Shag climbed into the left seat. Vance leaned over with a Florida chart folded to show the panhandle area near Tallahassee. "Here," he said, tapping the chart. "Just north of the coast. It's directly between these towns of Sumatra and Sopchoppy. We pick up New River and follow it south until we get a homing signal from the ground. There's an old duster strip there, a lot of high pine trees around the swamp. It's all set."

Shag studied the chart, looked out on the night world, saw the glow of Tallahassee to the north and eased the Ju-52 on a more westerly course. They had a half-moon and that would pick up a good reflection off New River. Johnny Crouse-Hinds had flown their Cherokee ahead of them, and Phil Bergellini and Frank Bemis had gone on the day before in the truck with fuel and supplies. Shag judged them to be about twenty miles from their destination when the homing light flashed on the panel. "They're ready and waiting," he said to Vance. He started down from their cruising altitude. They had to time it just right now.

"There. I've got him," Vance said suddenly. "Two o'clock low my position."

Shag rolled into a steep bank, saw the flashing strobes of the Cherokee flying low, far beneath them. Vance had one radio set on the frequency of 123.45. "Red Bandit, this is Ironsides. We got visual on you. Go ahead and do your routine."

"Roger that," came the voice from the Cherokee. Johnny was good at this. He had a job to do—to get attention to the Cherokee—and he winged off to the northwest toward a nearby town.

Still lower they caught the blinking lights on the otherwise completely dark strip, and then the bright beams of the truck went on to illuminate the flat grass waiting for them. Shag brought her in nice and easy, watched the truck turning, and followed its taillights until he inched his way beneath high trees. He steered the big airplane into a copse of trees and shut her down. They went to work immediately, hanging camouflage netting from the trees, draping it over the airplane, and then cutting down bushes and branches to add to the netting. Forty minutes later the Ju-52 was invisible.

But they could expect company. Engine sounds from the sky at night signaled to the law that a drug run could be underway and it was time to play the old shell game again. In a few minutes they heard an engine overhead, sputtering and coughing badly. Frank took the truck back to the strip and turned on his lights to guide Johnny in. They parked the Cherokee in the open, released the engine cowls, and opened her for inspection. A few deft maneuvers under a flashlight and a frayed fuel line appeared in the engine. Johnny, Frank Bemis, and Phil Bergellini stayed with the Cherokee and in a few minutes had a good campfire going. The truck vanished beneath the camouflage netting along with the Ju-52.

Shag, Vance, Pam, and Lew remained in the big airplane, hidden from sight and with machine guns hot and at the ready. It took less than thirty minutes for them to spot the headlights winding along the narrow road that cut the swamp, and they didn't need a close-up look to know it was a county sheriff on his way to check out the plane with engine troubles that a lot of people had reported.

The sheriff's car pulled up. This was a smart one. He was on his radio calling in and they knew other lawmen would be standing by for a callback. He also held a riot gun loosely in one hand, but it was only a second away from being used. They didn't wait for him to approach. Johnny walked out before the headlights, as brilliantly illuminated up as he could be, waving.

"Hi!"

The sheriff stood out of the light, watching everything, judging the airplane with the open engine cowl. "How many of you are there?" he called.

"Three! We got a busted fuel line and we lucked out with this strip here. We got it fixed but we figured we'd better wait for daylight before trying to take off. Say, can you make a radio call for us?"

They still couldn't see his face. "What's your need?"

"We're on a flight plan and unless we get word to some FAA station they'll have a whole search effort started for us. I guess the nearest one is Tallahassee. Say, I can't see you. Can I step out of the light?"

They knew the magic words were *flight plan*. No one trying to slip his way through isolated country was going to draw attention to himself by filing an easily checked flight plan.

"Sure. Come on over to the car," the sheriff called back.

Johnny went up to him grinning from ear to ear. "Damned glad to see you, Sheriff." He extended his hand. "Barton's my name. Chris Barton. We're out of Savannah and we were on our way to Pensacola. Could you get a call through to your station so they can pass on the word to the FAA that we're down but okay?"

The deputy made the radio call, waited for an answer to come back, and it did—precisely as they'd planned. There was an official record of the flight, and everything was as clean and up front as it could be.

"You sure you people are okay?" The deputy stood with them by their fire, as friendly as a pup getting a back scratch. Johnny took a swig from a bottle. "Fine, just fine. We got sandwiches with us and enough to drink us to sleep. We sure appreciate your helping us out. Those guys in the FAA get nervous when you don't close a flight plan, you know."

Of course, the sheriff didn't know that the flight plan had been filed by long-distance telephone, and that all the FAA knew was that a voice was on the other end of their telephone giving them the details of the aircraft, the number of people aboard, and their planned route. And everything matched perfectly.

There's nothing like having the federal government provide your cover for you.

The Cherokee left shortly after daybreak and went on to the next field, well into Texas, where Rademacher and Siedel were waiting with another truck and fuel and oil for the Ju-52. The day passed quietly in the swamp strip in north Florida. Darkness came, the poles and camouflage netting were removed, and the truck towed the big airplane free of the trees. Ten minutes later it was in the air and on its way to the remote desert strip in Texas where a similar rendezvous took place. This time the Ju-52 vanished beneath brown-and-tan netting and a lot of sand dumped along its edges, and the Cherokee and the truck remained in the open with tents pitched nearby. The day went without anyone coming within fifty miles of them, and that night they were in the air again. They landed in open country where fuel had been cached for them, loaded up, took off at once and landed again before dawn. No one was looking for them and their only need was to keep the Ju-52 from being seen by anyone, which was easy enough in the vast expanse of the desert country.

Their final landing would see them at their mining claim in New Mexico, but they had one last hurdle—a stretch of mountain country where they couldn't leave the airplane on the ground for a long period of time and there were no refueling facilities. Detailed planning paid off. Two weeks before they had bought an old DC-3 with long-range tanks. Crouse-Hinds and Bronstein flew to the field where the DC-3 was waiting, parked and tied the Cherokee down, and took off in the twin-engine Douglas. They landed on a mountaintop strip in West Texas, set up their blinking lights, and watched the Ju-52 slide in from the night sky. Hoses ran from the wing tanks of the DC-3 to the Ju-52, a portable generator began pumping, and an hour later the German airplane was refueled and on its way again. The DC-3 took off and landed at a major airport to refuel, then left again—as obvious to the world as if they'd carried neon signs.

Which, in a way, they did—with the words CLASSIC MINING in big, bright red letters along the fuselage and tail of the DC-3. They paid for their fuel by credit card, filed flight plans with the FAA, and did everything but tap-dance to attract attention.

At six o'clock the next morning the DC-3 came in for a dusty landing on the hard-ground airstrip of the Classic Mining facilities in New Mexico. Smoke drifted gently from an old bunkhouse, and lights gleamed through its windows. Crouse-Hinds swung the DC-3 around by the bunkhouse and shut down the engines. On the ground to meet the airplane were Shag, Pam, Vance, and Lew. There wasn't a single large building in sight.

And the Ju-52 had vanished once again.

25

Their world could have been on the moon. If someone had set up a mining camp on that distant chunk of lifeless rock it couldn't have been more isolated than the Classic Mining camp in New Mexico. Even the scorpions were scarce, and they never saw a snake and would have gladly fed any coyote stupid enough to shamble his way into their area. But coyotes aren't dumb so they stayed far away. The wind screamed down from a distant mountain and filled the air with a fine, invisible grit that clogged their nostrils and coated their bodies, and the humidity was so low they had to make a special trip to Fence Creek to buy a carton of Chapsticks so their lips wouldn't crack wide open and bleed. No cactus. Some scrub brush and all of it looked dead. There were two kinds of birds in the sky. Distant vultures on their way to some scavenging feast and the occasional metal craft that winged overhead; at night, when the jetliners passed over them at thirty to forty thousand feet, the sound reached into all their souls, for they were all pilots, except Pam, and she was a pilot's girl, which is just about as good, and when they heard that thunder whispering down from the highest mantle of the atmosphere, everything seemed less harsh than it had moments before.

Shag made them study maps and charts, he sent them aloft to learn the area from every angle and altitude, he took aerial photographs so they would know the section lines and old roads and other prominent topographical features and how to recognize what they had already come to name Boot Hill. The mine pushed its dark shaft into an upthrusting slope in otherwise ghastly and primitive open desert well to the southwest of Albuquerque. Although their surroundings didn't offer much visual pleasure, they were in the midst of high hills north of the Gallinas Mountains, and a long time ago someone had dreamed his dream of making a great gold strike here. What crazy geological survey brought on that God-forsaken plunge into financial catastrophe and personal obscurity they would never know. The nearest community was Fence Creek which, even if you counted the old hound dogs and the few horses as well as the people, hardly had a population worth noting. But it was a county seat and therefore it had telephones, stores, a post office, and such amenities as modern civilization offered up to foolhardy hermits.

Directly to the north of their newly christened Boot Hill was an area of not-too-ancient dark lava flows; walking a mile over this land twisted and frozen in its primal agony could cut the toughest boots to tattered ribbons. Stretching across the area to the northeast and the northwest was a piece of land that was less than blessed in the richness of its soil and not especially pleasing to the eye, but nevertheless very special land, for here was the reservation territory for the Navajo, Zuni, and Acoma Indians. There was precious little love between these communities and those of the round eyes, and it was just this lack of social intercourse that served to underscore their physical isolation.

Not one single road, complete from one end to the other, reached out from even the nearest community, Fence Creek. Long before this moment the seasonal swarms of huge cumulus clouds had gathered clannishly, and spent their fury upon the higher hills and mountains with what is politely known as garbage-moving rain. The sky erupts in sodden outrage to pour enormous quantities of water onto a land baked so dry and hard that almost none of that precious downflow is absorbed by the land, and instead it follows that quiet bid of gravity to run downhill and gathers its strength in sloping shallows and channels and gullies, and attacks the land with foaming, crushing tributaries. In years past every road to Boot Hill had been ripped away by such storms, and unless you had a vehicle that could span gorges and climb or shove aside boulders, you did not drive to their mining camp. There simply was no way and until the bulldozers and scrapers returned to patch and repair and fill or gouge new paths the only way to reach the camp was by air. Which suited them fine. There had been talk in Fence Creek of repairing a single road, but the strangers seemed perfectly satisfied with their own air transportation, which by now everyone in Fence Creek and also at the general aviation operations at Albuquerque Airport knew well, and since those idiots looking for uranium or whatever it was might be around only a short while, why spend the money to build a road that once again might lead straight to Nowheresville?

Besides the lack of roads, that place called Boot Hill also had no power lines, which meant no outside electricity and no telephones. They had that big old DC-3 and they flew in and out of there with whatever they needed, and to Fence Creek residents they were mighty good close neighbors thirty or forty miles away.

What no one in Fence Creek or Albuquerque knew was that the spur road leading off Highway 36 had been fixed by the crew from Classic Mining. They just hadn't bothered to tell anyone, and that's as good as no road at all.

"Every one of you people knows the rules," Shag said. He rested comfortably in a battered armchair in their kitchen-living-meeting-room bunkhouse. "That's why you were selected for this operation, among your other qualifications. Everything we take in goes to sustain the operation or pay for its future activities. The overages, and they'll start to get very big in a short time, will be distributed and paid into whatever type of accounts you want, and wherever you want, just so long as they don't point any fingers back in this direction. Sam here knows the tricks of the trade inside and out, and you can either use his experience or go out and screw up by yourself."

Sam was sprawled in the nailed-together wreckage of a wooden seat and grinned awkwardly in response to the sudden turning of heads in his direction. He looked at Shag, who nodded.

"The basic rule," Sam Bronstein said slowly, his inflections changing just enough so they knew he wasn't playing soldier anymore and had donned his legal hat, "is never to ruffle the good old Infernal Revenue Service." His voice had a timbre that brooked little argument and it was one of his most devastating weapons in a courtroom. Here it purred at easy idle and its effect was like a bass fiddle friendly to the ears and the soul. "The IRS is a strange breed of cat. You either stay completely unnoticed by them or you do everything but crawl into bed with them. Just as long as, one, you file a return, and two, you pay when necessary, they don't much care one way or the other how you latch onto the bread. They go by the rules. Most of what you hear about the IRS is crap. They're mostly a big gang of little people doing their jobs, and if you don't plug up their toilets there won't be any crap lying around for them to see. That's why we've set up different accounts in your names. One's visible and that's the one you paint bright red and bring to the attention of the money people out of Washington. The other account isn't in this country and we've worked out the least troublesome and best concealed of all possible ways. In fact, you can let it disappear in negotiable bonds and stocks and securities almost anywhere in the world if you want, and in fact that's what I recommend. Besides, once it's set up I'm the only person who will know what transactions took place."

Wolfgang Siedel peered at him through narrow and questioning eyes. "Only you? Not Shag, or," he gestured, "anyone else?"

"Only me," Sam repeated. "That way you never have to worry about anyone except me. And I sure as hell don't need any of your fucking money, so you're safe. Also, if you have questions, it keeps you from getting sweaty under the armpits about who to go looking for. And it also reduces to its absolute minimum the information about your own affairs. Now, once this whole thing is over—and Shag is the one who decides that—we separate ourselves absolutely from you in terms of any business connections. Questions? Or maybe some of you would rather play tennis."

"What the hell does that mean?" The question came from Phil Bergellini.

"It means that I know this part of the business better than anyone else. Period. You got questions, you're either dumber than I thought you were, or you want to know more, which means you're smarter than I thought you were."

"That's a crock," Crouse-Hinds told him bluntly. "You can go either way with that sort of cruddy remark."

"Precisely," came the answer from the unruffled Bronstein. "Aren't you glad I'm taking care of all those pennies you're going to be gathering?"

Crouse-Hinds grinned. "You'll never know it, mate, but I am. We checked you out down to your socks. You sure come out with high marks."

"And it never occurred to you that I've been out of school for more than a couple of days?"

They studied Sam carefully. "Which means what?" Frank Bemis asked.

"Which means that every query Johnny made, and which was answered to his satisfaction, was actually answered by people who either work for or with me," Sam said calmly. "Look, you either trust or you don't."

Shag's voice broke in. "If you have any questions, you're out right now," he said. They recognized the steel trap but these were men who never skirted an issue.

"What would happen," Bergellini asked, "if I wanted out, as you say, with no more questions. Like right now?"

"You leave here in the Gooney Bird and you're set

down at an international airport and you have five thousand clams in your pocket," Shag said. "You promise to leave the country until contacted at whatever is your destination and you swear to keep your mouth shut as long as you live, which won't be long at all if you break that oath to this group. That's how we cover one another. I trust you people and you trust me or you wouldn't be here. We don't need greed. It's like rabies and it eats away at the inside of your brain and destroys your reasoning. If you're in a pack of wolves and one starts foaming at the mouth then the others kill it instantly."

Phil beamed. "Sacred mother, but I like that," he said with enthusiasm.

Vance nodded at Sam. "You mentioned stocks before and outside connections?"

Sam nodded. "We, gentlemen, are the sole owners of Deutsches International Geological, Limited. On paper we're a holding subsidiary of Blomm and Voss in West Germany, but that's only a paper transaction, even if it's as solid as the Bank of England. The arrangement works for us—legal, neat, with a very long track record. Pam set it up. In fact, we're now looking for gold—by contract, anyway—for the parent company in Stuttgart."

"Gold?" Wolfgang echoed the word. "I thought it was uranium we were after."

"Everybody knows there's no uranium out here," Shag explained.

"But—"

"Hold it," Shag said quickly. "Everybody else knows and we know there's no uranium here. Pretty soon they're going to figure out that we really aren't as dumb as we look, that we're here looking for gold, and all our talk about uranium was a cover. But we'll drop just enough hints for people in Fence Creek and in Albuquerque to think they discovered what we're really doing here. And when we bring in some high-grade ore samples the word will spread like wildfire, and people will be beating themselves black and blue slapping their own backs to congratulate themselves on how smart they always were."

"There's gold here?" Wolfgang was more confused than ever.

Lew laughed aloud. "There will be. As soon as we buy the high-grade ore from a mine in northern Colorado and fly it down here and mix it with local dirt, and then take it to the assay office. Then we'll have a bloody real strike on our chapped hands, we will."

"Okay. Shall we get down to hard cases?" Shag looked at every man in the room. No questions.

"When do we get the motorcycles?" Shag asked.

Bergellini gestured. "Two days. With all equipment."

"Chutes and gear?"

"Everything's set," Wolfgang said quietly.

The atmosphere had changed. They hated the paperwork and legal crap and were glad to be a working team again. And by subscribing to a common code—for a mercenary is a man who must instantly trust the stranger fighting by his side, and to do that you've got to accept a code by which to live—they were as tightly knit and as committed to one another, in the face of death or any obstacle, as men who had been sworn into the best of so-called legal paramilitary forces. Which, with their skills and shared attitude of accepting odds because it makes the wine of life all the more heady, made them a very special group indeed.

"Vance, how about the UFO routines?"

Vance sat up straighter. "It's done. We've been using

flares and strobes and loudspeakers, the whole routine. Besides, out here the locals have been infested with UFO reports for years. Funny thing is, it's really a hotbed for this UFO stuff. Things have been whizzing through the sky for a long time. And we're not so far from a couple of missile and special research areas. So everyone around here sort of yawns when giant shapes move through the sky. The fanatics drool with joy and the nonbelievers pay no attention. You couldn't ask for better."

"Good," Shag said with approval. "Okay, gang, clear the table. It's time for studying the charts." Several minutes later there were charts and photographs spread across the table, and exhaustively detailed charts and maps tacked onto the walls of the room. Shag went to the chart of greatest interest.

"Study this area until you've memorized every major detail." Shag's thick finger tapped the paper. "See this section here? This is what's known as the Apache Indian Reservation, and it just happens to be in the middle of nowhere. To the east of the reservation is the Apache National Forest and on the opposite side, to the west, is Tonto National Forest."

Phil Bergellini crowded in for a closer look. "You mean this goddamn Indian name is for real?"

"Guess so," Shag said. "Look for yourself."

"Oh, I see it," Phil said. "But you know what Tonto is meaning? It means stupid. Dumbass. If they name a whole reservation then there must be one big bunch of dumb fucking Indians there."

"Okay, okay, hold the yuks down to a roar," Shag said loudly to break up the laughter. "They may call them stupid but they've gotten smarts pretty damn quick. Christ, this is like a girl-scout troop." His finger traced back to the Tonto National Forest. "Study the relief sections and the contour lines and you'll see this whole area is mountains and desert. It's mean country. Now, just north of here, this is Highway 40. It runs east and west through Flagstaff, east on down to Winslow and then to Holbrook. It's all in Arizona. If you take Highway 77 south from Holbrook in this wildass country you're headed straight for the Sitgreaves National Forest, and make a special note that this area lies just north of the Apache reservation. It has special meaning for us."

Shag left the charts and stood back from the group to observe them in a single glance. He relit his cigar and blew out a thick cloud of smoke. He studied it for a moment, seemingly absentminded, except they knew better. "It so happens," he continued after the pause, "that a few months ago some Indians stumbled on the richest uranium strike in the country. They just about fell over it because it's smack dab in the middle of Apache territory, and it's time to get even as far as they're concerned. The government has been having fits trying to get legal permission from the Indians to work the uranium."

Frank Bemis coughed. "That doesn't sound right, Shag. You know how we've treated the Indians. They had something we wanted and we went in and took it, raping a couple of thousand women and kids just for fun on the side. What's changed?"

"The whole world, Frank. It's all changed. The government needs the uranium. But the price of mass civil rights explosions and all that crap doesn't sit too well with them right now, so they're trying to play it by the rules. They don't want to stink up the works. So they're back to the old saw of trying to buy their way out of the situation, and they've offered the Apaches a down payment of three million dollars just to really study what looks like the great grandmother of all uranium finds."

Rademacher had a puzzled look on his face. "The Indians, they not crazy. They make deal?"

Shag nodded. "That they've done, but they insist on being paid their three mil in cash. In one-hundred-dollar bills, all freshly minted, packaged neatly. Sort of sticking in the legal knife for the fun of it. Thirty thousand green leaves aren't that bulky but they do make an impression. Look, let's not get off the theme here, because what I'm trying to tell you people is that three days from now the big ceremony takes place."

"Payday?" Crouse-Hinds' interest barometer was rising steadily as he began to anticipate what was coming.

"Payday," Shag confirmed. "Big ceremony; the works. The Apaches are insisting that the transfer of the cash take place—they've got the touch, all right—directly in Fort Apache." Shag returned to a hanging wall map. "And Fort Apache is," his finger stabbed the map, "right here." He swung around to face the group. "It's not the best-kept secret that the three million is being held in the Federal Reserve Bank at Flagstaff. And the government isn't worried about the information leak, because they've got more protection and firepower than Fort Knox."

Shag turned to receive a cup of black coffee from Pam. Wolfgang motioned for his attention. "I would guess you have worked out a plan to circumvent the defenses of the bank." He smiled. "I am right, no?"

"You are wrong, yes," Shag said. "No, Wolfgang, the story about the Flagstaff bank is a blind."

"Then—"

Sam Bronstein stepped in. "Look at the map again. See that town of Snowflake? Okay, follow Highway 77 down to a place called Taylor. A one-horse dump. But Taylor is so much more a turd than a town no one pays any attention to it. It's fifty miles north of Fort Apache. A small town, reached by only one road that's worth spit. One telephone line going in, one power line going in, and you've got it."

"So what is all this about Taylor?" Wolfgang was showing a touch of belligerence and Sam laughed at him.

"My fine young Prussian friend," Sam said softly, "money is my business, and that shitty little cupcake of a town called Taylor is where they've stashed the bread. *Kapish?*"

"This is a matter of logistics, details, timing, and reliable performance on everybody's part. One fuckup anywhere down the line," Shag stressed, "and it can all come unglued. So we're going to drill, twice, five, maybe twenty times, until we can do it in our sleep. Okay, let's start at the top. Gather round, chillun—"

26

The men cursed the sudden cold winds that whipped down from the mountains to the north and chilled them to the bone. Climbing the old telephone poles along Highway 77 was endurable for only two months out of the year. The rest of the time it was either unbearably hot or bitterly cold, and they were getting the first real taste of the latter. But they had a job to do, and north of the town of Taylor on Route 77 they strung a new line from pole to pole, and adjusted equipment along the bases of other poles. Shivering with the frigid winds, they sipped coffee from thermos jugs and drove south of Taylor to complete their work. When they were done they checked their watches. Every watch agreed precisely with every other watch.

They didn't call one another. That was the plan. Don't risk having communications shaft you when you need them most of all and everything can hang on a frazzled wire that shorts out a critical juncture in a black box. Set it up right the first time, go with your plan, and have a dozen contingencies on which to fall back if the unexpected happens. Rigid plans are fine only if there are a lot of back doors with swift access to them.

The telephones reaching northward from Taylor all the way to Snowflake went dead at 1:29 A.M. There was one witness to the strange cut in telephone communications. An old Indian drove his pickup truck along Route 77 when a blinding flash brought his arm up to shield his eyes. Before he could react a series of dazzling explosions followed and he had just enough time to see a shattered telephone pole crashing down on the cab of his truck. Nineteen more poles crashed down to the road, blocking the highway, cutting the power lines as well. Telephones serviced by this line in both Snowflake and Taylor went dead, and sections of countryside, as well as parts of each community, went instantly dark from the power breaks.

On a hill from which both towns could be seen, a dull boom of red-orange flame mushroomed from the base of a high, four-masted tower. Moments later the steel structure fell slowly to the ground, buckling as it crashed its way down the mountain slope and carrying with it the microwave antennas used for nonline communications.

At 1:31 A.M. two gasoline stations in Snowflake erupted in blinding explosions, followed by the deep *WHUMP!* of underground storage tanks ripping apart and sending flames roaring into the night sky. An underground gas line that fed a major part of the town was breached by the ground shock, spewed invisible vapors into the air, felt the touch of flaming debris tumbling before the wind, and set off another shattering blast. Within sixty seconds Snowflake was a community without power except from emergency generators. It was out of touch with the world by its normal telephone service, and was host to perplexed law-enforcement officers, who had no idea that several powerful scanning transmitters placed in their town earlier in the day were effectively jamming their radios. The jammers would operate for one hour, after which their batteries would go dead, tripping another relay that would release acid onto nitro blocks and utterly destroy the equipment.

The small town of Taylor was quiet. Not even the excitement of the impending Apache celebration kept people in the cold night air. They gathered in bars and clubs and were, for the most part, content to keep working on what promised to be a drunk that could last for several days.

At 1:42 A.M. the town snapped into darkness. Radios and televisions went dead. Homes, saloons, the small police station and firehouse—everything was dark. Telephones were dead and the police radios picked up only a strange whining and buzzing sound. That was all. People cursed, lit candles and kerosene lamps, used auto headlights and flashlights, and did their best to pick up on their drinking in anticipation of the great payoff from the split-tongued roundeyes.

"Hey, who's got the doughnuts?" Milt Sommers scratched his leg and yawned, then poured coffee from his thermos jug into a cup. Bill Parker held out the box of doughnuts.

"Thanks." Sommers sipped coffee in the darkened glass enclosure that made up the control tower at

Flagstaff's commercial airport. It was a beautiful night, but everyone had been caught unexpectedly by the cold winds. On the runway the wind was not only strong but gusting from side to side. A bitch for the pilots. They'd earn their pay for sure landing here to-night.

Otherwise it was a bore. There was more activity down below in the radar-control rooms. Down there they were working jetliners crossing the country or talking to an occasional military job on some obscure mission. But in the tower they hadn't had any aircraft movement for nearly forty minutes.

The red light flashed and a buzzer sounded. Sommers put down his coffee and tapped in the line to the traffic center below. A voice came clearly through the miniature plug in his left ear. "This Milty?"

"Yeah. What's up?"

"This is Charlie. Look, we're getting a crazy pickup on scope four down here."

"Oh, shit, not that damn Hindenburg again, guys."

"It ain't no zeppelin, smartass, but we're tracking it again and we've been paying a lot of attention to it. This time we have three stations on a simultaneous track, Milt, and we're all getting that same sort of fuzz, and it remains about a thousand feet across. Even if the edges are irregular, they're remaining cohesive in terms of ground track."

"Sure, sure, I know, Charlie, but this is the third time this week! And we're getting hell from headquarters for wasting their time and contributing unnecessarily to public panic and blah-blah-blah. The bottom line is we've been ordered not to report any more damn UFO's unless we can see them."

"Yeah, I know. So get off your ass, Milty, and take a look. Can you see anything out there?"

"Well, for Christ's sake, I got three hundred and sixty degrees out here. Gimme a direction."

"Try south."

"Okay. Stand by one."

Milt Sommers sighed and looked out the tower glass to the south. He'd had enough UFO crap to last him his whole—

What the hell was that? "Hey! Parker, c'mere," he said to his shift worker. He pointed. "See there? Green lights, but they're getting brighter and then they fade."

Parker already had powerful binoculars to his eyes. "I got 'em. Green and—hey! Yellow lights, sort of. But they're going in circles and . . . and now they're falling, very slowly, chasing each other in circles. Never saw anything like that. Jesus, what the hell is it?"

Sommers thumbed his transmit button. "Radar? Look, we got something in the south vector. Green lights and yellow lights and they're in a wide circle and they look like they're falling. You got any distance on your track?"

Radar came back at once. "I'll say we have! Twelve miles, and the scope is going crazy. There's a band about thirty miles long in which this scope has gone apeshit. Every sweep breaks up and the scope looks like a convention of fireflies and—"

"Good God! Look at it!"

They cruised in level flight at thirteen thousand feet. Pam crouched in the number-two hold of the Ju-52, a parachute harness with webbing and snaprings securing her to the plane. She dropped small packages through the open hatch beneath her. As each package fell away it was ripped open by the wind, scattering thousands of slim pieces of metal foil. They fluttered slowly to the ground, tossed every which way by the winds. And they happened to match quite closely the radar frequencies used by Flagstaff for air-traffic control. But what Flagstaff would receive was an enormous, slowly blossoming mushroom of electronic snow on all its scopes as the radar-sweep beams encountered the metallic chaff and shredded their signal. Pam released the last package, closed the hatch, and climbed back into the cabin. She picked up a headset and boom mike and called Lew in the turret. "How's it going back there, Lew?"

Standing upright in the turret, the wind pummeling him, Lew was having the time of his life. He was bundled into a heavy, quilted Luftwaffe flying suit, right down to the gloves and the fleece-lined leather helmet and goggles. He spoke into the microphone within his oxygen mask.

"It's a lovely bunch of coconuts, me love! Just bee-yootiful! And here we goes for another dose of the light fantastic!" Pam laughed. "Dis is der obscr-schutzer mitt orders vor der kapitan," he called to Shag in the left seat. "If you vould be zo kind, a big turn to der left is in order!"

Shag rolled the Ju-52 into a steady bank of fifteen degrees and in the turret Lew was standing erect with a heavy flare gun in each hand like a cowboy from an old Western movie transported to some temporal plane of higher idiocy. "Fire vun!" he shouted and squeezed the trigger of the left Very pistol, and a dazzling green flare streaked away from the airplane. "Fire two!" came the cry and from the pistol in his right hand issued a bright yellow flare. He reloaded and fired off flares again, then a third time. He looked down at six descending, sputtering green and yellow lights that formed a great broken circle.

The time rift opened—
Almost everybody in Taylor was under a roof or enjoying the growing revelry when the sound reached levels high enough to penetrate walls and windows and doors. It was a deep pulsating whine that grew louder and louder until it became a shrill warbling scream, mixed with heavy thunder and snarling machinery. People went outside to look into the sky, saw nothing or only a shape moving before stars, and then came the faint popping sounds they couldn't identify. More people came out to look up and someone grabbed a flashlight and there it was, one of them at least, barely visible, the outlines of a parachute. Then another, and still one more.

"Parachutes!" someone yelled.

They started running toward the chutes that were aimed with great precision and under control to land in a field at the north end of Taylor. Then they stopped at a new sound, the coughing snarl of motorcycle engines coming from behind them, roaring up the highway from the south. They turned, saw the single bright headlights, smaller but equally bright red lights as two motorcycles, one with a sidecar, bellowed into town toward the main intersection.

"My God . . . I don't believe it!" someone cried.

"They're Germans!" shouted another voice, "They're German soldiers!"

"You're crazy. They—"

A burst of machine-gun fire shattered the windows

of the main bar. Screams erupted as glass showered outward in all directions. The engines thundered up and down and tires squealed and people gaped in disbelief as helmeted and heavily armed SS troops came into view from both sides of the intersection. Voices shouted orders in German and what could not be understood verbally was clear enough with the pointed hands and threatening gestures with submachine guns. A police car, one of two such vehicles in town, came screeching around an intersection and its occupant came out quickly, reaching for his revolver.

"Nein! Hände hoch!" a voice cried and a machine-gun burst ripped the windshield and tires and shattered the fuel tank. The policeman dove for the ground as the car exploded, then he scrambled wildly to escape the flames. He didn't get far. A huge German sergeant towered over him, slammed a steel boot into his ribs and the officer felt bones yielding and a fiery pain in his side. The German reached down, removed the lawman's weapon and threw it aside contemptuously. The policeman was jerked to his feet by what felt like superhuman strength and the SS trooper pointed to the bar with the shattered windows, then motioned for everyone to get inside. A short burst with the machine gun ripped apart another storefront and everyone scurried for safety. They heard the German troops shouting among themselves, and the motorcycle with the sidecar, the machine gun mounted and ready, had stopped by the corner bank. A stunning woman in SS uniform with gleaming boots and long blond hair, a machine pistol in one hand, moved swiftly to the bank with an SS officer. They planted charges around the corner, moved to the side, and a devastating blast smashed through the center of the town. Smoke bil-

lowed out, whipped away by the wind. Then there came another explosion, muffled this time, as the bank vault doors were blown open. A German soldier ran down the main street and behind him there began a series of explosions as cars and trucks erupted in flames, lighting up the streets with ghastly flickering orange.

John Crouse-Hinds ran down the street slipping small plastic charges with jellied wrappings beneath or into each vehicle. Three-minute timers set them off and he was followed with one crashing explosion after another until the town center was one long line of burning and exploding vehicles. He stopped as Taylor's second police cruiser came around a corner almost on two tires. Johnny ran to the car, fired a burst into the windshield on the passenger side. The car skidded wildly to a halt and the officer within dove out, crouching, his gun coming up to fire. He spun around as a voice roared at him and a German boot came to catch him in the elbow. His weapon flew from his hand and he was jerked into the air and calmly and quietly the German sergeant broke his arm and flung him to the side. Gaston Rademacher looked down on him with yellow teeth bared in a great smile, and the policeman knew he was staring into the face of death.

The German sergeant winked and turned away to join his fellow soldiers. Someone took the wheel of the police cruiser, stopped by the bank, then roared off with smoking tires behind a German motorcycle and followed by the second motorcycle with the sidecar and that deadly machine gun.

At the edge of town, by the last house, a blinding

explosion tore the road apart and brought trees and telephone poles crashing down.

By the time the stunned and terrified townspeople of Taylor dared venture into the streets the only sound was the crackle of flames from more than twenty burning cars and trucks, the howling of the wind, and the barely heard cursing of the policeman nursing his broken arm, but grateful he was lucky enough to be—lucky? He felt a chill far colder and deeper than the night air. That giant had let him live. He gritted his teeth as the pain washed over him. No matter what, he'd be damned if he'd complain.

Flagstaff radar was frantic. "It's hovering to the south. We can barely make it out. It's been over, uh, you know where that town of Snowflake is? It's in that area and we can't tell if it's just hovering or—*the fucking thing's disappeared!*"

"Okay, bring her on in. Nothing's going to move for a long time north of us and the road's blocked to the south. The road's nice and open and the wind's right on your nose." Crouse-Hinds looked into the star-flecked sky and saw only the glowing exhaust flames from the Ju-52's engines. They turned the lights from the police cruiser and the motorcycles down the road and knew Shag would have it down pat. The wind was doing at least twenty and Shag brought her in steadily. He had three thousand feet of road. The Ju-52 touched down like a feather with a ground speed of barely over forty miles an hour, and Shag had her stopped in less than seven hundred feet.

Shag stayed at the controls as Vance and Lew ran to the cabin door. They jerked out the loading ramp and

it clanged down to the road surface. The men wrestled
the first motorcycle into the cabin and pushed it forward. Then came the detached sidecar with three million dollars in cash, followed by the second motorcycle. Johnny Crouse-Hinds went back to the police
cruiser and left a double charge of jellied plastic explosive inside the vehicle. He climbed aboard the airplane as soon as they'd shoved back the loading ramp,
pulled the door shut, and yelled to Shag to let her go.

Vance went to his control panel in the forward part
of the cabin, pushed in the cassette player, and the
loudspeakers buried in a belly hatch began a hideous
deep groaning sound that kept increasing in pitch and
volume. Shag went full forward on the throttles and
with short-field flaps set the Ju-52 had its tail up before they even moved, and eight hundred feet later
they had wheels off the ground. Vance snapped on the
lights. A row of dazzling aircraft landing lights in the
wings, three on each side and several along the fuselage, exploded silently, mixed white, blue, and orange
flares so bright that anyone looking at the airplane
lifting swiftly into the sky saw only those lights, the
effect the same as someone staring directly into the
bright headlights of a car approaching at night. You
see lights but never the car behind them.

And they didn't know there was an eyewitness to it
all. Shaken by the dark forms and the thunder on the
highway, shocked into slack-jawed fear by the terrifying crescendo of groaning sound rising to an ear-
shattering pitch, mystified by the crashing roar of engines and propellers he couldn't identify, and then
blinded by the flashing pattern of lights so bright they
were painful, the hapless old man who lived in a
shack—darkened by the power failure—two hundred

yards from the road lost his last vestiges of control when the police cruiser exploded with a roar that sent fiery wreckage raining down onto his roof.

Twenty minutes later the old man, totally bewildered, watched the wind whip flames through the collapsing wreckage of what had been his home.

27

It's the biggest little city in the United States. It lies in flatland so damn big you can see for almost three days straight ahead, but be careful you don't stumble over the thousands upon thousands of oil and gas wells that dot the landscape for more days on end. A man walking the Texas country around Midland would be hard put to believe there was anything else except desert and oil wells.

Until, that is, he came to Midland with its beautiful tall office buildings and giant banks rising vertically from the flatness. Not too long ago it was a cowtown, and then an exceptional cowtown, and then they discovered gold. Black and viscous and pumping upward like wealth-producing dark blood, which is what it was. Midland, Texas; glutted with natural riches, lying across Route 80 between Big Spring and Odessa. It was once a cowtown but now it had more money than it used to have cowpies, and they even imported their firewood, and one of the finest sections of the town, near its edge, was covered with a beautiful shopping center. The man who built it was a millionaire many times over and he hated shopping centers so he turned this one into a fantasyland of beautiful, wooded estatelike stores and plazas, banks, and restaurants, and a lush lawn more than three thousand feet long and five hundred feet wide with what just had to be the most beautiful grass in the entire state.

Now, the Live Oaks Shopping Plaza bank was something special. It was known in the banking industry as a funnel, because it was here that money from outlying districts came and was stored for the weekend before Monday-morning disbursement. To Sam Bronstein, much more important than the money was the well-conccaled fact that the Live Oaks Shopping Plaza bank was being used as another kind of funnel, for negotiable stocks and bonds. Twelve million dollars worth of bread in the form of paper currency is a staggering weight to handle. Twelve million dollars worth of negotiable stocks and bonds, which can be redeemed for more than half their value in *sub rosa* transactions almost anywhere in the world, is a dream.

The winds were perfect on a Thursday evening, and Shag Jordan and his team began winding down their clock at 9:40 that evening. Every radio station and television station in the city received a phone call.

"Uh, this is the dispatcher at the west rail yards. Listen, maybe they forgot about it, but we've got a bad problem here. A tank car has sprung a bad leak, and maybe the police ain't saying nothing because it could scare a lot of people, you know? But if they aren't told about this phosgene gas—what? Oh, sure. Johnson, Charlie Johnson, and I'm on the four-to-midnight shift. Look, that ain't important. This stuff is phosgene. You know what that is? It's a military shipment we had on a siding and it got bumped and somehow the tank car's sprung this leak, and the way the wind is blowing—damn right it's lethal, mister. One good whiff of this stuff and you shake hands with St. Peter a couple of minutes later. How the hell do I know why the police haven't issued any bulletins? When did cops get smart? Yeah, look, I got to go, because I ain't staying here any longer than I got to. I just didn't want a lot of innocent people to get hurt. What? Damn right they better evacuate! How many people here you think got gas masks, for Christ's sake!"

At precisely seventeen minutes past ten o'clock four tank cars in the West Side Marshaling Yards, which had been leased by the Odessa Natural Resources Corporation (created by Sam Bronstein for just this purpose ten days earlier), vented their sidewalls. Small plastic charges with nearly invisible antennas detonated and peeled back metal. Gas under pressure, already mixed with enough white smoke to make it visible, poured out in huge billowing clouds, carried by the wind toward the center of town. Within the first few minutes yardmen were on their knees, clutching their throats, gasping for air, retching violently. One man managed to get to a telephone, but he was unable to call and before he collapsed to the floor, puking wretchedly, he banged his hand against a master alarm. Sirens rang throughout the rail yard and lights flashed in the police station.

It took three minutes for the first police cruiser to reach the scene and another thirty seconds for both officers to feel they'd been slammed in the windpipe and chest and groin by sledgehammers. One man stumbled back to the police car and made strangling noises.

The rest was inevitable, and the effect snowballed

like an avalanche out of control. Word spread swiftly, the earlier-called radio and television stations interrupted normal broadcasting, every police and fire siren in town screamed for attention. Police cars and fire engines raced through residential areas warning occupants to get out of the city, to breathe through water-soaked towels (a worthless move but one to help allay the swiftly spreading panic), to drive away from the rail yards.

Midland Airport Control Tower received an emergency call. "This is the police. We've had a fire and explosion at the rail yards and poison gas is drifting downwind. You're safe where you are but you'd better shut down the airport immediately except for departures. Whatever you do don't let anyone land without police authority."

Step One set up the emergency.

Step Two released the poison gas. No one but the Ju-52 group knew there wasn't any poison gas. The tank cars that had been split open contained riot-control gas, which brings on copious weeping, chest pains, a feeling of strangulation, and violent nausea—and subsequent complete recovery from the concentrations that would exist through the city.

Step Three was to convince all concerned that they were being subjected to phosgene gas and tens of thousands of people could die.

Step Four assured some level of panic and absolute choking of all streets. Police cars, fire trucks, and anything else on wheels were locked within the snarled, frantic mass of traffic attempting to flee Midland.

Step Five closed down the airport. Closed it as tight as a drum as far as tower control was concerned. Vance Brady had made the phone call and he knew that no one working at that field was going to stay around a moment longer than necessary. In fact, if he knew human nature there'd be a swarm of planes leaving the airport—what is known as getting the hell out from under. He was right.

Step Six snarled all communications into and out of Midland. Rumor and panic feed upon themselves and in Midland they were like prairie fires before the wind. Besides, thousands of people were choking, gasping, weeping, and throwing up. It was real enough.

Step Seven came at 11:09 P.M., when Frank Bemis flew over an oil-tank storage farm on the other side of town from the Live Oaks Shopping Plaza. All Frank had to do was tune his radio transmitter to one two-six-point-seven-five and squeeze his mike button six times. The Cherokee was banged over on its side when the explosive charge went off at the base of the main tank and a holocaust of flames roared into the sky. The sight of the spectacular inferno and the sound of its hissing thunder increased the panic and concentrated attention on that part of town as well as the rail yard.

A truck rolled into Live Oaks Shopping Plaza on its regularly scheduled trash pickup run. It parked at the rear of the bank and Pam Kreiner led the way from the back of the truck, her autopistol at the ready. With her came John Crouse-Hinds, Gaston Rademacher, and Phil Bergellini, carrying submachine guns and heavy backpacks. They stood by the truck, sniffing the air.

"There's been a wind shift," Pam said. "Quickly, your masks." Moments later they were wearing gas masks, and Pam motioned for them to move. Not a soul was in sight, but time was limited and they didn't have any to spare for neatness.

Phil blew open the bank doors with a bazooka rocket charge. There wouldn't be any police cars, but there were ways to call for help and most assuredly police helicopters would be on their way here from Midland and outlying communities. They went inside, set the powerful demolition charges from their packs, ran outside the bank, and waited, crouched down behind a thick wall.

The explosion blew out the entire side of the bank and the wall of the vault within. Johnny and Phil went inside. Sam Bronstein had briefed them well and they found the separate small vault within the main vault. A burst from a submachine gun opened the light steel, and Phil went to work stuffing the documents into Johnny's backpack. He jerked it closed and slapped him on the shoulder. "Done. You sure we don't go after any cash? Damn, there's enough here to—"

A big hand spun Phil around. "You know the rules, mate. Follow the script. Let's go."

They disappeared into the shadows, listening to the distant scream of sirens and the bleating of thousands of automobile horns. Pam brought a portable transceiver to her lips. "Marker Beacon, this is Garbage One. Pull the plug. Repeat, pull the plug. The wind's out of the west. How long do you estimate? Over."

They heard the sound of engines high overhead. "Three minutes to the goal line. Get the other goodies set. Over and out."

High above them Shag had pulled back the throttles, gone to flat pitch on the props, and dumped forty degrees of flaps, coming out of the sky at better than two thousand feet a minute. He had studied the area below meticulously, and knew that as he rolled out toward the lights of the shopping plaza he could expect to see a bright flashing yellow light held by his team that would be visible only from the cockpit of the Ju-52. Pam held the light while the three men busied themselves with compact cylinders on each side of the open expanse of grass. She heard the whistling sound of the Ju-52 coming down, looked up and was able to see its reflection from the city lights. Then the dark shape settled to the grass in a perfect deadstick landing. Shag held the yoke back and went to power to reach them, swinging around as Lew Heath held open the cabin door.

"Get your blasted arses in here!" he shouted. "We're going to take off downwind! We've been monitoring the radios and there's a whole bloody pack of police choppers on their way in here! Hang on!" The cabin door slammed shut at the same moment that Shag went to full power. He let her run longer than usual because of the wind on his tail, lifted her off the ground and held her down to the last possible moment, and then horsed back on the yoke. Annie climbed skyward in a wild leap. They needed altitude fast and Shag pushed the throttles through overboost to 42 inches and they were climbing out at a thousand feet a minute. At fifteen hundred feet he brought back the power to normal takeoff maximum, climbing steadily. Pam worked her way to the cockpit, slipped on a headset, cursed at forgetting to remove the gas mask; she tore it off and slipped on the headset and thumbed the intercom.

"What was that about police helicopters?"

Shag's voice came into her earphones. "Someone

started putting the pieces together. Someone smart. There's a dozen choppers on their way in here right now and—" He pointed. "Christ, we didn't have a moment to lose. See them? About eleven o'clock from the nose. You can see their strobes."

A glowing formation sped low across the ground; the police helicopters.

"Did you have time to set up the reception committee?" he asked her.

"All set. Five-minute timers."

"Good." He leaned down suddenly and set their transponder to squawk the VFR code on 1200. He hadn't thought of it before. With everybody bailing out of Midland Airport in every plane that was available, they'd all be squawking 1200 and their own signal would be lost in the flurry of scope blips. He eased into a climbing left turn. "Almost five minutes," he said on intercom. "Let's see the show."

The police choppers were beautifully organized. These men had nailed more than one bank ripoff by some of the best people in the business. Two helicopters swept across the grassy expanse on the deck, came to a stop sideways so that the men in the cabin had direct lines of fire to the shattered bank entrance. Brilliant searchlights flashed on as two more choppers took up hovering positions on the flanks, all lights out, their gunners at the ready. Another flew high overhead, ready for anything, and the remaining helos dropped down and three men rushed from each machine toward the bank.

Nothing else moved. Nothing that was visible, anyway. At the sides of the long field the five-minute timers closed. The ends of the cylinders snapped open and from each cylinder a deflated bag was ejected. At the bottom of each bag was a tiny package, to which was attached a featherweight fishing line, tied securely to the heavy cylinders. With the clatter of helicopter engines, exhausts, and whirling blades, no one on the field heard the swift hiss of hydrogen into the deflated bags. Seconds later the balloons lifted from the ground, rising swiftly, trailing the fishing line that unreeled steadily from each canister.

The shortest line played out at two hundred feet. The fishing line pulled taut against the cylinder, and the sudden jerking motion freed a tiny detonator in the package at the bottom of the balloon. A half-pound of plastic explosives went off with a sharp cracking boom, igniting the hydrogen in the balloon in almost the same instant. A *whoosh* of flame billowed outward, lighting up the field, and then was gone.

Each hundred feet higher another fishing line snapped tight and another blast and accompanying fireball erupted over the field, only to vanish within seconds.

The police officers looked up, startled, confused—and ran like hell for cover. They'd never seen anything like it before, and neither had the thousands of people rushing through the jammed streets. By morning the panic-fed stories had mushroomed to a full-fledged attack by an enormous flying saucer a mile in length. Helped, no doubt, by hysterical phone calls to newspapers and television stations, all made by one unhysterical and bored Vance Brady.

Shag was proven right once again. Those men who were smart enough to separate the wheat from the chaff, the real from the nonsense, were drowned in the outcry, and it would take several days for everyday common sense to prevail. In the meantime he could slow them down just a bit more. Six thousand feet over the ground he turned off the transponder. Distant radars picked up the giant UFO and there were groans of "Oh, no, not again."

Twenty minutes later the UFO vanished.

28

Earlier that same evening, shortly before nine o'clock, the DC-3 transport with the words CLASSIC MINING emblazoned on the fuselage and tail slid down to a landing at Albuquerque Airport, with Sam Bronstein and Wolfgang Siedel in the cockpit. They closed the flight plan they'd filed while in the air, adding one more notch to the long list of absolute identifications they were setting up for the evening. They taxied to the general aircraft operations office, spent twenty minutes shooting the breeze with the not-so-pretty girl behind the counter, left a fueling order for the airplane, and rented a car. They drove to the Greyhound bus terminal, picked up an order of drill bits and other mining equipment, and drove to the airport motel where they would spend the night. They left a wakeup call for six o'clock and went to sleep knowing they'd dusted the trail behind them very well indeed.

Exactly six minutes after the Ju-52 came gently to earth at Boot Hill it was gone from sight. Every trace of the airplane had vanished, and five minutes after that everyone on the ground was back in dusty mining clothes. They went directly to the main bunkhouse, Pam wearing a pantsuit outfit, Lew and Phil dressed in nondescript clothes. On the table before them was the attaché case with the stocks and bonds so recently removed from the Midland bank. On the floor was Pam's baggage, packed the day before. Frank Bemis brought them all steaming coffee and they sat together at the table.

"Okay, let's run it through one last time," Shag said, the others nodding assent. "You two take Pam with you from here and fly to Stapleton Field in Denver. Lew, you've got an appointment for an ore assay and a meeting with a government mining expert, so that covers the why and the timing of the flight, and Frank is along as an extra pilot and hand. File your flight plan in the air, and remember, you report only two people aboard, right?"

"Got it," Lew said tersely.

"Good. You're as visible as possible in the air-control system but for a while you've got to play hide-and-seek on the ground. Keep Pam out of sight of any people at general aviation operations. They probably won't have more than two or three people there anyway. The best way will be for you, Lew, to get into their office and keep them occupied. Frank can go with Pam without being seen through the fence into the parking lot. It's a long walk to the main terminal from there but a lot of people do it and you'll fit right into the normal flow of pedestrian traffic."

Frank nodded.

"Now, the next step. Pam has a first-class ticket waiting for her under the name of Margaret Worthington, from Denver to San Francisco." He looked up as Pam was fitting a brown wig onto her head; moments later the beautiful blond was gone. He nodded his satisfaction. "Good. Now, Pam, what's your next step?"

"I land in San Francisco and rent a motel room at the airport; it's been confirmed in the name of Helen Arnheim. I pay cash for everything and insist upon a receipt. I check into the motel, where I change, into a black wig and a dress. I have two hours after checking into the motel to leave the room and get to Air Canada where I have a coach reservation to Ontario."

"What's your name?"

"Liz Denton."

"After you arrive in Ontario?"

"I check in at the Royal Hotel, still as Liz Denton. At eleven the next morning a man will come to my room. He'll be Robert Denton, a Canadian stockbroker. He's my husband. We go to his bank, where we're opening a safety-deposit box together. That way, having two keys to the box is perfectly normal. When Denton and I are alone in the vault, I place the securities in the safety-deposit box, make sure the clerk locks it with our key and the bank key, and we sign out. Denton and I drive to the airport, and I change on the way. I have a reservation from Ontario to New York, and—"

"Name?"

"Leah Starling. I live in New York where I'm a fashion designer."

"Go on."

"Leah Starling flies to Denver, changes planes for another flight to Colorado Springs. I wait at the airport, at the general aviation side of the field, where the Cherokee will pick me up. And it's back here to Boot Hill."

"If the Cherokee doesn't make it?"

"I wait six hours, then take a flight to Los Angeles and check in at the Sheraton-Universal Hotel near Universal Studios. I stay there until I'm contacted."

"Name?"

"At the Sheraton, I'm Fay Carter."

"If there's no word in seventy-two hours?"

"I assume the worst has happened and I start making inquiries."

"But never in person."

She nodded, and Shag turned to the others. "Three days after Pam leaves Ontario, Denton will attend to the securities. They'll be flown to Lisbon where the next transactions take place, and the only one of us who knows those details is Sam Bronstein. The securities will be exchanged for letters of credit and other negotiable papers, and finally there will be deposits in your numbered or named accounts, however you've set it up with Sam, wherever it's set up—Switzerland, Portugal, the Bahamas, Hong Kong. I don't know and don't want to know. Questions?"

Johnny rested his great bulk on his elbows. "We got twelve mil on paper, right? How much will that convert to?"

"About half."

Johnny's eyes bulged. "You mean we're giving up six million bleedin' dollars?"

"We're not giving up anything, Johnny. It's all paper. The securities are worthless unless they can be moved in the right places by the right people. It's a fair shake."

Johnny shook his head and grinned. "I guess that's being a success, then." He looked around at the others. "It's not so much what you makes that makes you a hero, it's what you give away to the other poor unfortunate millionaires that counts."

"You're getting the idea, fella," Shag told him. He turned to Vance. "How about it, Admiral? The Cherokee ready?"

"All set. I've turned it over and checked her out."

Shag rose to his feet. "Let's go."

At the airplane he held Pam tightly and kissed her briefly and hard. "Take care."

"I love you," she whispered in his ear, and turned quickly to climb into the small plane.

They watched until the flashing lights winked out from distance. Shag turned to the others. "Gentlemen, from this moment on you're digging for gold. Stay dirty, spit a lot, and above all, no matter how difficult it may be, act dumber than you really are."

By his side, Johnny sighed. "Act dumber, is it? I just gave up a share of six million dollars—that's nearly three million pounds—how much dumber can you get!"

"You'll see. We'll be having company soon."

Johnny drew up short. "Company, eh? And who might you be expecting, Shag?"

Shag held up one finger. "The Federal Bureau of Investigation." Two fingers. "Central Intelligence Agency." Three fingers. "Secret Service." Four fingers. "Drug Enforcement Agency."

"Drugs? We haven't come near—"

A full hand was outstretched. "Border Patrol." Six fingers. "New Mexico Highway Patrol." Seven fingers. "County sheriff, and—"

"Spare me, spare me the details," Johnny gave in. "By now I have the idea."

They walked slowly back to the bunkhouse. "Three million for the Indians. That was for starters. Then this job for twelve million worth of securities and bonds. That really ticked them off. By now they're trying to figure out how to tie in that caper in the swamp. Doesn't matter that we ripped off someone they'd like to nail. We got away with it—whatever it might be to them. We've been giving them the finger and they're going to check everything. So remember to keep your fly zipped. The one between your legs and between your lips."

The State Department didn't know how the stocks got out of the country. They dragged James Curtin onto the carpet and gave him absolute hell. Curtin, in turn, pointed the finger at Bill Woodburn from Customs, and he in turn gave State the finger because Customs worried about what came into the country instead of the other way around. Jake Torbay of the CIA wasn't asked into the scene, but since State confirmed the stolen securities had gone beyond the borders of the United States he could properly claim the possibility of Communist involvement and he jumped in with both feet. Hugh Harris of the FBI wanted to soak his head in a bucket of warm water to drown out the rising clamor all around him, but he was yanked from his Palm Beach office and hung out to dry by the head of the Bureau. They also gave him unprecedented authority in selecting a special team and since he had a perverse sense of humor, as well as a fine recognition of that rare commodity called intelligence, he put in a special requisition to borrow Red Thompson from the FAA. The administrator of the FAA, deluged day and night with examples of sagging morale on the part of his air-traffic controllers, yielded to the Bureau and ordered Thompson to represent the FAA on the special task force investigating the theft of three million dollars in cash from its secret storage place in Taylor, Arizona; the loss of twelve million dollars in securities from the shopping plaza in Midland, Texas; and, last but by no means least, "to find that goddamned Jewish UFO of yours! I hope that'll teach you to keep your stupid sense of humor to yourself."

Red Thompson seriously considered telling the FAA administrator to make like a gyro atop Red's extended middle finger, but he only had another fourteen months in his job before he was eligible to retire, and he had dreams of returning to the kind of flying that was fun. He hadn't had any in a long time. He kept his middle finger curled up in the palm of his hand and called Harris at his office.

"This the big FBI man? Fuck you."

"Hey, hello, Red. I was waiting to hear from you."

Red wanted to throw up into the phone. "How many of you assholes am I stuck with?"

Harris coughed apologetically. "All of us."

"I finally found out how it feels to be crucified. Okay, hero, is it true I run the show?"

"Uh, not officially, Red. The Bureau's been put in charge and—"

"I run the show."

"Okay, okay," Harris said hastily. Thompson was his only shot and they both knew it. "Where do we start?"

"Washington assigned us a Gulfstream jet. Everybody meets at Lauderdale International in three hours. We take off then for Midland. 'Bye."

"Hey, wait. I can't get them together by then!"

"You better, Prince Charming. Because two hours and fifty-nine minutes from now I close the doors and head west. Ciao, baby."

* * *

"Hey, Shag!" Sam Bronstein stepped into the mine shaft and shouted. "Company coming!"

Shag emerged from the cool darkness of the worthless mine, shading his eyes. He blinked several times and heard the whopping sound of the helicopter before he could focus. A big bastard from the sound of it. They must have commandeered one of the air force helos from that big military field near Albuquerque. Well, he'd been expecting them. In fact, they were a bit slow. He'd expected them at least a full day before now, which only meant that the confusion they'd sown had been more effective than he anticipated.

Everybody gathered by the airstrip except Vance. Shag had thought about that one for a while. "Admiral, when they show up they'll probably work out of the air force shop at Albuquerque. That means there's a chance somebody might recognize you. Everybody in the blue suit changes assignments every few years, right? So why take the chance. If we get company and it's the air force toting around the people, you make yourself scarce."

Vance was gone as they watched the big Sikorsky settle down on the runway in a screaming whirlwind of dust. Shag checked it out carefully. One high-ranking officer in a flight suit. Harmless; he'd been assigned as escort for just this flight. That meant he was local, he knew the area, and he was basically a bloodhound, but without the nose for it. Shag forgot him. He studied the civilians, the way they walked, the way their eyes moved as they looked around them. He dismissed two of them immediately and he was surprised that three men from that group fitted into the dangerous category. They were smart and they were professional.

Shag spit out dust and wiped the back of his hand along his face. "Thanks for the dust storm," he told the group. "Just what we needed."

A man in a dark suit, rumpled and sweat-stained, gestured his apology. "Sorry about that. We didn't mean to—"

"Hey, next time just drop it in a couple hundred yards down the strip. You got four thousand feet, for Christ's sake."

"I said we were sorry." Shag judged him a pro. He'd let this civilian shake him just a bit but he rocked right back. It was all there, the authoritative tone, the hunching of the shoulder muscles.

Shag almost laughed aloud as the man in the dark suit followed the script by extending a badge and ID card. "Hugh Harris, FBI. Mind if we—"

"I didn't see that tin star, mister. It was like a windshield wiper it went by so fast."

Harris didn't move for a moment. He withdrew the wallet case again and held it up steadily. Shag read it. "Ah. Hugh *R.* Harris. That makes a difference." He extended his hand. "Welcome to Boot Hill, Harris. My name is Jordan. What can we do for you? If you're interested in buying shares of Classic Mining, you're just in time."

Harris couldn't help the smile that tugged at the corner of his mouth. "No, thanks. We're here on official business."

"Shoot."

"You know about the problem at Midland, Texas?"

Shag scratched under his arm. "Not much. Just what we pick up on the radio. Big explosion in the rail yards there, or something. A train derailed and dumped a whole load of chlorine, and they had to evacuate the town. We know that much. Why?"

"Been there recently?"

"Midland? I've never been there. Never had no call to. Why do you want to know?"

"I'll ask the questions, if you don't mind."

Now's the time. Get this fucker off balance. Use the old body-language bit.

Shag stepped closer to Harris until they were inches apart, and he loomed over the FBI man. "Stick your badge up your ass, Mr. FBI man." His voice came out with a grizzly's warning to it. "Nobody asked you in here. You're on private property leased to us for a claim. Don't high-hat me, mister, and don't tell me that all the questions are down your one-way street. You want to play it that way, I'm ordering you off this property."

Shag had already seen the two gunners still with the helicopter. They were really loaded for going tiger-hunting, so the best thing to do was throw them off the track. He was still locking eyes with Harris when Johnny walked up to them, and he was bigger than Shag.

"All right, now, Jordan, just cool it. We both know what these bastards want," Johnny said. He put a meaty hand on Shag's arm. "We don't have to tell 'em a bloody thing. We've filed our report up in Denver and—"

Harris looked from Shag to Johnny. "What report?"

"Come off it, mate. We knew we'd never get away with that fairy tale of looking for uranium, but ever since we found that lode the old mine company missed, we've been expecting you people to crowd in here. You figure out some way to break our claim here? Well, let me tap your skull with some news, mister whoever-you-are. We're filed all proper and legal, we are, and—"

"Hold it," Harris said quickly. "No one's interested in your mine and I hope you find the mother lode in here."

Johnny blinked. "You mean there's no trouble with our claim? Let me tell you, ever since we filed, we've been expecting trouble."

"Not from me, I assure you," Harris said.

Johnny looked at Shag. "If our claim is clean, then what's he here for?"

Shag shrugged. He had started to respond but saw a tough man with thinning red hair leaving the group to join their confab. This one was even more the pro. He didn't bother with showing ID cards or badges or anything else.

"I overheard your name. Jordan, right? I'm Thompson, with the FAA out of Opa Locka."

Shag took it as it was offered—no problem. "You're a long way from home, then."

"Special assignment. This is—well, not an official investigation, but a sort of feeling something out. Do you mind if we look around? I'd appreciate it."

"Not at all. Go right ahead. We just like hands off our equipment. You know, look but don't touch."

Thompson nodded. "You have more than these two ships here?" He gestured at the DC-3 and the Cherokee.

"Uh uh. We might not be able to hang on to the Three much longer. Drinks a lot of that expensive juice."

"You fly the ore out of here, Jordan?"

"Look, Thompson, you came on fair and square. Don't fuck it up now. You know you can't carry enough ore in that thing to make it worth the effort even if we'd found a platinum lode. So don't ask questions to which you already have answers, okay? You could find out everything you need without leaving Albuquerque because we're on file with a dozen federal agencies. You want to look? Okay, look. But don't bullshit me, for Christ's sake."

Thompson showed a rueful grin. "I deserved that. Okay. Mind if I get a close-up on the Gooney?"

"C'mon." They walked past the big hangar, its doors yawning wide, the sand-blown floor littered with old machinery. Then they were at the DC-3, strolling around it slowly. "I got about ten grand worth of time in the old Gooney," Thompson said idly.

"You must be a hundred years old."

"I feel like it sometimes. Especially in this heat." Thompson stopped by the left gear. "That tire's way down into the tread. It would never pass an FAA inspection, you know."

Shag held his gaze. "The FAA never comes out here."

Thompson returned his stare. "No, I guess not. All this heat. Mad dogs and Englishmen, that sort of thing." He kept walking. He could have made a legal point about that tire, but he passed it off so casually—dammit, he was trying to be friendly instead of official, and who comes all the way out into the middle of this blasted hell to be friendly?

"Look, Thompson, come over here with me. Toward that hill." They walked away together. "I don't know what your small army is looking for, but you stand on top of that goddamned hill in front of us, right where that wind sock is, and you can see everything except down in the belly of the mine, and you're welcome to that trip now or anytime you want it."

Thompson held his silence until he stood atop the hill that overlooked the airstrip and the mining camp.

"It's the end of the world here."

"It's worth it if we prove out that lode."

"If you don't?"

Shag laughed. "Every mother's son of us has been broke before, mister. You win some, you lose some."

"See any German planes around here lately?"

"Any what?"

"German planes," Thompson repeated.

Shag thought. "About a week ago, come to think of it." He could almost feel the FAA man tighten his belly muscles.

"What kind? Where?"

"Hansa business jet. You know, that screwy thing with the wings swept forward. It was at Combs-Gates up in Denver. We made a trip there and saw it on the line."

"How about UFO's?"

Shag didn't answer for a while. "You're kidding. Come on, now, man, tell me you're laying the Sunday comics on me."

"I'm serious."

"So's my cock when I'm horny."

"Dammit, man, I really am asking. Have you seen or heard or noticed anything unusual in the air?"

"I really believe you're serious. But I don't get it. The FAA and the FBI and whoever's in that crowd with you. You're on a witch-hunt for flying saucers?"

"Look, Jordan, I'm already embarrassed. I'm just doing my job and I would really appreciate—"

"Okay, okay; I understand. Look, man, this is the desert, you know? We have inversion layers out here. We have planes taking off at night from Albuquerque and their lights bounce off the layers and we got ghost lights racing through the sky. I can't prove that's what they are, but—"

"Anything else?"

"Sure. You see everything in the desert. Boloids, you know, those green meteors that break up coming down through the atmosphere. We had a bunch of them last week. Hell of a show. But you want the nitty-gritty, right? Sorry, Thompson. No saucers or spaceships around here."

They walked down the hill. "Okay, thanks." Thompson kept his silence until they were almost back to the helicopter. He turned around and threw a ragged sort of salute to Shag. "Thanks for your trouble. And get that tire fixed before someone from the FAA sees it."

Shag grinned at him. The helicopter kicked up another dust storm as it fired up and lifted off.

Harris sat next to Thompson, who was deep in thought. Jake Torbay watched him closely as well. "Anything?"

Thompson shook his head. "Nothing."

"Then why the preoccupation?"

"Nothing I could put my finger on. But something bothers me. I have a sixth sense about airplanes, and I can't shake the feeling that those people were doing a number on us."

Torbay leaned closer. "What kind?"

"That there was another airplane out there and they were hiding it from us."

"Shit. Unless they dismantled the thing and carried it inside their mine shaft. Forget it, Red. You've had too much desert sun."

"Shag? Got to do some work on Annie. Have someone open up for me, will you?"

Shag waved to Frank Bemis. "I'll take care of it. Hang in there a moment."

Shag walked up the same hill where he had stood with Red Thompson from the FAA. He came to a stop by the steel pole that held the wind sock. He grasped the pole, twisted it to the right, bent it at an angle of forty-five degrees, and returned it to the vertical.

That triggered the switch for the big hangar doors. The hill on which Shag stood wasn't a hill at all, but a geodesic dome a hundred and fifty feet wide, with sliding doors thirty feet high that opened a space just over a hundred feet wide. Through which the wings of a Ju-52 fit very well indeed. They had built that dome in a hurry, which was easy enough with a crowd of strong men and interlocking aluminum girders. The top of the dome was covered with lightweight sand cement. Over that they poured desert sand, scrub bush, and rocks.

Nobody ever saw the hill because it was precisely what it looked like—a hill.

Who goes outside and looks for the sky?

29

She stood on the other side of the gate, and he'd never seen anything so beautiful in all his life. Even the weather lightened his heart. It was crisp and cool and not a cloud in the sky and all the way to Colorado Springs you could see in every direction for a hundred miles. Perfect weather for a guy to pick up his girl. He was astounded at how deeply this woman had gotten under his skin, at how much he missed Pam Kreiner. He shut down the engine, climbed from the Cherokee, and went straight to her. Not a word passed between them as he took her in his arms and kissed her deeply, almost urgently, and then held her close and squeezed until she gasped. He released his crushing bear hug. "God, I missed you," he told her.

She slipped her arm through his. "I feel I've been away from you for a year." A shudder passed through her, a release of pent-up feelings, and then it was all warm and just the way it should be. He brought her bags to the airplane and five minutes later they were rolling down the runway and lifting into the air. She snuggled up against him.

"You know how to fly with one hand?"

"Better than that," he said, and engaged the autopilot. They held their embrace for a long time, but finally his instinct brought one eyeball rolling around to the sky before them. They both sighed together, laughed like kids at themselves, and settled down comfortably for the flight over rugged mountains.

"How did it go?" he asked.

"Clockwork. Everything in order—one, two, three, zap. Has Sam confirmed the delivery?"

He nodded. She moved her fingers gently along the back of his neck. He growled. "Too damn bad we can't make love in this thing."

"We could, in the back seat."

"I hate dividing my attention."

"Oh. The plane. There is an autopilot, isn't there?"

"You're trying to get me into bad habits. I have a date with you tonight."

"Date," she confirmed. "How's everything at Boot Hill?"

He told her of the visit from the government group. "In words you've taught me, my darling, what's the bottom line?" she asked.

He let out a deep breath. "It's time to knock it off."

She tensed. "Do you mean that? Really?"

He nodded. "I've talked with Sam and the others, and the natural urge, of course, is to keep at what we're doing because it's been so successful. But instinct and common sense say to quit while we're ahead. We've done just about everything we wanted. Not quite a million dollars clear for everybody, but close enough so that it doesn't matter. Everyone agrees the airplanes belong to the original group of four. Vance,

Lew, you, and me, but they didn't care about that anyway. Our job now is to disband, do it properly, don't leave any empty spaces through which the feds can crawl after us. Right now even the cops are serious about hunting down that giant saucer so many people have seen on radar, to say nothing of all those eyewitnesses who feed on wild hopes and rumors. Everybody wants their UFO's to become real and that's been our best smokescreen. But by now the government's getting serious. They'll have brought Interpol into it. They feed everything into those computers of theirs and come up with what seems to be the best leads, and they'll go after everything with a microscope to get their first solid lead."

She lit up a cigarette, thought for a while. "Are we in any danger?"

"Not yet. Close, but not close enough to have us run for the exits. That FAA cat, Thompson. He's got more brains in one finger than that whole crowd with him put together. He knows this ghost plane is real. He can't put his finger on what's happening, but he knows it's real and he won't let up. He'll have checked out everything that happened in South America and Central America, and I'm sure he was brought into the picture in Florida, and the fact that he showed up here means it's a coast-to-coast effort."

"A short career. I thought I was a knockout in that leather uniform and the long blond hair."

He laughed. "You're a knockout any way you look at it. But back to the mining camp. We flew in a load of very high-grade gold dust. Real nuggets and the like, mixed it in with our stuff, and we've been spreading the word about a tremendous mother lode discovery. It's all working just as we planned, Pam. With the dollar in trouble around the world, and with gold prices going out of sight, what's more natural than for us to sell out to a major mining conglomerate in Europe that has all the bread and the organization to buy us out? Sam's taking care of that paperwork right now, in fact. We'll go to Fence Creek and throw a big bash and get stinking drunk and shoot off our mouths and spill everything. And then we split."

She squeezed his hand. "God, I'm glad to hear everything you've told me." She thought over his words. "What about us, love?"

He glanced at her. "Maybe we'll get lost for a while in Hong Kong or go to New Zealand, or maybe Italy. Nah, the beaches in Italy are all scummed up with oil. Switzerland. Anywhere you like."

"Think you could last a whole year on a honeymoon?"

"A year? I gave up that dream long ago, love, and now someone's given it back to me. I'm ready for a lifetime."

She sat straight and her eyes misted. "Thank you, Shag."

There was silence until a thought startled her. "Shag! I just realized, I mean—"

He squeezed her hand. "What's wrong?"

"Annie. What do we do with Annie?"

He grinned. "You're going to meet an old friend of mine. His name is Black Eagle."

"Black Eagle?"

"He's an Indian. Wears a feather and leather clothes and looks like a half-breed out of the hills. But he's also a brilliant lawyer and he likes money, and intrigue is his wine, so he's going to help us get shot down—after which we all disappear."

"Shot down? I'm sorry. I know I sound like an echo

chamber, but I really don't understand. What do you mean, shot down? That's ridiculous!"

"Isn't it, though. I don't want to spoil the party by telling you any more. You'll see when we land. We've removed everything personal from the camp. Whatever's left won't tell anybody a thing. Oh, I forgot to mention one important step in all this."

She waited. "That sale we were talking about to the German mining outfit? That conglomerate in Europe?"

"Yes?"

"It's going to break down. It's not going to go through."

"Shag Jordan, you're confusing me!"

"Well, imagine how the feds are going to feel, and they don't know anything that you know."

She sat back in quiet thought. *The chase. That's what keeps this man going. The heady wine of the chase, of outsmarting the best there is. Oh, well. Who am I to want a quiet home life, anyway?*

Black Eagle swallowed hard and clung tightly to his seat as the ancient German bomber thundered away from the dirt strip, banked into an alarmingly steep turn, and started its climb into the afternoon sky on a north-northeast heading. He looked at Pam Kreiner and smiled weakly. "Is he always a lunatic like this?" he asked over the sound of the engines.

"Most always," she said, smiling at the tall and dark man across the cabin from her. Shag was right; Black Eagle was a put-on and behind that crazy feather and his leather jerkins was a sharp mind and an animal instinct. A fearsome combination.

Black Eagle looked back at her, shook his head in wonder at the machine gun in its ball-socket mount in the window. This lovely woman with that invisible steel within her; she matched the machine gun perfectly. And that crazy Englishman in the machine-gun turret far behind them. Too much, too much. In the cockpit sat Shag Jordan and that quiet one they called Vance Brady. Five people in the machine out of time. He still couldn't believe where he was or what he was doing.

"This is really quite mad, you know," he said to Pam, picking up their conversation. Then he smiled broadly. "But I've never been paid better. My fee is almost astronomical when you think about it. Your man, Jordan, he never blinked an eye when I told him."

She offered a thin smile. "Then you must be worth it," she said, "or you wouldn't have been accepted within this circle."

"There is that, too," he admitted.

"Shag said you two knew each other from before, that there was something in your past. In fact, he referred to you as an old friend."

He studied her carefully. "I am pleased to hear that."

"Do you know that without even blinking an eye you change from legal to eagle?"

He laughed. "Beautiful! I must never forget that. It fits the costume and the routine equally well."

"Pam looked out through the window. "I think we'd better hold this until later. We've never flown before in daylight and Shag said things might get rather interesting." She patted the firing handle of the machine gun. "Do loud noises bother you, Mr., ah, Black Eagle?"

"Not at all. I play drums in the tribal band."

"How quaint."

* * *

They climbed steadily across the Cibola National Forest to fourteen thousand feet, where Shag rolled into an easterly heading and set their course for Santa Fe. This would carry them along a large cluster of heavily populated areas, but from the ground they'd be just another plane high in the air. Except that this time, Shag wasn't trying to hide. He wanted to be seen, preferably by another pilot who might get curious enough to come in for a close look at this impossible thing grinding its way through the skies. Everything had to be timed perfectly. They had to attract attention, scare the hell out of people, and do their next job without wasting a moment. There had to be enough time, anyway, to keep the government from closing in on them. This was Shag's master stroke, and Black Eagle, who sat high in the council of the Mescalero Apaches, was a vital cog in his maneuverings. If all went as he hoped then he'd be driving the FAA and the FBI completely wild. Everything they'd been chasing for months would appear right under their noses, confirming their wildest suspicions—and then it would all vanish again, but in a manner no one could possibly anticipate and that no one would believe.

They flew with their transponder turned on, fitting into the electronic chess game of air-traffic control, the same as any other airplane represented by the clear, bright blip on a radar scope. Shag was timing everything so they would reach Santa Fe at sundown. This was important. He needed the setting sun at a precise angle for his play, and he also needed the darkness that would follow quickly in the desert sky.

The DME gave them a readout of forty-three nautical miles from Santa Fe when he switched off the transponder. The same radar that had been tracking their course on the 1200 code for VFR flight would show that the blip had disappeared. Normal enough, for that could happen when a pilot turned off his equipment, descended too low for line-of-sight following, or had equipment failure. But none of that happened now, for the Ju-52 was still at altitude and at the same instant the VFR blip vanished—the enormous UFO snapped into existence on every radar screen within their range, and that covered an area well over a hundred miles across.

They listened to the frequency for Santa Fe Approach Control. Shag looked at Vance. "They've taken the bait." He thumbed the intercom switch. "Okay, you people back there. We should have some company pretty soon. You know what to do."

They heard Santa Fe talking to another pilot. "Cessna Six-three-three Quebec, we've got a strange target about ten miles east of your position. Would you mind deviating to take a look for us?"

"Sure, Santa Fe," came the reply. "What's up there?"

"Three-three Quebec, turn right to a heading of zero-eight-zero. We show a target ten miles from your eleven o'clock position and—"

"Santa Fe, I've got something visual ahead of me. I'm closing pretty good."

"Roger, three-three Quebec. We show the target as a thousand feet in diameter. Can you confirm? Over."

"How big? Say again."

"That's one-zero-zero-zero in diameter."

"Your computer's blown a fuse, Santa Fe. That's an airplane out there ahead of me and it sure ain't no thousand feet anywhere. It's an airplane. You copy?"

"Santa Fe here and we copy an aircraft. Can you identify the aircraft, please?"

"Uh, Santa Fe, I'm not sure. The gear is down and it looks like—no, I thought maybe it was a DC-3 but, oh, Jesus, I think I've lost my marbles—"

Silence. The 310 pilot went to full power on a steadily closing curve. He stared wide-eyed at the shape of the ancient German bomber growing steadily in size as he closed the distance, and the swastikas and crosses were bad enough, but that turret gunner standing out in the airstream—

He pulled alongside, coming back hard on the power. He wanted to talk to Santa Fe Control, but his throat was unbelievably dry and he felt suspended from reality as the turret gunner waved at him and motioned him to slide in closer. He responded, closing the distance until he could see the man smile beneath his goggles. He was completely mesmerized as the impossible apparition swung the machine gun about slowly and then he saw the muzzle of the gun sparkling bright cherry red and the next instant the 310 staggered as a hail of bullets shattered the windows of the rear seat and then crashed into the tail. The rudder pedals jerked wildly beneath his feet and stark terror overwhelmed him. Panic-stricken, he jammed the control yoke forward and plunged earthward and away from that impossible nightmare. He was sobbing from fear, and the intensity of what had happened churned his stomach and he retched violently all across the instrument panel and the control yoke in his hand. Only the scream of the wind through the torn windows brought him back to his senses. Instinct told him to reduce power and gentle the vibrating, shaking airplane out of its death dive.

* * *

"Looked pretty good from up here," Shag said.

"Nice and pretty it was," Lew called back from the turret.

"You stitch him a good one, baby?"

"Just like a good surgeon, Mr. Jordan. Chewed up his rear seat, got the windows, I did, and gave him a burst in the tail for good measure. He went downstairs in a hurry, but he was under full control. I never harmed a hair on his head."

"You get your sharpshooter's medal in your breakfast cereal tomorrow."

"Stick it, mate."

Black Eagle leaned closer to Pam. "They shot up that plane—"

She nodded. "They didn't even scratch the pilot. Lew's very good."

"But he'll report it!"

She smiled. She'd learned a lot from Shag. "No one will believe him. When he lands with his outrageous story of a German bomber with three engines and men firing machine guns at him, they'll arrest him. They'll figure he was on a drug run and he got double-crossed. He'll talk himself blue in the face for a week before they'll even start to listen. You're a lawyer. You know the police. If you were a cop would you believe him?"

Black Eagle smiled. "Never. But after a while I'd be getting curious, and I'd have to listen to his ravings, because I'd have nothing on which to keep him in the slammer."

"You're smart, but you sure talk funny for an Indian."

Black Eagle made a steeple of his fingers. "Would you like to see my routine as a priest?"

* * *

Shag cut off the rap session with Lew, punched in one radio already tuned to 123.45, and spoke into the mike. "Ladybug, Ladybug, you read Dragonfly here? Let's hear your wings flutter, sweetheart."

He waited several seconds for the response. "Gotcha, big guy. Hang loose, girls. The man with the steel eye is on his way and you can start your song and dance right, ah, right now will do fine."

"Gotcha."

Shag shoved the props full forward and brought in full throttle. Annie screamed with the sudden power and the howling propellers as Shag brought the big three-engined plane around to the north of Santa Fe, turned to put the sun directly behind him, and then, with the wheels almost scraping treetops and roofs, the sound devastating, he thundered smack down the middle of Santa Fe. Right through town center, lower than a line of buildings, the powerful gear ripping aside power lines, sparking transformers with sudden flashes of violet flame. He rolled steeply to the left, flattened out along a wide boulevard, and stunned everyone in sight as they howled through the city. Pam crouched in the belly hatch, dropping flare grenades as fast as she could pull the pins and dump them through the open space beneath her. As he completed his wild run, Pam was coming back into the cabin. She grabbed the machine gun and opened fire with a long belt of blanks, terrifying everyone who heard the deadly sound. The Junkers heeled over sharply and pulled up directly toward the huge sun hanging along the horizon until it was a great silhouette vanishing into time.

A deeper sound, purring-smooth, winding up to a cry of whistling death, sounded over the city, and disbelief compounded disbelief as a shark-mouthed P-40 fighter plunged from high altitude with tremendous speed, racing after its quarry, guns hammering, the Germans firing back. Smoke exploded from the left engine of the German bomber. It heeled over dangerously to one side, righted itself, staggered as the P-40 closed in tight and fired steadily, and then the right engine was pouring back thick smoke. At the edge of town reared a high bluff from which the bomber was seen by hundreds of eyewitnesses as it plunged earthward. There was a long moment of silence and then a tremendous, deep, ground-shaking explosion. A great fireball mushroomed into the air.

The shark-mouthed fighter disappeared. Sirens screamed as police cars and fire trucks raced over the rise to reach the plane just shot down. They found an enormous, smoking crater, pieces of burning debris scattered in all directions. The biggest piece left was from the tail, with the swastika blackened on the thick, corrugated metal.

30

It was dark within ten minutes and Shag kept her as low as he dared, holding high cruise power to keep her moving at 150 miles an hour along the two hundred miles to Lincoln National Forest, some fifty miles west of Roswell. When there were no ground lights below, Shag eased up for some altitude and Black Eagle came into the cockpit to stand between him and Vance. They clamped a headset with a boom mike onto the Indian's head so they could talk back and forth in the red lighted cockpit. The charts didn't count for much down here. Every road, every settlement, and every cluster of lights told Black Eagle what he needed to know for their position and where to continue flying. They were into a new area now, where the Sacramento Mountains ran through both the north and south areas of the Lincoln National Forest, each end separated by the Mescalero Apache Reservation. And it was within the sacred ground of the reservation country, where the whites did not come, that a road had been altered. The road stretched wide and straight and with the sound of the engines from the air, brushfires leaped up to mark out a flare path for their approach and landing.

"Jordan, keep this crazy machine of yours in tight," warned Black Eagle. "Be sure to touch down just beyond the first lights. And if you have any respect for Indian life, mine especially, stop this son of a bitch by the last fire. Just beyond that is solid cliff and I don't think even this locomotive of yours would do well against a small mountain."

"Jesus, shut up, will you?"

Black Eagle bit his lip, remained silent, nodded in appreciation as Shag worked the throttles and prop controls, hit the fuel pump, rolled down the full flaps, changed trim, scanned all the gauges and controls, and dropped alarmingly without power toward the fires. He had the tail down and the Ju-52 stopped with a thousand feet still ahead of them. "Taxi to the last fire," Black Eagle instructed. "Turn her around to point the other way and shut her down." Shag rolled to the end, stamped smartly on left brake and hit the right engine, and she wheeled about. He ran her to 1500 on the props, then pulled the colored knobs back, waited sixty seconds, and cut Annie's umbilical cord. The thunder fell away as he brought the mixtures to idle cutoff. "Stay where you are," said Black Eagle, and then was gone.

The fires were going out and dim flashlight beams played on the ground around them. They felt the airplane creak, then it started rolling backward. Vance turned to Shag with a look of alarm on his face.

"Cool it, Admiral. It's all part of the game plan. That rock face is as false as your grandmother's teeth. We're being winched into a cave."

Several minutes later they heard stone walls rumbling and then lights came on all about them. Shag stood up in the cockpit. "It's the biggest damn cave I've ever seen. Jesus. It must be two hundred feet wide at the entrance. I bet it goes back half a mile or more. This is one secret the Mescaleros still haven't shared with the Great White Father in Washington. Let's get down."

They met with Black Eagle. "It is done. Your flying machine shall be safe here and—"

"Cut the Tonto routine, Max."

Black Eagle sighed. "Right on. Okay, the Council has some suspicions but a quarter million greenbacks buys a whole pile of silence. It also buys the van waiting for you about a half-mile down the road. And my word that no one knows anything about tonight until you say so. Do your people know and understand our bargain?"

"I like you better as a dumb redskin. They know, baby. You did a neat job."

They walked in the darkness to the waiting van. "Tell me something, Shag. Where the hell did that fighter plane come from? When he cut in behind us I felt like one of Hirohito's unfortunates about to go to his ancestors."

"That P-40?" Shag laughed. "An old friend of my father's owns that bird. He stole it back in 1945 just when the war ended and record-keeping was a lot looser than it is now. He flew it to a ranch he has near Grand Junction, about thirty miles from anywhere else. Ghost town. He rerouted all the local roads around his place and his airstrip just happens to be the main street of his town. He's a weirdo. Got battle-happy, I guess, and he won't have anything to do with anybody except people he knows for a long time, and he's known me since I was a tadpole. Since that war ended he's been polishing and cleaning and maintaining that old fighter because—well, I guess his mind runs in circles and by the time he's into the real world something snaps and he returns to the old days."

Black Eagle nodded. "He wasn't firing blanks at us."

"Oh, I know. That's part of it. There's going to be an army of federal inspectors all over that place. They're probably there already. I want them to find the .50-caliber slugs from that fighter. Christ, he let loose with enough of it. You could see it hitting the streets along the town."

"Think your act will work?" Black Eagle pressed.

"For a while. Long enough, anyway. They'll bring in their experts. Same thing they had before in Lauderdale. I mean those bombs. No damage, nobody killed, probably nobody even hurt. The .50–calibers will throw them off for a while, but then they'll sift through that crater and go through the wreckage. I just didn't have the heart to kill some poor unknowing bastards and bury them with the rest of that ersatz wreckage we blew into the air when we went over. Oh, there's parts of engines and props and instruments, that sort of thing. We had the stuff back in Florida and we trucked it out and buried it here a few weeks back."

"You've planned it this way all along, then?"

"This ain't a crapshoot, Max."

"Well, what about the bodies that aren't there?"

"Some people will argue we bailed out. That should be a dandy of a manhunt. They'll be looking under every cactus for a hundred miles around."

They stood by the van. "I'll be in touch, Max. Thanks."

"Black Eagle and all his warriors thank the Great White One."

"Be careful you don't stick that feather up your ass."

"See you, tiger."

They shook hands and Shag climbed into the back of the van with Pam. Vance drove and Lew took the right front seat. They'd be driving all night to return to the mining claim in New Mexico. For the first time they would need that road they'd built in the desert.

"What now, Great White One?" Lew asked.

Shag waited until Pam lit up his cigar. He uncorked a bottle and took a long swallow, passed it up forward. "We're miners, right? We're struggling to stay alive out there in the desert and the heat. We go back and we work the mine. We fly the DC-3 and the Cherokee from here to there and we file flight plans and we stick out like sore thumbs. The boys are already gone. They lit out when we didn't have enough bread to make ends meet. That was set up a long time back, remember?"

"How long do we stay in that sandpile?" Vance asked.

"Long enough for everyone in Fence Creek to find out they were right about us from the start. That we're all assholes who've wasted all our money working a dead mine. Our flash-in-the-pan gold strike is going to give out pretty soon. Drive on, sweetheart, and be careful of the speed limit. You can't be too careful these days."

He pulled Pam close to him and rested his head in her lap.

"He's asleep," she told Vance and Lew a few moments later.

31

Shag walked in first, carrying the heavy leather sack over his shoulder. His dusty and frayed clothes looked like hell, and with long and uncombed hair he didn't look much better. He smelled like a wet goat, which also tends to attract attention. Following him into the assay office in Albuquerque, Pam differed only in gender, her face leathery and dried, her shoulders sagging with a bone-whipped weariness that needs no words. Tim Wylie felt instant sympathy as he greeted them. He'd gotten to know and like this crazy bunch. First their high hopes in their ridiculous get-rich-quick uranium hunt and then their flash-in-the-pan gold strike. Oh, sure, there were a thousand men like this Jordan fellow that Wylie could remember. You could always find a clump of good ore that promised the world but was a long way from being a lode. It was a shame the way the desert was eating these people alive. Wylie made a silent bet they wouldn't last more than another month or two.

He nodded to them. " 'Morning, ma'am. Morning, Mr. Jordan. Good day to you both."

" 'Morning." With a grunt Shag heaved the sack onto the counter. "You got the results of the last batch we sent in?"

Tim Wylie nodded again. "I sure hate to be the one to give you such bad news, Mr. Jordan."

Shag stopped in the process of striking a match to light up a cigar butt. That was one of his better moves. At first he'd been in here with a solid-gold Dunhill lighter and expensive cigars, and now he was using a match to light up this malodorous disaster. Wylie was supposed to notice it all and talk it up after they left. Shag let the hesitation last long enough to drop the match and strike another. He looked through the cloud of smoke at the assay man.

"How do you mean that, sir?" he asked.

"Well, Mr. Jordan, it's like this. Those batches you all brought in here last month? What you got there was a lot of dirt and just barely enough gold to count it for every ton of ore. That claim you're on—maybe this is none of my business, but you've been real nice and friendly, and—"

"Lay it out straight, Mr. Wylie." By his side Pam looked at Wylie with the eyes of a hound dog about to be run over by a garbage truck.

"Sir, that mine is plumb worked out, that's what. It's bleached dry and you're sure doing a lot of work right down to skin and bones with damned—beg your pardon, ma'am—little future to it. Why, you can't pull enough gold out of that dirt to run your operation, let alone to feed a crew of ten people. Besides—"

Shag let his shoulders slump. He leaned an elbow wearily on the counter. "Ten? Make that four. The rest of the crew—well, they took off. Can't blame them because we just didn't have the money to pay them anymore."

Wylie digested that slowly. "They still around these parts, Mr. Jordan?"

Well, well, Shag thought. So Thompson and his bunch didn't just leave. This place is bugged. Wylie's been told what to ask. Beautiful. Saves me the trouble of setting up false leads—

"Nah. What for? Couple of 'em went down to Africa to work on those gold dredges that Consolidated is running. They sure got a hell of an operation. They used those dredges in New Guinea for a while, then took 'em apart and shipped them to Africa. Maybe," Shag sighed, "if we had that kind of equipment we might have dug deeper and found what we were after."

Tim Wylie shook his head. "No, sirree, don't even think that way, Mr. Jordan. You're chasing a gopher down a tunnel that's got no end to it. You still own that big plane, don't you?"

"Yeah. Own it but can hardly fly it. Damn gas costs more than we can afford for that size ship. We're doing most of our flying in the Cherokee. At least that little son of a bitch is economical."

"Mr. Jordan, if you want to sell that plane and get out with something in your pocket, you let me know. I got friends at the airport who deal in planes and there's always a market for a good cargo hauler around here."

"Thanks. I'll keep that in mind. In the meantime, would you check out this new stuff for us?"

Wylie opened the leather sack and reached in an old and experienced hand. He still had his hand in the sack, hadn't even bothered to look at it, when he began to shake his head slowly. "Mr. Jordan, don't get your hopes up, please."

"We won't. How much time you want?"

Wylie knew the samples were worthless, but he felt compelled to carry it through. "Give me about two hours, okay?" He brightened his expression. "That'll give you folks a chance to get a good meal or do some shopping."

"See you."

They left and stood in the withering heat. "Shag, let's get a hotel room. I can't stand much more of the way you smell."

"Jesus, neither can I. I'll have some food sent up while we bathe."

"I'm sure the restaurant would appreciate that." She laughed heartily and they clasped hands as they walked the several blocks to the hotel.

Shag turned on the television in the room and kept the water running in the tub until he felt the noise level was high enough to screen out the bugs he knew had been placed in the hotel room the moment they'd registered. Then they both got into the tub. "Turn around. I'll scrub your back," he told her. His body close against hers, he brought his mouth to her ear. "Watch everything you say. They've already planted the bugs in the room, and they'll be listening to every word. You know how to carry it."

She nodded and her voice rose as he turned off the water. "Shag, this is the first time I've felt clean in a month. Can we quit? Please? You've got that job offer in Canada. You can fly that float plane and I can run the restaurant. My God, after all these months out here even frostbite sounds good to me!"

Hope you mothers are listening good, Shag said to himself.

* * *

She didn't speak freely until they were back in the air. Shag motioned her to silence with a finger against his lips, then moved a small electronic monitor in a complete circle around him. He nodded finally and slipped the monitor back into a pocket. "It's clean," he told her. "But you never know. Sometimes they're efficient and sometimes they're paranoid."

She smiled. "Like we're supposed to be about our gold mine."

"That old man was sincere. He was really trying to do us a favor by telling us to pack it in. We're going to pay attention to what he says. More important, those people in the back rooms who were prompting his questions, who taped everything, also listened in. By now their patience is running thin and they're getting confused."

"Do they really suspect us, Shag? I don't want to be an alarmist, but—"

"No, love, they suspect us and everybody else who might even have a chance of ripping them off. Consider their position and—" Shag interrupted himself, opened the small vent window by his left, and threw away the stinking rope he'd been smoking. He reached inside his jacket and pulled out a choice Jamaican cigar and lit up. He'd turned on the autopilot and he sat back, relaxed. "Okay, consider their position. They haven't got any real leads. We're driving them crazy. We're lunatics on a chase-the-gold kick. We have enough money to have gotten it ourselves without stealing it and not enough money to pour it loosely down a rat hole. Every which way they turn we're clean. Our backgrounds are less than pristine and we're the footloose type and they know some of the gang are mercenaries. So they've got to suspect us, love, but they also suspect a hundred other operations and a thousand other individuals who fit our type, and they've got a small army doing gumshoe and bugging operations on every mother's son."

She nodded and her laughter was like a silver bell to him. "And all they've come up with is—"

"A UFO that comes and goes, an airplane out of time they know is real but can't prove, and a bitter dispute within their own camp. Plus all the loot that's missing, a Cessna pilot who got the shit scared out of him for a year and nobody really believes wasn't caught up in a drug bust that went sour. What gets them even more upset is the way our crew just disappeared. You know, the whole gang of six. They had them all in their grasp and when they made a fist they found everybody trickling through their fingers like fine sand. Those guys are experts at vanishing."

"What if they track them down?"

"So? That's why I got Sam into this act. They can find them all they want. Everything's covered. Everything's *legal*. Sam made sure those bastards are even paying income tax, filing reports. They're so clean they squeak."

"They're a remarkable bunch, Shag."

He smiled. "I'm glad you said that." He nodded to himself. "They defied all the rules. I don't mean the caper, I mean among and with themselves. Six men who are strong, tough, independent, who have killed and almost been killed but don't like to kill. You know, that was one of the secrets of this whole group. Gaston is one of those people who could snuff out a man's life like squeezing a bug between his fingers but he'd rather let the man live. When there's a choice those people always chose not to come down on anybody in their way."

"I don't think I'll ever understand that code. You've all killed—"

"That we have," he affirmed.

"But even Gaston, or Johnny . . ." She shook her head. "They don't fit the picture."

"What about Sam?" Shag said. "He's the toughest one of the crowd because he deals in death. But it's all business and it's never personal. Did you know that Sam is a millionaire several times over?"

She was astonished. "I knew he'd made out well, but nothing like that."

"Well, he is, and he came along on this caper for the fun of it and because he knew killing was way down on the list. Sam and I flew some missions together and between us we wiped more people than you want to know about. It was a war; that justified it. But no one in our crowd is a killer by type, and that means someone who wants to or has to kill or enjoys it. This crowd enjoys the fight, the risk, the head-in-the-noose bit, and they'll take their chances with anyone or anything, but if they can get together for a drink when it's all over, including the guys they were fighting, they'd rather have it that way."

"What about Lew and Vance? What will they do when this is all over?"

"If I know Lew he's a lot more tired than he lets on. He won't go back to England because of what it's become. He'll head for what smacks of a frontier. It could be Australia or Singapore; I'd put my money on that. Lew could buy into an airline operation or even set up his own charter work, and he'll be happy for a while. And then some really juicy war will break out somewhere and he'll dive into the middle of it. He's a slave to the Siren's call."

She smiled. "That puts it well enough. Is Vance the same way?"

He shook his head. "No. Vance has something in him that's both a curse and a blessing, Pam. He feels deeper than almost anybody we'll ever know. I swear the son of a bitch should have been born a Jew, because he knows how to suffer so damned well! But hey, I didn't mean to lay his soul naked for you. I think Vance is going to disappear for a while. He has enough money now to spend the next bunch of years in great comfort, but not the way most people think of comfort. That doesn't mean luxury in his book. Comfort is freedom from having to consider your next meal, where it's coming from, or even thinking between first class and coach. It's knowing he can spend some time in the total luxury of being free to think, feel, search, experience, test, judge, taste, to open his sensory endings wide for whatever he wants to experience. Call it seeking out the truth. He got his ass into a hell of a lot of trouble once, and lost everything in the world except one thing, because he disobeyed orders and didn't kill a million people. That was back in the days when he commanded an atomic-bomb crew."

As Pam absorbed all this, Shag rolled in some nose down trim. The changed attitude of the airplane brought her from her thoughts. "You said Vance lost everything in the world except one thing. Can you tell me what that was?"

"His self-respect. He goes to sleep at night with a clean conscience."

"Then he's a rare and very fortunate human being."

"That he is, hon."

"Can you stand another question?" Shag nodded affirmatively. "Good. When we wrap up all this, what happens with the old girl?"

He glanced at her. "Annie?"

"Right. Annie. I've become very fond of her."

"God, so have we. We can leave her in that cave with the Mescaleros. She'll be safe enough there. But—"

She caught his hesitation. "But?" she echoed.

He was dropping flaps, rolling in to the dusty runway. "Later. When we're all together tonight. I think we'd better plan on flying out to dinner somewhere. What I have to say can't be said at Boot Hill."

Pam bit her tongue. There was a time to knock off the questions and the time was right then.

They flew to El Paso. Wheels up to touchdown took less than ninety minutes in the DC-3, and they parked at the executive terminal. Shag pressed a sawbuck into the hand of the line chief. "You keep that Gooney Bird parked right out here in front of your operations shack," he instructed. "I want her under full lights, right out in plain view for all the world to see."

"Got it."

"We're going down to Juárez for dinner. Anybody asks, you feel free to tell them anything you want. Get us a cab. When we get back that piece of green in your palm has two twin brothers."

"Thanks, Mr. Jordan."

Shag came to a dead halt. "How'd you know my name?"

"We get a regular list of aircraft numbers and owners we keep in the fuel truck. You're on it."

"Narcs?"

"Yes, sir."

"Assholes. For Christ's sake, kid, turn on some extra lights."

The line chief grinned. "I sort of figured it that

way, Mr. Jordan. Some guys are in that line and other guys just don't fit."

"And I don't?"

"You're way over that."

"You a psychic or something?"

"A psychology major and I'm good at it. I work here to get through the university."

Shag nodded. "You're so smart, you tell me where we're having dinner."

"Easy. Where no one would expect it and the food's great. Irma's."

"Cathouse, right?"

"Yes, sir. It's also where the Juárez chief of police goes for dinner. The restaurant and that cathouse might as well be in two different worlds."

They took the cab across the border to Irma's and the kid was right. There was this three-story cathouse that did a roaring business, and a bar where the undecided studs hemmed and hawed before they were dragged by the groin to an upstairs room, and a restaurant, where they had the best food in the city. Shag knew that a twenty-dollar bill would get them a private room for dinner, and an extra twenty would keep an armed Mexican cop at the door all through dinner, and few places in the world were safer to talk. Just for old times' sake he scanned the room with the monitor. It was clean.

They were into dark Mexican coffee and a shot of fiery golden liqueur before Shag clubbed them between the eyes.

"I've been holding out on you," he said. No one said anything. When you got that kind of opening you waited, and after a decently short interval Shag went on. "I want one more shot. I didn't say anything about it before because I wanted it only for us. I really didn't know this was going to come up until the last couple of days, but—" He shrugged. "It's an unexpected opportunity and it could be worth a couple of million." They were getting restless and he cut them off. "Sit on it for a moment. We don't need the money; we all know that without dragging that subject through the mud. But it would be nice to have it, I guess."

"It never hurts," Vance murmured.

Shag was studying Pam. "You look upset."

"I am. But it's not my place to question. I told you I wouldn't unless you broke my own rules. So far you never have. Don't mind me."

He nodded. "I found out about this, or I got the first hint about it, oh, maybe a month ago. I've been checking it out quietly, buying information. You know the assay office in Fence Creek? And the one in Albuquerque? They're both part of Wells Fargo. That outfit handles mining offices, banks, armored cars, payrolls, jewelry shipments; the works. Normally a Wells Fargo hit isn't worth the trouble. But this one is special. In fact, it's a very special delivery job in one truck. They've got it wrapped in a tight cocoon. No schedule on the books, but I've found out when and where that truck will be. I want to hit it."

Lew ordered tequila and salt. It helped him think better. He went through the ritual of downing the blazing liquor and licking salt from the back of his hand. He blinked watery eyes. "What's in the truck?"

"I don't know."

"That's stupid, isn't it?" Vance broke in. "You should at least have some idea. Gold, securities, fat bundles of cash, diamonds, comic books; you know."

Shag pressed both hands flat on the table. "I don't know what's in the goddamned truck. I do know that it's way off the regular schedule, there's no obvious reason why it's going to make the run that's scheduled for it, and it could be anything. But sure as God made little green apples it ain't your everyday shipment."

"You really want to hit a truck without knowing what's in it?" Lew was incredulous. He worked over some more salt and tequila.

"You need a lemon to do it right," Pam said.

He looked up and blinked. "What?"

"Here. I'll show you." She went through the ritual as if she'd done it all her life. "Bravo," he exclaimed and kissed the back of her hand. "The salt's on the other one," she smiled.

"The security for this thing is wild," Shag said, just a shade too quietly. It was Vance's turn to smile as Lew came erect and studied him. Pam rolled her eyes and kept silent. "In fact, there's more security to mislead people about the routing than there is about the truck itself. And the fact that it's traveling alone, whatever the hell is inside, is a blind so it won't attract too much attention. They've even got three armored convoys going in other directions, carrying money, to shift attention from this truck."

"We're pushing it, you know," Vance said quietly.

"Annie?" Lew asked. His normal eloquence faded beneath the tequila.

"Annie," Shag confirmed. "It's the only way. Our cover still works. That splattered radar return and the machine out of time. It's got a ways to go yet. Especially since it's all calmed down so much."

"We wouldn't dare go back to Boot Hill," Pam interjected.

"We're not going back to that sandpit," Shag told her. "Not tonight, not ever."

"Oh?" Vance's verbalized grunt spoke for them all.

"Tomorrow morning two miners will drive to Boot Hill," Shag said. "They'll get a paycheck in a post-office box every week from a bank in Chicago. Their job is to work the mine, get their money, which is rather generous, and know nothing about nothing."

"You mean," Lew said with wide eyes, "you had this all figured before we got here tonight?"

"Uh huh."

Pam motioned for attention. "But our clothes, our things, what about—"

"They're proof we're returning. They stay there. Forget them."

"The DC-3, Shag," Vance put in. "We need it to—"

"It stays right where it is. On the El Paso ramp. A cabdriver gives an envelope to that kid on the line. In the envelope is a hundred-dollar bill and a note to move the airplane to long-term parking, fuel the bird, keep it ready for takeoff at any moment."

"And we just waltz back across the border into El Paso?"

"No. We go south to an airstrip thirty miles from here. We fly north and land at Tucson and we go through customs, and we go on record for the flight, and we do everything legal and proper. Ain't no law, my faithful, that says we have to return Stateside through El Paso. And before you ask, the chief of police of the fair city of Juárez has it all set for us. The transaction, just in case you're nosey, was cash."

"Jesus Christ," Lew said.

"He's not part of the deal," Shag cracked back. "All right, dammit, now's the time to ask the questions and raise the fuss."

"If we don't agree with you?" Vance asked.

"The rules haven't changed, Admiral. One nay outweighs two ayes in this navy."

"There's four of us here and I only counted three votes," Vance reminded Shag.

"I don't vote," Pam said. "Where the man goes I go."

"Okay," Vance yielded. "Let's have the rest of it."

"I thought you'd never get around to it," Shag said, grinning. He lit a cigar, filled the small room with smoke, withdrew a chart from an inside pocket and laid it on the table before them. "Before we go any further there's one rule. On this stint we don't backtrack. We can't afford to. We make the hit and we keep right on trucking. Agreed?"

"The details first," Vance pressed.

They studied the chart. "See along here?" Shag explained, his finger tracing distances on the chart. "They're even moving that armored truck on remote roads, through primitive areas, and I still haven't figured out why. Look here; Tucson. Go due north to Catalina, a few miles beyond that, and then a road cuts through an area that's as barren as the moon. Highways 80 and 89 run together along here and it's about as abandoned as can be. See why? That superhighway, I-10, runs along here. Pam, gimme a pencil. Okay, now follow me along here." The pencil followed his words. "I figure we bring the iron bird down about here, and we time it for dusk. These people do most of this kind of travel at night, but they always like to get a head start and they don't want to be sitting still in the dark. So they get going at just about sundown. We make the scene here," he marked an X on the chart, "and then we cut to the north-northwest, up to Lake Mead. This gets set up well ahead of time, of course. D-Day is eight days from now."

He turned the chart sideways, the smoke getting

thicker with his own rising excitement. "Now, here are the White Hills southeast of Las Vegas. You'd never believe a place could be so isolated and so barren that close to Vegas, but it is. It's like pictures I've seen of Mars. I mean desolate, absolutely nothing, and the area is filled with those old dry lake beds where we can land the Ju at night. The damn things stretch a couple of miles."

He leaned back and took a glass of tequila from Lew's hand. "We land and taxi right up to an overhang. By the time we get there we've got a motor home waiting, camouflage netting, the works. Then one of us drives from the parking place to one of the resort marinas on Lake Mead, and there'll be a boat ready and waiting. One of you has to be in that boat on the far north fork of the lake. It's isolated there and there won't be anyone else there at the time, and—"

Pam looked up sharply, as if she were fighting her way out of being hypnotized by Shag's intensity. "A boat? In the lake? Why?"

"Because," Shag said gently, "as much as I hate to do this, the iron works simply has to go. I take off in the dark and I wait for just that first light of dawn and I start her down, power back, the controls tied in place. I go out the cabin door on a static line—"

Pam was aghast, her face white, fingernails digging into her palm. "I don't believe all this," she said in a hoarse whisper. "You're going to take off at night, alone, tie the controls, dive to a thousand feet and bail out at that altitude? Into the water?"

"Sure," he said, confused by her vehemence. "With the static line that chute will be opening within thirty feet of my going out the door. That's why we need the boat. To pick me up."

"You're crazy!" She was almost screaming.

Vance held her arm, brought her back into her seat quietly. Shag had an amused smile on his face. "Of course I am. That's why these things work."

"But, Shag—"

"No, Pam, he's right," Vance broke in. "The craziest thing about all this is that he's right. Bailing out like that is perfectly safe. I'll do it myself if it bothers you that much."

"My idea, my flight," Shag said in a tone that brooked no argument.

Lew stared at him with bloodshot eyes. "How deep is the bleedin' water?"

"That's even better," Shag replied. "Seven hundred feet and a strong current along the bottom. Iron Annie goes to a watery grave, but she goes out in style." He looked about the table. "Agreed?"

Lew nodded, extended his glass. "Up the bloody Queen!"

"Quaint, but unnecessary," Vance said. "It's a go."

Shag looked at Pam, who had buried her face in her hands. "Pam, say something," he told her. "Whatever it is, say it now and not later."

There was pain in her eyes. "What's there to say? I love you." She stood up and looked down on them. "You assholes."

32

They took off in darkness eight days later from the crude airstrip stretching before the cave of the Mescalero Apaches. Fires flickered along the dirt runway and Shag needed every bit of help he could get, including the cold air of the night. Annie was loaded well over her maximum gross weight of twenty-three thousand pounds and even those powerful tires humped down into the soft dirt. The wing tanks were filled with six hundred gallons of fuel, and they'd loaded a line of fifty-five-gallon drums into the cabin, with a pumping system to offload from the cabin into either wing as they drank fuel during flight. This extended their range and endurance so that they could fly most of the night and still have almost full tanks when they landed before daybreak.

Shag wound up the engines to full power but he was still uncertain about getting off before they reached the end of the dirt strip. "Do you remember how high those trees were at the end?" he asked Vance.

Even in the dim red light of the cockpit Vance's expression was unmistakable. "Too high and too damned close to us. We're pushing mighty hard, mister."

Shag thought that over for a few moments. If anything, Vance was Mr. Unflappable when it came to takeoff distances and the room needed to clear obstacles. Finally Shag nodded. "Okay, we cob them through the gate." He turned to Lew standing behind and to his right. "You take the power," he instructed, and as he spoke he snapped the overboost control to full open. "No thirty-six inches for this one," he stressed. "Take her right up to forty-five inches and hold her there until I bring the nose down. She's loaded like a pregnant elephant and those trees are getting higher every moment. Got it?"

"I'll make her sing, never fear," Lew promised.

"Pam, you belted in?"

Her voice crackled in his headset. "All ready back here."

Shag nodded to the others in the cockpit and Vance came back full on the yoke with him. Shag's right hand jockeyed the throttles to an even setting on the gauges and he stood on the brakes as he advanced power and then he felt Lew's hand over his own and he released the throttle knobs and went to the yoke with both hands. Even the brakes weren't holding anymore. She was dragging herself through the dirt. He had thought of a tail-low run with the twenty-five degrees of flaps, but that meant a bit more drag so he popped the brakes and let her roll a hundred feet before he shoved forward on the yoke. The tail was up and Annie's fuselage was level with the ground, the engines screaming painfully all around them as the prop blades tore at the air, and they accelerated with surprising speed for all their weight. Shag held her down until she was ready, then beyond that until the needle showed ninety, but he was watching the flickering fires and when there were only three spots of flame still before him, he came back on the yoke and she was in the air instantly. Shag knew she was solid and he hauled the yoke back hard, keeping her speed at ninety and trading off acceleration for climb rate. In the darkness they never saw the trees and they were five hundred feet above takeoff level when he pushed forward on the yoke to gain speed and Lew brought back the engines to thirty-six inches of manifold pressure. They kept normal takeoff power until they had two thousand feet above ground level on the altimeter. From then on it was a quiet, smooth flight in darkness, the transponder code set for normal VFR recognition so they would melt into normal night traffic flow, and their world was the familiar muted thunder of the three engines, the marvelous stability of a heavy airplane that had returned to its domain. They transferred fuel as they floated through the mantle of night, only their engine exhausts showing any sign of their passing, and then they were at their destination.

"We're early," Shag noted, easing into a wide descending turn and coming down at barely two hundred feet a minute. It was a wise move for they would be dropping into rough country and they needed daylight to judge depth, distance, and where they would land. First light came slowly, then ever more swiftly, and the thin slice of the new day along the horizon developed into ridges and abutments and definable curvatures and bends of the earth below.

"Got the airstrip," Vance said into the intercom. "Two o'clock my position. If you start left now and come down at about seven hundred a minute you'll be lining up on a long final."

Shag came back on power, shoved the props to flat pitch, and hauled back steadily on the big wheel below and to his right for full flaps. The long-abandoned airstrip in the heart of Arizona's Aravaipa Canyon Primitive Area kept expanding before him and he touched down gently, letting her roll to the far end. He motioned Lew forward. "See that grove of trees? You get out and take a close look. If the surface is okay I'll taxi in as close as I can get and we'll cover her up there."

Lew climbed outside and ran ahead of the waiting Ju-52. Apparently the surface tension was to his satisfaction, for he motioned Shag to taxi around to his right and swing the plane sharply. Shag inched her forward until the wingtip scratched through leafy branches and then Lew gave them the shutdown signal. Shag locked the brakes and let her wind down, punching off the power and switches. "Let's move," he said tersely, and all four of them went to work at once, dragging out the lightweight camouflage netting to drape downward from the trees so as to obscure the airplane from all but a close-up study. The flight had been about four hundred miles, including their turns and the wait for first light, and that meant they still had plenty of fuel in the wings. They offloaded the fuel drums and concealed them beneath the grove of trees.

"Okay, we take turns sleeping," Shag said. "Two down and two up. We're only twenty miles from that highway and the truck will be leaving Tucson straight from Davis-Monthan at dusk. That ought to make it about seven, which is about as close to sunset as it gets. And," he said tiredly, "if they hold to their schedule they'll be just east of Newman Peak, where we want them, with enough light remaining to make our move.

We take off as late as we can, just about seven, and we stay over open country until we go for the highway. Pam and I will take the first watch."

Pete Jefferson shifted in his seat, grateful for the cooling air swirling past him. He dangled a cigarette from his lips and tugged his shoulders against the restraining harness. He didn't care for the seat belt and harness but it was a rule of the company. Anybody who rode in the front cab of a Wells Fargo truck wore the belt and harness at all times. They looked ahead and to the sides through armored glass that would stop a .44 Magnum, but there was always the danger of a truck being overturned or smashing into a barrier, and the belt and harness would let a man live through that better than a man in a fighter cockpit.

Jefferson nodded to the man by his side. "Looks like a good run tonight. How's the coffee?"

"Be right with you." Scott Julian lifted a safety no-spill flask from its warmer and held it out to his partner. Jefferson sipped slowly. "Um. Helps. Going to be a long haul. Wonder what the hell we're carrying. I got the word they sent out three decoy runs to get attention away from us."

Julian rested a foot on the thickly padded dashboard. He glanced through the window into the truck body. Behind thick armor-plated steel another four men were seated, studying the road behind them, more alert than was their habit. "I don't know," he said finally. "But I don't like it. You know what I mean? We're so isolated out here. That load is heavy enough for gold or platinum—"

"Shit. It could be anything. You know how they work this stuff," Jefferson said with the wisdom of a man who'd handled this sort of run for years. "I remember one time we carried a box, must have weighed four hundred pounds. It was all lead. They had about ten pounds of paper inside. I heard about that later. They never let us know what we've got."

Julian nodded. "Well, that way we don't have to worry about it." He laughed nervously. "Wouldn't it be something if we were carrying biological agents?"

"Carrying what?"

"You know. Germ-warfare stuff."

"Why would we carry that?"

"I didn't say we were carrying it. It's just that if we were we'd never even know it. And what's better than this rig?" He gestured to take in their rolling fort. "We're sealed in, air conditioned, armed to the teeth. Maybe we're carrying toothpaste. I don't know."

Pete Jefferson grunted. "Fill this coffee can up again, willya?"

"Sure."

Silence fell between them. The end of the day was turning the sky into a beautiful lilac that reflected all around them. It was like nowhere else, this stretch of 80-89. The two-lane highway ran absolutely straight, not a break as far as they could see ahead of or behind them. Even the power lines ran well off to the side, high enough on the slopes to be above any sudden cataract of water that sometimes spilled through this country during the brief but violent thunderstorm season. On each side they saw deep gullies and washes, land tortured by a baking sun most of the year and lashed every now and then with knifelike water tearing down the barren slopes to each side. The armored truck felt like a tank, rolling at precisely 55 miles an hour, every mile of the way registered by a sealed wire recorder. Jefferson turned on their headlights. The sun shone with a painful brilliance on the horizon ahead of him. He pulled down a gray-tinted visor. "Goddamn sun."

"It'll be down in a couple of minutes," his partner said.

They drove steadily, but in the rear of the truck a security guard tensed. "Hey, did you guys see that?"

"See what?"

"Look. Way back down the road. I saw a flash on the highway." The others crowded to the back windows.

"Nothing there now."

"Look. See it? Like a smoke cloud. Way back. I saw a bright flash. It came and went."

"Could be someone turning on his headlights. You know, there's nothing there, guy turns on his lights and you see it as a flash. Or maybe it was the sun off a windshield."

"Hey, he's right. That smoke, or dust, or whatever it is. It's higher now. You can see the sun reflecting off—"

"Nope. It's headlights. One, anyway. Must be a motorcycle." The guard placed binoculars before his eyes. "It's a motorcycle, all right. Got a sidecar. Don't see much of them. Must be one of them bike-gang guys. Looks like they're wearing German helmets."

They were. German helmets and German uniforms. Pam, long blond hair streaming under the helmet, whipping in the wind, Lew in the sidecar. They'd stopped long enough after coming out from a deep wash to set off explosive charges that ripped the highway open, tore a deep, wide gash in the paved surface right where it extended over a bridge crossing a dry stream bed. The road behind them was now impassable. Pam speeded up.

* * *

Henry Roland picked up his microphone. "Jefferson, we got something crazy back here. Can you see that motorcycle in your rearview mirror?"

Jefferson looked back, saw the single bright headlight. "Yeah. What about it?" The intercom mike picked up his words and carried them through a speaker to the security team.

"Well, it ain't no ordinary bike. There was a flash back on the road and now here comes this motorcycle and it's got a sidecar. It's got to be doing a hundred or better, and we've got the binocs on it and—holy shit, they've got some kind of gun in that sidecar. It looks like a machine gun, for Christ's sake!"

Without a word the four men loaded their weapons, two riot guns and two submachine guns. They pulled aside small panels and the machine-gun barrels went into their firing slots. "I don't know what the hell is going on, but I don't like it," said one guard. "You guys be ready for anything."

Jefferson's voice came from up front. "Hey, some sort of flash in the road. Miles ahead of us and—good God!"

Lights blazing, a huge shape descended from the darkening sky, lower and lower until they saw the winged form touch down on the highway before them. Jefferson threw up an arm to ward off the dazzling light that ripped into his eyes and his foot went by reflex to the brake. That goddamned thing was still coming toward them and then it was turning and Jefferson and Julian stared with wide and disbelieving eyes as their headlights played on the side of a German bomber completely blocking the road.

"There's a plane ahead of us!" Jefferson shouted. "It's blocking the road and—"

His words were cut off as a blast of machine-gun fire smashed into the windshield. The armed glass held but the windshield crazed over immediately, making it almost impossible to see. The next moment the truck seemed to be exploding beneath them as the machine-gun fire zeroed in on their front tires. Jefferson fought desperately for control but he had almost no steering left and there was the scream and stench of burning rubber as he swerved crazily. He couldn't hold it straight and their left wheels slid on gravel and then off the side of the road and they were going over. Men's voices yelled and cursed as the armored truck tilted crazily and then metal screeched as they went over on their side, held by their straps, the truck banging and slamming to a halt against boulders, coming to a bone-jarring stop in a gully. The wheels spun crazily and the truck shuddered as the engine stalled.

The guards struggled to get to their weapons. They saw a figure standing in the motorcycle sidecar and there came a blast of flame and then a tremendous explosion against the back of the truck. Metal screamed in protest and the armor plating buckled. It held, but the impact hurled two men back, semiconscious, stunned from the blow. Both submachine guns had been thrown from their slots.

Then it went quiet, and they could hear rumbling engines from that crazy machine on the road before them. A voice with a thick German accent called to them through a loudspeaker.

"Inside the truck! Schnell! If you vish to remain alife you vill come out in der open at vunce! Ozzervise ve vill use a panzerfaust to set you on fire! Schnell! You vill burn alife in five zeconds! Come out mitt your hands in der air! Hans hoch! Rauss!"

From the other side a burst of machine-gun fire tore at the truck. "Jesus, we're trapped. They mean business out there. They got a bazooka or something behind us. We'll fry if we don't get out of here. Listen, you guys, do as they say. We can't stop them. And no guns or we're done for!"

Shag watched from the cockpit and Vance stood ready by the turret machine gun. Five men came out slowly, staggering, carrying an unconscious form with them. They showed their disbelief as a German SS sergeant, wearing helmet and wide goggles, covered them with a machine gun. And that other one, the blonde carrying a machine pistol. They stood with their hands high as the SS sergeant ran to the truck and looked inside. He saw ten metal cases, and he turned to the truck crew.

"Quickly or you are dead men. You vill carry those cases to the flying machine. Move quickly or ve vill cut you down."

They moved. It took two men to carry each case. They stumbled in the rough ground and half-carried and half-dragged the cases to the Ju-52, their eyes wide as they saw the German markings clearly now. Shag had come down from the cockpit and they saw a burly German officer. As they heaved a case into the cabin door, every move covered by three machine guns, the officer dragged it forward into the bomber. Several minutes later the cases had been transferred.

The SS sergeant was behind them. "If you vant to stay alife do as I say. Take your friend ofer zere and start away from here. Valk avay and do not turn around. Quickly, now!"

They went back to the still unconscious guard. Two men picked him up and they stumbled across the broken ground. "Whatever you do don't turn around," Jefferson hissed at them. "Them fuckers mean business and I don't want a backful of lead. Just keep moving."

They froze for a moment as an enormous explosion lit up the desert all around them, followed by a second blast as a rocket shell tore into the armored truck. "Keep moving, goddammit," Jefferson said desperately. "And don't turn around, for God's sake!"

Another tremendous explosion lit up the desert and more flames leaped into the sky. Flames threw ghastly shadows all around them.

Quiet for several moments and then a new sound. Engines turning up and then a deep-throated cry of thunder. "Everybody down! Go flat, go flat!" Jefferson yelled.

Thunder swelled and washed over them. Jefferson rolled over onto his back and lifted his head just in time to see the dark shape lifting away from the earth and disappearing into the night. In the road the motorcycle and sidecar were shattered, blazing wreckage, and at that same moment the fuel tanks of the armored truck exploded. Jefferson rolled over, face down, covering his head with his arms as flaming debris rained down. Then all they could hear was the crackling of flames.

33

Shag had never felt so good. He'd never expected to be in this cockpit again, running the odds, breaking them, defying all the rules, and they'd pulled it off in the neatest operation they had ever done. He stayed low as he darted across the mountain country, heading for the dry lake bed they'd planned on reaching in the dark. This one would be easy, with Las Vegas and the surrounding towns providing ready-made beacons to guide them in. Pam sat in the seat to his right and she saw the satisfaction on his face. She shook her head slowly and smiled with him. She thumbed the intercom. "You've got canary feathers all over your face, Jordan," she told him.

"Yeah, I guess so," he told her, and the smile widened to a grin. "I guess it's what makes the blood run hot. And we don't even know what we've got back there. I—" He cut himself short as Lew came into the cockpit. Even in the dim red light they saw the shock on Lew's face. He was drenched in sweat and shaking.

"What the hell's the matter!" Shag yelled. But Lew

had no headset and he couldn't hear in that thundering roar of the Ju-52 cockpit. Shag grabbed the engineer headset and shoved it angrily at Lew. The man was moving in slow motion as he fumbled with the headset. His hands were shaking so badly he had to try several times before he had the earphones and the boom mike in place.

"You, uh, you should . . . I mean, you better come back here," Lew stammered.

Shag looked at him with narrowed eyes, flicking his gaze between Lew's tortured face and the instruments. Without lights on the ground in this isolated area to provide horizon reference their whole world of safe flight rested on the red-glowing dials before the pilot. "Can you handle this thing?" Shag asked.

The vacant look on Lew's face disturbed Shag, and he was reluctant to trust this shaken man with the controls. Yet Lew could fly anything and Pam would be in the cockpit to be certain he paid attention to what was needed. After a strange pause Lew nodded. "Uh, righto, of course." He shuddered like a wet dog flinging away water from his coat, and the vapid look faded. "Sorry, Shag. I can handle it. You better get to Vance."

Shag climbed from his seat, stood close to Pam in the cockpit with one hand on the yoke before her. He waited until Lew was strapped in. "Hold her due north. Same altitude," he instructed. Lew nodded and shoved him gently back into the cabin.

He had the strangest feeling when he stooped out through the cockpit door that he had been looking at a death mask on the face of Lew Heath. The crescendo of noise fell sharply as he stood upright in the Ju-52 cabin. He was surprised to find Pam right behind him. "Lew told me to come back here," she said simply, and he nodded.

One light glowed in the cabin and in that light he *was* looking into a face—a mask—of death as Vance stared at him and Pam. Shag was swiftly losing patience because the man before him was literally in shock, as if he'd been struck by a cobra.

"What the hell is going on?" Shag demanded.

"The apocalypse."

Shag was dumbfounded. Was this man in a trance? "What did you say?" he asked again.

Vance held a flashlight on one of the containers removed from the armored truck. "The apocalypse," he repeated. "Look for yourself. But before you do I want to warn you about something—you're going to be holding Hell in your hands."

They went closer to the metal container and saw that Vance and Lew had opened the outside cover. The flashlight showed another metal container within, revealing strange studs, elaborate protrusions, and sharply etched printing within the metal. The light shook badly and Shag took the flashlight from Vance and handed it to Pam. He glanced up at Vance again. "What's in here?"

"I've been here before. This is your first time. Find out for yourself what it's like, goddammit."

"Shit." He ignored Vance for the moment, peered closer until he could read the largest letters: MARK 62 TN SYSTEM.

Serial numbers and technical data followed. He studied it for a while, noticed wires leading to the side of the crate, recognized an explosive-rigged detonator that would have to be disarmed before the inner container could be opened safely. But he was more disturbed by the reactions of these men who had flaunted death a hundred times with him. Shag sat down on another container. He took the time deliberately to light a cigar. He pointed to a container. "Sit down," he told Vance.

Vance swayed as they bumped through mild turbulence. He was reacting in slow motion. "C'mon, Admiral," Shag said quietly. "Take a seat and talk to me."

Vance moved slowly until he was seated and then he gripped the container beneath him as if he might fall off. He stared at Shag.. "Do you know what—" He swallowed hard, tried to speak again, couldn't.

Pam reached into her purse and removed a flask. She removed the cap and handed it to Vance. "Brandy. Go on. Take a long one."

Vance nodded. He took half the flask without stopping, handed it back to Pam, never taking his eyes from Shag. "You better take a shot. You're going to need it."

"Stop the damned theatrics," Shag snapped. "Get on with it."

"Always the same," Vance chuckled, and the switch was so great it startled Shag and Pam. "Just get right on with business no matter what."

"That's the general idea." Shag leaned back against the cabin wall. "You look like you can talk now without coming unglued. Go."

"All right." Vance took a deep breath, let it out suddenly as if purging himself. "Mark Sixty-two. TN System. Critical assembly is fifty-one-point-nine pounds." He stopped.

"Vance?" Pam's voice was soothing. "I don't understand. What does TN mean?"

He looked up at her and the death mask was gone, as if he had made some incomprehensible inner peace with himself. Now that he had come to grips with this *thing*, whatever it was, he had regained his composure.

"TN?" he repeated. "It stands for thermonuclear."

His words hit Shag with the impact of a truck. He stiffened, every muscle so tight they were cramping all over his body. He forced himself to breathe deeply. Jesus, two of them were bad enough. He'd have to show cool all the way through this.

"Thermonuclear?" Pam echoed. "You mean—" Her hand flew to her mouth as if saying another word would have been catastrophic.

Vance's voice was a monotone. "Mark Sixty-two Thermonuclear Weapons System. Warhead core fifty-one-point-nine pounds. Uranium two-three-five core trigger, implosion system, model sixteen. Outer jacket lithium-hydride-barium, gold cones for neutron—never mind. There's an easier way to say it. The Mark Sixty-two has a yield of three hundred megatons."

They stared at one another. Pam moved closer to Shag, gripped his shoulder. Vance looked like an avenging angel now. "Do you know what that means? That's three hundred million fucking tons of explosive yield for each one of these warheads!" He stood up suddenly, his arm sweeping in a wild gesture. "There are ten of them in here. Can you add it up? Do you know what it spells out? In this airplane, right now, under your ass, there is three billion tons, *three billion tons*, of explosive power!"

He sat down, calm again in one of those remarkable shifts of mood. "I may as well say this quietly. Screaming won't help, although God knows I want to scream. One, just one, of these warheads in the right place, detonated for maximum effect, can kill anywhere from fifty to two hundred million human beings. Shall I describe the fireball? The fireball alone? At Hiroshima and Nagasaki it was maybe one or two thousand feet in diameter. One of these things detonated on the ground has a fireball fifty miles across. You know how big that is? One ground burst will devour all of San Francisco and all of Oakland in a single swallow and the temperature will be over a hundred million degrees and that's just the core of the explosion. Shall I tell you about the shock wave that punches out at two thousand miles an hour? Or that the blast wave thirty to fifty miles outward from the fireball will knock down any city in the world? Or that an air burst of one of these things, if you blow it at a height of ten or twenty miles, will blind every living creature that looks at it for a distance of five hundred miles in every direction? It burns out the eyeballs, destroys the optic nerves. And I haven't started on the thermal yield and the direct radiation and the crater that's a couple of miles across and the fallout that's lethal a thousand miles downwind and—"

He buried his face in his hands and sobbed. And everything that Shag had known before of that moment when Vance refused to cross the fail-safe line and went home to a court-martial and disgrace from his own country paled to a weak dot in memory, because now he understood, he truly understood. Shag sat quietly, Pam's fingernails digging through his shirt into his shoulder. The shock had numbed both of them.

Then Shag shook himself free. He knew that the immediate danger was in how they reacted. You had to push it aside, attend to the moment at hand. One step at a time. He was back in control of himself. He removed Pam's hand gently and placed his own hand on Vance's shoulder. "Answer some questions, Admiral. It's important." He saw Vance look up.

"Do you know how to work these things?"

Vance nodded.

"Are they safe the way they are now? I mean, could we set them off accidentally?"

"No. There's a coded sequence to follow. Unless you follow that sequence you'll detonate an explosive charge that will wreck the mechanism and the thermonuclear system will blow apart. You could drop them in a fire and they won't blow."

Shag let out a long sigh of relief. It was like safe nitro, if you could imagine something like that. Or Pandora's Box, just so long as you sat tightly on the lid.

"Shag. My God, what are we going to do?"

Shag stood up and looked down at Vance. "Close up this case. Pam, you help him. Secure everything with that webbing. We can't ignore the facts of life. We're in the air and we've got to land before daylight. So let's cool it, okay? Just cool it and play it nice and slow. We're going to land where we planned, in the White Hills near Red Lake, and then we make this ironmonger disappear, and then we think."

He went back into the cockpit and took over the controls in the left seat. No matter what, he had an airplane to fly.

34

Shag tuned in his transmitter to 121.6. He knew his exact position from the horizon lights of the Las Vegas basin, and he was tuned in to Vegas VORTAC for a perfect DME mileage readout. Over the darkness-shrouded dry lake where they'd set up their equipment, he clicked his transmitter seven times. The radio signal opened the power to dry-cell batteries and a dull line of yellow lights appeared in the inky surface. Shag knew the precise altitude above sea level of the dry lake and he rolled the Ju-52 around to final a thousand feet above the surface and let her drift down along a slight crosswind. The lights grew in size, he slipped the wheels over the crossbar glowing up at him, and they were down, rolling along the line of yellow.

"I'm damned glad we were here before," he told Pam as they taxied close to a sheer bluff at the end of the lake bed. "Because right now there's a whole army and air force and everybody else in the government, and every law-enforcement agency in the country, looking for those crates we got behind us." He clicked his transmitter three times and the yellow lights went out, then he rolled down the underwing landing light. "There, see that road?" he told Pam. "We taxi along that. It goes around the flanks of that cliff and it's the last place anyone would ever look for a large airplane." The brilliant light beneath the wing gave them a clear view of the road, and Lew was running ahead with two flashlights. Shag brought the airplane to a stop between two high canyon walls, a natural cut in a steep crest. To each side rock towered hundreds of feet above them, but the way in and out was clear. If he taxied straight ahead and veered to the left a bit, he had at least three thousand feet of hard-packed dry mud for future takeoff. But that was later.

He shut down the engines. No one needed any prodding. They had prepared for concealment before their landing, but what had been a caper before was now serious beyond all imagination. They had driven hooks into the rock walls and now they slipped nylon lines through the eyebolts and stretched out their camouflage netting. Pam and Lew ran back to the strip where they had landed, picking up the landing lights and wiring, running back to the Ju-52 under its cover.

"It's not enough!" Vance yelled. "Get some brush—anything—and start wiping out those tire tracks. They'll be combing every open area with special cameras. Come on, do it!" They slashed away brush, wiped out the tire treads of the airplane right on down to her place of concealment between the towering rock cliffs. "Get some brush and throw it on the netting," Vance ordered. "When they take pictures of these areas we've got to have shadows at low light to throw across the netting or it'll stand out like a sore thumb." They worked feverishly, cutting their hands, but disregarding the pain to beat the clock. Brush and cactus lay tumbled across the netting.

Vance was right. From the air, either to the naked eye or on film, the netting had become a natural projection of the desert surface. The brush was already dry and not even special photographic processes would show a spectrum variation between the flora still in the ground from that heaped across the netting. They collapsed, beneath a wing, sweating and short of breath. They could afford a brief respite now. They were seventy miles southeast of Las Vegas and some twenty miles from the lakefront settlement of Temple Bar, but from appearances they could have been a thousand miles from the nearest town.

Vance finally sat up. "Okay, everybody. No fires, no smoking, nothing to give off any heat. They've got the word out everywhere and they'll be using anything that flies, and the reconnaissance satellites, to cover every square inch of ground. They'll be looking for us in the infrared especially and we don't want to give them anything to point at us. Shag, we'd better get in that Land-Rover and get the hell out of here before first light. Otherwise, even the dust trail could give them a hint and they won't pass up anything."

Shag nodded. They grabbed the few personal things they needed. "Hold it," Vance said. "Anybody carrying?"

Lew opened his jacket to show a .357 Magnum in a shoulder holster. "Put it in the plane," Vance ordered. "If we get stopped for anything, including a taillight that may be out, there can't be a single lead for anybody." Lew tossed the gun inside the cabin and closed the door.

"All right," Shag snapped, "let's roll."

They drove away from the butte and the concealed bomber. Their plans had been altered to an inconceivably drastic degree, but they still had the motor home stashed and that boat on the lake, and if ever there was a time for vanishing this was it. There was no driving north or even northeast because that way lay the Colorado River and the Grand Canyon. Instead, snatching the advantage of the last minutes of full darkness, Shag turned west, bumping and thudding their way around the small town of Dolan Springs. He picked up a reasonably smooth dirt road and drove at a steady pace until they reached Highway 93. From there it was an easy drive, mixing in with normal traffic, sparse as it was at this hour, to the lake marina. They parked the Land-Rover, leaving nothing with any identification behind them, climbed into the motor home, and drove twenty minutes to another marina. It took less than five minutes to transfer everything into the rented houseboat tied to the dock. It was the kind of lease deal common enough to this area; you took the boat by the month.

They remained strangely silent as first light silhouetted the stark ridges of mountains all around them, moving slowly under power out toward the center of the lake. The pressure built within them during those anticlimatic hours as the sun rose higher and the desert heat washed down across the lake. Their silence was almost enforced, demanded by their minds, an unspoken agreement just to let things be for this moment and try to get the pounding in their skulls to abate. By the time the sun was high overhead Vance was blind drunk, as numb as if he'd been turned to granite. They dragged him inside the cabin and tucked him in tightly. He stared sightlessly at the three of them, closed his eyes, and was asleep instantly.

Lew stayed by the wheel, deep in his own thoughts. Pam rested with her body touching Shag. She needed the human contact desperately, needed his presence. She was overwhelmed by it all, worse than the others, for their lives had for years been punctuated by death and destruction and killing. She lacked that advantage and her only hope was her tight emotional grip on Shag.

But there was no escaping the question that rammed into their guts and screamed silently at them. They had ten three-hundred-megaton thermonuclear bombs in their possession.

What the hell were they going to do with them?

They drifted slowly all that day and night and all the day following, staying on the lake as if its expanse could afford them insulation against reality. Even that short period of time helped them. They stopped running in mental circles, started edging closer to the knowledge that they must make a decision of some kind.

They turned toward shore, to a different marina, and shortly after nightfall, when the restaurant was filled and people were occupied, Shag and Pam went ashore and bought newspapers and assorted toilet goods. Pam made several telephone calls to girl friends in Las Vegas. Shag waited for her with a face of stone. "That could be a stupid thing to do," he said critically.

She took his arm. "You forget I'm a fast learner. I have some to-the-death girl friends in Vegas. And just so you'll know, you and I have been registered for the last five days at the Sundowner Motel—"

"Where the hell is that?"

"Small place out toward Nellis, the air-force field. We've been registered there for five days, and Lew and Vance have been registered at the Mint, downtown, for seven days. Not only that, sir, but the registry books have been signed and those particular rooms are shown as occupied since those dates, and payment was made in cash, with receipts. There's also a restaurant, the Angus Special, where the cocktail waitress recalls very clearly that we've been to dinner several times. The girls are also collecting showroom receipts, you know, stuff like that. We've been driving a 1979 Capri, and by tomorrow morning the car will have at least four hundred miles on the odometer. There are other details, the most important of which is that no one has been asking questions as to the whereabouts of one Pam Kreiner who, rumor has it, went home to Germany a couple of months ago."

He kissed her lightly. "I take it all back. That's beautiful. Registrations, car rentals, eyewitnesses, receipts; the works. We just might need it."

She nodded. "It also fits in with our being seen here tonight. We just left town for a couple of days to get away from it all. You know, months in the salt mines and that sort of thing? What could be more natural than to want to be surrounded by water after that hellhole of a gold mine?"

They went back to the houseboat and eased into the darkness. Shag spread the newspapers before them on a table. "Nothing," he said after a careful scrutiny. "Absolutely nothing, and this is the early-morning paper. The holdup of a Wells Fargo truck should be at least a small news item. But it's like it never happened."

Vance, unshaven, seated on the deck with his back against a wall, sipped at his coffee. "What did you expect? The serial numbers of the missing bombs?" He laughed without humor. "They don't need noise. They need those warheads. And I don't think I need to tell you the greatest manhunt in history is underway right now. If they even think there's a tie-in with anybody, this is the one time civil rights and privacy laws are just so much crap. They're going to come down with sledgehammers on even the first suspicion of a lead. They'll break arms and legs and use drugs and crack skulls and torture and—"

"Not too surprising," Lew broke in quietly. "You Yanks don't really know what a bloodthirsty lot you are."

"Up yours," Vance said easily. "What would you do in their place?"

"Break arms and legs and the rest of that bloody rot, of course," came the reply. "But the best thing that's happened to us is that we're the last ones they'll suspect."

They looked at him in surprise. "Come off it now," Lew went on. "You know they've already notified the Kremlin on that hot line or whatever it is the Big Man has in Washington. They've got to. The first people they're going to suspect is a well-organized terrorist group with international machinery. You've got your fair share of underground organizations here, right? Weathermen or whatever it is these subversive nuts call themselves. I guarantee you they've been bashing a few skulls around. They've hit every one of them." He grinned. "I can just see all those wogs in the PLO, what with your people telling the Arabs in no uncertain terms to find out and right now, if they're tied in, in any way. All the rules are out the window, mate. They'll suspect a foreign government, maybe a couple of them. The Japanese Red Army, maybe. Anybody, because they've got to figure that whoever it was knocked off that truck knew about the bombs well in advance. See?"

Shag chewed on an unlit cigar. "Jesus. I think you put your finger on it." A heavy fist smashed into his palm. "Damn! You've got to be right! It's the very insanity of it all. That German bomber, those weapons and uniforms. They'll have to figure it was all leading up to the big hit. Everything they did before was to finance their operation." He broke out into sudden laughter. "Want to bet they've come down with everything they've got on Basil Dorsch, our old pal from Peru?"

Vance seemed to come alive. "I'll be damned if I don't think you're right." He sat up straight. "They'll have tracked down every lead, checked out every witness, gone all the way back and at least one of those trails has got to have taken them back down to South America, and there are going to be a lot of fingers pointing to Basil Dorsch. It'll be a witch-hunt for Nazis, for sure." He sighed, smiling. "Who would ever have thought of it? Comeuppance is delivered unto us, after all." He looked at the others. "I know it's crazy, but that makes me feel a lot better. Whatever's left of the old crowd down in South America, you can bet they've all been flushed by now."

Shag lit up the cigar. As with the others, adrenaline pounded through his system with every moment. "Of course. If you were running this show, trying to find ten thermonukes, would you even consider that four idiots like us stumbled onto those bombs, by accident? No way, baby! Not in a million years. But they'll be checking out—"

He stopped short. "If I'm right, then someone has already done us a hell of a big favor."

"Who?" Pam voiced the question for the three of them.

"Scenic Airlines, that's who," Shag snapped. "And you know why? They fly scenic tours down the Grand Canyon."

"So what?" Lew pushed.

"They rebuilt two old Ford Tri-Motors, that's what."

They looked at one another and whooped with laughter. "Yes, by damn!" Vance shouted. "The old Tin Goose, bless her swaybacked hide! After what they heard from those truck guards, that would be the first place they'd look. We've got to get to a phone and find out!"

"Please," Pam begged. "What on earth is a Tin Goose and what's it got to do with us?"

Lew smiled at her. "It's a Ford, m'love. When Ford used to make airplanes. Three engines, just like Annie. Fixed gear, just like Annie. And corrugated metal, just like Annie. Of course, Annie's low wing and the Goose is high wing, and Annie's a lot bigger and heavier, but in the dark? I thinks they're right. That would be the first place they'd look. They've probably got every last mother's son of them behind bars right now, and—" He turned around and went into the cabin, a moment later stuck his head out. "We've got a radiophone on this thing. Want to give it a shot?"

Shag thought it over and nodded. "Pam, you do it.

Get the operator, don't give our number, give one close to it, and see if we can be put through to Scenic Airlines. Get the reservations desk for two seats for tomorrow."

They waited as she put the call through. When she hung up the phone she nodded. "They are out of business for a while. Maintenance problems, the girl said."

"Maintenance, my ass," Vance chortled.

"Lew, take her in," Shag said suddenly. "We've got work to do. Let's go to where we've got that motor home parked." Lew speeded up the engines and started for shore.

Shag turned to Vance. "When we get in we drive to that trailer park toward Nellis. They've got transients coming and going. I've got to get a pickup truck of some kind and take out five drums of fuel to the Ju-52 and fill her tanks. We'll bring extra batteries just in case we need them. We'll make this the last trip on the road. If we have to go back again soon we do it by air. Right in and right the hell out again, and—"

"Shag."

He looked up at Pam's interruption, waiting. "Are you planning to fly the Ju soon?" He was so filled with the excitement of renewed action that he failed to notice the strange, almost detached look on her face.

"Soon?" He shrugged. "Hell, I don't know. I want those tanks filled just in case it becomes necessary to fly out of there in a hurry. And it would have to be a one-way trip. There's no way we can go wandering around in that iron works anymore. Too slow, too dangerous." He shook his head. "You're on the right track, though. We'll have to get something a lot faster and with a lot of range built into it. Maybe a Rockwell Commander. Turboprop job. Or a straight jet. No; the turboprop would be better. Attract less attention. We could do it with a King Air. Something like that. We'll need speed and range when the time comes to move those bombs." He turned to talk with Vance, failing to see Pam's chalk-white face.

35

"Okay, it's all done. The Ju-52's fueled and ready to turn over. I don't think we've got a security problem. Nothing is pointing at us. I've made the deal for a Turbo Commander. It can carry all of us and those ten crates as well, and still give us all the range we need." Shag paused to swallow the rest of his drink. He'd been without sleep for a day and a night and he needed something to bring him down to the rest of them. They were crowded into their motor home in the desert trailer park, the television blaring just as it was in the hundred motor homes and trailers all around them. It covered their conversation well.

"We've got to come to a decision as to how we're going to handle the hardware," Shag reminded them, as he had a dozen times already.

"Well, we don't need a Turbo Commander, then," Vance said acidly. "What's happened to your brains, man?"

Shag glowered at him. They'd never been this tense

with one another. "All right, Admiral. Let's have your side of it."

"We have to move those bombs out of the country."

"To where?" Lew demanded.

"I don't know that yet. But we need speed and a hell of a lot of range. A 707 or a DC-8 would do it. We could fill her to the gills with fuel, and without any real cargo or passenger load we could get six thousand miles out of a cargo job." He thought over what he said. "There's a couple of ways to do it. The best would be to lease one with a crew. They wouldn't have to know what we had for cargo, and we could load thirty or forty crates aboard, so our ten would mix in with the rest."

"Where?" Lew demanded again. "We just can't go tripping around the bloody world, you know. And unless it's all set up ahead of time we haven't anyplace to go. Why, now, 'ere we are, we says, with ten pieces of hardware that can blow up half the mucking world, and we'll have the bridal suite, we will, please."

"I hate to admit it but he's right," Vance said. "Do you realize this is the first time we haven't had our plans tied down to the last tiny detail?"

"We needs a customer, we do," Lew said, quietly, deadly serious now. "We needs to set up a deal and have everything lined up neat, like tin soldiers in a row. And the best man to do that, no questions asked, is Sam Bronstein. We know him and we can trust him, and besides, we don't even have to tell him a bloody thing. Sam's a good trooper and he'll go along with us, knowing we'll let him in sooner or later."

"A customer?" They turned to Pam. "Who would buy—"

"Woman," Lew said with a deep breath, "we could sell these to the Arabs for a clean billion dollars. You understand that number? *One—billion—dollars*, delivered anywhere and anyhow we want, and no problems. We could carry the stuff to any field on the east coast in that Turbo Commander, transfer the cargo to the jet we lease, and we can handle the rest of the trip nonstop. They'll have to play it our way because they'll never know if we might set one of those things off by remote control or timer. They're a bloody suspicious lot, anyway."

"If we sell them it takes the pressure away from us," Shag said, voicing his thoughts aloud. "The government will find out soon enough and they'll go after those things with a strike force that no one could even think of stopping. Shit, the Russians would probably join in. And once they have those nukes back the pressure will fade away. If we play it right they don't even need to know we were involved."

"You'd really sell them to a foreign—" Pam didn't finish. Shag saw it coming and he stopped the rest of her words.

"You think we could ransom these things back to our government?"

"We could try," she said quietly.

"No dice," he said emphatically. "There's no way they wouldn't put the finger on us sooner or later. And they'd have assassination teams with a lifetime job of finding us and snuffing us. No, it's got to be some outfit other than here. Someone with a lot of bread who's willing to part with it for our little toys. And we can't leave the things where they are, because someone could find the Ju by accident, and they could get into the wrong hands. If we—"

Pam's voice stung them like a whip. "What did you say?" Her face was contorted, the cords of her neck as tight as bowstrings. She was incredulous, and ready to explode. "I couldn't have heard you right," she said, every word biting through clenched teeth. "God help me, I couldn't have heard that!"

Shag reached out to her, but in an instant she was on her feet and her hand slashed out like a striking cat. An astonished Shag saw blood trickle across the back of his hand where her nails had clawed him.

"Don't touch me," she spat, her voice hard and angry, cutting through every sound around them. Her eyes were wide and her face strained. "What the hell do you animals mean—*into the wrong hands*! What are you crazy bastards anyway? Saints? Angels?"

Her voice rose to a high, snarling buzzsaw. "You fucking bastards, you've made Jesse James and Al Capone and Dillinger and even Genghis Khan look like schoolchildren! You've killed and stolen and murdered and lied and cheated and I know because I was right there with you. But how can you talk about the wrong hands! My God in Heaven but you're all crazy. You're going to sell those things that could tear apart half a planet and bring on another war and—"

"That's enough!" Shag was on his feet, his own anger a burning fury in his eyes. "Sure, we play the game rough, baby, but we're out in front and don't you ever forget it. We take our chances and we keep it on a one-to-one basis, and if we get killed that's the breaks. We may not be saints but there's a line that we never cross. Sure we've got a bunch of hydrogen bombs on our hands, but we didn't plan it that way. You know that. You were there! If we'd known what was in that truck we'd never have gone near it in a thousand years. But it's happened and we've got them. We've got a tiger by the tail and we can't let go, so we may as well get what we can out of the deal. Lew's right.

Those things are worth a cool billion to us with no questions asked, and—"

"You're a liar, Shag Jordan."

The quiet statement hit him like a blow. His eyes narrowed. But before he could speak she walked up to him, stared him down. "You're a liar," she repeated. "You said you've never crossed that line? You have now. All three of you. You sell those bombs and you could be condemning helpless people, children, to a horrible death. A billion dollars, you say? That's pretty good business. A buck for every life. One billion dollars for one billion lives. I'll bet you could win the best business deal of the year award with that one."

Vance moved forward. "Hold it right there, Miss Kreiner. Don't you give me this goody-goody shit about morality. Remember me? Remember who I am? The guy who refused to kill a city and got his ass busted for it? I—"

"You make me sick. Spread your legs, Brady, because I think I'm going to puke. You and him and him," she grated, her finger jabbing at each man in turn. "So you got the short end of the stick. So fucking what! You're not the first to get the fickle finger of fate up your pretty pink ass, and you're sure as hell not going to be the last. Each one of you is like me. A whore. A prostitute. But at least I picked my company. Goddammit, listen to what I'm saying to you! I've been a hooker and I spent years getting paid to fuck people. But you three are worse than the lowest slut that ever lived! You got a bad break and you've been screwing society and life with every shot you could get since that moment. You're bleeding hearts for yourselves and you hide it behind your tight-jock macho horseshit. You go out and take your chances on getting killed because deep down inside you're all afraid of facing up to the everyday problems of life. You're copouts, all of you. You've been wallowing in your own self-pity because somewhere along the line you got shafted. Big fucking deal. That goes for you and it goes for me as well. But the one thing I never lost was style, and whores—like you and me—need that more than anything in the world. And until a few minutes ago I was feeding myself the same shit you've been living on."

She took a deep, shuddering breath, almost fighting for air. "You pegged it perfectly, Shag, when you said you three always dealt on a one-to-one basis, that you all took your shots right out in front. All four of us have done that, but the past is gone forever and it can't ever be brought back again because of what's happened." The tears started rolling down her cheeks without her even being aware of them. "I love all three of you crazy sons of bitches and—and—" She stared wide-eyed and sobbing at them and then the thing that had been building up in her came rushing to the surface and jerked from her like a primal scream.

"My God, don't you understand? Wouldn't you like to do the right thing for once in your stinking lives! Just once?"

36

Sam Bronstein climbed into the sleek Learjet, every line of his powerful body animal sleek in his black Italian silk suit. The door closed behind him, and in the thickly carpeted interior of the machine already coming to life he sat in a deep armchair, leaning back, studying the man who had come to dominate so much of his life. "It's good to see you, Shag," he said, and they clasped hands. Sam leaned forward to kiss Pam gently on the cheek. He looked around him, saw Vance and Lew at the controls. They started rolling forward, and Sam kept his silence as they taxied to the active and San Francisco Tower cleared them for immediate takeoff. The world sped away, the bumps ended as they rotated and the gear thumped into its wells. Vance took the machine upstairs at a steep angle with a howling rush of power, but inside the cabin it was quiet, almost hushed. "We're going to fifty-one thousand," Shag said after the long pause. "Nonstop to Boston. Drink?"

"Straight. No ice."

"Still Scotch?"

Sam nodded. He waited until Shag and Pam had their own drinks, then he opened his attaché case and took out a slim folder. "All right, let's get down to cases," he said. "I have many questions for you, but I'll run down my list first.

"And first is London. The payments were sufficient and the extra fees have melted away all the usual red tape. JetAir has for the past several weeks functioned as a viable international travel agency. It specializes in global luxury tours by charted 747, with scheduled stopovers in major cities, each stop from three to five days, with all details in the very elaborate brochures. JetAir has major offices throughout the world, each with a full staff ready. Finances are handled by the firm of Smythe, Battson, Carter and Williamson, which believes the full financial support for this operation is actually a ploy by which an Arab sheik is concealing a personal skim from the petroleum operations of his now very rich and decadent father."

"Good. It fits perfectly," Shag said.

"Better than that," Sam noted. "The funds are moved through Italy and West Germany, and Paris as well, so that there appears to be a smooth fiscal flow through interchanges of banks on the Continent. And, of course, that attends to North Africa as well. We are funneling some of the funds from West Germany back to Israel. By the way, where did you set up the JetAir offices in Vegas?"

"Two," Pam told him. "A small and very luxurious suite at the airport, and a main business suite in the Frontier Hotel. We also maintain a private apartment suite there as well."

"Very good. The television shop?"

"Boulder City. We thought even the slight geographical separation would work out best." She waited until Sam motioned her to go on. "The shop is run by Lew Heath, and it deals primarily in special order, customized work. Boulder Electronics right now has a contract to customize twenty video-recorder and television-screen systems, all very elaborate, and intended for installation in large aircraft. The contract is with JetAir, by the way."

"Excellent."

"Boulder Electronics also spends much of its time doing special installation work for the more expensive motor homes and houseboats in the marina resort area of Lake Mead. The trucks are well known and have become a familiar sight."

"And the other business?"

"That's AEC for Airborne Electronic Command. It's run by a man called Vance Brady, and he has his shop at Thunderbird Field just outside Las Vegas itself. He does special avionics work. He deals in major lines such as Bendix, Sperry, Collins, Narco, King—the best. He installs complete systems in business aircraft and he specializes in inertial navigation systems such as omega and loran and other very advanced and sophisticated electronics. AEC maintains another shop at Fort Lauderdale International Airport in Florida."

"Congratulations on your business acumen, Ms. Kreiner."

She smiled.

Sam went back to his folder. "A Boeing 747 SP has been leased for one year through Singapore Airways. This is a normal procedure for this organization, which at the present time has eight other large turbine aircraft on similar lease agreements. The crews are British, by the way, and they include two complete shifts of flight crews and cabin attendants. They have clearance for flights into and out of all cities on the JetAir itineraries. They are also aware that on each flight, JetAir executives have private access to a sealed-off area of the main cabin, in the rear of the main passenger deck. The aircraft has been modified to permit passage between compartments on each side of the rear fuselage. And, according to the specifications laid down in your dossier, all equipment in this compartment is to be installed and maintained by Boulder Electronics and AEC."

"When will the ship be ready?" Shag asked.

"As soon as those two companies complete their installations. I have also arranged for sixty-two passengers who have made their advance reservations, paid in full, for the sum of fifteen thousand dollars each. They have been most carefully selected and will pay the greatest attention to the fascinating sights their tour promises to bring to them."

Shag held his glass before his lips. "Problems?"

"None. International currency is a most remarkable lubricant."

"Security interference?"

"The State Department is very pleased with the operation of JetAir as it promises to promote understanding and goodwill among the countries involved."

"Where do you go from Boston?"

Sam glanced through the window at a world ten miles below them. "New York," he answered finally. "I have an appointment with the Swedish delegation to the United Nations." He extended his glass to Pam for a refill. "It goes well. How about your flight?"

"We talked with the man who runs Argosy Airways. They operate out of Lauderdale Executive and they have a direct line to the governor of the Bahamas. We're expected."

Sam smiled. "Good old Kingler. I know him from days of old. I'll make a few calls myself once I'm in my Boston office. Things will go easier if he has my personal assurance as to the private transfer of the funds involved. That way any hesitation will be eliminated."

"I really don't believe all this, you know," Pam said. "There's so much respectability here it stinks. Are you the same people I used to fly with?"

Sam patted her hand. "My dear, during a lifetime a man often plays both saint and devil."

She sighed. "Now you sound like him," she said, sliding her arm through Shag's.

Sam studied them both. "I could do worse."

Two and a half hours out of Boston the Learjet was slicing a swift furrow from high altitude on its clearance to the city of Nassau on New Providence Island in the Bahamas. Anston Kingler, new governor of the island nation, was right on the ball. The tower parked them in an area reserved for government aircraft and watched by armed guards, and the moment they stepped through the door of the executive jet a long black limousine pulled up to the aircraft. Lew and Vance, wearing the uniforms of business aircraft pilots, remained with the Lear. Shag sat in silence with Pam as they drove across a narrow, high-arching bridge to a private villa. They drove through a short tunnel to emerge in an underground garage, and three minutes later Kingler was greeting them.

He shook hands in a strong grip with Shag, bowed to Pam, went through the motions of the gracious host. "I received a call from our mutual friend in Boston," Kingler started without preamble. "From what I have been told your time is more precious than gold and you are on a very tight schedule." He stood by his desk, tall and imposing, a handsome black man in his early fifties with a tight crop of silvery hair. He was dressed casually but impeccably, and he stood silent for several moments as a servant brought drinks to his guests. When the room was empty he favored Shag with a brief nod to pick up their converation.

"We appreciate your own time," Shag said quietly. "Did our former contacts, and that final call from Boston, answer all your questions, sir?"

Kingler laughed and they saw him loosening. He took a seat by them. "I feel you address very few people with that word. I mean *sir*, of course. I am flattered."

"I know your background, Mr. President. Much better than you may realize. I use the term with you with absolute sincerity and respect."

Kingler nodded his gratitude. "You are also a diplomat, I see."

"Anything but, I'm afraid," Shag returned.

"Well, you must learn quickly, then. To save a great deal of sparring we have agreed to the terms of your representative. You will have a lease, an absolute lease with the normal provisos of no crimes against humanity being involved—"

"That is the last thing in our minds," Shag murmured.

"And so forth," Kingler said to wrap up the preliminaries. "The lease is for twenty years but the papers read an outright purchase. Violet Cay has thirty-eight square miles. Not very big, but remote and really quite delightful. We will, as you requested, provide a permanent police garrison and attend to all legal details, worked out with your own solicitors, for filing the necessary papers and making the required moves in the right place. I have already made arrangements for other governments to open relations with you on a diplomatic and business level. And, as I say, the documents will display unquestioned title and status for the period specified. As I understand it there will be declared a free territory."

"That's correct, Mr. President."

"I am curious. No gambling, trafficking—"

"None of that, sir. As we specified, your own inspection may take place at any time and without notification."

Kingler tapped fingers on his knee. "Remarkable. I have been trying to second-guess you from the very start, Mr. Jordan. I fear I have not succeeded."

"And you will not," Shag promised. "The figure is acceptable?"

"Three million in British currency. It is acceptable. Concern yourselves not at all with such matters. Our Boston friend and I have dealt before. There are no problems."

"Thank you, sir." Shag and Pam stood up, followed by Kingler.

"One last matter," Kingler said as he walked with them to the waiting limousine. "There is a government charter being prepared, I understand."

"Yes, sir."

"That means a government," smiled Kingler, "and a government means a name, does it not?"

"Jericho."

"Jericho?" Kingler nodded, then smiled broadly. "It has a dual cutting edge, I think."

"You think well, sir," Shag told him and they shook hands.

"Where do you go now, Mr. Jordan?"

"Las Vegas, Mr. President. There we will begin a luxury trip around the world by chartered 747."

Anston Kingler studied him in a new light. "Opulence seems to be a part of your system," he said, a bit sharply. But Shag refused the bait.

"Not at all, not at all," he said with a broad smile. "Our travel is luxurious but not necessarily our business. In fact, one of the sites we shall visit is among the Holy of Holies. The grounds of Jericho. There is a great truth to be found there."

"I confess, sir, you baffle me," Kingler said.

"Then I am grateful to you, Mr. President. Because that is a sign of of our success. Good-bye, sir."

She was huge and she cruised at six hundred miles an hour at forty thousand feet and inside her pressurized hull she was thickly carpeted and featured luxury that would have widened the eyes of a sultan of old. The 747 is an enormous machine, and the JetAir conversion presented a dining area and lounge, sleeping compartments, all manner of entertainment, and instant attention from stewards and stewardesses. There were two baths and four showers aboard the great winged liner of the air ocean, six chefs, and nearly every manner of elegance one might envision.

Except that every "paying guest" had been screened and selected with the most exquisite care.

At the rear of the enormous passenger deck a section had been closed off. It evoked little curiosity on the part of the passengers, who before takeoff were even shown its intricate electronic systems for "global navigation and satellite communications, using this incredibly advanced computer, model Mark Fifty-two." Six technicians worked in the restricted area under the direct supervision of Lew Heath and Vance Brady, who had brought aboard the aircraft VTR and TV systems with special programming.

Unfortunately, Heath and Brady had precious little time to enjoy the splendid and fascinating itinerary of the global tour. Lew Heath sprawled in a comfortable armchair at the lounge during a steady cruise eight miles high, nursing a tall, cool drink. A young lady took the chair by his side. "You look tired, my friend. Much too tired for a wonderful journey like this."

Lew saluted her with his glass. "Here's to the magic carpet."

"Ah, is that a note of irritation?" Lew tried to place her, but she was too cosmopolitan. She had a dozen different backgrounds and they were all perfect. He admired this woman; she was one of the most magnificent females he had ever seen. She reminded him of fine English steel, the kind you find in an officer's sword.

"I apologize," he told her. "Miss—"

"Dianne Stark. Malaysia. I schooled in Bern." Her smile was dazzling.

And she's too professional and too quick with the words to stall questions. So she's our mark. Well, well . . .

"Heath, Lew Heath," he said to her. "Sorry about being a grump. It's those bloody video recorders and players we brought along. They're giving us fits."

"Electronics interest me. My father deals with aircraft." She nodded to a bartender for a refill for them both. "Would you mind telling me about your problem? Perhaps," and her laughter was ambrosia over ice, "it will take away some of your problems."

"It's not that difficult, really." He hesitated. "Are you sure this won't bore you?"

"I shall call you Lew because our backgrounds are similar. You will not bore a woman who has her masters in electrical engineering."

There's the trap. She really does know what the hell this is all about. Oh, you bastards are smart, all right. Keep it cool and steady, Heath. You won't fool this one.

"You don't need a bloody masters to understand this," he said with just the right touch of self-deprecation. "You know those video players we have aboard? Movies, special shows, scenic ground and air previews of where we're going? Well, that works out fine, but we're also using the VTR—the video recording equipment—to shoot aerial and ground scenes as we go along, so that the people aboard this flight will be able to have a complete video record to take home with them. The playback material is working all right, but the recorders—" He made a sour face and shook his head. "They're off in their mag flux and we're getting high-band interference with the film as we take it. I don't know," he said ruefully. "It could be our altitude, or maybe there's sunspot activity, or even a magnetic field from the engines. But whatever it is, it means we work when we're on the ground. Fortunately, JetAir has contacts wherever we land and we can exchange some equipment and work on the rest of it during the layovers." Lew climbed to his feet. "Do forgive me. I should never talk business with a beautiful woman. Dianne, it's been a pleasure."

She nodded, her lips glistening, eyes incredibly alive. "The same, Lew. If you have time, invite me to your shop. I'm certain it would be fascinating."

He set down his glass. "As soon as we catch up, that's a promise. 'Bye."

And that was that. She should be turning in an interesting report. He suppressed his grin until he locked the electronics workshop door behind him.

* * *

San Francisco nonstop to New York. Four days on the town, everything arranged. Restaurants, discos, Broadway theaters. Full security protection for all guests. Lew and Vance worked day and night to repair balky equipment, cabled their next stop to have certain components ready. JetAir sent technicians to help them, and then time ran out.

A magnificent flight to London. Gossamer veils of the high aurora shifting over them. A whispering electrical atmosphere of silent music. In the back of the 747 SP Lew and Vance cursed their equipment. "Three days of fun and lovely times in London for them," he growled, "and it's day-and-night slavin' away at this bleedin' electronic muckery for us."

"Take a night off," Vance told him. "I've got a full crew from London JetAir on this job."

Lew thought about it. "Righto, Admiral. A good idea. Besides, the lovely lady is panting for my bod."

"Dianne Stark? That luscious—"

Lew held up a hand. "Never mind. Spare me. I have sweated through the nights dreaming of her ravishing my fair skin. Tonight I shall turn her pantherish talents loose on me."

"She could have any man she wants, you idiot."

"But she wants me. That tell you anything?"

"Uh huh. She's demented or she has ulterior motives."

"Well, there's nothing like some happy screaming between the sheets to while away the wee hours. Ta-ta."

He returned to the aircraft the next day totally exhausted, with a stupid smile plastered on his face.

London was great and Paris was a bitch. The equipment drove them up a wall. They had the JetAir staff going mad hunting electronic spare parts all over Europe.

In Berlin they heard stories of the wild revelry led by Pam and Shag. They didn't see any of it. They were chained to their work.

Moscow was a pain in the ass, although the guests loved the ballet and an all-out effort by the Soviet government to spread the red carpet for the passengers of JetAir Flight 1. In Rome, Lew remained with the aircraft and Dianne Stark "accidentally" ran into Vance in a salon and did some more body ravishing. "She seemed preoccupied, though," Vance later described it to Lew. They both grinned.

On to Cairo and a bustling, frenetic visit via camel and air-conditioned buses to tombs and pyramids. A strange journey as an expression of the extraordinary goodwill between Egypt and Israel; the passengers drove beneath the Suez Canal in a wide and gleaming tunnel, rolled through old battlefields, and reached their hotel in Tel Aviv, with four days and nights in the Holy Land awaiting them.

The Israeli army provided security for the group, although it appeared unnecessary. Shag and Pam left the escorted tour and drove to the grounds at Jericho. They walked through narrow, crowded streets and stood finally by a memorial to the men and women who had died in the fight for Israel's independence. At a café they had dark, powerful coffee and sweetcakes, and were joined by an Israeli army major.

The visit did not last long, and in the blink of an eye Sam Bronstein was gone from sight.

The long flight to New Delhi was made with most of the passengers asleep. They made up for their lassitude with the intense interest at their landing in Peking, and waiting for them at the next stop was a whirlwind of travel and entertainment by the Japanese government in Tokyo.

Finally there was a nonstop cruise from Japan to San Francisco with a farewell dinner high over the Pacific Ocean. They shook hands all around. The first globe-trotting luxury tour of JetAir had proven an overwhelming success.

They hit the mining camp in a devastating assault by helicopter and fast armored cars, and when the dust settled, the army team, its ranks swelled by agents from a half-dozen federal agencies, had for their pains two frightened men who'd been faithfully yet futilely working the mine, but were satisfied with their weekly paychecks. Two miners who had never seen their employers but received their checks by mail in Fence Creek. And their dog, an old floppy-eared hound who fell over in a quivering shock when the helicopters descended like the wrath of God and set up instant violent sandstorms.

The federal teams assembled behind locked doors in the air base at Albuquerque. "They're still one jump ahead of us," Hugh Harris of the FBI said wearily. "All this time we sat back and waited and waited and they were gone. Goddamn it, I want my hands on them!" He turned to Torbay of the CIA. "Jake, anything on those two men from the mine?"

Torbay shook his head. "We've pumped enough drugs into those two to make them addicts for life. They don't know shit. Period. It's exactly like they said. They were hired by phone and they get paid by mail, including their expenses. That's all they know."

James Curtin from State gestured impatiently. "Well, what about their damn airplane in El Paso?

Didn't that give us some kind of a lead?" He glared at the FAA man.

Red Thompson leaned back in his chair, balanced precariously on the two back legs. "It gave us a lead, all right," he said. "Just what they wanted. The kid on the ramp told us everything. He had no reason not to. A fat tip, nice people who even told him where they were going. He got his book out, showed us the time they landed, the cab he called. We spoke to the driver who took them to Irma's—"

"What's that?" Curtin snapped.

"Cathouse, restaurant, bar, all rolled into one happy business. They had dinner there. We have the waitresses, the manager—no one hid anything from us except the chief of police. His name is Santos and we got the distinct impression he was holding out on us."

Jake Torbay studied Thompson. "Did you put the squeeze on him?"

"The Mexican government gave us full cooperation and sent in their best agents. They were under orders to brook no nonsense and to come down hard on anyone who interfered in their investigation. They took Santos to their interrogation headquarters, beat the hell out of him and threatened to kill him if he didn't 'fess up. He spit in their face."

"And? What happened, dammit!" Curtin yelled.

"What happened is confirmation that we should keep these things in our own hands," Thompson said with disarming pleasantness. "He didn't talk and they kept their promise. They shot him. They were very satisfied because they'd followed orders. And they also snuffed the only real lead we had down there."

Hugh Harris tapped papers before him. "Well, not quite. The computer gave us their names. They surfaced again in Arizona. What we don't know is what they did between Juárez and going through customs in Arizona."

They turned to Bill Woodburn. Before anyone could speak he stuttered badly. "I—I don't know w-what happened. I m-mean, nobody t-told me about t-this."

"Jesus Christ," Torbay said with open disgust.

"What about that damned German bomber?" Curtin pressed. "Red was right from the beginning, it looks like. I mean, too many people saw the damn thing! I don't care if it came through a time tunnel or what. It's been seen by people on the ground and in the air and it shot up that Cessna—"

"And shot up Lauderdale airport with phantom bullets and bombs," Harris reminded him.

"I don't give a shit!" Curtin yelled. "I'm no fan of Thompson's but he's right. He's *got* to be right! There are too many leads, all the way back to South America. And that bastard, Dorsch. What happened with him?"

"He took poison."

Torbay's disgust at bunglers almost crawled about the table between them. "Harris, don't we have a make on these people?"

The FBI man nodded. "We have their names. At least five names and five descriptions for each of them. And every time we close in they vanish. Into thin air. We don't know who's real and who's not, and to answer the questions I know you're going to ask, we've arrested one hundred and thirty-seven people who could be them. We still have a dozen in detention, but I think we're wasting our time."

They heard a knock on the door but before they could respond it opened and an air-force colonel stepped through. He closed the door behind him, pressed a wall button, and they heard a slight hum. "I'm Colonel Robert Hawkins. DOD security. I think we have that make on one of those people you're looking for."

Torbay shot a fierce look at the colonel. "How the hell did you know what we were talking about? Have you got this room bugged?"

Hawkins wasn't fazed. "Of course. You people haven't exactly been drowning in success, have you? For all we know there's a tie-in right in this room. Don't protest, gentlemen. It's happened before. The White House is now actively considering a major effort to overthrow the government of the United States by means of violence. You'll forgive the official language but those are my orders. That hum you hear now means the bugs are no longer effective in this room."

"Screw all that," Harris said. "What's the make?"

"It lends credence to the White House theory. We picked up a very good fingerprint from that DC-3 in El Paso. It matches one we have on file."

"We didn't get a thing from that," Harris said.

"That's immaterial from our position," Hawkins said, brushing aside the remark from the FBI. "Do you want to protest your efficiency or hear what I have to say?" Harris turned red, but nodded.

"The name is Vance Sims Brady, former colonel with the Special Strike Force, Strategic Air Command. A B-52 pilot and an expert with nuclear weapons. He was court-martialed out of the service and after that he chose to disappear from sight. He was rather badly disgraced."

"What happened to him?" Thompson asked.

"That's not important now," came the cold answer.

"The fuck it isn't, you pompous idiot! Anything is

important! Stop your Dr. Strangelove act and spill it."

Hawkins froze but couldn't beat down the iron gaze from the FAA man. Finally the colonel nodded and related briefly what had happened with Vance Brady.

Hugh Harris slumped in his seat. "Oh, great. Just great. You know what we have on our hands? A moralist. And you know what a moralist is? Dedicated, utterly loyal to his cause, filled with burning fervor, and this one is also one of the best men ever to fly with the Strategic Air Command. If we had trained him to do what he's doing we couldn't have done as well." He looked at Hawkins with open contempt. "Tell us again how unimportant it was for you people to screw up this man."

Red Thompson moved quickly into the widening breach. "Okay, all of you, knock it off. Does the White House have this information, Colonel?"

"Yes, sir. They do now."

"And?"

"I was told to inform Mr. Harris that the FBI chief will be calling him any moment from—" The phone rang and he picked it up personally. He listened for several moments, then handed the phone to Hugh Harris. "It's from the White House. The FBI director is with the President."

Harris looked around the room, took the phone, listened for several minutes, handed it back to Hawkins. He studied the other men with him. "You can check with your offices later, but you'll all receive the same orders I just got. Brady, and the others, may be heading for New York. Our orders are to apprehend them. No agent, I repeat, no agent from any service or agency is to even approach them with a weapon. *No weapons of any kind*. They are to be taken alive. We can use physical force, drugs, gas, ultrasonics, but they are to be taken alive and, if at all possible, not harmed in any way."

He sighed. "Otherwise, knowing Brady, if we screw up we are all liable to wake up in the morning very, very dead."

37

They moved with clockwork precision, the springs wound by Sam Bronstein and the mechanism well oiled by a small and efficient army. The Learjet rolled off LaGuardia Airport's main runway in Queens, taxied to a waiting limousine at Butler Aviation, and without a pause they were on their way across the high bridge into Manhattan and swinging south along the East River Drive. Their driver was sealed off from them by bulletproof glass, and his orders had been expressed with unmistakable clarity. A very large and dangerous man had spoken quietly to him. "Deliver these people as per your instructions and don't let *anything* stop you. There will be a gray sedan in front of you and a brown-and-yellow van directly behind. Those are your cover vehicles. If you get stopped by the police for anything—get the hell out of there. Your cover will move in."

They were staying one faltering step ahead of the vast government forces closing in on them from all sides. They knew only too well how such programs worked. The mass of the investigative and tracking teams remain stalled only until that moment they get their first break and then, like a dam under tremendous pressure, the breach in the wall splits wider and wider and you become inundated with a flood tide of legal strongarms. They were running the string to its limit and time had suddenly reversed to favor them.

"Ain't a bit of doubt anymore, is there, now," Lew said quietly, inflecting the words as a statement, not a question. "See there? Two choppers over the river, following us, and another behind us and likely a few more we don't even see."

Shag looked idly at the powerful military gunships pacing them down the highway. "Doesn't much matter anymore. They've fingered us and that means they've got positive ID on Vance, and that now works in our favor."

Pam was startled by his remark. "I don't understand that. Secrecy has been everything. The cover names, the false identification, even the doubles made up to look like us, and now you say we have an advantage because they've identified Vance?"

Shag nodded and he saw Vance smile. "That's right, hon. They know who he is, a former member of a crack bomber strike force, an expert with thermonuclear weapons. He can take them apart and put them back together blindfolded. They've got to link us with those missing bombs. It's one thing to have those weapons in the hands of people who can't handle the safety devices, or know how to rig the warheads. But with Vance in the picture they're frightened, and they have good reason to be. They have no way of knowing whether or not killing him will set off a reaction we arranged earlier. One or all of the bombs might go off. From their viewpoint he may hate his country enough to turn against it. After Watergate and Nixon and Agnew and the rest of that crowd, what with the attorney general twisted as badly as he was—well, why go over the whole sordid story? The point is that they're spooked, and badly. This won't be the first good reason they've had to suspect a power group of trying to dump the rotten apples in Washington. They're spooked and edgy and so their imaginations demand that they be as careful as possible. They're walking on eggs and if you crack the shell it's going to be the biggest thermonuclear omelet they ever saw. They'll be cool."

Vance had a deathlike smile on his face. "Besides, in a little while we'll answer all their questions." He tried to hold down his own edginess, though it was a tough battle. "Is everything set for us tonight?"

She squeezed his hand. "It's set. I've talked with Sam twice tonight for updates. It's all arranged." She glanced at the three men. "No wonder the United Nations is such a political pigpen. You can buy on the black market there just like any other sordid street in the world. If you want time that's not on the agenda you pay the right people in the right places. We've done that. Four hundred thousand dollars for the General Assembly to be together for another meeting, for a speech, but it's all arranged for us to grab their attention."

A sigh shivered through her. "It's so crazy! I understand so much more now why you three have acted the way—well, what's gone on these last years with you. If you have something to say that's important no one wants to listen, so you've got to bribe people just to bring together other people you need to talk to."

Brady's nerves taunted him. "But, I mean, what you said, there aren't any problems?"

"Relax, Admiral," Shag answered for her. "It's our ball game from here on in. Two hours from now and they'll be twisting their ears to hear what we have to say. They won't be able to turn us off then. It will be the first time in more years than anyone can remember that words will be louder than their guns." He gestured by the window. "Look at those choppers out there. Gunships. Loaded with cannon and machine guns and rockets and everybody edgy and itchy on the triggers and they can't understand why it doesn't mean a thing anymore. That's politics, Admiral. When you can't make things work in the back rooms you send in the tin soldiers to argue for you. We're pulling teeth tonight."

"You seem damned sure of yourself," Vance countered.

"Oh, I am, I am," Shag said, and he was completely relaxed. "Just put yourself in their place and what can you do? One will get you fifty they know us now down to the last detail and they're under orders to take us, but under no conditions are weapons to be used." His face turned serious. "You're still all set up? Everything working okay?"

They patted their bodies, felt for equipment beneath their outer garments. They all nodded. "Good. I want everything hot. There's no backing down. If those people go apeshit you've got to close those switches. Don't think if you have to use them. Just do it."

Lew turned back from looking through the car window. "That's just the escort. There'll be a party to greet us."

"He's right," Vance said. "Let's arrange the order right now. I'm the one they've got to identify beyond all question, so I suggest I speak for us. If I know them they'll have someone who knows me well, another pilot or a crew member I flew with. They'll want him to identify me beyond any question."

Shag gestured idly. "You got it, Superstar."

Silence fell upon them and they watched the city lights whipping by, the heavy evening traffic, the buildings across the river. They passed beneath the Queensboro Bridge. It was only a matter of minutes now.

The black limo eased to the right and rode the up-sloping ramp from East River Drive to the main entrance of the United Nations Building. Evening sessions weren't that unusual at the UN, and the area was brightly lit in every direction. They studied the bustle of traffic, the television and radio vans.

"Someone's let out word there's something different tonight," Shag said. "They don't bring in their heavy news equipment for regular meetings. It's already set up inside."

Pam nodded. "Like I said, it's a pigpen. You buy and sell. Someone made a phone call and gets paid for the news tip."

"So much the better," Lew murmured.

The limo stopped and the driver came around to open the door. They stepped onto the concrete walk. "Well, they've already got it under control," Shag noted. "Look at the crowd. Too dispersed, too orderly. Want to bet there isn't a single visitor in that bunch? They're all part of the government team."

"The choppers have taken up flanking positions," Vance said.

"Up theirs," came Lew's instant rejoinder. "Will you forget those silly things, Admiral? Quit worrying about them. They haven't anything else to do. Just concentrate on what's in front of us. Here they come now."

Shag and Lew each carried an attaché case. They wanted Vance's hands completely free. They moved along the walk to the main entrance of the great glass tower and then they saw the wall. At least a hundred of them, dressed in everything from dark suits to casual sports clothes, but they were unmistakable. All you had to do was look at their eyes. Three men separated themselves from the group standing its ground and approached them, stopped several feet away.

Shag's group stood still, watching. One man came up to face Vance Brady, peering at him closely. "Hello, Vance. It's been a long time." He extended his hand and Vance didn't take it. There was a brief moment of embarrassment and the stranger let his arm fall by his side. Vance didn't turn his eyes away from the man before him. He spoke loud enough for Shag and the others to hear him clearly.

"His name is Arthur Jenkins. He's a colonel in SAC intelligence. We flew together and he was on my court-martial board. He's made a positive identification." Jenkins stood stone-faced.

Another man walked up to them. "My name is Hugh Harris. FBI. I'm sure you know this entire area is filled with our men. There's no way you can make it away from here. Those are our helicopters up there, heavily armed gunships and—"

"No shit," Shag said.

Harris was startled. He hadn't expected a completely casual attitude. It threw him, but he recovered quickly. "We would appreciate it if we could handle this whole affair quietly."

"Bug off," he was told, and Harris pressed his lips together. "I don't think you understand—"

"Vance, tell them," Shag broke in.

Whatever trepidation had unnerved Vance before was now gone. He was as cool as if he was back in a B-52 cockpit. He raised his voice just enough for the men before him to hear him clearly.

"Art, I want you to listen to me very closely. I know you're wired for sound and that there are audio and video pickups on us. I'm not going to repeat this," Vance said, his voice as cold as steel. "And that goes for your FBI friend and the rest of the crowd all around us. Now, look carefully, Art."

Vance opened his jacket slowly. Jenkins and Harris looked hard at the wiring harness and controls strapped to his body. "Shag, Lew, Pam. Show them."

They opened their jackets and the group standing between them and the UN entrance saw the same wiring harness. The jackets closed.

"Do you understand what these are, Art?" Vance said to the colonel. "Each harness is a complete electronic control system monitored to our EEG and EKG patterns, and our alpha readouts as well. If there is physical shock to our systems, to any one of us, or if we go into an alpha wave pattern, the biofeedback that registers complete rest or sleep that would be induced by drugs or a gas, will trigger the detonator systems. Each of us is wearing two pounds of plastic explosives. If it goes off with any one of us that person will be torn to pieces and so will the other three. There is nothing you can use to threaten us. Do you understand?"

Art Jenkins was white. He nodded slowly. Vance looked at the FBI agent. "Do you understand?"

"Yes," Harris said.

"Good. It goes further than that and I want your superiors to hear everything I'm saying."

"They can hear you," Harris confirmed.

"Then understand this too," Vance said to his unseen audience. "Any stupid move on your part will trigger our immediate deaths. I could go into more detail now, but we do have an appointment and you're delaying us. So there will be no doubt I want you to hear this number. Five-nine-six-six-six-two-three-one-four-eight. That's the serial number from a Mark Sixty-two. It has been armed and it is triggered just one sequence short of detonation. So have the others. Unless we are free every two hours to transmit a certain signal on a constantly changing computer random code, that last sequence will close and—" He smiled coldly. "I'll let your imagination do the rest. Now, we're coming through. Harris, get your thugs out of our way because if we're stopped then all the lights go out. Do you read me, mister?"

Harris gestured. The way opened as the government agents melted aside.

The four of them walked into the United Nations.

38

They walked slowly, in silence, into the great hall of the General Assembly. As if by magic a dark-skinned man stood before them, studied their faces, then bowed slightly. "This way, please," he said, and led them up and along one of the tiered rows. They sat down slowly in wide, contoured seats. Before each of them was a microphone, a headset for immediate translation of any speaker in a foreign language, telephones, and a printed schedule for the evening assembly. Shag looked about him slowly, carefully. He had an idea that Sam Bronstein was somewhere in the vast chamber, but in that sea of faces there seemed no way to be certain.

Lew tapped him on the arm. "I've spotted at least forty set up as cover on us," he said easily to Shag.

"There's a lot more than that," came the reply. Shag turned to Pam. "They're watching us with everything from all different angles. And we know we're all wired for sound here. Straight microphone pickups as well as their special antennas for zeroing in. Very neat." He looked up and stared into the empty space of the center of the assembly and smiled. "Rest easily, gentlemen," he said to thin air. "We're in good health. I suggest you study your TV monitors carefully. It's now one hour and fifty minutes since our last coded transmission. If you watch you can see how it works." He nodded to Pam. "Go ahead."

She placed an attaché case on the conference tier before her, opened it wide to reveal a computer keyboard, several digital readouts and other instruments that did not indicate what their readings meant. She placed a thin headphone by her ear, unreeled a wire antenna, punched several buttons to initiate her transmission, studied a digital readback, and then her fingers flew across the keyboard. A green light flashed on and they heard a short, clear tone signal.

"We are secure for another two hours," Shag announced. Around them the bustle of voices and movement began to fade, overhead lights dimmed slightly and several spotlights illuminated the speaker's rostrum and the desk of the secretariat. They only half-listened to the voices intoning from the rostrum. An hour of drivel was to take place before they were scheduled to speak. "I can hardly believe this is all happening," Pam whispered to Shag. "Look at this schedule." Her finger pointed to the next event: JERICHO. "It's so hard to accept that we're really *here*."

He tapped the nameplate that had been face down by their equipment, studied it, then placed it on a level slightly higher than their desk surface. JERICHO stood out like a sore thumb. To their right were black dignitaries from Tanzania. Norwegian representatives stretched along the tier to their left. There was no name on the tier directly behind them or directly before them, and they knew that in the name of "security" the representatives normally assigned to these spaces had yielded to the requests of the government to move in special agents for "protection."

The hour passed slowly. Lew had not spoken since his first few words. Vance was like stone. To Shag and Pam it was like watching a three-dimensional play being acted out before them.

Then the rostrum was clear and an official announced into his microphone in English, his words being translated instantly for every non-English-speaking group represented in the assembly, the next item on the schedule. "We will hear now from the representative of the new government of—" The voice hesitated and then the name was almost forced out, squeezed through a sudden disbelief, "of . . . Jericho." The announcement was met by a mild stir, and as Vance rose to his feet, Shag right behind him with an attaché case, they were accorded casual interest. There was some idle laughter and an increase in the background conversation. There had been countless little idiocies just like this moment in the history of the United Nations, and there were countless bids for membership in the organization, or someone arranged for a moment such as this to air some governmental grievance. To the delegates assembled in the great hall this was one of the annoying but necessary little interludes in the grinding process of international affairs. It was like letting the poor kid at the end of the block have his brief say. If the observers watching Vance and Shag proceed to the rostrum were intrigued at all, it was by what method had been taken to reach this point and, in one of the poorer-kept secrets of this organization, how much had been paid and to whom.

And what a strange name they had chosen. Was it supposed to have religious significance, as if this biblical name carried with it some strange moral power to command their attention? Jericho, indeed.

Perhaps, the delegates tittered to one another, they were going to play a trumpet and bring down the walls of the great assembly. Interest increased slightly as the two men reached the rostrum, took their seats, conversed briefly with one another. Then the bearded one placed a sheaf of papers on the table, a move met with audible groans. Well, at least they were limited in their time.

He had left the papers on the table and approached the dais with its microphones.

The secretary's voice boomed out through loudspeakers and into headsets. "We will hear now from the representative of the nation of Jericho. Mr. Shag Jordan, if you please."

He stood as straight and hard as steel, and just before he spoke Pam's words burned in his mind. *Wouldn't you like to do the right thing for once in your stinking lives! Just once?*

And the answer swept through him like a fresh, cooling breeze. *You bet, lover. Hang onto your seat . . .*

"I am here," he began, "with representatives of my government, to be recognized by the members of this assembly and to be accepted as a member nation of this planet." He remained silent for a moment as a murmur spread through the hall, and it was then that interest picked up. Finally an absolute hush fell over the General Assembly. There was the inevitable protocol as the secretary followed his script.

"May we inquire, sir, as to the nature of the political system of Jericho?"

Shag nodded to the man seated well to his right amidst his cluster of aides, turned back to let his eyes sweep the delegates, and then continued with a voice of absolute authority.

"It is survival. Yours, and ours."

The secretary cleared his throat. "That is commendable, good sir. Of course we are all interested in such a matter. It is why we are here. However, please let me remind you—"

"Be quiet." Shag's words were like ice water. "Listen to me; all of you." He hesitated for a moment. "I will not waste your time. I advise you to exercise more than the idle tolerance you are showing. We are here to tell you we are holding all of you hostage."

Again the murmur rushed like wind through the hall, louder this time, confused. "We are going to read a list of numbers to you," he said in a ringing voice. "Pay attention to those numbers. They spell life or death. We are not here to barter. We are not here for a dialogue. We are here to threaten you, and we have the means to make that threat come true. As you hear these numbers I advise you to write them down. You may then confirm them with the delegate from the United States. Those same numbers are in the possession of the delegate from the Soviet Union. So that you will understand, these numbers can also be your death warrant. Understand this point—you, *here*, are not the hostages of which I spoke."

Again, he paused for effect. "I am talking of four billion human beings."

The murmur rose to an uproar. Delegates stood, shouted at him, wondered aloud how this buffoon had reached the dais. Shouts flew to the secretary to remove this madman from the assembly. Shag waited a second before speaking directly into the microphones before him.

"SHUT UP, GODDAMMIT!"

The effect was instantaneous. Shock, dismay, utter disbelief. He took a paper from Vance Brady. "The numbers. In the event you may find what I say of less than compelling interest, these are the serial numbers that spell death. Note them carefully. Do not watch me—study the faces of the representatives of the United States and the Soviet Union. Look at the men who know they are in a room with people capable of bringing about the destruction of this entire world! For the serial numbers I give you now are those of the Mark Sixty-two Thermonuclear Weapons System of the United States Air Force.

"We will begin with the first device. The serial number is five-nine-six-six-six-two-three-one-four-eight. That bomb is now planted somewhere in the city of San Francisco."

Not a sound.

"Five-nine-six-two-two-seven-seven-one-eight-three. That bomb is in the city of New York."

He listed them all.

London.

Paris.

Rome.

Cairo.

Moscow.

Peking.

Berlin.

New Delhi.

"Those weapons were planted only recently in each of the cities mentioned. They were flown to each city by a chartered airliner on a tour of the globe. Each bomb was contained in a television recorder and play-back system and is equipped with four separate deto-nation devices. Interference with any one device will detonate the thermonuclear system. The time sequenc-ers for these devices must be reset every couple of hours to prevent the triggered sequence from closing and detonating any weapon. If any one weapon ex-plodes there will be a global sweep of destruction such as this world has never known. One bomb going off sets off the others and there is no way to stop the pro-cess. Any one detonation sets off an electromagnetic sig-nature and a radioactive signature to trigger the oth-ers.

"Your governments can confirm what I am saying. The chartered aircraft was a Boeing 747 SP of JetAir and visited each city I have just listed. You may have further confirmation from the delegate of the U.S.S.R., since a Soviet agent under the cover name of Dianne Stark was aboard that aircraft and was in each city at the time the weapons were emplaced."

Shag paused again. He knew calls were being made, his words were being confirmed, and governments around the world were screaming at American diplo-mats and the White House to confirm the truth of the serial numbers and that the bombs really were missing. Then he raised his hand and silence fell as swiftly as if a switch had been thrown.

"We could have arranged to explode one bomb as proof of everything I am telling you tonight. But that is childish nonsense. To kill hundreds of millions of innocent people to prove anything to this assembly is murder. So we have committed all the way. There are four of us in our group known to the intelligence services of my government. They know the truth. If one bomb goes off then all will go off."

He looked slowly around the stunned, tiered rows. "Are you aware of what a Mark Sixty-two is? Each of these ten weapons has the explosive yield of more than three hundred million tons in power. Each bomb is equal to three hundred megatons. All together they can release three gigatons—*three billion tons of explosive energy*—all at the same time. The cumulative effect of these devices—" He stopped suddenly and they were almost falling from their seats.

"You will now hear Vance Brady. He is a former colonel and pilot with the Strategic Air Command of the United States Air Force. Many years ago he refused to press an attack during an alert against a Russian city and for this he was court-martialed with dishonor. There is no dishonor now in his presence. He is a weapons expert. He will tell you what will happen if those ten bombs explode."

Shag stepped aside for Vance.

"I am a specialist in death and destruction. That is my science, my profession." Had he been the Fallen Angel he could not have been more devastating. "The detonation of these ten bombs will produce a casualty list which will be, at its minimum, one billion human beings. The effect maximizes with outer efficiency of all factors at approximately two-point-five billion human beings. That is for direct result of concussion, blast wave, earthquake effect exceeding the maxium of the Richter scale, radiated effects, tidal waves, and similar categories. It does not include the short-term and long-term effects of radioactive dispersal, fallout, and global carriage through stratospheric winds. The minimum calculated loss due to this secondary effect of these weapons is at least point-nine-six billion lives, and the outer scale varies as high as two billion because of the cumulative effects of livestock destruction, deterioration of crops, disruption of global weather patterns, all in addition to the lethal effects directly. There is no way, based on past studies of such events as the Krakatoa and Vesuvius volcanic eruptions, to predict with accuracy ultraviolet obscuration and its potential side effects. At that point, of course, a few tens of millions of human lives lost or gained is purely academic. I do not wish to annoy you with details, so the severely deleterious effects of genetic sterility, mutation, and other side effects I leave to your own research."

He looked around the assembly and a thin smile appeared on his face. He bowed. "I thank you for your great courtesy in listening so carefully." He returned to his seat and Shag moved again to the dais.

"So there will be no question of anything, you may regard us as fanatics. As madmen. Call us anything you wish. It is of no concern to us. But mark this, all of you:

"This is your last chance. It is true that we may be irrational. That is not our problem. It is yours. Somehow, in some mysterious way, we have acquired the means to do the right thing for this planet at its most dangerous moment since man first appeared. This is that moment. We are convinced that no matter what the reason, you all subscribe to a program of political insanity and an ultimate, inescapable nuclear war that will ravage this globe.

"So be it!" His eyes seemed to glow like burning coals. "I say to all of you who hear me now, and those who will hear later these words as they are recorded, that it begins now, tonight, this hour, this instant. We are not—"

A scuffle erupted along a lower tier. The leading delegate of Red China had climbed to his feet, shaking with rage, and as he had done so many times in the past, he turned abruptly to stalk from the great hall. He did not go far. A huge black man stood in his way. The Chinese delegate motioned impatiently for him to stand aside. The reaction was a crunching blow from the fist of the black man directly into the face of the Chinese delegate. His shattered nose sprayed blood in all directions and the Chinese diplomat collapsed unconscious to the floor. The black man turned and looked at Shag. Unsmiling, he bowed. Shag nodded.

"We are not blind idealists. If you wish to massacre one another with conventional weapons that is your choice. Indulge in all the wars you will. But unless the great weapons are done away with, unless production ceases immediately on nuclear weapons and strategic delivery systems, unless the weapons already existing are destroyed to the satisfaction of those investigative groups you choose yourselves, then as God is my witness, I swear to you we will detonate those ten giant bombs. We have made our decision. We stand at a wall that may not be crossed, and so we have chosen our name. Jericho. It is our belief that it is far better that half this planet should die by the sword now— than all the planet should perish by the nuclear flame tomorrow.

"You may now vote on the acceptance or the rejection of Jericho as a member of this assembly, of the family of nations. I—" He changed his mind abruptly, walked back to where Vance Brady was now standing, and in utter silence they returned to their seats.

The silence continued as Pam opened her attaché case and punched in the radio-transmitted code that would keep the great hydrogen bombs from exploding.

For at least another two hours.

39

They stood outside the General Assembly, overlooking the East River, the night wind tugging at their clothes. Pam clung desperately to Shag's arm. Her knees were weak, her soul drained of emotion. They were surrounded by agents of the United States, the Soviet Union, and Interpol. Others stood just behind, watching and listening.

Shag clasped Vance's hand and they held each other's without a word. He did the same with Lew. "We can't ever be in a group again," he told them. "You know we have to separate. Each of us will have the coded device to reset the triggering sequence. Vance goes one way; Lew, you go yours; and Pam and I must go ours. I've received word already from Sam. He'll follow the same pattern. I don't know the details and I don't want to know them and neither do you. That's our only safety. We'll have a way of contacting one another to be sure we never lose the capability of setting off those things."

They nodded. Tears streaked Lew's face but he seemed unaware of them.

"It's time to say good-bye. I thought you would like to know we're going to do one more thing, and we'd like to believe you'll be there with us in spirit. Pam and I are getting married."

She threw herself into Vance's arms, squeezed him as tightly as she could, and then she and Lew shared their tears.

Then they left, none knowing where the others would go.

And it happened, you know. SALT dissolved from a cauldron of controversy to almost frantic agreement. There really wasn't much choice. After the shock dissipated it seemed there was almost a sense of relief about it all.

The production of the great missiles and the bombers and the nuclear submarines ended overnight. Inspection teams went everywhere to oversee the dismantling of silos and the city-killers poised within. The missile-launching nuclear submarines rode to port on the surface and were broken up. The big bombers were blown apart with explosive charges and melted down. Fanatical inspection groups went to bomb production centers and tracked down the production of every pound of uranium 235 and plutonium the world over.

Even the lesser wars lost their steam. Any one bomb in Europe or Africa or Asia meant devastating effects for thousands of miles away. If the Mark Sixty-two exploded in Cairo it would devastate Egypt and most of the Arab lands, it would bury Israel in horrifying radioactive debris like a massive tidal wave and it would inundate Iran and Turkey and vast sections of the Soviet Union and continue on to enormous areas of the Far East. There was really no escape.

Only the Red Chinese remained bombastic and swore that no matter how much devastation might be wrought, China would survive with enough people to fight another war. Their willingness to accept vast losses of their own people and their trumpeted truculence about war brought about a sworn oath by every major nation on the planet for annihilation of Red China without nuclear devices. The bellicose threats faded.

Shag and Pam didn't care about riots and revolutions and border wars. They didn't know if the big gamble would work. But it was worth it.

Wouldn't you like to do the right thing for once in your stinking lives! Just once?

Win, lose, or draw—they were giving it their best shot.

"Maybe, just maybe," he told her a month later, "people have really been hoping for something like this all along. So they could have the decision taken from their hands, and nobody loses face this way."

"Maybe," she said.

Maybe. Every month, every year, there were fewer bombs and the huge bombers were gone and the great missiles scrapped and the deadly submarines broken into pieces. No matter how you looked at it, people breathed easier, slept a bit better.

Maybe.

Epilogue

Atop a high mesa in a remote part of Arizona known as the White Hills, they built a great acrylic dome, impervious to weather. Lights shone on and within the dome by day and by night, and inside the air was cooled and controlled, for here was the shrine. People came here, some as pilgrims of a new faith, some in thanksgiving, some out of curiosity. But they came by the millions to this Holy of Holies, shining and gleaming under the lights, this ancient, corrugated machine with three engines that had made it all possible, that had saved the world.

Dell Bestsellers

AMERICAN CAESAR

★ ★ ★ ★ ★

Douglas MacArthur 1880-1964

#1 NATIONAL BESTSELLER!
BY WILLIAM MANCHESTER

The author of *The Glory and the Dream* and *The Death of a President* brilliantly portrays the most controversial, most complex, and most hated or loved American general since Robert E. Lee: Douglas MacArthur! "William Manchester has written a masterful biography. Anybody who has ever wondered whether General MacArthur was a military genius or a political demagogue will find here evidence of both."—John Bartlow Martin. "Fascinating. Dramatic."—*Time*. "A thrilling and profoundly ponderable piece of work."—*Newsweek*. "Electric. Splendid reading. Like MacArthur himself—larger than life."—*The New York Times*.

A Dell Book $3.50

SHARKY'S MACHINE

WILLIAM DIEHL

THE MOST SENSATIONAL THRILLER OF THE YEAR!

For Sharky, a hard-driving cop, it all begins as a routine Vice Squad assignment. Until he listens to the shocking, erotic tapes that send him searching for a call girl known as Domino. And what began as a job, becomes an obsession. "COMPELLING. THE COMPLETE THRILLER."—*Newsweek*

A Dell Book $2.50

The
Thirteenth
Hour

John Lee
Author of *THE NINTH MAN*

Pursued by the SS, threatened by the Russian advance, Captain Henry Bascom has only cunning and sheer luck on his side. But when he becomes the sole witness to an incredible Nazi plot to save Hitler, he knows he will need more than cunning and luck to survive!

A Dell Book $2.50   (18751-6)